The Abduction

"Breathless."
Philadelphia Inquirer

"Deftly plotted political fun."
Library Journal

"Truly dirty politics and crime . . .
Hits a nerve . . . As timely as today's headlines."
San Francisco Chronicle

The Pardon

"Rings true to the emotional realities of
contemporary life. Readers will turn the pages
of *The Pardon* faster than a bailiff can
swear in a witness."
People

"A gripping mélange of courtroom drama and
psychotic manipulation, *The Pardon* possesses gritty
veracity, genuine characters that elicit sympathy, and
superb plotting and pacing . . .
A bonafide blockbuster."
Boston Herald

"Powerful . . . I read *The Pardon* in one sitting—
one exciting night of thrills and chills."
James Patterson

Books by James Grippando

The Swyteck series

WHEN DARKNESS FALLS
GOT THE LOOK
HEAR NO EVIL
LAST TO DIE
BEYOND SUSPICION
THE PARDON

Other Avon Books

A KING'S RANSOM
UNDER COVER OF DARKNESS
FOUND MONEY
THE ABDUCTION
THE INFORMANT

James Grippando

THE
INFORMANT

AVON BOOKS
An Imprint of HarperCollins*Publishers*

For Tiffany

This is a work of fiction. Names, characters, places, and incidents are products of the author's imagination or are used fictitiously and are not to be construed as real. Any resemblance to actual events, locales, organizations, or persons, living or dead, is entirely coincidental.

AVON BOOKS
An Imprint of HarperCollins*Publishers*
10 East 53rd Street
New York, New York 10022-5299

Copyright © 1996 by James Grippando
Excerpt from *Beyond Suspicion* copyright © 2002 by James Grippando
ISBN: 0-06-101220-3
www.avonbooks.com

First Avon Books paperback printing: November 2000
First HarperPaperbacks printing: August 1997
First HarperCollins hardcover printing: September 1996

Avon Trademark Reg. U.S. Pat. Off. and in Other Countries,
Marca Registrada, Hecho en U.S.A.
HarperCollins® is a trademark of HarperCollins Publishers Inc.

Printed in the U.S.A.

10 9

ACKNOWLEDGMENTS

The thank-you list is a long one, but one person stands out—my wife, Tiffany, for sharing the high points and for making the low ones completely irrelevant.

I'm especially pleased that the real pros who teamed up for my first book came together for a second. My editor, Rick Horgan, was again a great teacher, this time showing me the value of a well-structured outline, not to mention an ample supply of midnight oil. My literary agents, Artie and Richard Pine, have me convinced that no one in the business does it better than they do, but only because their remarkable actions speak louder than words. And Joan Sanger, true to form, provided helpful commentary on early drafts.

They say you should write what you know about, but it sure doesn't hurt to have smart friends. Rick Castillo, M.D., and Julietta Rodriguez, Ph.D., helped show me the way into the mind of a serial killer. Detective James Hall and the Yakima County Sheriff's Office got me as close to jail as I ever want to get. Jerry Houlihan and Rebekah Poston lent their considerable legal expertise on bank secrecy and offshore banking. "Miss Magg," in the Candler County Sheriff's Office, and David Moore, Candler County Coroner, showed a good deal of southern hospitality in helping me create the fictional town of Hainesville, Georgia. The folks in the social sciences department of the Broward County Library helped more than they know, as did the many journalists and law enforcement personnel I interviewed along the way, including Professor Bruce Garrison of the University of Miami College of Communications and Chief Warrant Officer Dan Waldschmidt of the United States Coast Guard. My thanks to all of you.

I'm also grateful for helpful comments and support from Eleanor Raynor, Judy Russell, Carlos Sires, Terri Gavulic, and Nancy Lehner. Finally, I deeply appreciate the genuine enthusiasm shown by my friends at Steel Hector & Davis, especially my friend and secretary of nine years, Bonnie Kahn-DeVreeze.

PART
ONE

Chapter 1

Gerty Kincaid expected the worst.

An Arctic front was dipping through Dixie, and southeast Georgia was bracing for its first blast of winter. By nightfall, said the weatherman, it might even snow. After seventy-eight years, Gerty wasn't tickled by the novelty. In the small town of Hainesville, January at its worst meant ice storms and downed power lines—not fluffy white snowfalls and a winter wonderland. There was no sophisticated meteorological explanation for it. That was just the way it was—and always would be.

That simple logic was like the town creed.

Life in Hainesville, they said, was as predictable as the sweet smell of azaleas in the spring and the April crop of onions. Vidalia onions, to be exact. They were the town's bona fide claim to fame, but it wasn't very southern to brag, so nobody claimed it. Hainesville was a one-stoplight town, population 532. It relied on one schoolhouse, a white clapboard rectangle serving kindergarten through twelfth grade. The First Baptist Church was the sole house of worship, built of bricks from the red Georgia clay. And there was just one doctor, a semiretired family physician who'd been honored with a parade, marching band, and key to the city when she moved down from Atlanta.

By early Friday evening a wind sock full of bitter northeasterlies was blowing through town. The smell of charred oak wafted from the chimneys of old homes with no electric heaters. Gerty was bundled up warmly in her beige trench coat and plaid wool scarf as she hurried up the curved sidewalk that led to her front door. Covered by a thin glaze of icy rain, the front steps and pathway glistened in the dim yellow porch light. It was slick and treacherous. She could have walked it blindfolded, however, having lived in the same old two-story, white frame house for nearly fifty years, the last ten alone as a widow.

She tucked her shopping bag under her arm while digging through her purse for the keys. The brass ring was enormous, cluttered with house keys, car keys, keys to an old shed that had burned down in '67—even keys to luggage she'd never actually locked. She kept them all on one ring, having promised herself that the day she could no longer tell the good ones from the bad would be the day she'd accept her daughter's persistent invitation to move in with her.

"Ah, fiddlesticks," she muttered. Her fingers ached with arthritis, and the tattered knit gloves only made it harder to grab the right key. The key ring jingled and jangled like a wind chime in her shaky hand. Finally she got it. With a quick shove the door opened, and she rushed inside to keep out the cold.

An eerie yellow glow from the porch streamed through the slatted windows on the door, lighting the needlepoint words of wisdom in the gold-leaf frame hanging on the wall. Gerty had designed and stitched it herself. THERE BUT FOR THE GRACE OF GOD GO I, it read. Southern for "Better you than me."

She flipped the light switch in the foyer, but the expected illumination didn't come. *Must be a power shortage.* But then she realized the porch light was still burning outside the door. *Maybe a blown fuse?*

It took a minute to hang her coat and scarf neatly on the rack. Then she fumbled for her key again in the dim yellow light. She needed the key to secure the lock. Her granddaughter, now a big-city girl with self-proclaimed street smarts, had come down from Richmond over Thanksgiving and replaced the old-fashioned chain and dead bolt with new high-security locks, the kind that required a key to get *out* of your own house. The idea was to keep burglars from reaching through the window from the outside to unlock the door on the inside.

It seemed like overkill to Gerty. What was next, a blood test to sit down at your own dinner table? She knew it defeated the purpose, but she'd developed the habit of letting herself in, then leaving her keys right in the lock on the front door.

As her eyes slowly adjusted to the darkness, she started across the living room. The curved back of the Victorian sofa was visible in the shadows. A shaft of light from the porch reflected off the oak-framed mirror above the fireplace. The century-old floor-boards creaked beneath her feet.

"General Lee?" she called out. "Where are you, baby?" Her voice had an apologetic tone. She'd promised to be home no later than five o'clock, and the general was one kitty who didn't like his dinner late.

"Come on, sweety. Mommy's sorry she's late."

She stopped at the table by the staircase to try the crystal lamp. It didn't light. The whole living room appeared to be without power. Strangely, though, the time displayed on the digital clock on the table seemed about right, and she watched one of the digits fall, which confirmed it was working. Seven-forty-two P.M.

She started down the narrow hall toward the kitchen. Halfway down, she was completely beyond the outer limits of the faint glow from the porch. She'd reached total darkness. With each additional step she relied more on memory than on vision. She slid her hand across the wall to feel for the light switch. A quick flip of the button brought an erratic flicker from the fluorescent bulb over the stove, giving her a start. Her pulse quickened, but the calm returned as she scanned the familiar old kitchen.

"General—" she started to say, then stopped. The bright crimson droplet on the floor caught her attention. At first she thought it might be coffee she'd spilled earlier in the day, but it seemed thicker and redder. She took a paper towel from the countertop and bent down to dab it. She blinked at the way it smeared across the linoleum.

She rose slowly and noticed a whole string of deep red drops, each about a foot or two apart, reaching from one end of the kitchen to the other. Most of them were small, but some were as big as quarters. The trail ended at the back door, which had a pass-through in the lower half that allowed her pets to come and go.

"General Lee?" Her voice shook with concern. Had he cut his paw in the darkness? she wondered. Was he hemorrhaging? Maybe he crawled outside to die in the weeds. In a panic she rushed for the back door, but it was locked and there was no key in the dead bolt.

"Damn these new locks!"

She raced from the kitchen, retracing her steps through the pitch-dark hallway and into the living room. Her breath was short and her heart was pounding as she neared the front door and reached for the keys in the lock, right where she'd left them. She froze.

The keys weren't there.

She stared in disbelief. Her hands began to shake, but she was standing completely still when the floorboard creaked directly behind her.

She wheeled and gasped, looking straight into the eyes of a dark silhouette—a huge man dressed from head to foot in some kind of black hood and tight-fitting bodysuit. She was about to scream, but his hand jerked forward and grasped her throat. His quickness stunned her. The strength of his grip made her knees buckle.

"I can't . . . breathe." Her voice broke as she fought for air.

"I don't . . . care." He used the same broken cadence, mocking her struggle.

As his grip tightened, the knife appeared. It hung before her eyes with the flat side toward her, and she saw her own terror in the eerie reflection. She could hear his voice, even make out a few words. He was talking *at* her, demanding something. The intense fear and pain made it all seem jumbled. The room began to blur. But the voice grew louder.

Chapter 2

Special Agent Victoria Santos was staring down the barrel of the gun, watching the marksman take aim from just thirty feet away. He was in the classic stance with feet spread wide, arms extended, and both hands on the revolver. His gun moved erratically from left to right; his eyes darted up and down. He had all the telltale signs of a nervous young cop trying desperately to get a bead on the man behind the hostage.

Her captor held her tightly with a knife pressed to her throat and one arm twisted behind her back. His breath felt hot on the back of her neck. The cop had kept him talking for nearly two minutes, but he was growing ever more angry and showing no interest in taking her alive.

"Drop the knife!" the cop finally shouted.

"Drop dead!"

"Drop it, now!"

The knife pressed against her jugular. A shot rang out.

"*Ow*," she cried.

Deep, red rivulets ran down her forehead, onto her plastic safety goggles.

The lights came up in the packed auditorium as Kevin Price, director of the FBI's Hostage Negotiation Training Seminar, tossed the rubber knife aside and stepped toward the microphone at center stage. He was a thirty-year veteran, gray-haired and ruggedly handsome. A dark blue FBI raincoat had shielded his striped tie and starched white shirt from the exploding mock bullet. "Thank you very much, Officer Crowling."

The embarrassed volunteer placed the training gun on the prop table, then stepped quickly off the stage.

"The point of these crisis simulations is not to single anybody out," Price continued. "Rather, it's to show that in real life, it's frighteningly easy to end up with a dead hostage. A face-to-face confrontation is one of the most volatile situations an officer can encounter. It draws on instinct, but also on proper training. It requires split-second application of some basic negotiating skills. There *are* right and wrong things to say and do."

Victoria wiped the last vestiges of red dye from her forehead. "Let's take a fifteen-minute break," she said, "and when we come back we'll talk about some alternatives to shooting the hostage in the head."

A light round of laughter rose from the crowd, followed by the hum and bustle of two hundred cops heading for two rest rooms.

Victoria removed her raincoat. The waterproof material had made her hot beneath the spotlights, but she couldn't feel too indignant—it had protected her suit from the pinkish red splatter. She smiled at Price as she rubbed the center of her forehead. "I must look like Cyclops."

He stepped closer to check where the mock bullet had impacted. In two-inch heels she stood eye-to-eye with him—six feet even.

"A third eye can come in handy," he said with a straight face. Then he smiled. "Seriously, it doesn't look too bad. I wish there were another way to give these demos authenticity."

"It's okay," she said as she folded up the raincoat. "Let me ask you something, though. We've done this seminar how many times now?"

"Oh, geez. Six years, three or four road shows a year. Probably thirty or forty times, I'd guess."

"Don't take this the wrong way, but why is it that I'm always the hostage and you're always the hostage taker?"

A funny look came across his face, like he'd never really thought about it. "I guess I didn't think it mattered."

She shrugged. "Maybe it does, maybe it doesn't. I just want you to know I can play both roles. Besides," she said with a disarming smile, "I'd really *love* the chance to slit your throat."

"I'll keep it in mind," he said with a smirk.

One of the event coordinators emerged from behind the stage curtain. "Agent Santos?" she said. "You have a phone call. They said it's important."

Victoria felt sudden apprehension. For the past four months, she'd been the FBI's task force coordinator in the multistate search for a geographically transient serial killer. By far, it was her most important assignment since transferring from hostage negotiation to the Child Abduction and Serial Killer Unit in Quantico, Virginia. Too often, an "important" message meant very bad news.

"You can take it in the office," the assistant said. Victoria followed her behind the stage. They meandered through a dark path of pulleys, ropes and props until they reached the office near the rest rooms. It was a windowless room no bigger than a closet, with books and papers stacked high in every available space. The desk was so cluttered it might have been impossible to find the phone had it not been for the red blinking hold button. Victoria closed the door for privacy and picked up the receiver.

"Santos," she answered.

"Pete Weston here. Sorry to bother you in the middle of your road show, but you told me to call as soon as I had anything."

She rubbed the last bit of red dye from her eyebrows, then blinked hard, switching completely out of her training mode. Dr. Weston was a DNA expert in the FBI laboratory at headquarters, one of hundreds of experts she relied on for support.

"Don't apologize," she said. "Thanks for working a Saturday. Got my results?"

"Yes, but you won't be happy."

She sighed, but showed no surprise. "What did you find?"

"Well, I looked at the specimens from the Eugene, Oregon, scene first. You remember we had some drops of blood in the bathroom, around the sink and tub, well away from the body. Unfortunately, I'm afraid you can rule out your theory that the killer cut himself and left behind a trail of his own blood."

"How do you know?"

"On a hunch I compared the unidentified blood from Oregon to the blood of the other four victims—Cleveland, New York, Arkansas, Miami. I got a match with Miami. He must have taken it with him from the Miami victim, or maybe it had just collected on his knife or soaked into his clothing. He could have frozen it to preserve it, then brought it with him to Oregon and sprinkled it at the scene."

"He's collecting blood now?" she said warily.

"In a way, yes. But it doesn't mean you have a vampire on your hands. If you did, you'd probably have me examining blood from blenders and coffee cups by now."

Victoria said nothing, though she tended to agree. From the psychological profile she'd helped construct, she already knew the killer was no raving lunatic spewing his own blood, hair and fibers for the police to gather in their evidence bags—the so-called disorganized sociopath. Beyond that, though, no one was sure *what* they were after. The mixed signals were what made the case so baffling, and the thought of yet another dead end brought a knot to her stomach. "How sure are you about the match with Miami?"

"Virtually certain."

"That's certain enough for me," she said. "Given the case history, I guess it was pretty unrealistic to

13

hope for a break that big. Thanks anyway, Doc. You do good work."

She hung up, then pushed aside a stack of books to sit on the edge of the desk. After a minute of thought, she dug in her purse for her Dictaphone.

"Saturday, January eleventh," she began. "Lab results suggest further modification of profile. Savagery of attacks, level of carnage left behind at crime scenes, absence of actual sexual penetration continue to suggest disorganized qualities. Level of staging and increasing manipulation of evidence, however, indicates a keen presence of mind and well-conceived plan to taunt police and/or thwart the investigation, consistent with an intelligent and organized serial killer."

She paused and took a deep breath, as if suddenly comprehending the size of their problem. She switched the Dictaphone back on. "In short," she said solemnly, "subject can be classified neither as organized nor disorganized. It appears as though we're dealing with a unique sociopathic hybrid. One killer, with attributes of both."

Church let out at noon on that clear but cold Sunday. A call came in to the Candler County sheriff's office in Metter around twelve-forty-five. The clerical staff didn't work weekends, but it was time to order new supplies for the detention center on the other side of the sally port, so Barbara Easton was working overtime. The Bible had taught her never to work on Sunday, but she was a nineteen-year-old single mother who needed food on the table. "Sheriff's office," she answered in a polite southern drawl.

"Good afternoon." The man's voice was completely calm, lacking any sense of urgency. His speech, however, was thick and gravelly, seemingly disguised. "I want to report a homicide."

"A *homicide*? You mean someone was murdered?"

"That's the only kind of homicide I know of."

"Where! I'll call for an ambulance."

"Too late. I told you: She's dead."

"Okay, uhm. Just calm down, all right?" She was fidgeting with her hair, speaking more to herself than the caller. "Are you sure she's dead?"

"Dead sure. I'm the one who killed her."

Her mouth opened but words didn't follow. "You—" her voice cracked, "you're calling to report your own murder?"

"It's not *my* murder, missy. I'm not dead. I'm the murderer."

The patronizing tone gave his words even more impact. Her hands started to shake, and her mind went blank. "Are you—is this some kind of joke?"

"Let me put it to you as plain as I can, lady. The last person I talked to is now a bloody mess on her bedroom floor."

A lump came to her throat. She'd been a secretary only a month. Her training hadn't covered *this*, but her instincts told her to get him to talk to a cop. "Sir, would you like to speak to the sheriff?"

"I'd like to speak to *somebody* who knows what the hell they're doing. Make it fast."

"Just one sec." Her shaky finger hit the HOLD button,

then she dropped the receiver and peeled down the hall. "Sheriff!" she shouted. "Come quick!"

Sheriff John Dutton was in the back, chatting with his deputy by the Mr. Coffee machine. He was fifty-two years old, fair-skinned and freckled with wavy red hair that was turning precipitously gray. Twenty-eight years of cruising in patrol cars and pigging out at the local Egg 'N You Diner had put an extra thirty pounds around his waist. Barbara was panting and wide-eyed with panic when she reached him.

"Man's on the line," she blurted. Her chest was heaving as she tried to catch her breath. "Says he killed someone."

He blinked in disbelief, but her eyes told him she was deadly serious. He dropped his chocolate dough-nut on the counter and sprinted to the phone. A ring-ful of keys jingled on his belt loop, and his heavy thighs rubbed together to the tune of tight polyester slacks. He jumped in the chair and caught his breath. "Did he say anything else?" he asked quickly, before getting on the line.

"Nuh-uh. Just that he killed someone. His voice sounds kind of funny, though. Like maybe he's disguising it."

He grabbed the receiver, then paused and grimaced. For years he'd been pushing for an upgraded phone system, but the county budget didn't even allow for automatic recording of calls to the new 911 service, let alone to the sheriff's office. "Fetch me my Dictaphone," he barked.

Barbara scrambled across the room to his desk, rifled through a drawer full of pens, pencils, and crumpled candy bar wrappers, and came up with the Dictaphone. She hustled back to the sheriff, who picked up the receiver and switched on the Dictaphone, holding it by the earpiece. He cleared the nervous tickle from his throat and pushed the blinking button on the telephone. "Hello, this is Sheriff John Dutton. Who am I speaking to?"

"Prince Charles of Wales," came the sarcastic reply. "I'm not about to tell you who I am, fool."

"Okay, no problem. No problem at all." He spoke in the even, understanding tone that had kept dozens of domestic disturbances from turning into bloodbaths. "I hear there's an incident you want to report."

"It's no *incident*. It's a homicide."

"You want to tell me about it?"

"What do you want to hear, Sheriff? How she begged me not to do it? Or how she screamed when I did?"

. He drew a deep breath, forcing himself to show no emotion. "So the victim's a woman, I take it."

"Now we're getting somewhere."

"Who is she?" He closed his eyes and waited, fearing he might know her.

"Name's Gerty. Lives over in Hainesville."

He brought his hand to his forehead, grimacing with anguish. Hainesville had but one Gerty; the world knew but one Gerty. He bit back his anger and forced himself to maintain a congenial tone— anything to keep the guy talking. "You sure you don't wanna tell me who you are now, pardner?"

"Sure thing. I'm your next-door neighbor, asshole.

I'm the guy standing behind you in the checkout line at the Piggly Wiggly."

"You got a name?"

"One more stupid question, Sheriff, and I'm going to have to ask you to put the girl back on the line."

"Fair enough. Just stay on the line, okay?" He took a sip of cold coffee from Barbara's Styrofoam cup, ignoring the lipstick on the rim. "Tell me this much: Did you know Gerty—or did she know you?"

"Never met her before. Never even laid eyes on her."

"Then why in the world would you kill her?"

"Because I'm a bad person."

"Well, you must have some kind of reason. You don't just kill somebody for no reason."

"You're thinking *way* too logically, Sheriff."

"I just want to know why you did it. That's all."

"All right. I'll tell you why." The voice tightened with anger. His speech became slow and deliberate, with eerie pauses between words, as if some other part of him were answering: "Because . . . I . . . *felt* like it."

The sheriff winced. It sounded like he meant it— the guy just *felt* like it. "Where's she now? Where's the body?"

The man sighed, then there was silence. Precious seconds passed. The sheriff felt his throat going dry. He feared he was losing him. "Come on, pardner. Let's not play games. Where'd you put the body?"

"I didn't *put* her anywhere. I can't believe you hick-town cops haven't gotten over there yet. Shit, man, if I had to sit around waiting for you and Barney Fife to find her, no one would *ever* recognize my work."

"Why? How long ago did you kill her? Just tell me that."

"Two days ago."

"Why'd you wait so long to call us?"

"I wasn't through with her."

"What does *that* mean?"

He let out a deep, sarcastic sigh of boredom. "It means that now I *am* through with her."

"You son of a bitch. What did you *do to her*!" He was on the edge of his seat, his face flushed with anger.

"Sorry, Sheriff," he said coolly. "That was your final stupid question."

The line clicked, and then came the dial tone.

Chapter 3

two rapes, nine robberies and a fatal drive-by shooting. After thirteen years with the *Miami Tribune*, Mike Posten had seen enough crime to recite the daily tally without emotion, like "two eggs and toast with a side of bacon."

At six feet two he could be intimidating when necessary, and some of the characters he met made it absolutely necessary. He was easy to talk to but not a "smooth talker," with warm brown eyes and a disarming smile that had once made him a bit of a heartthrob after hours. His J-school professors had told him that even though he was no pretty boy, he had the talent and presence to go far at a major television network. For him, however, the printed word was the most rewarding form of journalism. The morning newspaper was the world's equilibrium. As irreverent as he could be sometimes, he maintained a dedication to his craft that had earned him a Pulitzer and the grudging admiration of his colleagues.

That Monday morning had been particularly busy, and Mike had wasted most of it in Miami's "Little Havana" area trying to interview some drunk with vomit on his shoes who said he'd found a nice pair of sneakers in the Dumpster with the feet still in them. Normally Mike would have kept right on working through lunch, but today was a personal matter.

Lunch-hour traffic was moving briskly across MacArthur Causeway. The six east-west lanes almost seemed to float in the blue-green waters of Biscayne Bay, connecting the skyscrapers of downtown Miami to the neighboring island of Miami Beach. Along the south stretched Government Cut, a narrow waterway for cruise and cargo ships that probed like a mile-long finger from the Atlantic. Waterfront mansions rimmed the private residential islands to the north, home at one time or another to the likes of Al Capone and Julio Iglesias.

Mike and Karen Posten drove in separate cars from their marriage counselor's office to the restaurant on Miami Beach. She led in her Infiniti. He followed in his black Saab convertible. It was a metaphor, he thought, for the current state of their marriage—separate, with him in pursuit. Two months ago, she'd suggested he take an apartment. She swore there was no other lover. There was no physical, mental or substance abuse. No money problems. And most of all, no passion. After eight years of marriage, they'd become two very successful people who took each other for granted. At least that's what their counselor had told them.

"Lost her," Mike muttered as he turned north on

21

Ocean Drive. Probably a dozen cars looked exactly like hers—it was south Florida's current luxury vehicle-of-choice. He would have bet a week's salary that one of these days while eavesdropping on police radio he'd hear not that the suspect had fled in a white four-door sedan but that he was *not* driving an emerald black Infiniti.

He spotted his wife a few blocks ahead, entering one of the sidewalk cafés that made South Beach so popular. Parking was impossible on Ocean Drive, so he curbed his convertible at the valet stand, right behind a flaming red Porsche with a personalized license plate reading UNWED MD. If ever a case could be made in support of drive-by shootings, this guy had to be it.

Ocean Drive was, by local consensus at least, the most colorful strip of restored Art Deco hotels in the world. On a sunny afternoon like this one, it was a prime cruising lane for people watchers and scantily clad beachgoers. Tourists sipped espresso and conversed in a dozen different languages. Speeding Rollerbladers weaved in and out of pedestrians, excusing everything from sweaty sideswipes to head-on collisions with a glib, "Sorry, dude."

Mike had never considered himself one of South Beach's so-called beautiful people, though his thirty-eight-year-old body was still fit, trimmed by years of discipline at the rowing machine and an undying passion for competitive sports—basketball and racquetball being his favorites. His hairline had given him a brief scare in his early thirties, but the recession had stopped quickly, and it was clear now that his thick, dark mane with flecks of gray would survive middle age.

Karen was already seated at a wrought-iron table beneath a Cinzano umbrella by the time he got his valet ticket. He made eye contact and waved from across the restaurant. She seemed a little out of place in her pearl necklace and navy blue business suit, but she still looked great, fanning herself with the menu. Her thick auburn hair was shoulder length, slightly longer on the left than the right—a daring cut for the newest partner at Saunders & Sires, Miami's largest and, by all accounts, stodgiest law firm. At thirty-two she was six years younger than Mike, but she had an uncanny ability to look younger or more mature as the circumstances demanded. Either way, she was striking—deceptively so for a woman who'd finished at the top of her law school class and served as editor in chief of the *University of Miami Law Review*.

Mike arrived just as the waiter was setting two salads on the table.

"I'm kind of in a hurry," said Karen, "so I went ahead and ordered for you. Grilled chicken Caesar."

"Sounds good." He pulled up a chair, unfurled the cloth napkin, and then winced curiously at the distinctive shiny metal bowl holding his salad.

"The salads come in dog bowls," explained Karen. "That's why it's called the Dog Gone Café. Clever, huh?"

"Oh, it's beyond clever," he said, smirking. "I'd say it rivals the kind of trendy logic that would have the Russian Tea Room serving entrées in teacups."

They made small talk for a while, then ate in silence, not for lack of anything to say but for lack of nerve to say it. The bowls were nearly empty before either could steer the conversation in a serious direction.

"Session went well today," said Mike. "Don't you think?"

"Better," she said, shrugging. "I think we still have a ways to go, though."

He looked at his bowl. He was starting to feel like a dog. *Throw me a bone, Karen.*

"Mike, please don't take this the wrong way, but I really wish you wouldn't always look to me for status reports. It seems like all you ever want to know is how close we are to solving the problem. But you don't ever really talk about what we have to do to fix things."

"Sorry. I was just feeling pretty good about what Dr. Newsome said about our psychological profiles today—that we're so much alike."

Her brow furrowed. "That's not what she was suggesting. She said we're the psychological mirror image of each other."

"Which means we're exactly the same."

"It means we're total *opposites*. When you look in the mirror, everything's reversed."

He averted his eyes, befuddled. "I guess that's one way of looking at it."

"Anything else, folks?" the waiter interrupted.

"No, thanks," said Karen. She checked her watch. "Sorry, but I have to scoot back to the firm. I'm deposing a bank vice president at two-thirty."

"You mean you're not staying for the Milk-Bone soufflé?"

She smiled and opened her purse.

"My treat," he said. "You can pay when we dine at the Russian Tea Room."

"Deal."

They said good-bye and exchanged a nothing kiss. He watched as she walked to her car, hoping she'd look back, maybe give him a smile. He didn't get one.

He ordered another Evian with lemon, then turned his attention to the people parade along the extrawide sidewalk on Ocean Drive. A statuesque brunette clad in a strategically ripped dago-T scurried toward the Ford Agency. A geriatric retiree inched along on his walker. Amazing, he thought, South Beach was the one place on earth where even the homophobic cop down from Brooklyn seemed to blend right in with the flamboyant transvestite walking six poodles on a leash. Peaceful coexistence. So why did every conversation with Karen feel like a boxing match?

At ten after two he called his office voice mail on his portable phone, then dialed the answering machine back at his apartment. Actually, Zack's apartment. As he waited for the fourth ring, it suddenly occurred to him that for nearly two decades he'd had the same best friend. Karen didn't seem to keep in touch with anyone longer than a few months. Maybe they *were* opposites.

"Hello," Zack answered.

"Dumbshit, what'd you pick up for? I'm calling in for messages."

"Gee, it's good to hear your voice too, man."

"Sorry. I'm not exactly having a banner day."

"No problem. Anyway, the light's not blinking on your machine, so I guess nobody loves you. But you did get a package this morning. Kind of weird. It's got "urgent, open immediately" written all over it, but it came second-day, non-Saturday delivery—which means a three-day delay."

"From who?"

"Not sure. Can't read the name on the delivery invoice. Looks like it was mailed from Atlanta."

"Go ahead and open it." Mike heard the package tearing open, then he couldn't hear anything as a Jeep full of bikini-clad Brazilians rolled down Ocean Boulevard with the boom box blasting.

"Hmmm," said Zack. "This is strange."

"What?"

"Just a sheet of paper. Nothing on it but some woman's name. Typed. Do you know a Gertrude Kincaid?"

Mike froze. He'd been following the gruesome trail of "tongue murders" ever since the third victim had turned up in Miami. "Actually, I'm doing a story on her."

"She one of your sources?"

"No. A victim. Looks like she's body number six for that serial killer I've been covering. Her name just came over the wire this morning. Small town in Georgia. Police found her body yesterday, but they think it happened sometime Friday."

"*Friday?*"

"Yeah, why?"

"Like I said, the package took three days to get here. It was sent on Thursday."

Mike could suddenly hear himself breathing. "Don't touch anything, all right? Just leave everything right where it is. I'll be there in a minute." He switched off the phone and ran to his car.

Chapter 4

a record-breaking cold front was working through south-central Georgia that Monday afternoon. Gray skies cast an eerie pall over a brown, rolling landscape that seemed shocked by the blast of Arctic air. Livestock herded together in the open fields along Highway 46, sheltering each other from the cold north wind. At the end of the long line of barbed-wire fencing, bare oaks and azaleas lined the quiet streets of Hainesville.

Special Agent Victoria Santos parked her rented Oldsmobile at the curb in front of 501 Peach Street. "Kincaid" was the name on the mailbox at the end of the driveway. As she opened her car door a blue-and-white van marked ACTION NEWS pulled away from the curb. She presumed several other media types had already come and gone in the past twenty-four hours since the body had been discovered. A curious neighbor watched from beyond the white picket fence as she ducked under the yellow police tape and headed up the brick driveway. Three men wearing the brown leather jackets and dark brown trousers of the Candler County Sheriff's Department were standing on the covered front porch, on the official business side of yet another line of yellow police tape stretched across the top step. It was cold enough for her to see their breath steam. Little puffs of conversation came from all directions, each seeming to talk over the other.

Victoria rubbed her hands together and pulled her trench coat tight, cursing the cold beneath her breath. It was a far cry from the steaminess of Cuba, where she'd been born thirty-three years ago, or, for that matter, the warmth of Miami Beach, where she'd spent her childhood. She'd spent the last ten years up north, after graduating from the FBI Academy, but her blood still hadn't thickened. Strangely, it had been warmer in Virginia this morning than in Georgia, and she hadn't had time to check the weather before flying to Savannah, let alone pack appropriately. She'd left on a Bubird—the Bureau's name for its own aircraft—directly from the Quantico airstrip, five minutes after taking an urgent call from her supervisor.

"Santos, FBI," she announced with a flash of her credentials. She was standing on the top step, just shy of the police tape. "I'm looking for Sheriff John Dutton."

The conversation stopped, and their stares made her mildly self-conscious. She was taller than the sheriff, but she felt much shorter standing one step below the men on the porch. They looked at her as though they might have found her attractive at a bake sale or church picnic. Here, however, she was definitely the intruder.

Sheriff Dutton stepped forward, hands resting irreverently on his hips. He came close enough for her to read his name bar pinned to his jacket, but he didn't formally introduce himself. "You're the help they sent down from Washington, I take it."

"Not Washington, exactly. I work out of Quantico, Virginia. Thanks for notifying us."

"Wasn't *my* idea to notify anybody. It was the State Attorney who wanted to call in the feds. Hell if I know why—we take care of our own here." He gave Victoria an assessing look. "I'll just remind you once, miss, *I'm* the one running this investigation."

Less than five minutes on the scene, she thought, and already she was knee-deep in testosterone. "I fully intend to respect your authority, Sheriff. However, you should know that my reasons for being here are not casual. I've spent the last four months working with local law enforcement in five states on five previous murders that may be related to this one."

"Do say . . . Well, right now, this is the only murder we're concerned about. In Hainesville, ain't nothin' more important than a matter of local concern."

"I can appreciate that."

"Then I hope you also appreciate that things are well under control. Crime scene's secure. I did it myself, to reduce the chance of any disturbance. Filled out the initial report. Sketched a floor plan, took photographs and a videotape. You can look at any of that. But I'm not about to have anybody who shows up with a badge poking around inside willy-nilly."

"Rest assured, I want to work *with* you to catch this

killer. We can talk about the crime scene later. First, though, I'd like to see the body."

"It's long gone. The body van picked it up yesterday. Georgia Bureau of Investigation routed it to the branch crime lab in Macon."

"I know, I'm on my way there. I was just hoping you'd come with me, maybe give me some background. I'm sure I could use your insights as well. Can I count on you, please?"

She did everything short of batting her eyes, struggling to keep a straight face. With her forensic background she could practically have performed the autopsy herself, and she hardly needed a county sheriff to show her around a morgue. Politics, however, made it important at the outset to reassure the locals that they weren't being squeezed out of their own investigation.

"All right," he said, seemingly disarmed. "I'll drive."

In two minutes they were in the squad car, headed west on I-16. Cunningham's funeral home normally served as Hainesville's morgue. The local coroner, a paramedic at Candler County Hospital, had already ruled the death suspicious, so the body had been transferred to the Georgia State Crime Lab for examination by a trained forensic pathologist. It was over an hour's ride, mostly on interstate, so there was plenty of time for Victoria to review her notes.

"What can you tell me about Mrs. Kincaid?" she asked, finally looking up from her sheaf of papers. The wipers squeaked across the windshield, clearing away a few slushy drops that were on the verge of becoming Candler County's first significant snowfall in more than five years.

"Seventy-eight-year-old widow. Her husband was a state legislator who died when she was in her early forties. She never remarried, raised a two-year-old daughter by her lonesome and fifteen years ago was elected Hainesville's first woman mayor. She retired a couple years back, but still went to every city council meeting. Lived alone, drove herself wherever she wanted to go and chewed the hell out of anyone who suggested she was getting too old to do it. LBJ was president the last time she'd missed a Sunday-morning service, and she couldn't have been sick more than a few days in her life. That's why it was so conspicuous when she wasn't in the front pew singing yesterday morning." He took his eyes from the road and looked at her directly. "That's why it's so important I catch the animal who killed her."

"And that's why I'm here. To help."

"I *know* why you're here," he scoffed. "You think we're a bunch of dumb rednecks who can't handle a homicide because there ain't been nobody killed in Hainesville since the bad guys wore blue and the good guys wore gray. Well, that ain't the case, miss. We know our stuff here."

"I'm sure you do. But whether you're good or bad cops has nothing to do with my being here." She paused, trying to think of some way to explain her visit without insulting. "Have you ever heard of CASKU, Sheriff?"

He furrowed his brow, searching, but he was plainly drawing a blank. "Heard of it, yeah. Stands for . . . for somethin'."

"It's an acronym for the FBI's Child Abduction and Serial Killer Unit, based in Quantico. It's fairly new, created specifically to provide operational assistance to any local, state or federal law enforcement agency involved in the investigation of a child abduction or serial murder case. My job is to make sure you get the services you need—crime analysis, formulation of investigative strategies, technical and forensic resource coordination, use of the FBI Evidence Response Teams or FBI laboratory services. I also coordinate our analysis of the behavioral characteristics of unknown serial killers. It's called 'profiling.'"

"Now that you've described it, I *have* heard of it. You're the guys responsible for those god-awful forms."

"You must mean the VI-CAP form—Violent Criminal Apprehension Program. They *are* long, but the key to the profiling program is to make sure the information fed back to Quantico is as complete and accurate as possible, so it's worth the effort. The whole program started with actual interviews of convicted killers like Manson, Richard Speck and Ted Bundy. Now it's grown into a huge database that includes profiles of virtually every known serial killer in modern time. The idea was to figure out what makes these guys tick, what drives them, what they feel and don't feel before, during and after the murders. The learning curve is ongoing, but special agents back at Quantico can now look at the evidence in a given case and construct a psychological profile of the killer. For the investigators in the field, a solid profile gives them somebody to look for."

"But if this is the sixth murder, like you say, there must already be a profile."

"Not a good one. This is a particularly tough case. We figure the killer's probably a man, but only because female serial killers are so rare. The classic victim's female, between the age of fifteen and thirty. Here, we've got three men and—counting Mrs. Kincaid—three women, their ages ranging from thirty-one to seventy-eight. The classic serial killer is a sadistic sexual psychopath who strikes within his own ethnic group. In this case, none of the victims was sexually assaulted, three are white, two are black and one's Hispanic. If that's not confounding enough, they come from six different states, six very different communities. Manhattan. Eugene, Oregon. Miami. Cleveland. Fayetteville, Arkansas. And now Hainesville."

"Don't see much of a common thread there. What makes you think they're all related?"

"That's another benefit of VI-CAP. The computer helps link up crimes from different jurisdictions that might otherwise never be connected—you know, the old joke about a killer signing his name on the victim's forehead in Oregon, while the cops in Cleveland are looking for the same guy but don't know a thing about it. VI-CAP gave us a match after the third victim was found in Miami. It was the bizarre MO. Granted, it's still the only thing that links the victims to each other or to any one person who could be their killer, but it's a strong link—more like a signature than an MO. All were stabbed, multiple times. And each one had their tongue extracted from their mouth."

Dutton cringed, thinking how much it hurt just to bite his own tongue. The image of the dried blood on

Gerty's lips suddenly returned. "When you say extracted," he said warily, "you mean cut, I suppose."

"Partly." She stared out the window, deep in her own thoughts of five other victims who came before Gerty. "But mostly I mean ripped."

She heard the sheriff breathe a heavy sigh, and they rode the rest of the way to the morgue in silence.

"Looks like myocardial infarction," said Dr. Percy Ackerman, medical examiner. He was short and stocky with a very round head covered by a salt-and-pepper stubble that was no longer than a five-o'clock shadow. He stood at the head of the autopsy table, bearing the stains of various bodily fluids on his green surgical scrubs and latex gloves.

Victoria peered down at the old woman's naked, gray body. Two deep incisions ran laterally from shoulder to shoulder, across her breasts at a downward angle and meeting at the sternum. A long, deeper cut ran from breastbone to groin, forming the stem in the coroner's classic "Y" incision. The liver, spleen, kidneys and intestines were laid out neatly beside a slab of ribs on the dissection tray behind Dr. Ackerman. The cadaver was literally a shell of a human being, strangely reminiscent of the hollowed-out half of a watermelon on a table of hors d'oeuvres. Victoria smeared another dab of Vicks Vapo-Rub beneath her nostrils, taking extra care to cut the odor. At moments like these she would swear that a degree in medicine was the only thing separating serial killers from forensic pathologists. That, and a conscience.

"You mean Gerty died of a heart attack?" Sheriff Dutton asked incredulously.

"I'm saying she was literally scared to death. Medically speaking, extreme terror or fear can cause a sudden and massive release of epinephrine—better known as adrenaline—causing ventricular fibrillation of the heart. That seems to be what happened here. I would point out, though, that her rather advanced arteriosclerosis made her somewhat susceptible to V-fib."

"Well," said Victoria, "you can't crack somebody over the head with a lead pipe and then defend yourself by saying his skull was too thin. A killer has to take his victim with all her weakness, all her vulnerabilities. The mechanism of death may have been myocardial infarction, but surely you agree that the manner of death was still homicide."

"Absolutely."

She walked around to the other side of the table, looking more closely. "Tell me more about what scared her. Was it something the killer did to her? Or does it look like she just saw him standing in the doorway and that was all her poor heart could take?"

"Gerty Kincaid was no scaredy-cat," the sheriff scoffed.

"In this case," sighed Dr. Ackerman, "I'd say she was too strong for her own good. An immediate death of natural causes would have been a blessing."

Victoria glanced at the clear plastic bag on the tray, holding a flat, reddish brown wedge of flesh. The color ran from her cheeks, and the torrents of cold air from the ducts overhead suddenly seemed colder.

"You think the tongue came out before she was dead, then."

"Actually, it wasn't completely removed until I did the examination."

Victoria shot him a look of concern.

"The killer had taken it better than three-quarters of the way," said Ackerman, slightly defensive. "That's what made the State Attorney call you in the first place, thinking it was connected to these tongue murders in the news. It was just hanging by a shred. I took it the rest of the way to inspect the wound."

"All right," she said. "But this is important: Do you think the killer did his part before or after death?"

"I'd say it was *perimortem*—at or near the time of death. We've got various signs of torture. Look here," he said as he turned one of the hands palm up. "Nails dug into the skin on the inside of the palms. She actually punctured the skin and drew blood. I'd say digging in *that* deeply is consistent with sustained, excruciating pain—the kind of pain you might expect to be associated with someone trying to rip the tongue right out of your mouth."

"We've seen that on a few of the other victims," Victoria said quietly. "What about time of death?"

"She was starting to swell with gas buildup. A few blisters had already formed under the skin, and fluids were leaking from her nose and vagina. So I fixed the time of death sometime on Friday, figuring she'd been dead maybe two and a half days. It's hard to pinpoint an exact time."

Victoria nodded. His conclusions seemed sound, but she suspected that his estimation of the time of death

...as no doubt influenced by newspaper reports that Gerty Kincaid was last seen alive on Friday morning.

Dr. Ackerman carried on about livor mortis patterns and the details of his examination for another twenty minutes, until Victoria announced it was time to leave. She and Sheriff Dutton walked in silence to the parking lot. The sun had just set. Gray skies were turning black, and the temperature had dropped even further. Tiny drops of water on the hood of the squad car had actually frozen.

"Is he any good?" she asked casually as they piled into the car.

Dutton switched on the heater, but it blasted only cold air. "Who, Dr. Ackerman? Best damn pathologist in Georgia—maybe even the whole southeastern United States. Doesn't have some goofy nickname, like the Grim Reaper or Dr. Blood and Guts, and he doesn't eat ketchup sandwiches while doin' his autopsies, neither. Just because he's originally from south Georgia don't mean he's some backwoods flunky you see in a made-for-TV movie."

"I wasn't implying he should be dressing deer. Don't take this too personally, Sheriff, but you seem to get awfully defensive every time I ask you a question."

He paused, seeming to measure his response as the squad car came to a halt at the corner of Oglethorpe and Second Avenue. "Me—defensive? Maybe. But I think it's more along the lines of those women who say they have to work twice as hard to get half as much. When it comes to law enforcement, a small-town cop's probably a lot like being a woman in the FBI. Nobody thinks you can play with the big boys."

Victoria smiled with her eyes. She wasn't sure she liked him, but she suddenly understood him.

He lit up a cigarette. "I mean, people must ask you all the time why a woman like you would want to chase serial killers for a living."

"Yeah," she said, smiling thinly. "Sometimes after knocking off a bottle of Mylanta for dinner, I even ask myself that question."

He took a long drag on his cigarette. "Why *do* you do it?"

She stared out the window, said nothing for a long moment, then turned back to him. "For the victims."

The sheriff cracked the window to release the cigarette smoke. "You do seem to care more than most. I could tell from your questions that you were hoping poor old Gerty had died before that monster started ripping out her tongue."

"That wasn't just compassion. I read the transcript you faxed me of that phone call—the so-called confession. Toward the end he said he wasn't through with her until a couple of days after he killed her. That's one of the things that was so intriguing to the FBI profilers. That he would actually have the bravado to call the sheriff's office in the first place was a sign that he was beginning to thrive on the attention. But beyond that, we thought this might be the first case where he did something to the victim after the killing. Postmortem mutilation would change the profile considerably. But that's not the way it happened, according to your Dr. Ackerman. The killer attempted to extract the tongue at or near the time of death, just like the other cases."

"But why did he stop in this case, before the tongue was all the way out? You think somebody scared him off?"

"No. I think he stopped because she died of a heart attack. It tells me this psycho has no use for a dead victim. His signature isn't ripping out people's tongues, dead or alive. His signature is torture."

Dutton felt his mouth go dry. "Okay, you say the perp has no use for dead victims, but I've got the guy on tape saying he waited two days to call and tell us about the murder because he wasn't through with the body yet. Where does that leave us?"

"I'd say it leaves two possibilities. One, the caller *is* the killer, but he's throwing red herrings into his story about postcrime behavior, intentionally trying to mislead us. Or two, he's not the killer at all—but for some crazy reason, he wants us to think he is."

"Why would anyone want that?"

She sighed and shook her head. "Your guess is as good as mine. One thing's for sure, though. That phone call and the tape recording have to remain absolutely confidential. The last thing this investigation needs is nationwide media coverage of a phone call that may have been designed to get everyone looking for the wrong guy."

"Don't worry. That's one good thing about a small department. No leaks."

"I certainly hope so," she muttered under her breath, knowing there was no such thing as a police department without leaks.

Chapter 5

mike sped along the coastline on Bayshore Drive, toward the cluster of bare sailboat masts that projected like a wintry forest from Coconut Grove Marina. He reached the Yacht Harbor condominium just after three o'clock and took the elevator straight up to Zack's twentieth-floor suite.

Although a knee injury had ended Zack's NBA career as a rookie, a huge signing bonus made a second career unnecessary. After Mike helped get him a brief stint as a *Tribune* sportswriter, he quit to pursue his passion—flying. He bought a fleet of seaplanes that took legitimate businessmen from Miami to Palm Beach or Key West and back. Sometimes he'd just take tourists up for the view. The best feeling, though, was when he went up alone, zipping along the coast over turquoise reefs or due west over the wavy brown saw grass that blanketed the Everglades—a near seven-footer imagining what it would be like to be seven *hundred* feet tall.

The view from Zack's penthouse was just as spectacular,

with a wall of windows and wraparound balcony overlooking Biscayne Bay and the Miami skyline. Inside were mirrored walls, polished floors of Brazilian marble, and modern Italian furniture that looked so uncomfortable it *had* to be expensive.

"It's in your room," said Zack, directing Mike as he breezed through the dining room.

Mike had been living in the guest bedroom for the past two months, ever since Karen suggested he take an apartment. At the foot of his unmade bed lay an open pizza delivery box and television remote. On his pillow was the open FedEx package from Georgia, right where Zack had left it. He stepped around the pile of unfolded laundry on the floor and sat on the edge of the bed for a closer inspection. Zack was in the open doorway, leaning against the frame and licking the bright orange residue of a party-size bag of Cheetos from the tips of his fingers.

"I guess you shouldn't touch it," said Zack.

"Good point, Sherlock. I'd hate to smear one of your paw prints."

"Come on, man. I wasn't being nosy. You *told* me to open it." He wiped his hands on his sweatshirt, watching as Mike scrutinized the FedEx invoice—without touching it. "So, you gonna call the cops?"

Mike sighed. "I'll speak to the brass at the paper first, but I gotta believe that's what we'll do. I mean, if this guy sent the package on Thursday and this Kincaid woman wasn't attacked until Friday . . . well, if he isn't the killer, who else could he be?"

"Why would he send it to you, though, as opposed to any other reporter?"

"For all I know he did send it to others. We don't know that I've been singled out—not yet. Actually, what bothers me more right now is how he knew to send it here, to your condo."

Zack stroked his chin, thinking. "That kind of makes me think maybe you *have* been singled out, dude. Could be his own little power play. It's his way of saying that he knows you're separated, that you're living somewhere other than your usual home address. If you were just another reporter on a long mailing list, I don't think he'd go to all that trouble to check out your marital status."

Mike paused, weighing what his friend had just said. "Good point. Actually, when you think about it, it makes some sense that he'd pick me, since I work for the *Tribune*."

"What's so special about the *Tribune*?"

"You figure, if he's going to contact a newspaper, it would probably be in one of the five cities where victims have turned up. Miami's one of them. And the *Tribune* has a huge readership."

"Yeah, but didn't one of the killings take place in New York?" Zack said, smirking. "They got something there called the *New York Times*, don't they?"

Mike was about to make a suitable gesture when the phone rang. He and Zack exchanged expectant glances. *Now what?* Finally, on the fourth ring, Mike snatched it up. "Hello."

"Did you get my package, Posten?"

Mike's mouth opened, but it took a moment for his words to flow. "Who is this?"

"Rule number one, asshole: no questions."

Mike glanced at Zack, who moved closer to the phone. "Yeah, I got your package," Mike said. "It's right here. Saw your little note, too."

"Impressed?"

"Yeah, sure. Takes a big set of balls to torture a seventy-eight-year-old woman. Who's next on your list, day-old puppies with their eyes still closed?"

"You're missing the point, smartass. I didn't kill her. I just *predicted* it."

Mike's brow furrowed. "What do you mean?"

"Exactly what I said. I shipped the package to you on Thursday, and the killer whacked poor old Gerty on Friday. I predicted she'd be next, and I was right. I know who the next one's going to be, too. And the one after that, and the one after that. I've cracked the killer's pattern, and I'm the only one who ever will. Because nobody thinks the way he does—except for me."

Mike's head swirled, but he struggled to stay focused. "This is a very sick game you're playing."

"It's no game. It's business. There's something in it for you, something for me. I know you'd love to hear my predictions—get the scoop on the competition. What reporter wouldn't? I'll give it to you, and *only* to you. A nice big exclusive story. All you gotta do is give me something in return."

"Like what?"

"Money, for starters. Lots of it. Fifty thousand dollars for my next prediction."

"You dirtbag, I'm not about to pay a penny to you or any other source. You've got the wrong reporter."

"Oh, I've got the right one all right. Stay in the

game, and maybe I'll tell you why. Citibank. The account number's on the back of the package. It's in the name of Ernest Gill. Make a cash deposit by Friday."

"You deaf? I said I'm not paying."

"Oh, you'll pay," the caller said smugly. "You have no choice but to pay. Because if you don't, I'll keep making my predictions, the day before the murder. And you'll keep on getting them. The day after they find the body."

"What the hell kind of a prediction is that?"

"A worthless one. Which only goes to show: You get what you pay for."

"Listen—"

"No, *you* listen. Don't even think about the cops, or my next prediction might hit very close to home. Understand?"

Mike started to object, but the line suddenly went dead.

Chapter 6

the *Tribune* headquarters sat right off sparkling Biscayne Bay, with a fifth-floor newsroom offering picture-window views of the Port of Miami and Miami Beach. Curiously, the editorial board was quartered on the fifth floor, south end, in probably the only waterfront office space in Miami with no windows. Neither that, however, nor the beige wallpaper was the real reason the rank and file called it "the ivory tower."

The largest office belonged to Aaron Fields. At age sixty-two he'd been publisher for the past five years, a member of the board for seventeen. He had the people skills of a consummate politician, which meant that people still liked him even after they discovered he was a mile wide and an inch deep. Thick silver hair and a thin smile of confidence gave him the look of success. He dressed the part, too, sporting custom suits that cost more than some reporters earned in a month—certainly more than Mike had earned thirteen years ago, when Fields had first hired him.

His impressive desk, credenza and wall unit were matching teak and rosewood, all custom designed to the contours of his office. Remington bronzes were perched on marble pedestals along the wall, the way rich, unathletic men who had never ridden horseback often expressed their love for the Wild West. Behind him was his collection of rare books, none of which he'd ever had time to read.

"Are you suggesting we pay this lunatic?" said Fields. His Cole-Haan wing tips were propped up on his desk, and he was leaning back in his chair, hands clasped behind his head.

Mike shifted uncomfortably in a wing chair, then glanced at Charlie Gelber, executive editor, seated on the couch. Mike had been talking for twenty minutes, laying it all out. "At this point I'm just looking for guidance."

"We simply don't pay informants," Gelber said indignantly. "We're not the *National Enquirer*."

Mike struggled not to roll his eyes. Gelber was a forty-eight-year-old creative type with an effeminate voice that became even more affected when he tried to be stern or sarcastic. A habit of crossing his legs like a woman and bringing a hand to his cheek like Jack Benny fed rumors that he was gay. Long ago, however, Mike had come to the very firm conclusion that Gelber didn't smile nearly enough to be gay, straight or otherwise sexually active.

"Paying him isn't the real issue," said Mike. "The question is, do we have an opportunity here to help stop a serial killer who's already struck once in our own city and is now up to victim number six nationwide."

"Well, excuse me, Michael." Gelber cocked his head—and there went the hand to the cheek. "But catching the bad guys is Eliot Ness's job."

Fields dragged his feet off the desk and onto the floor. "Tell me this, Mike: Do you think he's the killer or don't you?"

"Could be. Or he could be working in tandem with the killer. Or maybe he really is simply the evil—maybe even clairvoyant—genius he claims to be. To tell you the truth, I'm not sure which of those would be worse. All I know right now is that he wants his money, and if he doesn't get it, I'm sure I'm going to get another call about another dead body."

Fields ran a hand through his hair, troubled. "You don't really believe that paying him is going to stop a murder, do you? Either way—whether he's the killer or just an informant—his financial incentive is to keep these serial murders running longer than *A Chorus Line*. And let's face it: The only way he can validate his predictions is to let the murders happen. We may be the first to get the scoop after victim number seven goes down, but I don't think we're ever going to get these *predictions*, as he calls them, in time to stop number seven, number eight or number twenty-nine."

"You may be right," said Mike. "But I've been following this story from the beginning, and my law enforcement sources tell me they're not even close to naming a suspect. Creating a dialogue with this guy could be the only way to yield a clue that might finally stop the killing. It's like when the *Times* and *Post* published the Unabomber's manifesto to help stop the bombings. It worked in that case. There's no guarantee that we'll save lives, but we have a responsibility to try, at least. We can't just throw up our hands and say we don't pay informants, then pretend like nobody ever called me."

"Fine." Gelber was up and pacing on a Persian rug, waving his arm with emotion. "Let's say we *do* pay him. What if it turns out he really *is* the killer? How do you think our readers will react when they find out we've been giving a serial killer a financial incentive to keep on killing?"

"I thought of that. And that's why we shouldn't go out on this limb alone. I think we should work with the FBI on this."

Gelber stopped short. "*What?* We're independent journalists, not assistant deputies for federal agents. Are you *nuts?*"

"That's enough, Charlie," said Fields. His eyes narrowed and he spoke in a calm, even voice. "Mike, are you nuts?"

"I know there's an ethical dilemma here, and maybe Charlie has a point. Maybe a journalist should *never* tell the FBI about an informant—even one who might help solve serial killings, or who might himself be the serial killer. But this particular informant isn't just offering information about crimes that someone else has already committed. He's demanding money for his predictions about *future* victims—and *he* may very well be the killer. That's almost extortion. It's a unique situation where there simply aren't any rules."

"There's one hard-and-fast rule," said Gelber. "Journalists are independent."

"Look," said Mike, "all the sanctimonious bullshit

in the world doesn't mean we *never* cooperate with law enforcement. Remember back in July '83? I was just two months on the job when terrorists kidnapped the wife of that former Salvadoran ambassador here in Miami. I uncovered it right after it happened, but the FBI asked us—asked *you*, Aaron—to keep the story from the public because the kidnappers threatened to kill the ambassador's wife if he called in the cops. So we didn't run the story, and neither did anyone else in the Miami media. When they caught the guys a week later the FBI even issued a public statement crediting the Miami media for our cooperation."

"What's your point?" snapped Gelber.

"Simple. Sometimes public safety has to take precedence over journalistic independence and the public's right to know."

"So what are you proposing in this case?" asked Fields. "I want specifics."

"A compromise—one that lets us retain a level of independence and that still gives the police the information they need to catch the killer. We pay the informant for his predictions, but the FBI secretly supplies the money. They pay informants all the time, so they should go for it, and this way the *Tribune* technically wouldn't be violating its own policy against checkbook journalism. But there'll be no telephone taps or other intrusion by law enforcement into my conversations with the informant. The FBI will get only those clues that I decide to pass along to them."

"It's pretty risky," said Fields. "What's in it for us?"

"We help catch a serial killer," said Mike. "But if you're looking for some kind of quid pro quo, I suppose we could ask for some kind of exclusive if the FBI makes an arrest."

Gelber grimaced. "This would be a huge mistake. I wouldn't be worried if we knew Mike's source was the killer. No one would fault us for going to the FBI in that situation. But here we don't know; in fact, he's telling us he's *not* the killer. If we start running to the FBI every time we *think* that *maybe* one of our informants has committed a crime, our phones will stop ringing."

Fields leaned back and stared at the ceiling, thinking. "Tough call," he said, sighing. "What you're proposing, Mike, probably can't be defended if it turns out your informant really is just an anonymous source out to make a buck, no matter how mercenary or reprehensible we think that is. Are you willing to go out on a limb over this?"

Mike's eyes became lasers. "I know this much. I'm not willing to sacrifice another victim if there's a chance we can help catch this psycho. Are you?"

The room went silent. Fields drew a deep breath and glanced at Gelber. But there was no more argument. "I'll arrange the meeting," he said.

Chapter 7

nightfall made mirrors out of the windows overlooking Biscayne Bay, and without the vista the newsroom had the stark and gaping ambience of a high school gymnasium. Beige walls were the perfect complement to the industrial carpet and fluorescent lighting high overhead. A twisted network of dividers compartmentalized the room into open workstations for nearly a hundred fifty reporters and staff writers, each with their own video display terminal, gray metal desk, and modern telephone that emitted a muffled chirp instead of the good old-fashioned ring. It was relatively quiet now, but in peak business hours the incessant buzz of a hundred different conversations swirled above them. Mike's pod was somewhere in the middle, like the wedge of cheese in a sprawling rat maze.

He leaned back in his chair, his face lighted only by the glow of his computer terminal in the screen-saver mode. He smirked at the familiar preprogrammed message that flashed across the screen in big green letters from left to right, an old Vince Lombardi quote that Aaron Fields had drilled into his brain from day one. "Be fired with enthusiasm. Or you will be fired—with enthusiasm."

For thirteen years that creed had kept him working late, night after night. How many times had he called Karen to cancel plans at the last minute? How many times had he simply forgotten to call, or even apologize?

He glanced at her photo on his desk—a honeymoon shot taken six years ago, back when he thought divorce was for the other fifty percent. Karen, wearing shorts and a cable-knit sweater, was perched atop a pile of huge gray boulders along the coast of Maine, the surf crashing in the background. There, he'd truly fallen for her: He slipped after snapping the photo and tumbled into a crevice. She climbed down to him, recklessly, as if the most important thing in the world was to reach him.

He was okay, so they sat there on the jagged coastline and watched the sun set, just talking. They were great talkers back then, took pleasure in exchanging small secrets.

Karen had a theory about that—one that made perfect sense to a newspaper reporter who dealt with anonymous sources. "Only two kinds of people can talk without inhibitions," she said. "Strangers or lovers. Everyone in between is just negotiating."

"So," he said, "unless there's love—"

"In some ways, you're actually better off being strangers."

After six years of marriage, he had to wonder when

it was that they'd been reduced to "negotiating"—and whether they'd finally reached the point where they were better off strangers.

His phone rang and he snatched it up, thinking maybe it was Karen. To his disappointment, it was Aaron Fields.

"I knew I'd catch you at work," the publisher said with approval. "Listen, I just wanted to let you know I'm making a slight change in your proposal to the FBI."

"What kind of change?"

"I agree that we can't have the FBI eavesdropping on your phone conversations. The idea of a bug in a newsroom makes me very nervous. But instead of you just passing the informant's tip along to the FBI, we're proposing that the FBI get its information just like everybody else—by reading your stories in the *Tribune*. We retain exclusive control over what we print and don't print."

"What do you mean '*print*'? Who says this guy is telling the truth?"

"He's proven himself reliable with Gerty Kincaid."

"Come on," Mike scoffed. "You always insisted we verify—"

"Things change," Fields interrupted. "I'm not telling you to abandon your standards. Throw in all the qualifiers you want—'unconfirmed reports . . . it's alleged' . . . all that. But the paper needs the sales bump this story will give us."

Mike was speechless.

"Charlie's in agreement with me on this," said Fields. "Printing a story after each call from your informant is more in line with our role as independent journalists than passing tips directly to the FBI anyway."

"I'm still not comfortable—"

"Mike, your instincts were right: We have to help stop this killer. But if we pay money for the tips and don't write the stories, your informant will know we're working with the police. Trust me, okay? This is the only way it'll work. Now, get back to work, you slacker," he joked, then hung up.

Mike breathed a heavy sigh, not sure what to think. He switched off his desk lamp.

Somehow, he didn't feel much like working late anymore.

A slushy rain had been falling all day. By 9:00 P.M. temperatures were in the teens and downtown Atlanta was encased in ice. Most businesses had closed early that afternoon so that people could get home safely before dark. Those who hadn't left fast enough were now parked on the interstate, cursing the winter storm and a five-car pileup that had traffic blocked for miles.

A blast of cold wind nearly knocked Cybil Holland to the frozen sidewalk as she emerged from the Ritz-Carlton on Peachtree Street. No vacancy. It was the same at all of the downtown hotels. At this point everyone, Cybil included, had given up any hope of getting home tonight.

She cinched up her Burberry trench coat, turned up the lapels and headed directly into the chilly north wind toward the subway station at Peachtree Plaza. The Ritz had promised her a room at their Buckhead

Hotel in midtown, but it was up to her to figure out how to get there. MARTA was her only hope.

She walked with her head down, bucking the wind and intermittent icy flakes that bit her on the cheeks and forehead. It was too dark and windy to tell for sure, but the precipitation seemed to be falling heavier in the streetlamps' fuzzy light. Across the street, the store windows at Macy's had glazed over with a thick layer of ice. The Ritz was only a block behind her and already she felt like she'd trudged a mile, freezing and suddenly nervous—increasingly aware that she was alone on the streets.

Without gloves her hands were stinging. She blew on them and her breath steamed, fogging a big heart-shaped diamond in a platinum setting with emerald baguettes. Out of street smarts she turned her ring inward to conceal the stones. She walked as fast as she could, planting her high-heeled shoes carefully on the ice-slicked sidewalk. The incline was slight, but the ice and gusty wind made it like climbing a ski jump. Her feet slipped as she reached the corner. To break the fall she threw her hand out in front of her when, out of nowhere, someone hit her broadside and knocked her to the sidewalk.

She was facedown, sliding then bouncing down concrete steps, bearing the weight of whoever had slammed into her. They landed with a thud at the base of the steps in the pitch-dark bowels of a restaurant delivery pit, somewhere below street level. A gloved hand muted her scream as she stared up in fright at the man in a ski mask.

Kneeling beside her, he grabbed her by the hair,

snapped her head forward and back, slamming it against the concrete. He watched the eyes roll up into her head, then rifled through her purse. A nice wad of bills—a couple hundreds and some crisp fifties.

"Rich bitch," he mumbled.

He pitched the empty purse aside and took her hand, which she'd clenched into a fist. He pried her pudgy fingers open to reveal the heart-shaped diamond cupped in her hand, like an oyster housing its pearl. He tugged at the ring, but it wouldn't budge. Another tug, but it was stuck on her knuckle.

"Come *on*, fatso."

He twisted it, even spit on her finger to help it slide off. No dice.

Quickly, he unzipped his leather jacket and pulled a diving knife from its sheath, exposing an eight-inch blade with a serrated edge. Then, just for an instant, he pressed the flat side of the shiny steel blade against her lips. It steamed. She was breathing, still alive. His eyes lit, as if he preferred it that way.

Like a butcher with his block, he flattened her hand on the bottom step, palm down, spreading the digits to isolate the ring. He positioned the blade directly on her knuckle, got up on his haunches and came down with all his weight. The bone cracked like a frozen twig, and the blade broke through to the icy concrete. He slid the ring off the bloody stub and gave the stones a closer look, smirking with satisfaction. A diamond *and* emeralds.

He stuffed the prize in his pocket and clutched the wad of cash. "California, here I come," he said quietly, then peeled off into the night.

Chapter 8

Victoria wasn't invited to the meeting in Miami with Aaron Fields. The Special Agent in Charge of the Miami Field Office attended, accompanied by David Shapiro, chief of the Child Abduction and Serial Killer Unit in Quantico. Not every payment to an informant was handled at this level, but the *Tribune*'s proposal was a bit unusual. Victoria heard about it that same evening, when she checked in with Shapiro for a routine status report. The decision, she was told, was flatly no.

The FBI headquarters was in the J. Edgar Hoover Building, but no one had ever called it that, even before the cross-dressing allegations. Most simply called it "ugly." The unsymmetrical tetrahedron covered an entire city block between Ninth and Tenth streets on Pennsylvania Avenue, seven stories high in the front and eleven in the rear, giving the impression that it was about to fall over backward. The exterior walls were unfinished concrete, punctuated with pock marks that looked like machine-gun fire. Victoria entered through the employee entrance on Pennsylvania at 9:00 A.M. and went directly to the office of Tom Dougherty, assistant director of the FBI's Criminal Investigative Division.

Dougherty was several levels of authority above her, outside her normal chain of command. His division directed the work of nearly eighty percent of the Bureau's agents, and he personally reviewed the undercover review board operation minutes to determine whether every category-one proposal was worth the expense and risk. Ordinarily, Victoria would no more try to see him without an appointment than she would just drop by the Oval Office. The bottom line, however, was that she liked the *Tribune's* proposal, and she couldn't in good conscience let her supervisors kill it simply because it lacked the one thing the FBI valued more than anything else: precedent.

Dougherty was a distinguished fifty-five years old, two years away from the Bureau's mandatory retirement age, with thick gray hair and a cleft in his chin. He dressed conservatively in a dark blue suit, white shirt and berry red tie. He was rushing out the door to a congressional hearing on Capitol Hill when she caught him outside his office. With his implied permission—he didn't tell her to get lost—she followed him down the hall, down the elevator, and out the door. His limousine driver was waiting at the curb, a handsome young man who was downright obsequious, showing Dougherty even more deference than she was. She followed him all the way to the open car door, trying to get his ear. Finally, he agreed to let her ride along.

She was nearly out of breath from nonstop speaking as the limo pulled into traffic. "I want you to know, sir, that I'm not one to go over the heads of my supervisors lightly."

"I appreciate that," he said dryly. "Because I'm extremely busy."

He seemed impatient as she continued to plead her case, checking his watch several times, signaling that time was short. She gave him as much information as she could compress into the short ride, but he seemed unmoved.

"I can't emphasize it enough," she said. "It's not every day we get this kind of cooperation from the media. It could provide the breakthrough we need. And compared to the amount of money this investigation has cost so far, the proposed payments to this informant are a bargain."

He looked up from the open file in his lap; the mention of money seemed to have grabbed his attention. "Obviously, the amount of the payments isn't the whole issue. The Justice Department pays about a hundred million dollars a year to informants, most of whom, frankly, are scumbags who never produce squat. The real problem is that we can't pay him a dime if he's the killer. We'll have political hell to pay if it turns out he's the killer and he gets away with the taxpayers' money—possibly hundreds of thousands of dollars when all is said and done."

"I totally agree. That's the key issue: Is the informant the killer."

He looked annoyed, but it was his normal expression. "Well, what do our analysts think?"

"They're leaning toward the view that he *is* the killer." Her voice grew tighter, and she looked Dougherty in the eye. "But I think they're wrong."

"Is that so?" he said with a condescending smile. His smirk slowly faded. "How long have you been with the CASK Unit?"

"Eighteen months. But I spent five years in hostage and crisis negotiation, where I learned a few things about the way the criminal mind works. The truth is, no one has thought more about this case over the last four months than I have. And I just don't believe this guy's the killer."

"Why not?"

"A lot of little things that I don't have near enough time to explain. But the best reason is Ernest Gill."

"Who?"

"Gill—it's a phony name the informant is using. I checked with a historian at the Smithsonian last night. Turns out there was an Irish sailor by that name on the SS *Californian*, back in 1912. His salary was five English pounds a month. A Boston newspaper paid him five hundred dollars for his story that Lord Stanley, the captain of his ship, saw distress flares fired from the *Titanic*, but he just kept on going."

"Seems strange that someone demanding money for his story would tie himself to a historical precedent."

"That's the point. Gill's story led to three formal government investigations into Lord Stanley, one in the U.S. and two in Britain. The newspaper may have paid him a lot of money for what sounded like an unbelievable story. But as far as anyone could tell, it looks like everything he said was true."

"So Mr. Gill is back again, getting paid to tell the truth."

"I guess that's his message."

"But—you've lost me now," he said with a grimace. "How does his use of the name Gill lead to the conclusion that the informant's not the killer?"

"Simple: It's too cute, amateurish, something you'd come across in a bad movie. It's the ploy of someone fairly dull-witted who *thinks* he's being clever. The killer's not at all like that. He's far more intelligent, far more savvy. At least, in my view he is."

Dougherty's look was incredulous. "That's all you've got to go on—his chosen alias is inconsistent with your profile?"

"Sometimes that's all it takes. It's like the Yorkshire Ripper case in the late seventies. Obviously I wasn't around back then, but I studied it in one of my courses at Quantico."

"What does that have to do with anything?"

"It was in England. After four years of investigation, the police had eight serial murders on their hands with no suspects—until someone mailed in a tape recording, claiming to be the killer. The Brits jumped all over it. They broadcast it on television and radio, hoping someone would recognize the voice. Hundreds of police officers went out in the field playing the tape for people who lived in the victims' neighborhoods, hoping they'd recognize the voice. Then finally, as a favor to the experts at Bramshill, one of our agents listened to it. Instantly, he knew it was bogus. There wasn't any scientific way for him to *know* that. But he was sure he was right, because the tape was inconsistent with the profile of the killer he'd constructed from the evidence. And you know what? He was right. The guy on the tape wasn't the killer. It was a hoax.

"I feel just as strongly about Mr. Gill. I'm not saying the informant's a crank. Somehow, he does appear to have some insight into the killings. But he's not the killer. Not in my book."

Dougherty breathed a heavy sigh. Victoria watched nervously as he mulled it over in his mind. The silence seemed insufferable. He shook his head and was about to speak, but she cut him off.

"I know I'm right, sir." She spoke firmly and with complete confidence.

He gave her a long, discerning look, but she didn't flinch. The car rolled to a stop at the guard gate at the Capitol.

"All right," he said finally, almost begrudgingly. "Put it in writing. Send me a memo requesting that we pay this informant based upon *your* firm professional opinion that the informant is not the killer. If you're willing to put your neck on the line, I'll get the money approved."

She smiled with relief, then opened the car door and shook his hand. "Thank you, sir. You won't regret it."

"I know *I* won't," he said flatly. "That's what your memo's for."

She stepped down from the limo and closed the door. Her smile faded as she stood alone at the guard gate, watching the big black limo pull away.

Chapter 9

Victoria arranged to meet Mike Posten at Mango's Café in Fort Lauderdale at 2:00 P.M. She'd wanted their first meeting to be out in the open so that their rendezvous would appear casual, and Mike had wanted it out of Miami so that he wouldn't run into anyone he knew.

Mango's was a corner café in the heart of the upscale shopping area on east Fort Lauderdale's Las Olas Boulevard. It was an older area that had gone up and down with the economy over the decades, but these days it was definitely up. Trendy art galleries, boutiques and antique shops flourished beneath a canopy of bushy palms and sprawling oaks that pointed the way to that famous beach where Connie Francis first sang "Where the Boys Are."

Victoria stopped at the entrance to the outdoor seating area, a cluster of little marbletop tables surrounded by a railing and manicured hedge running along the sidewalk. She'd seen Mike's picture in advance, but she would have spotted him without it.

He had to be the guy munching on tortilla chips, nervously looking around as if trying to figure out which one was the FBI agent, the wrinkled old Canadian speaking French to his left or the Claudia Schiffer look-alike to his right.

"Mind if I join you?" she said from behind.

He looked up, wiping his hands clean of the lemon he was squeezing into his Evian. He seemed startled by the attractive brunette wearing a sleeveless white shell and plaid shorts. Victoria took it in stride, by now well aware of the effect her slender figure and long bronze legs had on men.

"Actually, I'm waiting on someone," he said.

"I know. Me." She extended her hand. "My name's Victoria Santos. Probably wouldn't be very discreet of me to flash my credentials." She dropped into the seat across from him.

"I guess you weren't what I was expecting."

She smiled. "Not even the FBI wears trench coats when it's sunny and eighty degrees out."

The waitress brought menus, and Victoria ordered a Diet Coke. Mike emptied the rest of his bottled mineral water into a glass, then squeezed in another wedge of lemon.

"That's a scam, you know," said Victoria.

"What?"

"The whole bottled-water thing. You might as well be drinking tap water."

"Do you work for the FBI, or for the Surgeon General?"

"I just know these things. Has it ever occurred to you that *Evian* spelled backwards is *naive?*"

Mike chuckled. "Pretty funny for somebody who's

made a career out of chasing homicidal maniacs." He sipped his water, then dug a little. "How *did* you get into this line of work, anyway?"

"You dive right in, don't you?"

"Why not?" He pressed gently: "Your motivation was . . . ?"

She hesitated, then chose the glib response. "When I was a kid I had a thing for Efram Zimbalist Junior."

Mike nodded. "But Efram never chased serial killers. Why did you get involved with that?"

She sighed. *That same old question again.* "Well, looked at one way, it's the ultimate women's issue. Most serial killers are sexual sadists, and most of their victims are women."

He waited for more, but there was only silence. "That all you're going to say?"

"Excuse me?"

"Your answer. It's so . . . abstract, depersonalized. Almost sounds evasive."

She gave him a curious look. She'd used that answer hundreds of times before, and no one had ever called her on it.

He selected a tortilla chip and dipped it in salsa. "The 'victim' angle intrigues me, though. Makes me wonder whether there's something in your background that makes you feel like one."

"That's a very personal question."

"I'm a reporter," he said with a shrug. "There's no such thing as 'too personal.'"

She arched an eyebrow. "And I'm an FBI agent. There's no such thing as being too abstract or evasive."

"Another Evian, sir?" asked the waitress.

"No," he said, smirking at Victoria. "Just tap water."

"You learn fast." She smiled thinly, and then they ordered. A burger for him, something healthy called the "New Wave Salad" for her. When the waitress was gone, Victoria turned serious.

"We checked out the FedEx package you received. No fingerprints, except your roommate's and the delivery man's. Everything else, however, is as you suspected. It was definitely shipped on Thursday, and we're now as medically certain as we can be that Kincaid wasn't killed until Friday. I can't divulge certain details about our investigation, but I can tell you that the Candler County Sheriff got a rather obvious tip on Sunday morning that led him right to Kincaid's body. That didn't make much sense to us until we heard about your package. We think they're connected."

"How so?"

"Whoever sent you the package knew it was going to arrive on Monday. We think he tipped off the sheriff's office on Sunday out of frustration that nobody had found the body yet. Unless Kincaid was identified as victim number six before your FedEx arrived on Monday, her name wouldn't have meant anything to you. Also, the informant's whole claimed ability to predict the murders hinged on the medical examiner being able to confirm that Kincaid was murdered on Friday, the day *after* he sent the package. The longer the body went undiscovered, the more it would decompose, and the less precise the examiner could be about fixing a time of death."

"What kind of tip was it?"

"I'm sorry, I can't tell you that."

"Five minutes, and already we're in the 'no comment' zone?"

"I've told you all I can. Anyway, we welcome your cooperation, and we're willing to accept the terms your publisher laid out to my supervisor last night. But there are a few ground rules."

"Okay, shoot."

"We agree with your publisher that this isn't likely to be a one-shot deal. The informant's financial incentive is to feed you clues over time, bit by bit. So, first rule, whenever you hear from him, you call me at the number we gave you. Remember it, and don't write it down. By the way, do you have a pager?"

"Yeah, local."

"We'll get you a SkyPager so I can beep you from anywhere in the country. Anyway, whether you call me or I call you, we avoid discussing anything of substance on the phone. We'll meet for lunch or a drink, always in a very public place. Dress casually. Greet each other like friends, not business associates—certainly not like a reporter talking to the FBI. We smile and kid around, just in case somebody's watching."

Mike leaned forward, his eyes narrowed. "The deal is that you only get what I print in the *Tribune*, when I print it. My publisher doesn't want me holding private sessions."

"That's fine. But we should meet before each payment, just to talk logistics. We can't assume he's going to keep saying deposit fifty grand at Citibank. He may change his amount, he may even stop using banks altogether. I need to know that. The money is going to have to come from you—or at least *appear* as though it's coming from you. But I can't just give you a suitcase full of cash and have you pay it out as you see fit. I need some measure of control."

"Does that mean you'll keep paying even if he ups the amount?"

"We'll see. Fifty thousand won't raise too many bureaucratic eyebrows. But it'll definitely get sticky if things drag out too long and he starts doubling, maybe tripling his price."

Mike's mind whirred. "Sounds okay, I guess."

"Good. Because you may not like my second rule. Nobody can know about the *Tribune*'s arrangement with the FBI. So far it's you, your publisher, and your editor. That's already too many."

"Well, obviously my best friend Zack knows, too."

She sighed. "How good is he at keeping a secret?"

"Very good," Mike said. "Don't worry about Zack. Of course, I have to tell my wife, too."

"Why?"

"Because she's my *wife*."

Victoria smiled thinly. "Mike, I *am* with the FBI. I *know* the status of your marriage."

He shifted in his seat. "What difference does it make if we're separated? I can't keep something like this from Karen."

"You must. The only sensible way to play this game is to assume the informant is the killer, or that he's someone who's just as dangerous, if not more. The more people in the loop, the greater the risk to everyone."

Mike looked away. "All right," he said, sighing. "But if we have to keep her in the dark, that means she can't take steps to protect herself if something goes haywire. The informant's already hinted that the predictions could start hitting close to home if I went to the cops. I want her protected—twenty-four hours a day."

"We could do that without her even knowing it. I'll have to clear it through the Miami Field Office, but I'm sure they've got someone doing background checks on applicants for government jobs who'd think watching your wife is a major career opportunity." She checked her watch. "In fact, I'm meeting the profile coordinator there in forty minutes to talk about the Miami investigation. Sorry to eat and run, but I have to go."

"One more question," he said, catching her as she rose.

She paused. He had a look on his face that told her something was bothering him. "What is it?"

"Ever since I got the call, I've been racking my brain, asking myself, 'Why me?' With all the reporters in the country on this story, why would he single out *me* as his sounding board? I can't figure it—can you?"

She laid a ten-dollar bill on the table to cover her share of the tab, then looked him in the eye. "I guess the answer to that question depends, doesn't it?"

"On what?"

"On whether he's an informant," she said, arching an eyebrow. "Or whether he's the killer."

Their eyes locked in a tense stare, as if each was wondering what the other's guess was.

"Keep in touch," she said, rising. She turned and headed for the exit, leaving Mike alone to ponder his own question.

Chapter 10

O n Friday evening Karen headed home on
Miami's Metrorail, an elevated commuter train
that paralleled the six-lane parking lot that was
U.S. 1 during rush hour. The tracks and open-air stations rested on concrete pillars, fifty feet or higher
aboveground. From a window seat Karen looked down
on the power lines, treetops and barrel-tile roofs of
what used to be a quiet suburban neighborhood. These
days, however, all the doors and windows were covered
with iron security bars, and razor-wire fences protected
places of business. The speeding silver train came to a
stop at the Coconut Grove station. A few passengers
got off, but it was still standing room only. Karen was
three stops from home and deep in her thoughts, but as
the train left the station she stirred at the sight of a
guard on the platform with a pistol at his side.

Fortified houses. Trains with armed guards.
Compartments full of lonely travelers who never speak
or make eye contact with anyone around them. It got

her thinking about a summer trip she and Mike made back in the late eighties, when they took the Eurail to Berlin. Their train had stopped in the middle of the night, and just one look out the window gave her the eerie sensation of the East German border. Police dogs sniffing around. Armed military police dollying convex mirrors beneath the train to check for stowaways. She and Mike were sharing a six-person compartment with a young Polish couple who, it appeared, were smuggling food back to Warsaw. Mike had given them his duffel bag to make it a little easier. It was 2:00 A.M. before the passport check was over. As the train left the station Mike was nearly asleep on her shoulder. She flipped on the reading light and woke him with a nudge.

"Tell me something," she said quietly, so as not to wake the other couple. "If I lived on one side of the wall and you lived on the other, what would you do?"

His eyes blinked open, and he nuzzled against her breast. "Tunnel under it," he said confidently, "to be with you."

"What if you couldn't?"

"Then I'd sneak out. Bribe my way out. Pole-vault over it. Somehow, I'd get out."

"But what if there was just no way? Say it was impossible. You and I had to live separate, forever and ever."

His brow furrowed, as if he didn't like her rules. "I don't know what I'd do."

"Would you fall in love with someone else?"

"Karen," he winced.

"*Would you?*"

73

"No, never. Why would you even ask me that?"

She paused, then said quietly, "To see if you love me enough."

He took her hand. "Isn't *totally* 'enough'?"

She smiled sadly. It would be, she thought—but it would take nothing less than that to tell him something she'd been trying to tell him for a very long time. Still, she couldn't find the courage.

"Next stop, South Miami," came the crackling announcement from the Metrorail conductor. Karen shook off her memories and prepared for her stop.

The train slowed as it neared the station, and she moved toward the exit. Through the glass door that joined one car to the next she noticed a man in the next compartment who had seemed to move only when she moved. She glanced his way again for a better look. He looked away quickly, as if he'd been caught staring. He was mid-twenties, she'd say, and professional—pinstripes, power tie, briefcase. He looked like any other accountant or banker who rode the train every day. What bothered her, however, was that he looked even *more* like the guy at the mall she'd noticed last Tuesday night.

The train stopped, and the automatic doors opened. A few people got on, many more got off. She had a funny feeling—an intuition. Just as a test, she stayed on. Sure enough, so did Mr. Tuesday. The doors closed and the train pulled away, carrying both of them toward the next stop.

Her mind raced. He could be just some nice-looking guy trying to get the nerve up to say hello, she thought. Could be some weirdo who's been following her for a week. Or it could all be in her head. *Get off at the next stop*, she resolved. *If he gets off too, it isn't paranoia.*

The train stopped at the Datran Office Center—the last station on the southbound line. Everybody had to get off, she realized, which meant that his getting off here really wouldn't confirm he was after her. When the doors opened she moved with the flow across the open-air platform toward the escalators that took the stream of passengers down to ground level eighty feet below. Two or three people crowded onto each step. Gliding down, her eyes roamed the station in search of a guard, but she saw none. Halfway down, she checked over her shoulder, to the bottleneck of commuters at the top of the escalator. He, too, was going with the flow. Or he was following her.

The crowd fanned out at the bottom in a weekend charge to the turnstiles. Karen, however, did an immediate U-turn and jumped on the up escalator, which ran adjacent to the one going down. She was alone going up, since no one was city-bound in the evening rush hour. She was face-to-face with the steady stream coming down, slowly drawing closer to the man she wanted to see. She wanted to memorize his mug, and she wanted *him* to know she could finger him in a lineup if ever she had to.

Her heart pounded as the gap narrowed. She forced herself to take a good look, imagining she was describing him to the police. Six feet. Brown hair. Brown eyes. Possibly Latin. She searched frantically for some distinguishing feature, but her nerves got in the way. The closer she got, the more indescribable he became.

They had yet to make eye contact, and the moment they passed he completely looked away. *Not the behavior of a man who simply wants to get to know me.*

She reached the top just as he reached the bottom. The crowd had completely funneled down the escalator, leaving her alone on the platform. Her heart sank as she watched the train she'd rode in on—her planned route of escape—pull away from the station. Half the bulbs overhead had been smashed by vandals, she noticed, and the platform was even darker without the lights from the train. An eerie quiet filled the night, punctuated by the electric hum of six hundred volts running through the tracks.

She wondered if he'd follow her back up, but she was almost afraid to check. She reached into her purse and clutched her can of Mace. With half-steps, she tentatively made her way back to the top of the escalator. Peering down to ground level, she could see him only from the knees down, standing by a Pepsi billboard at the base of the escalator. He hadn't made his move yet. But he hadn't left the station.

She hated to take her eye off him, but she stepped quickly to the edge of the platform to check on another train. No sign of one. She scurried back to the escalator, then froze. *He's coming up!*

On impulse, she yanked the red emergency lever, shutting down the escalator. He looked up, and for the first time they made direct eye contact. Her heart stopped. She prayed he'd turn and run. He ran *toward* her, gobbling up two steps at a time.

She screamed, but he kept coming. Across the platform was an elevator. She ran for it. With a push of the call button the doors slowly opened. The rapid echo of footsteps warned he was still giving chase. As she jumped in the elevator she could see him closing in. She screamed again, hitting the button over and over to make the doors shut faster. He was just ten feet away when she gave up on the button, put the weight of her whole body behind the door, and pushed it shut.

She fell against the wall, gasping for breath. After a split second of relief, terror struck. The elevator was a dinosaur. He'd hit ground level before she would. She flung open the control panel and pulled the emergency stop, jerking the elevator to a halt and sounding the alarm. She grabbed the phone.

"Help me!" she shouted.

"Security," a man answered.

"A man—he's chasing me! Pinstripe suit, on the platform. Stop him, please! Stop him before he gets away!"

Chapter 11

by 4:00 P.M. Pacific time a thick, bone-chilling fog
had rolled in from San Francisco Bay, reducing
visibility at Union Square to about two city
blocks. The square was a restful and impeccably manicured park in the busy hub of the shopping district,
planted with palms, yews, boxwood, and flowers, all
centered on a towering memorial to Admiral Dewey's
victory at Manila Bay. Rush-hour traffic inched along
the wide streets bordering all four sides. At one end,
the palatial St. Francis Hotel sat with the permanence
of the Pantheon. Macy's Department Store flanked the
south side. Streams of pedestrians hurried along the
sidewalks, wrapped in warm winter trench coats to
keep off the chill.

Curt Rollins had never been to San Francisco
before, so the heavy fog fascinated him. It made him
think of London. Jack the Ripper.

"Cheerio, ol' chap," he said to a teenage girl in the
crosswalk. She made a gross-out face and scurried away.

He headed east on Post Street, toward the teeming rectangle that was the banking center between Kearny and Sansome Streets, the West Coast version of New York's Wall Street area. Along the way, he planted himself on the sidewalk to admire his reflection in the big plate-glass window outside F.A.O. Schwarz. He wore faded Levis, an Atlanta Braves baseball cap, and a thick navy-blue parka that made him look much bulkier than he was. Traces of dried brown feces besprinkled his leather gloves, but his secondhand clothes were otherwise clean, recent acquisitions from the Salvation Army. A pair of deep-tread hiking boots came in handy trudging up and down the steep city sidewalks. Walking made him winded, for at age thirty-two he had the body of a much older man. In the six years since prison he'd yet to find a job or a decent place to live. A thin face and jaundiced pallor bespoke vile habits and a lifetime of addictions. He was in perpetual need of a shave, a bath, a fix and a drink.

"Hey, fuck you, buddy!" he snapped at the window.

"No, fuck *you!*" his image shouted back. He grabbed his crotch like those Mafia types from New *Yawk* and continued on his way.

A bank marquee on the corner flashed the time of day. He hadn't given the *Tribune* a to-the-minute deadline, but he had said Friday, and by now the financial institutions on the East Coast had all closed for the weekend. It made him nervous to think about it: Either fifty grand was sitting in his account or it wasn't. It was time to find out.

Rounding the corner, he was singing a head-banging

song by his favorite rock group, Guns N'Roses, mimicking the screechy voice of his long-haired and tattoo-laden hero, Axl Rose. He was getting to the good part—something about an old lover buried out in the backyard—when he stopped in mid-note at the sight of an automatic teller machine dead ahead, facing the sidewalk. He didn't notice which bank owned it, and it didn't matter. The sign had the "Cirrus" logo, which told him his magnetic card would work. He traded his cap for his trusty ski mask to shield his face from the bank's security camera. He stepped up to the machine, bending slightly at the knees, so he'd look five or six inches shorter to anyone who might watch the video-taped transaction. The machine sucked in his card, and he eagerly punched in his code.

"Welcome, Mr. Ernest Gill," the display screen read.

Rollins smiled. That was the phony name he'd used to open the account weeks ago, before he'd even decided which reporter he was going to call. He hit the "balance inquiry" button and waited. His heart raced as he listened to the machine print his ticket. He'd opened the account with the minimum amount required, the leftover proceeds of a stolen Rolex watch. After all the planning and maneuvering, he was finally about to discover whether the gravy train had begun.

He snatched the printed ticket from the slot and read it: CURRENT BALANCE $50,100.00.

"Yessss," he hissed beneath his breath, like a tennis player serving an ace. He did a little dance, almost giddy with excitement. He'd promised himself he wouldn't touch any of the money until the scheme was completed, but he couldn't resist. After all, he'd have to replace the clothes on his back, now that the security camera had him on film. And all this travel was getting expensive, more than hocked jewelry could support.

He withdrew the daily maximum—six hundred bucks—and then pulled off the ski mask and merged into a stream of commuters brisk with purpose. He ran the last half-block to hop the cable car on California Street. He'd take it wherever it was going, so long as it was *away* from the ATM. Then tomorrow or the next day or whenever he felt like it, he'd find another bank with an ATM—maybe across town, maybe another state—and withdraw another six hundred.

Lunch money, he thought smugly, *compared to what Posten is going to pay me.*

It was 7:00 P.M. Friday, and Mike still hadn't finished his Sunday-edition exposé on violent crimes committed by tourists, a twist on the usual Miami-bashing story about tourists as victims. TOURISTS WHO COME PACKIN was the headline one of the copy editors wanted to slap on it. Even the *Tribune* wasn't above an occasional lapse into *Hard Copy* hyperbole.

"Hope you finish before Monday," the cleaning lady said as she emptied his trash into her big bin on wheels.

"If I don't, it's been nice working for you, boss." They exchanged smiles as she moved on to the next cubicle. He took another sip of bad coffee and turned back to the computer. He was massaging a paragraph about a murder at a Hialeah cockfight, trying *not* to make it sound like a fatal argument over a penis, when he heard a voice right behind him.

"Michael."

He looked up from his desk. Only one person ever called him "Michael," and she used that harsh tone only on the rarest of occasions. "Karen, hi. What are you doing here?"

"Zack said you'd be here," she said flatly.

He looked at her curiously. She was wearing a business suit, but she looked disheveled. The jacket wasn't quite straight, and her hair needed combing. Little beads of sweat glistened above her lip. She looked like she'd been running, and she was obviously mad. "Did I do something?"

Her face turned an even deeper shade of red.

Wrong question, he thought. She obviously would have just called if she weren't looking for a showdown, face-to-face. He quickly canvassed the newsroom, spotting a few Friday-evening stragglers who might overhear. "Can we discuss this in private?" he said, motioning toward the glass-encased conference room. She followed him inside and closed the door behind her. He offered a chair, but she wasn't taking.

"I can't believe you did this," she said.

"Did what?"

"Don't deny it. You'll only make it worse. He told me."

"Who's he? Told you *what?*"

"I caught a man following me on the Metro tonight. I thought he was some kind of nut, but when security nabbed him he said he was hired to protect me. Naturally," she scoffed, "he wouldn't say who hired him or why I need protection."

Mike's expression fell. He stood in silence, stunned.

Karen's eyes welled as her anger turned to disbelief. "You *did* hire him. I can see it on your face. God, I hoped it wasn't true, but now I'm glad I came all the way down here. You actually hired a private eye to spy on me while we're separated."

"No," he stammered. "That's not it at all. He's not a private eye. It's . . . it's for your protection. I wish I could explain, but I can't. Not now."

"I came here to sort this out. If you have an explanation, let's hear it. *Now.*"

He struggled to say something, but what could he say? That he was secretly cooperating with the FBI, and that he'd kept her in the dark because she couldn't be trusted to keep her mouth shut? *That* would really fix things. He needed time to think. "I'm sorry," he said, massaging a throbbing temple. "I really can't discuss this now."

Her lips quivered with anger. "Then we've got nothing to talk about." She flung open the door and rushed out.

"Karen, wait!"

She cut across the newsroom in seconds, past the night editor, eyes riveted on the exit. He had to break into a trot to catch her in the lobby. She was frantically pushing the elevator call button over and over again when he took her by the arm. As the doors opened she shook herself free.

"Please," he said with a pained expression. "This isn't what it seems."

She stared back coldly from inside the elevator. "Neither was our marriage." The doors closed, and she was gone.

He just stood there, like a man punched in the chest. Instinct told him to run after her, but he knew he'd made her too mad to reason with her, and this was no time for knee-jerk solutions anyway. First things first: He marched back to his cubicle to call Victoria and tell her he had to confess all to his wife—whether the FBI liked it or not.

The phone rang just as he reached for it. He did a double take, startled. He answered on the next ring. "Posten."

There was silence, then a dry reply. "You know, security at the *Tribune* is really lax."

Mike paused, though he instantly recognized the voice of his informant.

"It's you."

"And another thing: It's very stupid of you to leave your computer on while you go wandering around the building. You never know who might access your files while you're away from your desk."

"What are you talking about?"

"Switch on your computer, you'll see."

"It's already on."

"Good. Go to your control panel, bring up the screen-saver mode."

Mike clicked his mouse, exiting his files. The old Lombardi quote came up, his usual screen-saver message. "Okay, I'm there."

"Left-click twice with the mouse."

He hit it once, and the Lombardi quote disappeared.

With the second hit, a new message popped up. TIMOTHY COPELAND, it read in bold red letters. Mike felt his stomach tighten. "Where does he live? How do I stop this?"

"San Francisco," came the morose reply. "But you can't stop it. Happened early this morning, but I couldn't tell you about it till I got my money. Don't worry, though. Cops ain't found the body yet. You're the first to know. Besides me and the killer, you're the *only one* to know."

"This was supposed to be a *prediction*, not a news flash."

"It *is* a prediction. That's why I put it on your computer beforehand, so you'd know I wasn't just phoning you after the fact. Check with your tech-services people. I'm sure they'll be able to confirm that I input the name a few days ago."

"So what? It's no good to me now. It's too late to stop it."

"Don't get high-and-mighty on me. Admit it. You guys don't want to stop the news from happening. You just want to be the first to report it."

"Do you think this is clever?" Mike asked.

"It's not *clever*. It's brilliant. So don't bite the hand that feeds you. I might bite back."

"How can you just let these people die—for money?"

"People let other people die for money every day. A lot more money than I'm making. Cigarette companies do it. Chemical companies do it. Why the hell shouldn't *I* do it?"

"Because it's wrong."

"The only thing wrong, Mother Teresa, is *you* wasting our precious time. This is a big story. First homosexual victim, to add to your confusion. And it's the first victim who didn't live alone. Your killer's getting bolder. Timothy's gay lover is bound, gagged and unconscious, locked up in the closet. He won't know a thing. But he's very much alive."

"So the killings aren't random. He's targeting specific people."

"Not so fast. Next installment: a hundred thousand dollars, same account. By next Friday."

Mike rose from his chair and looked out over the maze of workstations, making sure no one could overhear. "What makes you think I'll keep paying you?"

"Because my information just keeps getting more valuable. Do you know how he takes the tongues?"

Mike hesitated. He felt almost morbid about it, but he sank into his chair and reached for a notepad. "No. Tell me."

"A diving knife. Two incisions at the base of the tongue, one on each side, each about a third of the tongue's width. Two little notches that give him something to grab hold of. Kind of like those corkscrews with the T-shaped handle. He puts on metallic butcher gloves—divers wear them for spear fishing. Not even eels or sharks can bite through them. And then he yanks. Usually once or twice. Sometimes three or four times. Until—" He made a clucking sound with his tongue, like a cork popping from a wine bottle.

Mike stopped writing in midsentence. For a horrific split second he envisioned it happening to one of the victims—*alive*. The pain and blood, the screams and tearing. Yet the description was so matter-of-fact, like hooking up a stereo. *If this guy's the killer, he's got ice in his veins.*

"What's the matter," the caller said with a snicker. "Cat got your tongue?"

Mike grimaced. "How do you know so much—so much detail?"

"How do you *think?*"

"Either you've seen it happen. Or you made it happen."

"Either way, you get your exclusive. Just stay tuned. And keep your payments current."

"Wait!" Mike said as the line clicked, but there was no reply. His hands were shaking as he hung up the phone. He drew a deep breath and closed his eyes tightly.

"What was that all about?"

He turned at the piercing voice from behind. It was Brenda Baines, a veteran reporter who'd started at the *Tribune* a year after Mike, and who'd lived in his shadow from day one on the job. Ever since he'd won his Pulitzer, a week didn't go by when she didn't announce to someone that he was Miami's most overrated reporter. She had straight, black hair and big green eyes that made her attractive in a severe but exotic way. She was standing behind a chest-high divider in the next pod of workstations. "Were you eavesdropping?" he said accusingly.

"I was just sitting here at my cubicle, couldn't help but overhear."

"How long have you been there?"

"Long enough to hear you say something about

paying a source," she said with a penetrating stare. "A rather flagrant violation of *Tribune* policy."

"Mind your own damn business."

"If somebody's breaking the rules around here, it *is* my business. And I know what I heard." She grabbed her purse, then turned and walked away.

Mike sank down in his chair and exhaled. "Timothy Copeland," he said quietly, feeling a wave of frustration crash over him. There wasn't supposed to be a seventh victim. No one in the newsroom was supposed to know anything about the money. And Karen— *What the hell am I going to do about Karen?*

He sat for a few more seconds, then, resigned, reached for the phone. He hit speed dial and waited.

"It's me, Mike," he said solemnly. The words came slowly. He felt unclean, almost nauseated by what he was about to say. "Aaron, I need page one tomorrow."

Chapter 12

"*A* *Tribune Exclusive*," boasted the morning's front page, "*by Michael Posten*."

Just after 7:00 A.M. the phone rang on Mike's nightstand. Victoria Santos had just finished reading the story and was already booked on the next flight to San Francisco—United, 9:35, out of Fort Lauderdale. They still had a strict rule against talking "business" on the phone, so Mike agreed to an eight o'clock breakfast meeting. If it were up to him, they would have just talked on the phone. As a reporter, he often found his own sources to be more forthcoming on the phone than in person. From experience, however, he knew that FBI agents preferred in-person meetings. They claimed it was because they wanted to assess demeanor, or that phone conversations were often cut short. The real reason, he suspected, boiled down to authority and subtle intimidation.

Begrudgingly, he threw on a pair of plaid shorts and his last clean shirt, a twelve-year-old memento from the Pope's last visit to Miami. Some Anglo trying to capitalize on Cuban America's love for His Holiness had unwittingly printed up ten thousand T-shirts reading LA PAPA, the Potato, instead of EL PAPA, the Pope. Mike had worn it to the press conference.

Forty minutes north on I-95 at the customary eighty miles per hour put him in Fort Lauderdale by eight o'clock. Victoria had picked Offerdahl's Bagel Gourmet on Seventeenth Street, one of the original shops owned by John Offerdahl, a former All-Pro Miami Dolphin middle linebacker. Mike ordered a toasted seven-grain with honey butter from the cheery young woman behind the counter, then joined Victoria at the round table for two she'd snagged by the window. She was dressed in nice-fitting jeans of eyelet denim and a red cotton sweater that was definitely airplane apparel.

"Mmmmm," said Victoria, taking a sip of her coffee and munching on her bagel. "I'm in heaven."

"Glad to hear it. The last twelve hours have pretty much been hell for me."

A flick of her tongue wiped the espresso mustache from her lip. "Sorry about that mix-up with your wife. We had a rookie covering her. Guy just plain panicked when she spotted him. He probably should have bolted. Instead, he tried to catch up with her and keep her from calling the cops. His intentions were good. Last thing we wanted was your informant to hear on the news that some South Miami cop had mistakenly arrested an FBI agent who was protecting your wife."

"Well, I don't know what he told her. But now she

thinks I'm a jealous husband who hired a private detective to spy on her."

Her eyes lit. "Let her keep on thinking that. It's perfect."

"It's not *perfect*. This is my wife—my *life*—we're talking about. I have to tell her."

"If you tell her, our deal's off."

"Okay," he said with a shrug. "Deal's off."

"Fine." She leaned forward on her elbows, assuming a datelike posture. "Just one thing I'd like to know, hotshot. What are you going to do when the money stops flowing and your informant gets *really* pissed?"

His bravado quickly faded, and he shook his head with resignation. "It's true what they say, isn't it. No good deed goes unpunished."

"I know you're feeling put-upon. But let me just say something about this situation with your wife. I'm speaking to you as a woman now, not as Special Agent Santos, okay?"

"Sure."

She took a breath, measuring her words. "I find it a little hasty on her part to be jumping to the conclusion that you hired a private detective to spy on her. *Hasty* isn't the right word. *Defensive*. It's like that line from *Hamlet*: 'The lady doth protest too much, methinks.' I'm not passing judgment, but maybe what's got her more uptight than the thought of you hiring a detective is the fear of what your detective might find out."

His eyes narrowed. "Do you know something I don't know? Or are you just assuming that as a journalist I'm in the habit of relying on wild speculation?"

"I'm just trying to help. I've seen the FBI send a lot

of men to prison who put too much faith in wives or girlfriends who weren't exactly trustworthy. I'd really hate for one of us to end up dead because you made the same mistake."

He sat back in his chair, arms folded. "Have you ever been married?"

"No. And I'm not against it. That's not where I'm coming from. I just haven't met the right guy."

"Well, I *have* met the right woman. You know, when Karen and I got married, she said that the only way two people can be totally open with each other is if they're lovers or strangers. It's been rough lately—most of it my fault, I guess—but if we lose trust, the best we'll ever have is that no-man's land in between." He leaned forward, emphasizing his resolve. "I'm going to tell her the truth."

She sat back, looked at him, seemed to be making up her mind. "Okay, you tell her, but make damn sure she realizes everything we have on the line here."

Mike smiled, satisfied with the small victory.

She checked her watch. "Anyway, looks like I've got a plane to catch in forty minutes. So what do you say we get down to business?"

He nodded in agreement, pushing his paper plate aside. "He wants a hundred thousand by Friday. Same account."

Her eyes widened. "Already he's *doubling* the demand? I'll have to speak to my unit chief, but with the kind of information you're getting, it should be approved. Just so you know: He's verifying the deposits with an ATM card, and he's withdrawing some funds at the same time. Six hundred bucks so far, the daily maximum."

"Pretty clever."

"Yeah. We can't post guards or mark the bills at every machine in the country. But ATMs do have cameras, and every transaction creates a record of exactly where he's been. He wore a ski mask to protect his identity, but some of these machines aren't all that fast, so it's a big risk for six hundred bucks a pop. My guess is, he's desperate for cash right now. But once the nest egg builds up to something really substantial, he'll want to make one big withdrawal, one quick transaction. When he does, we'll be all over him quicker than you can say insufficient funds."

"When do I get the money?"

"Probably Thursday. Don't deposit it until Friday, his deadline."

Mike shook his head, sighing. "Funny. I got into this hoping he was the killer. The thought of him possibly getting his hands on all this money makes me not so sure."

"Well, whoever he is, I don't think he's totally in it for the money. He's having some fun with us. Danced a jig in front of the camera outside the ATM machine in San Francisco, dressed like a bum."

She checked her watch. "Damn, I gotta get going." She gathered up her trash, then stopped. "Oh, one other thing. I know we agreed you'd have complete editorial license to print whatever you wanted, but please think before you print. You did some serious damage to our investigation by printing the details of how the tongues are extracted. That *was* the modus operandi. Now that you've made it public, it'll be harder to rule out copycats."

"So it was smart of him to reveal those details to me."

"Yeah, assuming he's the killer."

"Don't you think he is?"

She paused, thinking about the memo she'd written to Assistant Director Dougherty. "Let's just say there's disagreement within the FBI on that point. That's why we'd like you to get him talking less about the killing and more about the killer. We already know *what* this maniac does to his victims. We want to know *why*."

"He's nuts, that's why."

Her expression turned very serious. "No. I think he's evil, sadistic and knows exactly what he's doing. It makes a difference."

They rose together, and he held the door open. "Not to Timothy Copeland, it didn't. Made no difference at all."

She dug her car keys from her purse. "But it did to his roommate."

He nodded, seeing her point. "If the roommate *does* happen to know anything, you know my number."

She opened her car door, then turned back to him with tongue firmly in cheek. "That's what the FBI's here for—to make sure reporters get good material for their stories."

"Nice to know you have your priorities straight," he replied.

"Later," she called out through the window, then drove off.

Chapter 13

thirty minutes before sunrise Victoria parallel-parked her car at the curb outside Timothy Copeland's town house near Telegraph Hill, a pricey residential area of narrow alleys and small frame houses perched on San Francisco's alpine inclines. His was a Victorian-style flat, two story and brightly painted with a gabled roof. A tall Italian cypress evergreen shot up like a needle from a big pot on the front porch. Yellow police tape still covered the red front door.

Victoria had been over the crime scene several times in the past two days, but never at 5:30 A.M. As best they could tell, that was the time of Copeland's murder.

As a matter of practice, she made it a point to visit murder scenes at the same time of day the killer might have been there. Just knowing how cold it got at that particular hour could give her an idea of the clothing he'd worn, or help her figure out whether he'd hidden in the bushes or inside his car before making his approach. The comings and goings around the neighborhood might offer a lead on a possible witness. Most important, she could see everything just as the killer had seen it, and maybe understand why the victim hadn't seen him coming.

The quiet street was wet and dimly lit, and the dampness made for a bone-chilling night. She pulled her brown leather jacket tight to keep off the cold as the car door slammed with an empty thud. She stopped and listened. Urban quiet. To Victoria, there was nothing more eerie than busy city streets turned dark and deathly still.

From the sidewalk Victoria looked north and south, casing the neighborhood. Parked cars lined both sides of the street, but traffic was nonexistent. On the corner atop the hill she could see prosciutto hanging in the window of a small Italian grocery store, but it was dark inside and obviously closed. An old redbrick warehouse across the way looked as though it had recently been remodeled into expensive lofts and efficiencies. Only two apartments appeared lit in the whole building. She made a mental note of the night owls or early birds, whichever the case might be. Copeland's side of the street was lined with refurbished apartments, all very similar to his. Some had single-car garages, but they were all too close to the street to have a driveway. Narrow alleys ran between the buildings, just wide enough for garbage cans. Low-powered streetlamps lit each of the alleys, except for one—the one directly across the street.

Curious, Victoria took a flashlight from her car and crossed over.

It was uphill to the other side, and the sidewalk put her at eye level with the top of Copeland's doorframe. She glanced at the streetlamp overhead, but it was impossible to tell whether it had been tampered with or had simply burned out. She shined the flashlight down the dark alley. Trash cans lined either side, but the thing she noticed most was the continuing incline as the alley grew deeper. She glanced back at Copeland's town house, then stepped slowly into the alley, walking uphill.

The alley grew darker with each click of her heel, but the beam from her flashlight pointed the way. A small stream of water trickled in the gutter at her feet, racing toward the street. Gravity grabbed her as the grade grew steeper. She passed a cluster of trash cans, then stopped and turned around. It was like looking out of a tunnel— a telescope was more like it—right at eye level with Copeland's second story. She could see directly into the upstairs bedroom in which he'd perished.

With the flashlight she searched the ground around her. The cracked cement was wet, but she noticed several black dots that hadn't quite washed away. She got on one knee for a closer look. It was hard to tell, but it looked as if someone had crushed out a few cigarettes. A few swipes of the flashlight confirmed her guess. A soggy cigarette butt lay in the gutter, next to the trash can. Someone had been standing there having a smoke. Jeffrey Dahmer was a chain-smoker, she suddenly recalled. She rose slowly and gazed back at Copeland's bedroom.

He'd watched from right here, she realized. The killer had stalked him.

In a split second she shot from the alley and was jogging back across the street. She wanted to turn the bedroom lights on, then return to the alley to see what the killer might have seen. She tossed the flashlight into her car, then retrieved the house key and went inside.

The door closed behind her with a hollow echo. Strange, she thought, the way the ear always knew when there was no one home. She switched on the brass chandelier in the foyer, then headed upstairs on the Oriental runner. She moved quickly at first, then slower, until she stopped completely at the top of the stairs. The pictures on the wall made her feel like an intruder—stark reminders that this had been a home before it was a crime scene.

From the amount of carnage, she figured the police had arrived expecting to find two gay men with a plentiful supply of whips and chains on the premises. Copeland and his partner had been effectively married for the past nine years, though. Neither was the type to have met a sadistic killer in a pickup joint. Seeing the two of them together in the photograph suddenly reminded her of what Mike Posten had said about lovers and strangers—that they were the only people who could be truly open. He'd forgotten about *victims*. Murder victims, in particular, were the most completely open of all. The books they read, their favorite snack, the thickness of their pubic hair—all of it became a matter of public record for the world to behold.

She often felt guilty about that, as if the only people who deserved to know her own secrets were the victims she knew so well.

She continued toward the bedroom, then froze in the open doorway. She was looking through the dark bedroom, directly out the window. With the lights off she could see outside. She had a clear view of the parked cars on the street, the sidewalk, the apartments on the other side. The alley, however, was pitch-black. Anyone could have hidden there, and Copeland would never have known it.

She was about to switch on the bedroom light, then stopped. With narrowed eyes she stared out the window. She could have sworn that in the alley's dark recesses lurked a tiny, glowing orange dot. She inched closer to the window, leaving the bedroom lights off. Halfway across the room she stopped and took another hard look. Ever so slightly, the orange dot had seemed to move—but it was definitely still there, deep in the alley across the street.

Someone, she realized, was standing there smoking.

Her heart raced. She knew from countless other profiles created back at Quantico that, when it came to serial killers, the old stereotype was often true: They *did* return to the scene of the crime. They'd even been known to "help" with the manhunt, so curious were they about the progress of the case. She pulled her gun from the holster and raced downstairs. If she could get down in time, she might trap him in the alley.

At full speed she rushed out the door, down the front steps and across the street. She took cover behind a car parked in the front of the alley and aimed her pistol across the hood.

"FBI!" she shouted. "Come out with your hands up!"

She waited a moment, squinting as she searched for the orange dot. It was gone.

"FBI!" she shouted, then listened. She heard nothing at first, but then came a slamming noise from somewhere in back. She suddenly realized it wasn't a blind alley with only one way out—it must have had a rear exit. She jumped out from behind the car but stopped at the edge of darkness. She knew better than to run headlong into a dark alley, alone with no backup. She sprinted up the sidewalk a half-block to the next alley, which was lighted.

"Shit!" In the light, she could see plainly that the alley ran clear through.

She did the hundred-yard dash uphill, all the way through to the narrow street that ran along the back of the buildings. Her pace quickened as she rounded the corner and headed back up the block to the dark alley. She stopped twenty feet away from the back entrance. The wooden gate was wide open—the slamming noise, she realized, had been the sound of the orange dot getting away.

"Damn." She was breathing heavy from the all-out sprint. She looked one way, then the other, but the street was empty. With her gun drawn she stared into the blackness. The thought of being so close brought a tinge of fear, but she didn't let it show.

If he could somehow still see her, she wanted him to know: She was the one who'd crush him like his cigarette.

Chapter 14

On Wednesday morning Victoria and the field coordinator from the FBI's San Francisco office computer-interfaced via ISDN circuit with their videotape analyst in Washington, D.C. The security camera at the bank's automatic teller machine had recorded the informant's transaction last Friday afternoon, and Victoria had sent the tape back for analysis at the FBI laboratory's Video Support Unit on the third floor of the J. Edgar Hoover Building.

Special Agent Brent Schullman looked fiftyish with yellow-gray hair and a dogged expression that had probably served him well in his early years in the military police. He had the huge calloused hands of a man who liked to fix cars or work in the yard, which didn't seem to mesh with his designer suit and gold cuff links. Victoria figured his wife must do his shopping, and the way he cleaned his eyeglasses with his silk Armani necktie seemed to confirm her suspicion.

The two agents sat beside each other facing the

keyboard, computer and big twenty-inch color display monitor. Victoria worked the keyboard and mouse as the image appeared on the screen.

"Good morning," Dr. Edelman's voice resonated over the speaker.

Schullman did a double take, as if he'd expected to see the doctor's face appear on the bright blue screen. Victoria sensed his confusion. "We'll see the same thing here on our screen that he sees on his back in Washington," she explained.

"Good morning," she said into the speaker. "Dr. Edelman, I have Special Agent Brent Schullman here with me. He's the field coordinator and case agent for the San Francisco investigation. Actually," she smiled, "I think the real reason he's here is to see how his computer works."

A chuckle came over the line from Washington, but Schullman didn't seem to appreciate the humor.

"Anyway, Doctor, I know you haven't completed your analysis yet, but I just got word from the lab this morning that the cigarette remnants I found in the alley near Copeland's apartment were Marlboros, and the stock of paper indicates they were distributed and probably purchased on the East Coast. That makes it all the more evident that whoever was smoking in the alley probably didn't live around there and had no business being out there. It made me curious to know whether you've been able to find any evidence that the man in the ATM video is a cigarette smoker."

"Understood. Let's pull it up and I'll show you what I got."

The screen flickered, and the grainy black-and-white

image from the ATM security camera appeared on Victoria's monitor. It was a frozen pose, showing one of the clearest images of a man in a ski mask standing at the machine.

"As you can see," said Edelman, "there aren't any obvious signs this man's a smoker. No cigarette pack poking out of his pocket, et cetera. If I had a high-resolution color tape I could probably tell you whether his teeth were stained with nicotine. But not with an ATM tape. I searched for signs of ash on his clothing, but in black and white that's extremely difficult to pick up. The only thing I found is this," he said, zooming in on the right hand. "Notice the thumb." The zoom tightened until the screen filled with just the tip of the thumb. "See the little hole? The glove is burned right through to the skin."

"Like somebody who uses a cigarette lighter with his gloves on," said Victoria.

"Exactly."

"That seems a stretch," said Schullman. "How do you know it's a burn mark? Maybe he just takes his gloves off with his teeth and bit a hole through it."

The zoom tightened further, as tightly as it could without reducing the grainy footage to a meaningless collection of black-and-white dots. "Notice the fibers around the hole," said Edelman. "They're not frayed, the way you'd expect them to be with biting and pulling. They're singed. It's a burn mark."

They stared at the image together, until both she and Schullman seemed convinced. "All right," said Victoria. "Is there anything else?"

"That's it for now. I'll call you if I get anything more. So long."

"Thanks, Doctor," she said as the line disconnected. The screen turned a blank bright blue as she leaned back in her chair, thinking.

"You buy this burn-hole theory?" asked Schullman.

"If Edelman says it's a burn mark, I believe it's a burn mark."

"But where does it take you?"

"Hard to say. *Somebody* was watching me at Copeland's apartment, and whoever it was probably followed me there."

"What's your guess?"

"At first I thought it might have been the killer—a chain-smoker who stalks his victims and returns to the scene of the crime, curious about how the investigation is going. Now it looks like it could have been the informant. We know he was here in San Francisco, since he used the ATM here. And if Edelman's right, he's probably a smoker. I just don't know," she said, sighing. "All I saw was an orange dot in the darkness. It could have been the informant, could have been the killer."

"Seems to me you're overlooking an obvious possibility," said Schullman.

"What?"

"The informant *is* the killer."

Victoria said nothing as she clicked the mouse and turned off the computer.

Chapter 15

Late Friday evening Victoria cabbed it to the airport to catch the red-eye back to Washington, a five-hour nonstop that was supposed to leave San Francisco at 11:00 P.M. It was time to report to her supervisors. She'd spent most of the last six days working not with Schullman but with San Francisco Homicide, sharing everything she'd learned over the past three months and taking back little bits and pieces that might build on the collective knowledge of six—no, seven—different departments. One detective had compared it to earthquake seismology, how each murder was like another point on the Richter scale, increasing the intensity and complexity of the investigation exponentially rather than linearly. The analogy seemed to fit.

The victim's roommate had added a new twist to the murder, making Timothy Copeland the first who didn't live alone. Unfortunately, the killer had drugged him with an animal tranquilizer, and he didn't recall a thing. His very existence, though, was enough of a departure from the previous murders to make them all attuned to the possibility of a copycat killer, especially since Mike Posten's last article had blueprinted the way the killer had extracted the tongues.

Nearly a week had passed since she'd last spoken to Mike. She confirmed through her bank sources that he'd deposited a hundred thousand dollars in Ernest Gill's account, right on schedule. She'd thought about calling him once or twice during the week, then thought better of it. Strange, but sparring with him was the thing she liked most about her job right now. But talk about ambivalence: She knew their next conversation would probably mean another body.

She wondered whether trading jabs with Mike Posten was really all that much fun, or whether the rest of her job was simply too grim. Mutilated bodies, bloody crime scenes—experience had somewhat toughened her to such things. But something she'd never get used to was being a source of amusement for the boys in Homicide. Tonight had been the worst. Three detectives from SFPD had invited her along to happy hour, and she'd accepted just to kill time before heading to the airport. It was a noisy, smoky bar packed with the downtown professional crowd. Her foursome was shoulder-to-shoulder in a Naugahyde-seated booth, two on each side. Victoria sipped chardonnay, but the three men were soon plastered on two-for-one shots of tequila.

"Hey, Santos," slurred the oldest one. He was bald and so overweight that his jowls were hanging over his shirt collar. "What kinda name is that? Puerto Rican?"

"Cuban."

He licked the salt from his hand, belted back another shot, then sucked the lemon. His face cringed with a peculiar pleasure. "Cuban, huh? So, señorita," he said in a bad Mexican accent, "you wanna roll my cee-gar?"

The three men laughed heartily.

You wanna wear your cajones around your ears? she thought. But she just rolled her eyes and then checked her watch.

A wry smirk crept onto his face as he lit up a cigarette. "You know, my ex-partner went to high school in Florida. He told me all about you Cuban girls. Know what he told me?" He leaned across the table, as if to let her in on a secret. "Said third base is a snap, but that you never give up home plate. Have to save your virginity for marriage."

Please. She glared across the table, then gathered up her coat and purse. "Guess that's my cue to leave."

He grabbed her arm. "Hold on, sugar," he said with a smirk. "Stay for a while. We promise to respect your virginity." They burst out in laughter.

She sprung from the booth, then stopped and shot him a look. "Sergeant," she said, "the only thing more disgusting than the thought of your puny dick inside my body is the fact that you three goons think this is even remotely funny." She turned and left, ignoring a crack from one of them about how he loved it when she talked dirty.

She reached the airport three hours before her flight, but sitting alone in the Cloud Nine bar was far preferable to another thirty seconds with the Three

Stooges. By 10:00 P.M. she'd consumed all the "cheez" popcorn she could possibly stand, and she knew she'd strangle Ted Turner if she had to go "around the world in thirty minutes" even one more time with CNN. She was actually looking forward to that cramped airplane seat and the obligatory in-flight showing of last year's major box office disappointment.

The ice cubes clinked in the glass as she finished off another vodka tonic, her second. Having logged more than a million miles with the FBI, flying was a fear Victoria had gradually learned to suppress. *Sleeping* in a metal tube some thirty thousand feet above ground was still another mountain to climb. She was exhausted, however, and with a few more ounces of Russian-ade, tonight might be the night.

"Another Stoli and tonic?" the waitress asked.

Victoria handed up her empty glass. "Please."

She was seated at a table for two by a window overlooking the runway. People came and went from the tables around her with each arrival and departure announced over the loudspeaker. A snoring man with a backpack was stretched across five chairs at the table behind her, as if sleeping on his couch at home. A man dressed smartly in a business suit had taken the table beside her, burying his nose in some book, reading beneath the light from a neon beer sign. He looked about her age, with the kind of rugged good looks that usually snagged her attention. He had thick dark hair, and his large, athletic frame made the little plastic bar seats seem even more uncomfortable than usual. She'd been idly thinking about him ever since he'd sat down.

"Here you are, sir," the waitress said to him. "Dewar's and water. I'm sorry, did you say bottled water or regular water?"

He lifted his nose from his book, finally showing Victoria something other than his chiseled profile. "Regular's fine."

"Good choice," Victoria said to him as the waitress walked away.

"Excuse me?" he asked.

"That bottled-water thing's a scam, you know."

He smiled and raised his glass. "So I've heard. Cheers."

They sipped their drinks and exchanged glances. "You mind sharing a table?" he asked. "I'm a little too close to the smoking section over here."

She hesitated, then figured what the hell. If he turned out to be a creep, her plane was leaving in fifty-five minutes. "Sure," she said.

They shared the usual small talk—where they were from, where they were headed—then ordered another round of drinks, though this time she opted for a ginger ale. He was a broker who dealt in Corvettes, Bentleys, and other classic automobiles, on his way to yet another wealthy estate auction in Chicago that would prove you can't take it with you. As always, Victoria was appropriately vague about her "government job." Quickly changing subjects, she noticed the title of the self-help book he'd laid on the seat between them. "*How to Put Power and Passion into Your Relationship*," she read aloud. "So, what woman is making you read *this*?"

"Actually I'm not reading it. I just hold it up and

stare at it in public places, like airports, until some attractive woman strikes up a conversation. Works every time."

"And your wife doesn't mind?" she said with a smile.

He smiled back, then turned a little more serious. "Actually I'm not married. Not anymore."

"You say that like it's recent."

"The fat lady was singing long before it was legally over. We're still friends. It wasn't bitter. It was just . . . Ah, you don't want to hear it."

"No, go on—tell me."

"Well, to be honest"—he gave a sheepish expression—"it was sex."

Victoria gulped.

"Not that we didn't have it. We just didn't have it enough. No, it really wasn't even that." He looked down. "We didn't have it in enough different ways. You know what I mean?"

Her eyes widened as she sucked on an ice chip. "Well, yes, there *are* different ways."

"Am I making you uncomfortable?"

"Me?" she scoffed nervously. "Nah."

"Because I've really been looking for a woman's honest assessment of this."

"I don't mind being honest."

"Women usually don't. But try to talk about sex with another guy, and about the only thing you'll get out of the conversation is that *he* sure doesn't have any problems. Not that *I* had a problem, of course."

"Of course."

He laughed lightly. "Okay, the *problem*, if that's

what you want to call it, was that I married a woman whose basic attitude toward sex was that she didn't mind it. I knew this, of course, when I married her. Hell, I knew it the day I met her."

"You had sex the day you met?"

"No. You don't have to have sex with a woman to know whether she's into it. Men can just tell these things."

"Oh, yeah? How?"

"Her looks."

"You can tell whether a woman's into sex by what she looks like?"

"No. By how she looks—*at me*. Looks are very sexy. Like you, for instance. The way you kept glancing over at my table from the minute I sat down, peeking out from behind that wisp of hair that kept falling in your face. Very sexy."

She smiled with embarrassment. "So what do you make from that?"

"I'm not sure. But see? You're already thinking the way you should be thinking. All the little things translate to something else. That's how we know."

"So your wife didn't translate."

"She translated all right. I just defied the message. I kept hoping someday she'd hit that sexual peak everyone always talks about. But it never came. I tried everything. *I* knew *her* body from head to toe, but she still acted like I didn't have a body below my chin. I mean . . . you sure this isn't making you uncomfortable?"

"It's—no, I'm fine."

"My wife and I must have made love thousands of times, but I bet that if you had four other men in this bar drop their pants and lined us up, she wouldn't know my—my equipment from theirs." He seemed to blush. "I'd better stop there."

Victoria struggled for a response. Finally, words came to her lips. "Hey, I don't even know your *name*."

"I'm Mike," he said, extending his hand.

"Mike," she said with a smirk, thinking of someone else. "That's a nice name." She shook his hand, but it was more than a formality. They both held on a little longer than they might have. "I'm Victoria."

She looked at him again from behind that wisp of hair, the look he'd thought was sexy. "You know, another guy named Mike once told me that the only people who can be completely open with each other are lovers or strangers."

He nodded slowly. "There's a lot of truth in that. Hell, I think I was just more direct with you than I ever was with my wife."

There was a long but comfortable silence. Neither one looked away.

"You know," he said, "I travel to the Washington area quite a bit. Would you like to get together sometime? I mean, for lunch or maybe dinner?"

Her smile flattened, but she kept looking into his eyes. "Sure. Why don't you give me your business card?"

"Well, that doesn't make it very easy for me to call you when I come into town, does it."

She hesitated. Her standing rule was never to give her number to a stranger. But maybe that was the reason the only men she ever met were obnoxious cops at happy hour who asked her to "roll their cigars."

"You've got a point there," she said. She took a pen from her purse and put it to the cocktail napkin. "You realize, of course, that we'd no longer be strangers."

"That's okay. I promise I'll still be completely open with you. Except, no more stories about my ex-wife."

She chuckled to herself, still feeling a buzz from the vodka tonics. "That I can live with," she said with a smile.

At 5:00 A.M. Saturday, Curt Rollins was dressed all in black—jeans, sweatshirt, ski mask, and gloves. A black vinyl pouch strapped tightly around his waist contained everything he needed. He was on one knee in a cluster of bushes at the edge of the woods, hiding and watching. During five hours of surveillance the temperature had dropped twenty degrees, but it still wasn't cold enough to freeze the ground. He'd smoked half a pack of Marlboros and was on his last cigarette.

The secluded house at the top of the hill was completely dark, save for the outside porch light. This one would be easy. One story. No alarm, no pets, no neighbors. He could have made his move long ago, but something held him back. The white clapboard house with blue slatted shutters looked like hundreds, even thousands of others he'd seen in his lifetime. But the smell of sulfur from the tide, the cool wind whistling through the screened-in porch and the lonely tinkle of a wind chime gave this one a haunting familiarity. It reminded him of the first crime he'd ever committed, at age ten back in 1973. . . .

The sun was setting on another long and boring

summer weekday as he and his best friend Frank trudged along the dirt road, toward the lake. Any minute now the long shadows of the forest would cover the shoreline, and the croaking chorus of bullfrogs would begin. Curt was wearing his favorite Chicago Bears jersey and baggy hand-me-down jeans that he wouldn't grow into for another four years. He had a crew cut like his older brother in the Marines and a string of phony rub-on tattoos running up his arm.

"Let's go creepy crawling," said Frank.

Curt scrunched his face. "What's that?"

"Don't you know anything?"

"Nope," he said, crossing his eyes. "I'm a retart."

Frank gave him a swift kick in the rear. "It's not re*tart*, you retard. I told you to stop doing that, or we're not hanging out anymore." Frank was the smart one, but he was small for his age. He was always getting in fights with kids who called him "Franny" or "Shorty." Curt was the only kid he could hit without getting punched back.

"I read this book my mom bought," said Frank. "About a guy named Manson. His gang used to go sneaking into houses and open drawers and stuff while people were sleeping."

"I ain't going in nobody's house when they're home."

"You chicken?"

"No. It's just stupid."

Frank clucked like a hen. "You're so chicken you wouldn't even go in an empty house."

"Yes, I would."

"Prove it. Let's go inside the Dawson's summerhouse down by the lake."

The white clapboard summerhouse was at the top of the hill looking down on Loon Lake. It was still boarded up from the winter. With a stick Frank pried away one of the blue slatted shutters at the back of the house. Curt lifted him up so he could look inside. He broke one of the windowpanes, slid open the window and crawled inside. "Come on," he called from inside the house.

Curt pulled himself up by the windowsill. He tried going in headfirst but didn't have the arm strength. He threw one leg over the ledge and tried going in backward. He was inside from the waist down, blindly searching for the floor with his tiptoes when he lost his grip and tumbled inside. A table went over, and a lamp crashed to the floor.

Curt looked around. It was dark and stuffy inside, but from the light through the window he could see the porcelain lamp scattered on the floor in a hundred pieces. "Oh, no," he groaned.

On impulse, Frank dashed across the room to the matching lamp and knocked it off the table. He laughed, like he enjoyed it.

"What are you *doing?*"

He just laughed louder. A wild excitement filled his eyes as he stood there, surveying the room. He grabbed a poker from the fireplace and started knocking books from the shelves and pictures from the walls. Dishes, the television, knickknacks—everything, smashed. Curt screamed at him to stop, but the noise drowned him out.

He stopped suddenly, panting and completely out of breath. "Break something," he shouted.

Curt stood there, shaking.

"We're in this together. Break something!"

"I—I don't want to."

Frank held the poker in both hands and ran at him at full speed, knocking him to the ground. Curt was on his back, and his friend was on top, pressing the poker down on his throat. "Break something! Or I'll kill you!"

Curt looked up in fear, gasping for breath. "Okay," he grunted. Frank let him up, but he walked right behind him and held the poker like a baseball bat, threatening him. "The mirror," he said, pointing above the fireplace. "Knock it down."

Curt took a deep breath. Reluctantly, he climbed up on the stack of logs by the fireplace and tugged at the big oak-framed mirror, keeping one hand on the mantel for balance. It wouldn't budge.

"Harder!"

With two hands he gave a hard shove. The mirror shifted and Curt lost his balance. The stack of logs collapsed beneath him and he fell to the hardwood floor. The mirror landed on his foot with a thundering crash, shattering into tiny pieces. Curt cried out in pain.

"My leg!" Tears streamed down his face. A triangular piece of glass as big as a slice of pizza was protruding from his bloody calf.

"Don't be a sissy!"

"Let's get out of here!"

"You're getting blood all over the place. You're gonna get us caught!" Frank ran to the bedroom and came back with a bedsheet. He wrapped his hand in the sheet and pulled out the broken glass. Curt screamed.

"Stop being such a girl!"

Curt's voice was shaking, and he couldn't catch his breath. "I have to call my mom. I have to go to the doctor."

Frank tied the sheet around the leg, but the red soaked right through. "Creepy crawlers don't go to the doctor."

"I need stitches."

"I can do it. I watch my mom do it at the animal hospital all the time. It's easy. All I need is a needle and thread."

"No way! I'm going to the doctor."

"You *can't*. You can't tell anyone how it happened. This is like when we play army. Same rules."

"I don't want to play."

"This isn't *play*," he shouted. "You know the rule. What do you say if you're captured? Answer me! Or I'll kick you in the leg!"

"Don't kick me!" he cried. "Just name, rank and serial number, that's all."

"If you go to the doctor, you're a snitch. Snitches are the lowest form of life on earth. Take the pain. Just take it! . . ."

Rollins bit his lip, feeling it all over again. He blinked hard and shook off the memory. He looked to the east, where a faint orange glow was brightening the horizon. It would be light soon if he didn't move fast. He crushed out his cigarette, gathered up the handful of butts from the ground around him and stuffed them in his pouch so the police wouldn't find them. After three deep breaths, he sprung from the bushes and skulked across the yard, up toward the dark and deathly quiet home of the next scheduled victim.

Chapter 16

Karen's eyes blinked open at the crack of dawn. The bedroom walls were a pale sky blue. A poster-sized photo of Clearwater High School's Class of '82 covered the bedroom door. Kermit the Frog, Winnie-the-Pooh, and the rest of her childhood collection of stuffed animals stared at her from across the room. The rousing smell of coffee told her life was stirring in the kitchen. She checked the old heart-shaped Snoopy alarm clock on the nightstand, then lay back on her pillow and smiled to herself. Seven A.M. A whole extra hour of sleep today. *At least Mom sleeps in on the weekends.*

Although she'd instructed her secretary to tell everyone she was out of town on business, she'd actually gone home for a week away from Mike, their counselor and their well-intending mutual friends. She had things to sort out in her own mind, and it was impossible for her to be objective about their marriage while living in the home they'd built together, waking up every morning in the bed they used to share.

She put on her robe and slippers, brushed her hair, made a quick stop in the bathroom and shuffled sleepily toward the kitchen.

"Morning, dear," her mother said cheerfully. Her face was already made up, and she was dressed smartly in blue slacks and a pink blouse, wrapped in a big flower-print apron. She was standing at the stove, flipping pancakes on the griddle.

Karen gave her a peck on the cheek, then poured herself some coffee.

"Cream's on the table," her mother said. "I have an appointment at the beauty shop at eight. I thought maybe you'd want to come with me."

She smiled sadly. Even after a whole year, it still depressed her to think of her mother as a member of the widows club that met every Saturday morning at the Curl Up And Dye. She ran her fingers through her tangled hair and said, "I . . . don't think so."

Her mother brought a platter of pancakes to the table, then sat directly across from her. Karen's eyes widened incredulously at the mountainous stack. "Mom, it's just you and me, right? Or did you invite the neighborhood?"

"The perfect ones are on top. The not-so-perfect ones are underneath."

Karen lifted her plate like a beggar and smiled with appreciation. "I'll have a perfect one."

She smothered the cakes with the goodies she never kept in her own house—real butter with all the fat, real maple syrup with all the calories. She ate quietly, only half listening as her mother discussed their plans for the day. After a few bites, she put down her fork and flashed the troubled look that never in thirty-two years had failed to draw the appropriate response from her mother.

"What's wrong, dear?"

"Mom, did you ever keep secrets from Daddy?"

She shifted in her seat, a bit taken aback. "My, where did that come from?"

"Did you?"

Her coffee cup tinkled as she stirred nervously. "I suppose I did, sure."

"I don't mean little things. Big things."

"Everybody has secrets, Karen."

"What's the biggest secret you ever kept from him?"

"Oh, my," she said, sighing at the size of the question. "I don't know."

"I know it's personal. But it's really important."

She looked into her daughter's clouded eyes, and she could see it *was* important. "All right. Well . . ." She looked off toward the dining room, searching her mind. "I know. You remember your daddy's first Lincoln? The Mark Four, or whatever it was called back in the early seventies."

"He loved that car," Karen said with a nostalgic smile.

"Oh, did he *love* that car. I was the only person he would let drive it, besides himself."

"Actually, I don't even remember him letting *you* drive it."

"I drove it. Once. Got as far as the end of the driveway. Damn thing was so long I backed it right into the mailbox."

Karen laughed, then covered her mouth. "I'm sorry. That's not funny."

"At the time it was terrifying. Never in his whole

life had your father ever bought himself an expensive new car. It was just two weeks old, and I put a nasty dent in the fender."

"What did you do?"

"Luckily, your father was out of town on business. So I drove it to the body shop and had it fixed."

"Did you tell Daddy?"

"Never."

"Didn't you feel bad about that?"

"At times. But I figured, this was one of those unique situations where telling him what had happened would actually be selfish. My confession wouldn't make *him* feel better. It would only make *me* feel better, by easing my conscience. That new car was such a joy for him. Why spoil it?"

"That makes sense."

"Sure it does. But the problem, Karen, is that you can rationalize just about anything that way. You can rationalize lying about an *affair* that way. Why be so selfish as to tell your husband? It would only spoil his image of you."

"Then how did you draw the line?"

"I just drew it. And that's the real problem with secrets. It's like Nixon and Watergate. The cover-up is worse than the crime. Once you keep a secret from someone, it gets harder every day to tell the truth. After your father sold his car and bought a new one, I could have told him I put a dent in it. No big deal. A car is just a *thing*. But the fact that I'd kept it a secret from him for so long—that would have truly hurt him. And it's a Pandora's box. He'd start to think, gee, what other secrets does my wife keep from me?"

"So you never told him."

"No, I never did."

They sat in silence for a minute. Then her mother looked at her with concern and asked, "Sweetheart, is there something you're keeping from Mike?"

Karen stared down into her coffee cup. "Yes. And it's just like you said. I've kept it inside so long that I don't know how I can ever tell him."

"I'm sure if it's just a little thing, he'll understand."

"It's not a little thing. Not even close."

"How big *is* it?"

She looked up, and her eyes welled with tears. "Mom," her voice shook, "you know how big it is."

The older woman's eyes filled with sadness. She knew. And she could tell from the look on Karen's face that the years of silence had made it even more of a secret than it ever had been. She could see that, at least in her own mind, it had become unspeakable.

The morning sun was streaming into Zack's waterfront condo, but Mike was only half awake. His hair was sticking out in all directions from another sleepless night of tossing and turning, reflecting on a bizarre week. It was almost morbid the way congratulatory calls had streamed in from friends and colleagues at the *New York Times*, the *Washington Post*, and all over the country. His Saturday-edition exclusive was a Sunday headline everywhere else. The random nature of the brutal killings and the wide geographic dispersion had turned it into national news: Anyone, anywhere could be next. The best part, quipped Aaron Fields, was that even the *San Francisco Chronicle*—the paper of record in the victim's hometown—could only print the facts "as reported by the *Miami Tribune*."

Beautiful, he mused. *Thirteen years of busting hump, and the biggest story ever comes from opening a checkbook.*

Behind the hubbub, however, thoughts of yet another victim swirled distractingly. He was all too aware that after the last cash deposit, the killer had struck immediately. Every time he managed to take his mind off the murders, troubled thoughts of Karen made sleep even more elusive. He'd been trying to call her since Monday, but her secretary said she was "out of town, couldn't be reached." He hated to let this fester, but she obviously wasn't ready to let him explain the debacle at the Metrorail. Over and over he replayed in his mind the perfect conversation where he'd tell all and she'd forgive him totally. He wasn't sleeping, but he knew he was dreaming.

He was wearing gym shorts and a T-shirt, sipping hot coffee and staring sleepily at the television from Zack's leather couch, when the phone rang. He muted the early-Saturday-morning news and grabbed the cordless phone from the cocktail table.

"Thanks for the money, Posten."

A sudden burst of adrenaline lifted him from the couch. With the receiver pressed to his ear he walked out the sliding-glass door that led to the balcony. He stared out over the leafy green canopy of treetops below, wondering if his informant was as close as he sounded. "Don't *thank* me. This is extortion."

"Sorry. I keep forgetting that I'm *forcing* you to become the hottest crime reporter in America."

"Look, it's too early in the morning to play your silly games. Tell me who the killer is."

"You'll need a serious increase on your Visa limit for an answer to *that* question."

"Is it you?" said Mike.

In the sudden silence, Mike could hear a tinkling sound over the line, like wind chimes—or like the hypnotic sound of halyards tapping in the breeze against the bare masts of a thousand sailboats. On a hunch, he leaned out over the balcony railing, craning to see the pay phone right across the street by the marina. He could see the BellSouth logo on the shelter, but the corner of his own building jutted out just far enough to keep him from seeing whether anyone was at one of the phones. "How about it? Are you the killer?"

"Are you trying to trace this call? Is that why you're dragging it out, talking shit?"

"No."

"Wouldn't do you any good anyhow. It's a pay phone. I'll be in the next state before anyone can track it down."

A pay phone—and he sounded so close! Mike leaned over the railing again, straining even harder to see around the corner of his own building. He was twenty stories up, stretching out like a trapeze artist. The instant he looked down he lost his balance. He caught himself at the last second, arms flailing as he nearly dropped the phone. Still, he couldn't see. "I'm not tracing anything."

"Maybe you are, maybe you aren't. The fact that I'm even worried about it sucks. I chose *you* over thousands of other reporters, because I thought I could trust you."

"I'm as trustworthy as they get."

"Not good enough. I'm trusting you with my *life*, man. All you got on the line is your reputation."

"At least *one* of us is risking something of value."

"Always the wiseass, aren't you? Good thing we'll never meet. Could be dicey."

"Is that a threat?"

"I don't make threats. Only predictions—remember?"

Mike felt a knot in his stomach. "You still haven't answered my question. Are you the killer."

"I don't answer anything free of charge."

"That's what makes you so special, I guess."

"That's what makes me no different from anybody else. Nobody tells the truth for free. We're all looking for something in return. Power. Respect. Sex. Love. All I want is money. Hell—I'm *easy*."

"This is anything but easy."

"That's because you make it harder than it needs to be, looking in all kinds of places you shouldn't be looking."

"Where *should* I look?"

"Try the glove compartment of your wife's car."

"You son of a bitch. You leave my wife out of this."

"It's a real scoop, Posten. Victims eight and nine. Married couple. First double homicide. How bad do you want the story? Enough to drive over to the airport garage and hunt for your wife's car while she's out of town?"

Mike bristled at the thought of him following Karen, knowing her whereabouts. It drove home the chilling point that there was no protection from a faceless enemy. He looked out from the balcony in frustration, wishing he could just see around the corner of the high-rise. "From now on," he said angrily, "you deal directly with me, or we don't deal. Period."

" 'From now on'—I like the sound of that. It means you understand that this is a long-term relationship. That's good, because your next installment's another hundred grand. And I want it quick. I'll give you two working days. It's due on Tuesday."

"*Enough* already. Just *stop* the killing, damn it."

"Easy, hotshot. My time is just about up, so I'm hanging up now, just in case you *are* tracing. But stay right by the phone, because I'll call you right back. I promise I'll have something that's well worth a hundred thousand."

The line clicked. Immediately, Mike leaned out over the railing to see if anyone was walking away from the bank of pay phones. From his angle he couldn't even see that much. He considered hopping on the elevator or even running down the twenty flights of stairs. His cordless phone would only work inside the apartment, however, and he didn't want to miss the return call. Then his face lit up with an idea. He rushed to his closet and grabbed his binoculars, then raced out of the apartment, leaving the front door open as he peeled down the hall. He stopped at the window at the end of the corridor, hoping for a clear view of the pay phones. A big sprawling oak was blocking his line of sight.

"Dammit!" He hurriedly retraced his steps back toward the apartment, then stopped suddenly in front of a neighbor's unit. The north view! He pounded on the door, waited a few seconds, then pounded again. A sleepy man in pajamas answered with the chain on the door. He peeked out suspiciously through the crack.

"This is life or death! Let me in, *please*. I need to use your balcony!"

The man made a face, then groaned something in Spanish.

Shit! For the millionth time in Miami, Mike wished he were bilingual. "*Por favor,* uh . . ."

The phone rang back in Zack's apartment, and with the door open he could hear it echoing down the hallway.

"Let me inside, just for a second—*please!*"

The man shrugged and slammed the door.

The phone kept ringing. Mike sprinted back inside and snatched it up.

"What took you so long?" the voice asked.

Mike paused to catch his breath. The call sounded even closer than before. "Where *are* you?"

"Where I am, who I am. That's not important. Now, the killer—*he's* important. So get yourself a pen, and write fast. Here's your hundred-thousand-dollar story. Here's what the criminal psychiatrists of the world call a profile of a serial killer."

Mike stood in the doorway, torn. He could rush downstairs on nothing but a hunch that his caller was there, but with the limited range of his cordless phone he'd lose the connection and miss the story. His other option was to stay put and get the story—the whole hundred-thousand-dollar exclusive. His stomach churned with the same mercenary guilt that had tortured him last time, when he'd called Aaron Fields to reserve page one.

"I'm listening," he said as he stepped back inside and closed the door. "Talk to me."

Chapter 17

Victoria arrived at Washington National Airport with pleasant thoughts of a quick drive home and a long soak in a hot, sudsy bath. Before she even reached baggage claim, however, her plans had changed. Another agent met her at the gate with new orders. She got right back on another flight and landed in Tampa, Florida, at ten-thirty Saturday morning.

Clearwater Beach was a forty-minute drive from the airport. Victoria knew the way and drove on automatic pilot, glancing now and again at the glistening waves on a choppy Tampa Bay. Wrapped in her thoughts, she was recounting those pulse-pounding moments outside Timothy Copeland's apartment last Tuesday night, ending in a futile chase of the glowing orange dot down the dark alley. It seemed like a metaphor for the entire investigation: a flicker of hope, another blind alley.

She wondered if she'd really been that close to the killer, trying to understand the logic behind a serial killer watching her inspect the crime scene. She didn't have to stretch to find an analogue. Her training had taught her that serial killers—particularly intelligent ones—often insinuated themselves into the police investigation, sometimes just for the thrill of it, but more often to learn more about the investigation and the people conducting it. Ted Bundy had volunteered at a rape crisis center while he was murdering women in Seattle. Edmund Kemper, the California co-ed killer—with an IQ of 148, higher than Einstein's—had so befriended the police that when he finally called and confessed to the murders they thought it was a crank.

Her tired eyes suddenly flickered with an idea. She picked up her Dictaphone from the passenger seat, brought it to her lips, and hit RECORD. "Possible proactive measures. One. Hold community meetings in each affected neighborhood to discuss the murders. Publicize through the local media. Killer may appear at one or more, so monitor each meeting with plain-clothes or video surveillance. Two. Identify local bars or other social gathering places where officers investigating the murders in each city hang out. Be on the lookout for inquisitive civilians. Three . . ."

She paused, then sighed. She knew there was a third idea, but after a night on an airplane her mind had checked out. The exit ramp was just ahead anyway, so she switched off the Dictaphone and turned off the causeway.

In five minutes she was in a quiet old neighborhood sporting one ranch-style house after another, all built in the 1950s and 1960s. Most had been updated by younger couples in recent years with new barrel-tile roofs and bright pastel paint jobs. A few were still home to their original owners, marked by old jalousie windows and pink plastic flamingos on the lawn. She checked the street numbers, then parked the rental car at the curb at the end of the cul-de-sac.

She checked herself in the mirror. Terrible case of mushy airplane face, but it would have to do. She walked up the sidewalk and double-checked the address. Four-fifteen Bell Aire Lane. She rang the door bell and waited. A full-faced woman in her sixties answered. She looked like she'd just come from Saturday morning at the beauty parlor, with styled gray hair and a warm expression.

Victoria identified herself and flashed her badge. "Are you Edith Malone?"

Her brow furrowed with concern. "Yes," she said shakily. "What's this about?"

"Please don't be alarmed. I'm here for your daughter."

"My *daughter*? Why? I hope she's not in some kind of trouble."

Victoria tucked her badge away, then answered without emotion. "None of her own doing. May I come in please?"

Her hands were shaking as she opened the door. "Yes, sure. Come inside."

Victoria drove to the airport, where she and Karen boarded an eight-seat prop Buplane. Karen seemed bewildered, and Victoria was certainly sympathetic.

Here was a woman whose marital problems alone had driven her to her mother's for a week of reflection. Victoria tried to imagine how she would feel if some guy had chased her through a Metrorail station one week, only to have the FBI track her down halfway across the state the next. She explained everything, though, on the flight to Miami.

"Why wasn't I told any of this before?"

Victoria paused, considering her response. "The minute we learned that the informant planted the latest message in the glove compartment of your car, we felt you were in sufficient danger that we had to tell you. Your involvement was no longer indirect. It would be impossible for us to give you the level of protection you need now, unless you know what's going on. And you need to be able to take your own precautions, to protect yourself. For your own safety, we acted immediately, even before we had time to consult your husband."

"That wasn't my question. I want to know why I wasn't told *before*."

She started to respond, then checked herself. "That was a joint decision between your husband and the FBI."

"You mean Mike actually agreed to that?"

"Yes, but I don't want to speak out of turn. I think I'll let him explain when we land."

"I can't wait to hear this," she huffed.

They sat in silence for several minutes, each in her own thoughts as the engines hummed. Victoria glanced across the narrow aisle several times discreetly, and Karen seemed to be cooling down. Finally, their eyes met, and they exchanged awkward smiles.

"So," said Karen, "how do you like working with Mike?"

"Fine. No problem."

"Do you like him?"

"Like him? Yeah, sure. Then again, I spend most of my day trailing psychopathic sexual sadists. Let's face it: Saddam Hussein would be a breath of fresh air."

Karen smiled. "Yours *is* an unusual career choice. I can't help but wonder—"

"Why do I do it," Victoria finished the thought for her. "Your husband asked the same question. I gave him the ten-cent version."

"*Nobody* gives Mike the ten-cent version of anything."

"So I learned. He wasn't too happy. Made some crack about how I must have something in my background that makes me feel like a victim."

Karen's eyebrow arched with interest. "Meaning you do this for revenge?"

"I'm not a vigilante, if that's what you're wondering."

"I'm sorry, I didn't mean to imply that. I just meant I wouldn't fault you for feeling angry, you know, if you were a victim. I could understand how a woman would feel that way." She rubbed between her eyes, like a woman with a migraine. "If she were a victim."

Victoria blinked with confusion. "Are you okay?"

"Yeah, fine," she said with a "chin-up" smile. "I was just thinking how quickly people forget about the victims. That's the worst part about being one, I would imagine. Being around people who'd rather forget something you can never forget."

Victoria hesitated, then touched her lightly on the forearm. "Is there something you'd like to tell me?"

"No, not really. I guess the thought of a serial killer having just rummaged through my glove compartment has me a little spooked. I'm genuinely curious, though, one woman to another. Has doing this serial killer stuff helped you?"

"Helped me what?"

"With whatever it is that drove you to do it."

"I don't want you to think there's some big ugly secret here."

"I don't. I'd just really like to know."

"I'm not one to talk about myself," she said wearily. She glanced across the aisle and caught Karen's eye. She seemed sincere, not nosy. "Well, if you really want to know, I think it has something to do with my . . . shall we say, family history. I'm what they call a Jewban—half Jew, half Cuban. Sometimes I think my boss wishes I was handicapped, just to cover another minority, but that's another story.

"My maternal grandfather died in Auschwitz. My uncle—my father's brother—spent twenty-six years in one of Castro's political prisons. Family reunions were a real blast. A bunch of old drunks guzzling down Sangria made with Manischewitz wine, arguing over who was the most persecuted. At least that's how I saw it as a kid. As I got older, though, the stories started to fascinate. It made me want to understand the criminal mind—especially the minds of men who know the difference between right and wrong, yet who kill and kill again, with no remorse or any sign of a conscience."

133

"So you're one of those cops who likes to think like the killer."

"I wouldn't say that. I try to understand the killer by looking through the eyes of the victim. Which means I may not crawl as far inside the killer's head as some investigators do. But it gives me the passion to keep on looking when others might give up."

Karen nodded slowly. "I figured you were like that."

"Pro-victim, you mean?"

"No. The kind of woman who never gives up."

Victoria thought she sensed something in her tone, a defensiveness she sometimes got from wives of the men she worked with.

Silence lingered as they exchanged ambiguous glances. Then each just looked away, peering out the little oval window over the wing, toward Lake Okeechobee below.

Chapter 18

for the first time in two months, Mike went home. Fortunately, Karen was a creature of habit, so he'd had no trouble finding her car at the airport—she always parked on level K, "for *Karen*," so she wouldn't forget her spot.

Had he not been carrying an envelope with the names of two more victims, it would have felt good to pull into the familiar driveway and walk up the curved path of stepping stones that cut across the front lawn. Whatever might come of their marital problems, he would always think of this pink stucco house with white gingerbread trim as a happy place, filled with memories of happier times. He remembered the day he and Karen had planted the little hedges around the flower bed, five or six years ago. It rained like a hurricane halfway through the job. They ended up laughing and rolling in the mud, then they chased each other inside, scrubbed each other clean and spent every ounce of remaining energy making love to each other the rest of the day.

It pleased him to see everything still looking the same. Karen hadn't changed a thing. A good sign, he thought. The only problem was that the invitation home had come not from Karen, but Victoria Santos.

"Come on in," said Victoria, answering the door.

"Thanks. Nice of the FBI to invite me into my home."

Her phone call had been appropriately cryptic, though Mike had gleaned enough from her innuendo to know that Karen would be there and that she was finally in the loop. Still, his heart skipped a beat when he saw her sitting on the living-room couch. He wanted to give her a hug, but she rose slowly and seemed a little standoffish. Her coolness only heightened the guilt he felt for not having told her the truth from the beginning.

"I'm sorry you had to find out this way," he said softly.

"Me too," she said in a clipped voice.

Victoria stepped forward. "Just so you know, Mike, I picked Karen up this morning on orders from Washington. As soon as we heard that the informant had left the latest predictions in Karen's car, we figured it was only a matter of time before you told her everything. So we told her."

He was still reading Karen's expression, searching for some opening to seek her forgiveness. He suddenly turned toward Victoria, as if her words had just registered. "Let me stop you right there," he said sharply. "How in the hell did you know the informant had left something in Karen's car before I even called to tell you about it?"

Her expression fell. "I—I was on an airplane, unreachable. I guess I assumed you'd called somebody else."

"If I had called somebody else, don't you think they would have told me they were sending you to pick up my wife and tell her everything? I never called anybody."

She blinked hard, thinking. "Well, it's not really important *how* we knew. Somehow, we knew."

"You tapped my telephone, didn't you."

"No!" she said.

"You're lying. You promised to respect my integrity as a journalist. The deal was that the FBI supplied the money, and the only information you'd get was whatever I decided to print in the *Tribune*. You broke your promise not to eavesdrop on confidential conversations between me and my informant."

"*I* don't know that, Mike, and your mere accusation doesn't make it true."

"The *only* way you could have known about Karen's car is if the FBI had listened in on my phone call with my informant."

Victoria sank in silence, unable to argue.

Tension filled the room as Mike's look of disbelief turned quickly to anger. He started pacing, then forced himself to speak calmly. "You know, up until now I was having second thoughts about whether I should go public with the profile of the killer that my informant gave me. I remembered what you said last time, how my printing the details of how the tongue was extracted might impede your investigation. I thought revealing the kind of person the killer is might also be detrimental. Of course, the FBI doesn't need me to print anything, since you're listening to my conversations. But now, as far as I'm concerned the FBI can go straight to hell. If you can't keep a promise, then I'll print whatever I damn well please."

"Mike, I swear, if there was a wiretap, I personally knew nothing about it."

"Sure," he scoffed. "If you're going to continue lying to me, I think it's best if you just leave, Victoria. I need to speak to my wife."

"I understand you two need to talk. But we have business to discuss."

"I said it was time for you to leave," he said sternly.

She was about to protest, but one glance at Karen's mortified face made her think twice. "Fine," she said stiffly. "Good-bye, Karen."

Karen nodded, then Mike led Victoria to the foyer and opened the door. She stopped at the threshold and looked him in the eye.

"Let me tell you something, Mike. It's really unfair to make me out the bad guy in front of your wife. But let's put that aside. Whatever you decide to tell Karen about our arrangement, the fact remains that we've got a serial killer to catch. And whether you recognize it or not, the stakes have just gone up—*way* up. There was absolutely no logical reason for your informant to put the names of those victims in Karen's car. He could have FedExed them to you again, or used your computer again—or he could have put them in *your* glove compartment. His only purpose in using Karen was to demonstrate an increased level of control. He's telling you that he knows who your wife is, where she is, what she's doing."

"I know that."

"But I don't think you've thought it through. To be blunt: This means that if our experts in Quantico are wrong—if it turns out your informant is *not* the serial killer—then you're dealing with an informant who is himself exhibiting serious sociopathic tendencies. That's not a good thing," she said with a tinge of sarcasm, "and this is no time for you and I to be at each other's throats. So call me when you've cooled off. Because it's a little dangerous to quit the game before you even know who you're playing against. And I assure you: We *don't know*."

She turned quickly and headed down the steps.

Chapter 19

t he Sunday-morning *Tribune* landed with a thud on the Baines's doorstep. Brenda normally slept in on Sundays, but she was up early today. She'd been working on an investigative piece on Florida's death penalty for nearly two months, and the first of a five-part series was scheduled to run on page one in Sunday's edition. It was her biggest project in more than two years, and she was crawling out of her skin eager to see it.

Brenda had come to the *Tribune* nine years ago from the *Milwaukee Journal*. She was immediately tagged as the snowbird from the Dairy State with the milky white skin, but her shiny black hair and big green eyes made for an exotic combination worthy of a magazine cover. Both she and Mike had been single back then. They started the lunch routine soon after her arrival, which quickly led to dinners, dates, and three nights a week at Mike's apartment. It was while lying in bed that he'd told her the *Tribune* needed to fire its incompetent associate publisher. It was while lying in bed that she'd passed that along to the associate publisher.

Since then, she and Mike hadn't really seen eye to eye, so to speak.

She fumbled for her glasses on the nightstand and rolled out of bed as quickly as she could without waking her husband. They'd made love last night and she couldn't find her panties, but the slinky top to her silk nightie hung just low enough to cover the essentials. She hurried to the porch, and the wind lifted her negligee up to her face as she reached for the paper. She stood there on the porch, oblivious to her nakedness, stunned by the headline.

SERIAL KILLER STRIKES AGAIN. VICTIMS 8 AND 9 FOUND IN SOUTH CAROLINA. The kicker she read aloud: "A *Tribune* Exclusive, by Michael Posten."

Her face flushed red as she flipped frantically through the paper, searching for her piece. It wasn't there. They'd pulled it. "Son of a bitch!" she shrieked, sending the cat scurrying off the porch.

She tucked the paper under her arm and stormed back inside, slamming the door behind her. She went right back to the bedroom and threw the paper on the bed, waking her husband.

"Look at *this*."

He rubbed the sleep from his eyes, then read the headline and shook his head. "I'm so sorry, honey. Looks like that jerk went out and paid for another exclusive."

"Oh, no," she said with an angry glare. "He hasn't *begun* to pay for this one."

*   *   *

Victoria was growing tired of seven-day workweeks, but she was well overdue for a status report. At noon on Sunday she drove to her supervisor's house in rural Virginia.

February wasn't the prettiest time of year, as the scattered forest and rolling fields were bare and brown. The white frame house was two stories with a high-pitched roof, an old stone foundation and a wraparound porch. Built in the late 1700s, it had all the charm and inconvenience of a historic landmark plucked from a Williamsburg village.

She and David Shapiro sat in matching leather armchairs in the downstairs study. The dark wood decor would have made any time of day feel like midnight, but the cozy glow from the fireplace warmed their faces. Out of respect, Victoria had eschewed her usual weekend scruffies for dark wool slacks, heels and a cashmere turtleneck. Shapiro dressed more to her liking in jeans, hiking boots and an old Duke sweatshirt. A coffee-stained mug and crumpled pack of Camels lay on the end table beside him.

Shapiro was forty-nine years old with twenty-five years of law enforcement experience, mostly in violent crime. He'd started with the FBI in the Identification Division longer ago than he cared to recount. Impressive bronze plaques on the cherry-paneled wall commemorated his service as president of the International Homicide Investigators Association, program director of VI-CAP within the FBI's National Center for the Analysis of Violent Crime and, currently, chief of the Child Abduction and Serial Killer Unit. At five foot eight he was shorter than Victoria, but his piercing eyes could easily intimidate. He was a chain-smoker who rarely smiled. Even those who liked him said he had the jaundiced edge of a man who'd seen more unsolved murders than anyone in the world.

"Why didn't anybody tell me about a wiretap at the *Tribune?*" she asked pointedly.

Shapiro took a long drag from his third cigarette since her arrival. "There's no wiretap at the *Tribune*. The good old days of J. Edgar are gone. The FBI doesn't just slap a wiretap on a newspaper."

"Are you denying any eavesdropping on Mike's conversations with his informant?"

"I'm saying that it's been limited to Zack Newman's apartment. I wouldn't even bother trying for electronic surveillance at the *Tribune*, but it's a little easier to persuade a magistrate that you need a phone tap at a penthouse suite of an unmarried black male who flies seaplanes in and out of Miami."

She shook her head in disbelief. "We promised Posten that his conversations with his informant would be private. Period. We didn't limit it to conversations *in the newsroom*. If you didn't intend to honor the agreement, you should have told me."

"Why?" he said with a sharp glance. "So you could go over my head again? Maybe ask Assistant Director Dougherty personally to kill the proposed wiretap?"

Victoria sighed and averted her eyes toward the fire. "I'm sorry you're still angry, but I didn't go to

Headquarters to make you look bad. I just felt it was a terrible mistake to reject the *Tribune*'s offer. You presented your decision to me as final. I had nowhere else to turn."

He sipped his coffee. "I'm not saying that second-guessing me was wrong. I'm just saying it has consequences."

"What kind of consequences?"

"The wiretap's a good example. Agents who are in the habit of going over their supervisor's head shouldn't expect to be made privy to every little detail of the operation."

"This is not a little detail."

"It is in the big scheme. We have a serial killer to catch."

"If Posten backs out of the deal over a wiretap, we might *never* catch him."

"He's in too deep to back out now. If he's not afraid for himself, he has to be afraid for his wife. We're the only ones who can protect them. And if he stops cooperating, we stop protecting."

"I laid that on him before. That might not be strong enough anymore."

"Then *make* it strong enough," he said sharply.

Victoria took a deep breath, quelling her anger. "How do you suggest I do that?"

He lit up another cigarette. "Tell him the truth. Tell him that if he wasn't scared shitless talking to the informant before, he'd better be now. Because evidence is piling up that the informant is the killer."

"What are you talking about?"

"The tapes. We compared the voice of his informant

to the tape Sheriff Dutton gave us. That's why we decided to tap Posten's phone in the condo—to hear the informant. Both the electronic analysis and psycholinguistic examination point to one conclusion: The same person made the calls."

"How can they be so sure? The Hainesville caller was obviously disguising his voice, and it was a terrible recording on a little Dictaphone held up to the receiver."

"I trust our experts," he said flatly.

"All right. Assume they're right. Why does that lead you to the conclusion that the informant is the killer?"

"Why?" he said incredulously. "Because he *said* he was the killer when he called Dutton. Now, I know that's not a hundred percent conclusive, but we can't just dismiss it."

"But he's *not* the killer." She moved forward in her chair, speaking with resolve. "The informant could have been lying when he told Dutton he was the killer, just to throw us off the trail. Logically, the longer it takes us to catch the killer, the longer his gravy train keeps on running. But more important, calling the sheriff is just like the other kind of pranks I've been talking about from the very beginning. The man we're after isn't nearly playful enough to resort to gimmicks like the Ernest Gill checkbook journalism thing. And he wouldn't take unnecessary risks either, like sneaking into the *Tribune* to leave a clue on Posten's computer terminal or calling the sheriff's office to confess to the crime. Those are the juvenile pranks of some lightweight who's trying *way* too hard to be clever.

We're not looking for a rambunctious gamesman. We're looking for a smooth, efficient killing machine."

"Well, let's hope you're right," Shapiro said, seething, "because I'm telling you: Heads will roll if it turns out we're actually paying a serial killer for information on his own crimes. That was the reason I nixed this arrangement in the first place." Shapiro made a visible effort to calm himself. "Look, just put your ego aside for a minute, okay? Let's say you're wrong, and everyone else is right. Tell me: How are you going to keep the killer from getting away with the taxpayers' money?"

"So long as the funds stay in the banking system we can track them. I've got sources at CHIPS, FedWire, and SWIFT to cover wire transfers, and I'm working with FinCEN out of Detroit to follow the CTR trail for large cash deposits and withdrawals."

"What if he goes international, tries to hide behind bank secrecy?"

"Mutual Legal Assistance Treaties will help us there. They cover most of the major bank secrecy players— Switzerland, Mexico, the Bahamas, and twenty-some other countries."

"Suppose he goes someplace obscure."

"Then we'll have to count on bank insiders. Informants. I know that sounds a little risky, but you have to remember: The only way we get into a jam is if it turns out he's the killer *and* somehow I lose track of the money."

"Wrong. That's not how *we* get into a jam. That's how *you* do. You're the one who wrote the memo to Assistant Director Dougherty, assuring him the informant wasn't the killer."

She swallowed hard, then nodded with assurance. "That's right, sir. I wrote it. And I stand behind it."

"Yes," he said as he crushed out his cigarette. "And you stand alone."

Sunday afternoons were normally Mike's quiet time, but not today. The phone hadn't stopped ringing since his latest exclusive hit the newsstands. He was growing tired of the attention, and by four o'clock he'd stopped answering the phone. By five o'clock his answering machine stopped picking up because there was no more room for messages. A few calls came and went with a half-dozen rings. One, however, wouldn't stop ringing. Somewhere after the twentieth ring, Mike picked up the phone.

"You're the hottest thing in print now, aren't you, wonder boy."

The voice was scrambled by some kind of electronic device, making Mike bristle. It sounded a little like his informant, but it was too mechanical to be sure. "Who is this?"

"I'm your ticket to fame. It's all at my expense."

He paused, confused. "What's this all about? Who are you?"

"Never mind that. You were doing so well. Not just the scoop on the victims, but the details about the killings. Man, you had it exactly right. I was impressed. Even admired you. Then like a typical journalist, you turned and stabbed me in the back."

"You mean this morning's story?"

"No, I mean the *Peanuts* cartoon in the funnies, asshole."

"What was wrong with the story?"

"What was *right* with it?"

"You tell me."

"Nothing." His voice grew louder, the anger coming through even with a scrambler. "Not a damn thing. You couldn't resist, could you? You get a little momentum going, and all of a sudden you're an authority on everything. You know all about the killings, so you think you know all about the killer. Well, let me tell you something: You don't know shit about me."

"Then set me straight."

"Penile surrogate. Confused sexual identity. Possibly impotent. You left out every stereotype except how I hate pussy cats. Tired, cliché, bullshit. That's what your so-called psychological profile is. And you *knew* it was bullshit."

"Listen, just calm down, okay? I wouldn't print anything I didn't think was true."

"You *liar!* You'd print anything to sell a fucking newspaper. You don't care what you say or who you slam. Just so long as you're first. Better to be dead wrong than dead last. Isn't that what you news creeps say?"

"Hey, I'm sorry if—"

"Don't patronize me." He was speaking louder and faster with every word. "You think you're gonna get away with this, don't you?"

"I don't—"

"Shut up! You figure if you're wrong, so what? Today's deathless prose is tomorrow's kitty-litter lining. Well, for *me*, pal, it doesn't just go away. If it's in black-and-white today, it's in black-and-white forever. It doesn't end with the recycling bin. It's already on the Internet. You know what that means? Right now some twelve-year-old, slanty-eyed, snot-nosed little shit is laughing at me in Singapore. It's in the Library of Congress, you asshole. Know what that means? Little snot-nosed shits are gonna be laughing at me for the next two hundred and fifty fucking years. You understand me? It *never* ends."

"We can—"

"I said *shut up!* You libeled me. I've been *defamed*. And I'm *not* going to stand for it!"

"Look, I can fix it. What do you want me to do?"

His breathing was heavy and erratic, giving eerie life to the robotic sound of his electronically scrambled voice. "I want you," he said in a low, angry tone, "to *hold* your fucking tongue."

The phone slammed, and the killer was gone. Mike hung up slowly, then buried his head in his hands, shivering with the sinking realization that he'd finally met a man who sounded entirely capable of ripping out another's tongue—over and over again.

PART

TWO

Chapter 20

Victoria arrived in Quantico, Virginia, for a team meeting at nine o'clock Monday morning. They met two floors underground, in a windowless room with bright fluorescent lighting. David Shapiro, chief of the Child Abduction and Serial Killer Unit, sat at the far end of the long rectangular conference table, flanked on the right by Victoria, and on the left by two other CASKU agents, Steve Caldwell and Arnold Freeland. Bulging files stacked one atop the other rose from the table like broken columns from ancient ruins, each stack a different height. Nine altogether, one for each of the unsolved cases. On the wall directly behind Shapiro hung a colored map of the United States. Blue-headed pushpins projected from the random spots the killer had chosen, from Miami to San Francisco, Eugene to New York. On arrival, Victoria had noted two new ones in South Carolina—victims eight and nine, the first double homicide.

For an hour, they compared the different victims and crime scenes, making judgments about the killer that were based as much on intuition as past experience. Victoria's interest piqued when they turned to Mike's latest article.

"Let's start with the *Tribune* profile," said Shapiro.

"Totally bogus," said Victoria.

"Don't be so cavalier," said Caldwell. He was a fifty-year-old academic type with curly salt-and-pepper hair, black-rimmed glasses, and an unlit pipe clenched between his tobacco-stained teeth, best known as the Academy's full-time instructor in Sex Crimes and Applied Criminal Psychology. Caldwell had come to the CASKU "on loan" from the Investigative Support Unit, which was the new name for the original Behavioral Science Unit that had pioneered criminal profiling. The formation of CASKU had created a profiling turf war with the ISU, but when it was finally settled that CASKU would do its own profiling, the chief of the ISU sent Caldwell over to CASKU— ostensibly to help the new unit develop a profiling program, but more likely to rid himself of one highly intelligent but unbearably pompous pain in the ass.

"The *Tribune* profile is fairly consistent with the profile *we* created," Caldwell continued. "I do believe we're dealing with a sexually dysfunctional male. Possibly impotent, like Posten's article said, which is precisely the reason we see no evidence of penile penetration in any of the victims. In the most extreme scenario, we may even be dealing with a rapist who's had his penis bitten off or nearly bitten off during forced oral copulation, which would explain his rage and oral fixation. The tongue is a *quasi*-sexual organ he can sever from both men and women, so the mutilation is indeed sexually motivated. The wide range of victims reminds me to some degree of the Richard Ramirez case, the California Night Stalker. Except with Ramirez *both* the victims *and* the killing methods were so varied, you would never suspect one person of doing it. Here it's just the victims who vary. In either case, however, the variety doesn't change *the reason* he kills."

She shook her head. "I don't think the killer is the typical sexually dysfunctional woman hater. There are too many male victims. Something else is driving him. It's more domination. Manipulation. Control."

He took the pipe from his mouth, shaking his head in condescending fashion. "This is a classic psychosexual turmoil. I like to call it the Osiris complex."

"The *what* complex?"

"Osiris," he said with a haughty affectation, as if any dolt should have heard of it. "In Egyptian mythology, when the god Osiris is killed and dismembered, his companion retrieves all the body parts. Except she can't find the penis. So she makes a huge phallic replica and orders all Egyptians to worship it. It's the proverbial quest for the missing penis and veneration of its substitute. Here, the killer has made the tongue a substitute. In less extreme cases, the inadequate male who wishes to impress his wife or girlfriend might simply pay a plastic surgeon to inject fat cells into his scrotum. In more primitive cultures, like the sadhus of India, men tie a ten-pound weight around the penis and stretch it to lengths so absurd they can actually tie it into knots beneath their loincloth. If you can't see the sexual motivation behind these killings, Victoria, then you're simply overreacting to that last telephone call Posten received."

"I'm not reacting to anything. I felt this way before then."

He sighed impatiently. "Look, you're relatively new here. We have to start with the premise that while few, if any, serial killers are psychotic, nearly all are psychopathic sexual sadists. That's been true since the first documented serial killer, a nineteenth-century Frenchman who was a butcher by occupation, and who brought himself to orgasm by stabbing women to death. Why do you think we have so few women serial killers? The killer's obsession with perverse sexual fantasy is something I've come to understand not just through literature, but through countless interviews with serial killers—all of which, I might add, were conducted long before you ever got to thinking it might be *fun* to be an FBI agent."

She glared at the cheap shot, but tempered her response. "All right, Steven. Just for *fun*, why don't you consider the possibility that maybe this one doesn't fit your mold?"

Freeland jumped in. "I'm not choosing sides," he said, mindful of Caldwell's ego. "But I don't think it's totally absurd to postulate that if innocent people all over the country are suddenly getting their tongues cut out, it may be because they said the wrong thing, or possibly they spoke to someone they shouldn't have spoken to. Maybe the motivation isn't totally rooted in sexuality. He may be more mission oriented, like an assassin."

"When you think about it," said Victoria, "the fact

that he let Timothy Copeland's roommate live tends to support an assassin profile rather than random sexual slayings. The guy doesn't leave any more bodies than he has to, which is smart, since more victims means more physical evidence for us to study."

"Let's proceed on both fronts," said Shapiro, settling it. "Who wants to follow up on this?"

"I'm already on it," said Victoria. "I've been exploring whether the victims or the killer might be a government informant or somehow connected to one."

Shapiro raised an eyebrow. "Where do you stand?"

"I'm working with the Information Management Division to check the names of every confidential informant still alive, every person who's entered the federal witness protection program since Bobby Kennedy started it. None of them are victims. As far as we can tell so far, none of them are related to any of the victims, either."

He leaned back, folding his hands behind his head. "How about looking at it the other way. Any leads as to whether one of them might be the killer— or connected to the killer?"

"That's a bigger undertaking," she said. "At any given point in time we've got three thousand people in witness protection, about two hundred new ones going in every year. Plenty of people have entered it and turned bitter. They lose their past, lose their families, can't find a decent job once they start a new life. There's plenty more who considered going into it, put their life on the line by testifying, and then decided not to go through with it once they saw what it entailed. And that's just the *federal* program. We got fifty states to deal with on top of that."

"Keep at it, Victoria."

"We are. Of course, the witness protection programs are just the tip of the iceberg. At the federal level alone we've got volumes of informants who have nothing to do with the program. Add to that every person who might have a grudge against an informant and your list of suspects is endless. I've got everyone we can spare looking into it. Everyone with security clearance, that is."

Shapiro narrowed his eyes pensively. "Seems to me we're overlooking one obvious category."

"What's that?"

"Assuming this has anything to do with informants, it doesn't necessarily have to be *government* informants. The victims could be people who talked to the media. Or the killer could be some journalist's confidential source."

"That's a list of names we'll never see," she said. "Even if we were entitled to it legally, it'd be logistically impossible to get it."

"I agree. But for some reason this informant has singled out one reporter from a Miami newspaper. We at least need a list of *his* informants."

Caldwell scoffed, tapping his pipe on the table as he spoke. "I would hardly expect a Pulitzer Prize–winning journalist to betray the confidence of every informant he's ever dealt with. And I don't think there's any judge in America who would force him to do it, either. Confidential sources are protected by the First Amendment."

"I wasn't suggesting we ask a judge to force it out of him. But I think Victoria could persuade him."

A prurient gleam came to Caldwell's eye. "Sounds delicious. Do I hear the makings of an offer he can't refuse?"

"Enough of that," said Shapiro.

Victoria ignored it, speaking directly to Shapiro. "At the risk of breaking precedent, I agree with Steve. I can't see a journalist divulging his sources. After all, it was Posten's obsession with the need to protect a *potentially* legitimate source that was the basis for our unusual arrangement with the *Tribune* in the first place."

"I know it's a tough assignment," said Shapiro, "but your supervisors would be very impressed. Maybe even impressed enough to forget about a certain memo you wrote to Assistant Director Dougherty, saying the informant's not the killer."

She averted her eyes, then looked right back at him. "I'll see what I can do," she said, "but I'm not fooling myself. I know there's only one way you're going to forget about that memo."

"Oh? What's that?"

She looked around the table, meeting each set of eyes. "If I was right."

Chapter 21

Victoria arrived in Miami just after three o'clock that Monday afternoon. Over the next several days she would have to contact each of the twenty-six different state and local law enforcement agencies and eight different FBI field offices that were now searching for the same killer. With Mike's "profile" having been front-page news in Sunday's *Tribune*, it was important to explain how it did and, more important, *didn't* affect the FBI's profile of their UNSUB—FBI jargon for "unknown subject." Shapiro had told her to start in Miami.

The Miami task force meeting was held at the FBI's field office in northwest Miami, a large gray building that housed most of Miami's 380 agents—the fifth largest in the Bureau. Victoria checked in with the receptionist behind the bulletproof glass in the austere lobby on the second floor. Two plaques hung on the wall by the elevators to commemorate agents who had made the supreme sacrifice. Victoria recognized the names of Benjamin P. Grogan and Jerry Dove, two Miami agents who fell in a tragic shoot-out in which 140 rounds of ammunition were exchanged. Their deaths had prompted the FBI to ditch the traditional .38-caliber Smith & Wesson revolvers as the weapon of choice and issue semiautomatic handguns that wouldn't jam when bone fragments from an agent's shattered hand found their way into the chamber.

The Miami task force included various branches of state and local law enforcement, from Metro-Dade police to Florida state troopers. Nearly sixty officers filled the FBI's large training room on the ground floor. Victoria stood at the lectern in front, with a white rectangular grease board behind her. Nine FBI field agents stood along the side wall, and the local police officers and detectives working the case filled ten rows of classroom chairs with half-desktops. Looking out over the audience, Victoria noticed more gray hair than usual. It seemed that some experienced veterans had been brought back from retirement to help in the pursuit. With the *Miami Tribune* getting the scoop on every murder, the pressure was obviously mounting on local law enforcement to produce a breakthrough in the Miami case.

Miami was the serial killer's third strike, an interesting one from the standpoint of constructing the serial-killer profile. The body of a happily married, forty-two-year-old successful Cuban American businessman had been found in a canal. The killer had attacked him at night, when he was closing up his hardware store, then taken the tongueless body to the Everglades to dump it. Hiding the body, Victoria knew, was generally a sign of planning and sophistication. In contrast, the first two victims had been found in their homes, badly mutilated—a sign of overkill and irrationality. Miami thus provided one of the first major signs of a "mixed" killer, one who exhibited both "organized" and "disorganized" traits—which is to say, it was yet another anomaly in a long string of anomalies that had left police scratching their collective heads.

The audience quieted as copies of a nine-page double-spaced handout circulated from left to right across each row. Victoria switched on the microphone.

"Good afternoon," she said over the muffled sounds of shuffling paper. "Each of you should have a copy of the FBI's latest profile on our serial killer. There are some modifications from the earlier version, but not as many as you might expect. And that's the main message I want to deliver today: Don't be misled by the ghoulish portrait of the killer painted in Sunday's *Tribune*. You have to distinguish between what the killer looks like in the everyday world, and what he *becomes* when he's committing his crimes."

"So whatta we got?" said one of the detectives. "A modern-day Jekyll and Hyde?"

"That's a little melodramatic, but in a sense, the schizophrenic tendencies may be stronger than we originally thought. I'll get into that more in a minute. First, let's talk about that profile in the *Tribune*."

Victoria glanced at one of the agents by the door, who dimmed the lights. She switched on the overhead projector, then put up a transparency of Mike's article that lit up the wall behind her in the darkened room.

"Right off the bat, we can say this so-called profile is either the work of someone who doesn't know what they're talking about, or who is deliberately trying to mislead. For example," she said, pointing to the third line, "we're certain the killer's not a homosexual."

"One of his victims was queer," said one of the gray-haired officers in the front row.

Victoria winced at the slur. "One of his victims was also a seventy-eight-year-old woman. That doesn't make my grandmother a suspect."

She removed the transparency, leaving the projector light shining on the wall. "I don't intend to give a newspaper story too much credence by going through it line by line. You should focus on the FBI handout, not on what ran in the paper. There is just one other point I want to make about it, however."

She paused for a moment, making sure she had everyone's attention.

"The level of detail in that bogus profile reflects a great deal of familiarity with the crime scenes or, at the very least, the crime scene reports and photos—possibly even the preliminary police reports. And the terminology he uses reflects a certain . . . *sophistication* isn't really the right word. It's more of a working familiarity with police jargon."

"Are you saying that the guy calling the *Tribune* is a cop?" said the gray-hair again.

Victoria paused and looked as far as she could into the audience, though the light from the projector had reduced them to shadows. "I'm saying he could even be sitting in this room."

On cue, the agent at the wall suddenly switched on

the lights. She'd said it for effect, as part of their prearranged plan. They'd hoped on a long shot that the unexpected burst from darkness to light might catch a face in the audience with an incriminating expression. Several officers were glancing uneasily at their neighbors, but no one seemed particularly nervous or exhilarated. Goose eggs, however, were entirely consistent with the latest FBI profile.

Whoever he was, the man knew the tricks—*before* she could play them.

Chapter 22

Victoria parked the borrowed Mercury Grand Marquis in the far end of the asphalt lot to the east of the Airport Hilton. A group of field agents had invited her to dinner, but she preferred to decompress and prepare for the meeting with the Arkansas task force tomorrow afternoon in Fayetteville. It wouldn't be as large a group as the one in Miami, but the pressure would be just as palpable. None of the cities in which the killer had struck wanted to see it happen somewhere else. But what really drove the local investigations was the unstated fear that the killer would come back to their town and strike again.

The sun had set an hour ago, and the airport lights flickered in the darkness on the other side of the expressway. Large ficus trees cast shadows beneath the yellow lamps that lighted the parking lot. She locked the car door and started toward the hotel, watching the blinking red lights of a 747 landing in the distance.

The parking lot was full, and she was almost two hundred yards from the hotel entrance. She clutched her purse as she walked alone between cars. As she neared the sidewalk she heard footsteps behind her, matching her step for step. She quickened her pace. The footsteps quickened. She glanced over her shoulder and saw a lone, shadowy figure. She kept walking but stepped off the sidewalk. Behind her, the sound of the footsteps changed from the clicking of concrete to the dull thud of asphalt. She stepped back on the sidewalk—so did the footsteps. She readied herself to reach for her gun, then stopped quickly and wheeled around.

"Fancy meeting you here," came the voice in the darkness.

She sighed and relaxed her trigger finger. "That's a good way to get yourself shot, Posten."

"Sneaking up on you?" he said as he pulled an envelope from his pocket. "Or carrying around the latest FBI profile of our serial killer?"

"Where did you get that? We haven't released anything to the press."

"A guy doesn't work the crime beat for thirteen years and not make a few friends on the police force. How do you think I knew it was you in the Bucar?"

"So what are you doing, showing off? Am I supposed to be impressed that you can get your hands on the profile and follow me to a parking lot?"

"Easy, Victoria. I'm not here to make trouble, okay? I know the FBI doesn't like its profiles to be made public. All I want to know is whether you geniuses at Quantico think the guy who called me on Saturday to give me that profile is the same guy who called me yesterday to complain how inaccurate it was."

She swallowed hard, fiddling with the car keys in her jacket pocket. "Let me put it this way. The description of the killer in your story was so ugly and unflattering that in some ways it actually reinforces the view that the informant *is* the killer. He's the same man, and he hates himself for what he can't stop himself from doing."

"Come on," he scoffed. "The guy who called yesterday acted like a totally different person."

"Nothing's conclusive, but the consensus so far is that we're not looking for two different men, but one psychopath with a schizoid personality. He's psychologically at war with himself, playing both killer and informant, speaking to you in two different voices."

"They think he's schizophrenic?"

"Not a true schizophrenic. More like a schizoid personality disorder with compulsive features."

"Why do they think that?"

"I've seen studies saying that forty percent of serial killers have schizoid personality disorders."

"But why do you think that in *this* case?"

"Please," she said uneasily. "Don't ask me to reveal everything."

"I'm not. Just give me *something*, dammit. I'm not looking for a story. I just want to make sense of all this. I'm risking much more than my career here. You owe me *that* much."

She sighed. Seeing the anguish on his face made her feel like she did indeed owe him *something*—even if it was mostly the FBI's point of view rather than her own. "All right. But this has to be totally off the record."

He nodded.

"From what our experts have gathered, both the killer and the informant appear to be sociopathic personalities, though very different types. The killer is the antisocial psychopath. Theoretically, that should make him easier to catch, because this type is less cunning, tends to have messy murder scenes and leaves behind clues. The informant, however, is not antisocial. He's the kind of guy who could be your next-door neighbor. Very smart, very difficult to catch. The fact that the informant is the Ted Bundy type could explain why we've had such a difficult time catching the killer. If the killer and the informant are one man, the more savvy side of this schizoid personality may be covering the tracks left behind by his less sophisticated side."

Mike nodded slowly, taking it all in. "The idea of my informant being a sophisticate troubles me a little. Granted, over the phone he sounds pretty smooth. He's computer literate, because he was able to reprogram my screen saver to tell me about Timothy Copeland. But then there's the videotape from the ATM machine in San Francisco you told me about. He was dancing a jig like a lunatic, dressed like a crack addict who sleeps in the gutter."

"The analysts don't think that was a true manifestation of his killer personality, if that's what you're asking. That was purely a cover. He knew he was going to be videotaped when he used the cash machine, since most ATMs have security cameras. That's why he wore a ski mask. He's no dummy, Mike. Apparently he even knows something about wiretaps, because he's cut off every one of your phone conversations just in the nick of time to prevent us from tracing the call. We're dealing with a very complex personality disorder—if our experts are right."

"And you aren't troubled by the fact that the electronically garbled voice in the last call sounds like a totally different person."

"Our guy in the Signal Analysis Unit over in the Engineering Section says he could have been using some kind of variable-speed control device. Even beyond that, however, voice inflection can change drastically when different schizoid personalities emerge."

Mike mulled over what she'd just said, then shook his head. "I don't buy it—the informant and the killer being one person. Call it street intuition but I think there's a lunatic out there who's smarter than the killer, sicker than the killer, and who understands these murders better than you do. That scares the hell out of me. And I think it scares the hell out of you, too."

She stared back, then blinked. "I've got five cities to hit in the next three days. I'll be in touch." She turned and started toward the hotel, all too aware that she hadn't denied the accusation.

Chapter 23

m ike left the Hilton at seven-thirty and headed toward Zack's condo in the Grove, his home-away-from-home. At the T-shaped intersection at the end of Virginia Street, his headlights shined directly into the big picture windows of a dark green building that was Señor Frog's, a Mexican restaurant that, according to the sign above the door, had been in business SINCE 1109. That was actually its street number, but it *was* a Grove landmark. He and Karen used to go there for nine-layer nachos, margaritas, and laughs. That wasn't in the twelfth century, but sometimes it seemed that long ago.

His car phone rang as he rounded the corner. He finished the turn and answered it.

"Karen, hey," he said with a smile. "I was just thinking about you."

"Mike, you've got to get over here." Her voice sounded strained, almost agitated.

"What's wrong?"

"It's nuts. The phone hasn't stop ringing all night, and now they're parked outside the house."

"Who?"

"Who *else?* Your fellow sharks in the media. Congratulations. Tonight's lead story is my husband the journalist—the *checkbook* journalist."

His gut wrenched. "I'll be right there."

Mike pulled a quick U-turn and raced south to Coral Gables, past the University of Miami campus. A quick turn off Granada Boulevard and its walled-in estates put him a half-block from home, in the heart of a neighborhood that he and Karen could afford only on both their salaries. A canopy of leafy ficus trees and oaks laden with Spanish moss blocked out most of the moonlight. The lone streetlamp on the corner cast a dim yellowish light over his front yard. Squinting, he could make out the news logos of Channels 4, 7, and 10 on three satellite vans parked on the street. Another was blocking the driveway. Covering the sidewalk was a tangle of wires connected to a handful of men toting camcorders on their shoulders. Several others moved about in shirtsleeves in the warm night air. Mike recognized the woman with the big blond hair and microphone fixing her makeup in the side mirror of a van.

It seemed hard to fathom that the manner in which he'd reported the news had actually become the news. But being in the biz, so to speak, he knew that not even Miami had near enough crime to fill the expanded news hours of local TV shows.

To avoid the commotion, he drove to the next street that ran parallel to his. The houses in the

Riviera subdivision were laid out in rows of two, so that the fronts faced the street and the backs faced each other. He parked in front of the Old Spanish—style house that backed up against his own backyard. Quietly, he got out of his car and walked behind his neighbor's house, praying not to get shot. He walked faster as he approached the iron picket fence that separated the two backyards; then he jumped it and tumbled to the ground on the other side, on his own turf.

He picked himself up and stood in the darkness, looking across the kidney-shaped swimming pool and through the wall of French doors that ran across the back of his house. With the lights on in the family room he could see everything inside, including Karen sitting on the couch. She was wearing a blue knit sweater and shorts, with her legs extended and feet up on the coffee table. She was reading some magazine and sucking on— if memory served him—a Weight Watchers chocolate mousse fudge pop. He felt like he could have stood there all night, watching, and never been detected. He felt like *anyone* could have stood there all night—and the thought chilled him. He dashed across the lawn and tapped lightly on the French door.

Karen jumped at the noise and nearly shrieked, until she recognized his face through the little windowpane. She unlocked the door and let him in.

"Sorry," he said. "I couldn't come in the front. There's an army out there. Where the hell is your protection anyway?"

"They're parked out front. They're using a media van to look less conspicuous."

"Fat lot of good that does. What if I'd been—"

"A crazy serial killer?" she said, finishing his sentence. "They gave me an alarm in case anything goes wrong." She held up her wrist and displayed what looked like a watch, except that where the face should have been was a tiny red button. "They didn't want to be intrusive."

"Well, my fellow newshounds don't seem to have any qualms. Looks like our separation isn't common knowledge yet."

Karen frowned. "This story sure is common knowledge. It was all over the evening news: Pulitzer Prize–winning journalist pays off an informant who may be a serial killer. Where are they getting this stuff?"

"It has to be Brenda Baines. She overheard me on the phone with the guy that night you came by the newsroom, and she must have heard more than I thought. I'm not exactly on her Christmas list, you know. She's the only one I know who'd be vicious enough to leak something outside rather than take it up with the *Tribune*."

"It's terrible, what they're saying. Haven't you seen *any* of it?"

"No, actually. I was, uh, over at the Airport Hilton. With Victoria."

"Great," she said. "It's not enough that I have to overhear the two of you arguing like boyfriend and girlfriend in our own house. Now you're meeting at hotels."

"C'mon . . ."

"Sorry," she said with heavy sigh. "Listen to me, I sound like somebody out of a soap opera."

"Yes, you do," he said, smiling.

"I guess this is all starting to get to me. The FBI's on my tail. The media's on my doorstep. My husband's on a first-name basis with a serial killer." She turned and ran a hand through her hair, glancing at her reflection in the mirror. "And now this jealousy thing. I *hate* this."

"Sounds to me like you still value our marriage, that's all."

She looked into his eyes. "What should we do about that?"

"We could alert the media," he said, jerking his head toward the front door.

Her eyes brightened. "I got a better idea. Why don't we just forget about them, forget about everything. Just sit on the couch, me and you, and talk."

"I'd like that."

She smiled thinly, then turned serious. "I've been feeling like a hypocrite, the way I came down on you for not telling me about your arrangement with the FBI."

"What do you mean?"

"I have, well . . . secrets of my own—things I've wanted to tell you about for a very long time."

"What kind of secrets?" he asked warily.

"Things about myself. I've been beating myself up lately, blaming myself for not telling you. But there are two sides to this. I remember so many nights lying in bed, listening to you in the other room talking on the phone with your sources, trying to coax information out of them. You were always so patient with them, so understanding. Sometimes I wish you'd be more like that with me. Maybe I would have opened up more."

"Well," he said, "let's talk about it."

Suddenly, the SkyPager on his belt blared with a pulsating beep, signaling a message.

They exchanged glances. Time froze. Then finally he looked down.

"Damn. I think that's Aaron Field's home number."

"Can't it wait?"

"Karen, it's not every day my publisher calls me from home. He must be watching the news. I better return this."

She sighed and shook her head. "You'll have to plug in the phone. I pulled it when those reporters kept calling."

"It will just take a minute, I promise. Hold your thought."

"Right."

He dashed to her office and connected the phone. He paused to peer outside through the mini-blinds. The mob of reporters had grown larger. With a sinking sense of dread, he picked up the receiver to return Aaron's call.

Victoria showered and slipped into the white terry-cloth robe that came with her hotel room. Her wet hair was twisted up in a bath towel. Too tired and too busy to call any of her old friends in Miami for dinner, she ordered room service and ate in bed while reviewing the autopsy protocol from the Arkansas case. It wasn't until she was halfway into a protein-rich bean salad that she'd realized she was actually putting food in her mouth while reading about "petechiae in the conjunctiva," or tiny hemorrhages in the mucous membrane of the brain caused by increased pressure in the head at the time of death.

The phone rang on the nightstand. She answered and tucked the receiver beneath her chin. It was Tony Costello, an agent from the FBI's Atlanta Field Office who'd been Victoria's Georgia coordinator ever since the Gerty Kincaid murder.

"Victoria, hey. Sorry to bug you so late, but I think we got something for you on these tongue murders. Have you been watching the news at all?"

"No, I was just having a nice quiet dinner with a corpse."

"Huh?"

She shook her head. Chasing serial killers could do strange things to your sense of humor. "Never mind. What's up?"

"In a nutshell, there's some controversy brewing over Posten's coverage of the murders, and it's getting some coverage."

"What kind of controversy?"

"I'm not exactly sure, and that's not the reason I'm calling. What happened is that a guy in Atlanta—Reggie Holland—was watching the news, and the particular report he saw discussed in some detail the articles Posten has written about the murders, including that one he wrote after the Copeland murder in San Francisco. You know, where he describes how the killer cuts out the tongue—two small incisions on each side of the tongue using a diver's knife with a serrated edge."

"Right. The one I told him he shouldn't have written."

"Well, it may be a good thing that he did, because that's what got Holland's attention. His wife—Cybil is her name—was attacked in Atlanta on a Monday, the *day after* they found Gertrude Kincaid in Candler County."

"We got another victim?" she said apprehensively.

"Well, that's the issue. See, Mrs. Holland wasn't murdered and she didn't have her tongue slashed, but whoever attacked her sliced off her finger to get her engagement ring. They never caught him, and from what I've gathered so far, the Atlanta police don't really know very much, because she was knocked unconscious and hardly remembers anything. But by looking at the wound they've been able to figure out that, whoever he is, he used one heck of a big knife with a serrated edge—like a diver's knife—to cut off her finger."

"So, Mr. Holland thinks—"

"He thinks what *I* think. The killer struck in Hainesville over the weekend, and by Monday he was trying to disappear into Atlanta, the nearest big city. He got hard up for cash or whatever, and his wife with her diamond ring was in the wrong place at the wrong time."

Victoria grabbed the notepad from the files spread across the bedsheet, then jotted down a quick thought. She suddenly felt like this could be it—the killer had finally slipped. "Have you talked to the wife? Did she get a look at her attacker?"

"She didn't see a thing. Got blindsided, knocked

down a flight of stairs. Put her in a coma for almost a week."

"Did they recover the knife?"

"No."

"Well, then, what *do* we have?"

"The finger," he said. "They weren't able to reattach it, so it's sitting in a container of liquid nitrogen in the Georgia State Crime Lab in Decatur. The police wanted it preserved. Their hope was that if they ever recovered the knife, they could match the blade to the cut marks on the finger."

"If they don't have the knife by now, they're probably never going to find it."

"True," he said. "But if you get the right forensic pathologist, I was thinking maybe he could compare the stab wounds on our victim in Hainesville to the cuts on that finger sitting over at the crime lab. It would be nice to know if our killer is the same man who stole a diamond ring in Atlanta. I could have a team of agents scouring every pawnshop in the city, seeing if he hocked it. Maybe one of the shop owners even got a look at him."

Victoria sat up in her bed, her lips curling with a faint smile of hope. "This is good, Tony. Set up an appointment with the Georgia State Crime Lab for tomorrow morning. I'll make *sure* we have the right pathologist."

Chapter 24

m ike collected his thoughts for a moment before dialing the number. He actually called directory assistance first, just to make sure it was Aaron's home number that had flashed on his pager. It was. Aaron snatched up on the half-ring, as if he were sitting beside the phone waiting for the call.

"What the hell is going on, Mike?"

Mike caught his breath. "I don't know exactly. I'm just as blindsided by this as you are. But you're obviously upset—"

"Damn right I'm upset. We've got a major crisis here. The phone hasn't stopped ringing. And it's not penny-ante local stuff. *Newsweek*, *Time*, the network news. They're all on top of it now. *Nightline*'s even doing a spot tonight on ethics in journalism—focusing on the alleged payments we've made to your confidential source. I have to go on TV tonight to defend my own newspaper. It's like that big ethics debate back in eighty-eight, when everyone from Rivera to Koppel was asking whether those Miami reporters went too far by hiding in the bushes outside Gary Hart's town house. Only this is a thousand times worse. Two of my editors threatened to resign if I don't fire your ass."

Mike drew a deep breath. "What are we going to do?"

"We knew we'd have to go public with this eventually. Granted, we all hoped that would come *after* we'd caught ourselves a serial killer. I don't know who let the press in on our little secret, but it sure wasn't me. And it wasn't Charlie."

"Are you accusing *me?*"

"It had to be you. Maybe not on purpose, but somewhere you slipped. And we made it clear from the very beginning that if you did slip, you were the one who was going down. Not me. Not Charlie. And certainly not the *Tribune.* That was our deal."

Mike took a deep breath. "What are you saying?"

"I'm saying that, for the time being, I know only one way to handle this. I'm sorry, but I'm putting you on probation."

"For *what?*"

"I can't just ignore the editorial revolt on my own doorstep. I have to take *some* action."

"This is crap!"

"We've got no choice. You can't just come out and deny you're paying an informant. That would be a lie. And we can't reveal that you're working with the FBI, or your informant will stop calling, and we'll have blown everything we've tried to accomplish. Or worse, if your informant feels like you've double-crossed him, you might be putting your own *life* in danger. For better or worse, we've got to ride this out to the end."

"Aaron, this is my reputation we're talking about. Doesn't thirteen years count for anything?"

"Of course it does. That's how we got into this mess in the first place. If anyone but you had come up with this proposal I would have killed it immediately. And if it were anyone but you, I wouldn't be giving him a chance to redeem himself."

"*Redeem* myself? I must be missing something."

"I'm going to allow you to continue your coverage of the serial killings, even though you're on probation. The only condition is that I handle all inquiries about alleged payments to confidential sources. I'm not asking you to lie—just refer all questions to me."

"How do I justify that?"

"Tell the truth. It's an ongoing story, and you're concerned that any comments could jeopardize your relationship with your informant. The *Tribune* is handling the matter internally for now, and you're confident that your name will be cleared in the end. Period."

"This is insane."

"Trust me. No matter how much heat our competitors in the media put on us, I'll fend them off, so you can keep doing your job. Hopefully your stories will help catch the killer, and in the end we'll have no public relations problem to speak of. Just remember: We're in this box together. Right now, all we can do is let me play dumb and do a song and dance around the tough questions, until you can bring this thing to closure."

"Basically what you're saying is: Go catch myself a serial killer and all our problems are solved."

His voice rose with urgency. "Do you see another way?"

Mike sunk in his chair. "You're all heart, Aaron."

"I gotta go. Just stick with the program."

The line clicked in Mike's ear. He brought his hand to his forehead, his mind racing.

"Can we talk now?" said Karen. She was standing in the open doorway, arms folded.

He winced. "Sorry, but I gotta go talk some sense into Aaron. He's putting me on probation over this."

"Can't it wait until tomorrow morning?"

"It really can't. This is getting worse by the minute. He's going on *Nightline* tonight."

"That's not for another three hours."

He glanced at the clock, then back at Karen. His frustration was immense. "This is my *career*. Don't *you* think I should go?"

"I can't tell you what you should do."

He took another look at the clock, then back at her. He could see in her eyes that maybe it would have happened. If they had just stayed there on the couch with no interruptions, she would have opened up, maybe even asked him to spend the night.

"Karen, I *really* have to go."

"Then go."

He rose quickly and tried to kiss her on the lips, but she turned her cheek. His forced smile came out more like a grimace. He turned and hurried to the French doors. Karen followed and stood watching as he slid them back. He stopped on the lawn and looked back longingly, pleading with his eyes.

"I'll call you as soon as I get this straightened out. I promise."

She folded her arms tightly and shook her head. "Don't knock yourself out," she said as she reached out and shut the doors tight.

Karen waited for Mike's call, but it never came. She knew how important his career was to him, but he sure didn't seem to appreciate the importance of what she'd been trying to reveal. At midnight, she unplugged the phone and went to bed.

At 6:30 A.M. she reset her alarm for nine o'clock. She was still trying to fall asleep, and if she did, she wanted to get at least a couple of hours. Even after two months, sleeping without Mike was still awkward, and a week at her mother's had made the house feel even less like a home. The familiar noises from the kitchen weren't so familiar anymore. Passing cars on the street seemed to stop right outside the house. Hours passed as she lay in the darkness, eyes wide open, listening for footsteps. In the small hours of the night, an empty house was a frightfully noisy place.

Lying on her back, she thought about her so-called protection. Maybe the alarm wasn't enough. When she'd seen Mike, she'd frozen—hadn't even thought to push the button. Maybe the agents outside had gone for coffee or had fallen asleep. Maybe they were lying in a ditch with their tongues cut out.

Fading in and out of no-sleep and near-sleep, she

tried to imagine what Mike was going through, dealing with someone who might be a killer. She wondered if *she* could do it, if she could bring herself to converse with someone so psychotic. That thought stayed with her as her mind finally drifted, taking her to another level of consciousness, to another time in her life. . . .

A cold Canadian wind had invaded the college town of Ithaca, rising in furious gusts as a steady rain beat on her windowpane. It all added up to yet another night of staring at the ceiling. She hated living alone, and she resented the hell out of her old roommate for dropping out of school, stuffing the rent payments up her nose, and sticking her with the apartment for the entire spring semester.

She heard a thud outside, like a slam against the building. She sat up in bed and listened intently. The wind and rain howled outside her window, but all else was quiet. Slowly, she lay back against her pillow, listening so hard that she could hear the feathers compress to envelop her head.

Another thud, and she shot up in bed. Her mouth went dry, and her heart raced. She listened, but there was only silence. The digital alarm clock said 4:27. The phone sat right on the nightstand, but she'd had so many false alarms with the campus police they'd started referring to her as the little girl who cried wolf. She drew a deep breath, then pulled back the covers and slid out of bed.

She was wearing a long cotton jersey that came to the middle of her thighs, with bikini briefs underneath and thick white socks on her feet. One foot went slowly in front of the other as she entered the hallway, a long, dark tunnel with green sculptured carpet. She stopped at the living room. It was dark, lighted only by the faint glow of the night-light she'd placed in the kitchen. The furnace kicked on, giving her a start. She swallowed hard, calming her nerves. *Grow up*, she told herself. *Don't cry wolf again.*

She took a few more steps, then stopped and folded her arms tightly for warmth. It was chilly, down-right cold, even with the heater on. Outside, the wind whistled. Inside, the curtain blew—and she gasped at the sight of the open window and the rain pouring in. Before she could scream there was a hand on her mouth and a damp weight on her back that pushed her to her knees and then to her stomach. She kicked and twisted, but he was sitting on her kidneys. She couldn't breathe and couldn't shake free. Again she tried to scream, but his big, gloved hand squeezed tighter around her mouth, and as she gasped for air her nostrils filled with stinking smells of old leather gloves.

"Shut *up*," he grunted, breathing bourbon on her face. "Just shut—"

Up she came, like a rocket from the sheets. Her hands were shaking as she frantically looked left, then right, searching and disoriented in the darkness of her own bedroom. Sweat poured through her nightgown. But all was quiet.

She caught her breath and rubbed the knots in her neck. Dreaming again. That same nightmare. Worse than a nightmare. It was all too real.

If only it *were* a dream.

Chapter 25

torrents of icy air streamed from the air-conditioning vents in the ceiling, making the autopsy room of the Georgia State Crime Lab feel like a meat locker in a packinghouse. After an hour in the chill, Victoria Santos had to put on her long winter coat. For a hot-blooded Latin, she was a confessed wimp in the cold.

Bright lights glistened off the white sterile walls and buffed tile floor. A long mobile cart for transporting bodies to the morgue was parked against the wall. A shiny metal autopsy table was in the center of the room, riddled with small holes that allowed water and fluids to drain into the round metal tank below. It looked like the perforated face of a giant cheese grater balanced on a huge tin can. Atop the table sat the small-parts dissection tray. Atop the tray lay Cybil Holland's frozen finger.

Victoria stood on one side of the table, staring down at the purplish stub with the pink French manicure beneath the bright examination light. Beside her stood Dr. Leslie Harmon, a tall black woman from the Fulton County Medical Examiner's office who spent most of the time right in this room at the crime lab in Decatur. Tony Costello, the stocky Atlanta field agent, stood behind her in the shadows. On the other side of the table and hunched over the tray was Chester Burns, a fifty-nine-year-old internationally renowned forensic pathologist who smiled a lot, considering he was a walking encyclopedia on knives and stab wounds. Victoria had brought him down from the Bureau's Forensic Science Research and Training Center in Quantico.

"We got lucky," said Dr. Burns. He was smiling, as usual, but still staring down at the finger, squinting through gold-rimmed glasses. He was wearing a crisp white lab coat, and his short black hair was matted on his head, parted widely down the middle. He straightened up and stepped back from the tray. "The cut is very clean. Fortunately, her attacker didn't saw off the finger. Sawing would have shredded the tissue, splintered the bone. That would make my job a bear."

Victoria strained to listen. His words were sometimes hard to understand. Burns was deaf. Victoria had always found a bit of irony in that—the dead speaking to the deaf.

"See here," he said, pointing. "It sliced clean through, like a cleaver on a chopping block. Teeth marks from the knife's serrated edge are plainly visible."

Victoria leaned forward for a better look, close enough to see little blond hairs between the knuckles. "What can you tell so far?"

He smiled. "I can tell you're uncomfortable with my being deaf. You enunciate too hard. Just talk—I've read lips all my life."

She blinked with embarrassment. "Sorry. Let me rephrase the question anyway. What can *you* tell that *I* can't tell?"

"I'll have to make a cast and take more precise measurements to be sure. Study the photographs. I'll need a radiologist to confirm readings—"

"All of which will take days," Victoria interrupted. "I need to know *now*. Give me your gut reaction. Is this the work of our serial killer?"

"I'll never be able to tell you that."

"Why?"

"Maybe someone borrowed his knife."

"So, you do think the knife used on Gertrude Kincaid was the same knife used on Cybil Holland."

"If you're asking me whether I can I testify to that in court, my answer is no. If you're asking me whether I've seen enough to think it would be worth your while to follow up on this lead, the answer is definitely yes."

Victoria nodded. "That's what I wanted to know." She glanced behind her at Tony Costello. The sight of the six foot two, hard-nosed Italian shivering in his shirtsleeves made her smile inside—she'd warned him he'd want a coat. "Let's get out of here," she said.

Tony nodded eagerly and rubbed the circulation back into his hands as he followed her out the door into the lobby. After the icy autopsy room, the lobby felt like a sauna. He helped Victoria remove her coat, then looked her in the eye.

"Looks like your case has got a new priority—as in finding a ring with a heart-shaped diamond and emerald baguettes."

She looked into the middle distance, thinking. "Something's bothering me, though—something about the timing of all this."

"How do you mean?"

"Let's say it *was* the same knife—that whoever killed Mrs. Kincaid in south Georgia on Friday also attacked Mrs. Holland in Atlanta on Monday night."

"Your forensic pathologist just told you it's possible."

"But if that's the case, then our profilers back in Quantico need to seriously rethink their view that the informant's the killer."

"Why is that?"

"The informant picked a curious way of informing Posten that the next victim after Kincaid would be Timothy Copeland in San Francisco. He manipulated Posten's computer to flash Copeland's name on his video display monitor. He had to sneak into the building to do that. It was an illegal break-in, so our Miami office checked into it—dusted for fingerprints, the whole nine yards. Nothing turned up, but by checking the computer's memory, the systems manager was able to tell that the modifications were done at exactly eight-twenty-six A.M., Tuesday—actually three days before Copeland's murder."

"Which means?"

"Which means that if this schizophrenia theory is correct—if the informant is the killer—then he somehow got from Peachtree Street in downtown Atlanta to the *Tribune* headquarters in downtown Miami in less than twelve hours. He was in Atlanta one evening, and in Miami the next morning."

"Big deal. It's a two-hour flight."

"That's just the point. There *weren't* any flights. Last night, after you called me, I began thinking about the Atlanta–Miami connection, and checked into it. I thought maybe we could get some passenger manifests. But the same ice storm that stranded Cybil Holland in downtown Atlanta had the airport shut down for five hours on Monday night, till one o'clock in the morning."

"What about after one o'clock? He could have flown out as late as five-thirty or six and still gotten to Miami in time to manipulate the computer at eight-twenty-six."

Victoria shook her head. "Think about it. The guy's a wanted serial killer. He just sliced off a woman's finger. He probably has her diamond ring stuffed in his coat pocket, and he maybe even still has his favorite knife tucked away in his baggage. You think he'd sit around the airport for five hours like a caged rat, hoping to catch the next plane to Miami, whenever that might be?"

"Okay," Tony said, nodding in agreement. "So, he drove."

She sighed, troubled. "It's true that, at least according to the stereotypes, geographically transient serial killers love to take long drives. But it's a good fourteen-hour drive from Miami to Atlanta."

"It could be done in twelve. A buddy and I made it in thirteen down to Joe Robbie Stadium when we snagged Super Bowl tickets at the last minute. Granted, we had to take turns driving nonstop. I'm not sure I could have done it alone."

Those last words hung in the air, as if the proverbial light had gone on above their heads. Finally, he said what they were both thinking: "You think he shared the driving?"

"As in, him and the informant?"

Tony shrugged. "That's another option, isn't it. The two of them working together?"

"Like Bianchi and Buono," she said, thinking aloud.

"Who?"

"Kenneth Bianchi and Angelo Buono. They were cousins. Together, they were the California Hillside Strangler."

Tony rubbed his temple, as if overwhelmed. "Enough already. If I'm going to assemble a team of agents to start asking pawnshop owners if they've seen a guy trying to hock a diamond ring, you need to tell me what the hell we're looking for. Is it two guys working together, two guys outfoxing each other, or one crazy lunatic with multiple personalities?"

She looked past him, glancing toward the door to the autopsy room. "That's what we need to find out."

Chapter 26

m ike woke at precisely 7:30 A.M. He lay in bed and stared up at the whirling paddle fan over his bed, wondering why it was that whenever he didn't *have* to get up early his internal alarm clock worked like the countdown for a space-shuttle launching.

At 7:31 the empty feeling hit him. Probation. Last night's face-to-face meeting with Aaron had changed nothing. For the first time in thirteen years he didn't have to swing by the morgue before breakfast to say hello to the latest stiffs. There'd be no jailhouse coffee with the usual suspects, no visit to the emergency rooms for the bloody truth about last night's street fights. Damn, he missed it already.

His energy level was too high to sit around watching *Today*'s Willard Scott wish happy birthday to another hundred-year-old woman who still enjoys skydiving. He didn't care if he *was* on probation—if he dug out the stories, he knew Charlie Gelber wasn't going to turn them away. He killed the morning over at the police station, therefore, scrounging for leads on that distinguished congresswoman who was supposedly ducking from a drive-by shooting when her head had landed in the unzipped lap of a twenty-year-old passenger who was not her husband.

Angry as he was about the way the arrangement with the FBI had blown up in his face, Mike kept his afternoon banking appointment. Aaron had made it clear that the only way to defend the arrangement was to get results—which gave him no choice but to continue doing all he could to catch the killer. Accordingly, when a hundred thousand dollars of the FBI's money was wired to his account at three-thirty that afternoon, he promptly transferred the funds to the Citibank account of Ernest Gill, well under the informant's Tuesday deadline.

Afterward, Mike went for a long drive to clear his head. February was *the* reason he lived in Florida. Cool breezes, blue skies. The late-afternoon sun felt warm on his skin, like an old friend with the power to heal. With the ragtop down, even a drive on the interstate beat the hell out of the Chicago winters he'd endured growing up. The smell of sea salt in the air was a soothing substitute for road salt in your boots. His Saab was doing seventy as the road signs suddenly offered two very distinct choices: downtown or the beaches. He thought of the lyrics from an old Springsteen song, "Hungry Heart," about the guy who took a wrong turn and just kept going. Not a chance, he thought. Not for Mike Posten. No running allowed. Not unless it was on the proverbial treadmill, in search of the brass ring.

Suddenly, the thought of a broken promise jolted him. Karen. Last night, he'd promised to call her as soon as he'd straightened things out with Aaron.

Tuesdays and Thursdays were her nights for aerobics, he knew. Her class started at six o'clock. He turned down the exit ramp, drove by the florist for a bouquet of apologies, then took the back roads to the health club.

As he steered into the parking lot, the lead story on the hourly news update caught his attention on the radio. It was an excerpt from last night's show on *Nightline*, a sound bite of Aaron Fields responding to the charges of checkbook journalism. The convertible lurched to an abrupt halt as he slammed it into park and cranked up the volume.

"I've known Mike Posten for thirteen years," he intoned over the radio. "Let me say that I questioned him point-blank about this, and he has assured me that all reports of improper payments to a secret informant for exclusive stories about murders he himself may have committed are patently false."

Mike switched off the radio, noting the nifty way Aaron had inserted the qualifying word "improper" in front of "payments." *Should have been a politician, Aaron.*

He spotted Karen cutting across the parking lot, but she didn't see him—or if she did see him, she was ignoring him. She was dressed in a gray business suit with burgundy neckerchief—definitely courtroom attire—with her workout bag slung over her shoulder. Just as he started out of the car to catch her, his beeper rang.

"Not again," he groaned. He glanced at the display. EMERGENCY, the message read. CALL ME VS.

He made a face, torn inside. Part of him said catch up with Karen, part said call Victoria. It was like last night all over again, when Aaron Fields had called, where there were no right answers. "*Dammit.*" He snatched up his portable phone from the console and punched out the number. Victoria answered on one ring.

"This had better be a real emergency," he said as he watched Karen disappear into the health club.

"It's the Ernest Gill account at Citibank. The quarter of a million dollars we paid your informant."

"I made the deposit this afternoon. What about it?"

She paused, then said warily, "It's gone. All of it."

"Gone—how?"

"He moved it offshore. Wire transfer."

."Surely you must have anticipated *that.*"

"We've known for the past week he was moving money through a series of wire transfers. We were tracing it, never missing a beat. The trail led offshore this afternoon, right after you made the last transfer deposit. Antigua. They've got some of the strictest bank secrecy laws in the world. Tighter than Switzerland or the Cayman Islands."

"But if you know it's in Antigua, why can't you find out *where* in Antigua?"

"It's like dropping a coin in the ocean. You can see it break the surface, but you have no way of knowing where it's going to land. Antigua is one of the few bank secrecy havens that has no treaty with the United States for the exchange of banking information. I can get records from domestic banks showing transfers to Antigua, but the Antigua banks won't give us any records of how and when he moves the money once it's over there. I'll have to rely completely on insiders to piece things together. There was always a risk he'd try to hide behind bank secrecy, but I just didn't think your informant was savvy enough to pick one of the few places on earth that would be a total bitch for us."

Mike waved off an old man selling mangoes on the sidewalk. "Do you think he's cashing out? The game's over?"

"I don't know. That's why I'm calling you, though. We have to map out a strategy in case he calls again."

"He *better* call again. If we don't catch this guy, I'm going down as the sleazebag journalist who did nothing but give a serial killer the financial incentive to keep right on killing."

"Believe me," she said, thinking of her memo to Assistant Director Dougherty. "You're not out on that limb alone."

Chapter 27

the cuckoo clock on the wall chirped three times in the darkness, echoing throughout the small, two-bedroom house. No one flinched except the man in the hallway, a stranger in the house.

He was an imposing silhouette, dressed in a black rubberized diving suit, a fabric that would shed virtually no fibers for the benefit of police and their labs. A rubberized hood meant that not a single hair from his head would be left behind. Thin but durable diving gloves gave him full use of his fingers without leaving prints. His face was covered with black greasepaint, making his features completely indiscernible in the darkness. As the cuckoo clock finished its silly and sudden intrusion, his white teeth flashed in a bemused smile. He seemed to welcome the absurdity it had cast over a deadly serious situation.

Curt Rollins moved with quiet confidence down the narrow, dark corridor that led to the bedroom. He was becoming more sure of himself each day, learning more with each victim, the diving suit being his most recent adaptation. He walked without a sound, one step at time, deliberate but patient. He stopped at the end of the hall and glanced at the assortment of photographs covering the wall. It was like a big collage, only neater, because everything was framed. A group of college-age women all dressed in ski clothes, smiling and clinging to each other atop a snowy mountain. A diploma from George Washington University— Bachelor of Science, Class of 1981. A pretty blonde in her twenties with an older woman who had to be her mother.

Rollins gave the entire collection a quick once-over, until his gaze suddenly fixed on a black-and-white photo in a gold-leaf frame, right next to the diploma. It was a silver-haired man in a judge's black robe, probably in his seventies. Possibly her father, maybe her grandfather. He had a serious and distinguished look, posing before stacked shelves of law books, holding his horn-rimmed eyeglasses in his right hand. He wasn't really smiling, but he flashed a hint of that flat power smile that smacked of law-and-order and long prison terms. Rollins stared into the old judge's eyes, and the imaginary exchange made him bristle. He knew they'd never met, but he looked like every judge—including the crusty old bastard who'd sentenced him to prison nine years ago.

Rollins didn't like to think about that day, but the ugly memory burned clear, as if it had all happened yesterday. Even the smallest details had stuck with him. The white fluorescent light glaring off a polished marble floor. Rich mahogany paneling with shiny brass trim.

The young and nervous public defender who was assigned to his case. Most of all, he remembered the menacing, disgusted expression on the old judge's face as he peered down from the bench and pronounced final sentence.

"The prisoner shall please rise," said the bailiff.

Rollins and his lawyer stood side by side. The prosecutor stood to their left, behind the polished mahogany table that was closest to the empty jury box. Both the prosecutor and defense wore pinstripe suits, as if they were on the same team. An armed guard stood by the door, dressed in the standard gray slacks and crisp blue blazer. Several Chicago police officers in their midnight blue uniforms filled the gallery behind him, mere interested spectators on this auspicious morning. Everyone looked dignified, except the prisoner in the orange jumpsuit with his hands cuffed behind his back. He felt like the courtroom jester. All he needed was a pointy hat.

"Mr. Rollins," said the judge, almost spitting out his name.

He looked up at the judge's scowl, trying to hide his contempt. He said nothing.

The judge glared right back, pointing his gavel as he spoke. "I am always outraged when I see a police officer on the take. But this case has convinced me that there is no more despicable character on earth than an officer of the law who would sell to a drug dealer the name of a confidential government informant. I thank God he wasn't killed, and I wish I could put you away forever. I sentence you to the maximum term of seven years in prison."

With a bang of the gavel it was all over. Seven years in state prison. A death sentence for a cop.

The cuckoo clock blared once more, marking the quarter hour. Rollins took a deep breath, leaving his memories and focusing dead ahead. He was standing in the open doorway to the master bedroom. The scene didn't shock him, for it was much like the others. She was still on the bed, lying flat on her back. Her hands and feet were bound with an electrical cord. She was naked from the waist up, still wearing her pink panties with white lace trim. Stab wounds covered her stomach and chest, too many to count. Big puddles of blood had soaked through the white sheets. Her severed tongue rested on the pillow beside her.

Rollins moved closer to survey the evidence, but as he stepped into the room he was attacked from behind. Before he could react his arm was twisted up behind his back and there was a knife at his throat.

"Don't move," his assailant said.

Writhing in pain and racked with fear, Rollins went completely rigid, resisting every false move. His heart raced and he took short, panicky breaths. He could sense the sharp blade slowly cutting through the rubberized hood around his neck, working its way toward his bobbing Adam's apple. His mouth was so dry he could barely speak.

"Don't hurt me! Please. It's me—Curt. Curt Rollins."

"Curt?" There was surprise and anger in his tone, but his grasp only tightened. "You stupid son of a bitch."

Chapter 28

a shaft of morning sun from the skylight cut through the darkness in the black marble bathroom. From a glassed-in shower rose a thick cloud of steam, fogging the beveled mirrors and gold Italian fixtures on the sunken Roman tub. Crystal sconces on the wall dripped beads of condensation, like icicles melting in a warm mist.

Frank Hannon stood naked with the lights off, drenching his thick, sandy-blond hair in cascades of hot water. At six feet five, the top of his head nearly reached the shower nozzle. Blasts of water ricocheted in all directions from his rock-solid body. He closed his eyes to enjoy the warmth running down the ripples in his stomach. With his shoulders flexed like a bodybuilder a channel ran down the middle of his V-shaped back. The ritual was therapeutic. He could relax this way for hours after a kill.

This morning, however, his mind wouldn't rest. Curt Rollins was a nuisance he just hadn't figured on.

It all made sense, once he thought about it. Rollins, a former cop, was undoubtedly trained in stakeouts and surveying crime scenes. Who would be more qualified to tail a killer, gather up evidence, and then sell his story to the press? The thing he couldn't figure was how he *knew*.

The hypnotic sound of falling water took him back to their childhood, to the only thing he could think of. It was the day he and Curt had vandalized that house by the lake, more than twenty years ago. . . .

Nine-year-old Frank was hiding in the tree fort behind his house. The sun had set hours ago, and he'd been hiding alone in the darkness ever since Curt had limped home on his cut-up leg. Through the big maple leaves he could see the entire yard in the moonlight, all the way to the street. A white Bonneville pulled up and parked in the pea-gravel driveway. The engine cut off but the headlights stayed on. His father got out and stood in the yard.

"Frank!" he yelled, as if calling the dog.

Frank watched in silence as a blue Impala with a white vinyl roof pulled up behind the Bonneville. A skinny blond woman got out and lit up a cigarette. Curt's mom. She seemed all excited and nervous. She walked around the car and opened the passenger door. Curt hobbled out. He was on crutches and had a white bandage from his knee to his ankle. Frank knew in an instant that he'd been to Emergency.

Frank caught his breath at the sight of a third car pulling into the driveway. A police car. The county sheriff.

"Frank, get over here!" his father shouted.

He hurried down the tree trunk and cut across the lawn, then stopped at the end of the driveway. He was staring directly into the blinding headlights, which turned the grown-ups into dark, shadowy figures. Squinting, he could make out their faces. His father was scowling with arms folded. Curt's mom looked even madder than the time he'd swiped her underwear off the backyard clothesline. The sheriff was wearing his brown-and-beige uniform with a flat-brimmed hat, but it was the size of the gun in his holster that got Frank's attention. Curt hid behind his mother, afraid to even look at his friend.

"Did you break into that summerhouse?" his father demanded.

"No."

He slapped him across the face. "Don't lie to me!"

"I didn't do nothin'."

His father turned toward Curt and looked him in the eye. "Curt, did you break into that summerhouse?"

He hobbled on his crutches and hid farther behind his mother. "Yessir," he said quietly.

"Why'd you do it?"

Curt paused. "Because—because Frank made me."

Frank came at him with fists flying. "You're a rat! You're a little beady-eyed rat!"

The sheriff grabbed him and held him back. Frank was kicking and yelling, and he bit his hairy arm. The cop cried out in pain as Frank shook loose. His father grabbed him by the shirt and pinned him to the ground, kneeling on top of him to keep him from squirming away.

"You're a ratfink, Curt!" He was flat on his belly with his cheek against the grass. His father buried one knee squarely in his back.

The sheriff patted Curt affectionately on the head. "You did the right thing, young man. It's always best to tell the truth."

Frank's father grabbed him by the hair, nearly picking him up off the ground. The strong odor of bourbon flowed with his words. "You know where you going this time—*don't you*, you little shit."

Frank knew. His father had threatened him a month ago, after he got caught in the cemetery. Six months ago, a seventeen-year-old high school senior had been raped and stabbed to death, her naked body found in the woods. It was the town's biggest news in a decade, and a local newspaper had seen fit to describe her wounds in gruesome detail. Frank had devoured every bit of it. He kept the photos and newspaper clippings under his bed, including an obituary that said where she'd been buried. Every night, he'd crawl into bed, take off his pajamas and read the old stories. He thought about her, dreamed about her, imagined her telling him what it was like to have someone slit her throat. Her murder was never solved, and when it finally faded from the news Frank felt empty, unfulfilled. After a few weeks he started riding his bike past her house. He stopped a few times and watched from the sidewalk, even snuck up to the porch once and sat on her steps. He started stealing mail out of their box, rummaging through it for belated sympathy cards to her family or magazines she might have subscribed to. One night, he rode past the grocery store where she'd worked after school as a part-time cashier, and then he peddled to the cemetery to find her grave. The fresh sod hadn't completely taken root yet, so he could see exactly where she was. He was drawn to it and walked all the way around it. He stood on it, sat on it, even laid down on top of it—until he felt an uncontrollable urge to urinate on it. So he did, right on the headstone. A groundskeeper had caught him and called his parents. Lousy snitch.

His father yanked his hair again, snapping his head back. "I warned you, ya little bastard. Next time you stepped over the line, your skinny ass would land in jail. And I meant it. Sheriff, do what you gotta do."

The sheriff scowled as he took a roll of black electrical tape from his pants pocket, then knelt down and taped Frank's skinny wrists behind his back, like makeshift handcuffs.

"I'm not afraid of jail," Frank scoffed. "Not afraid of you, either, you stupid pig."

"You will address me as Sheriff Nettle," he said sternly. He grabbed Frank by the arm and lifted him to his feet.

His father gave a wink. "No special treatment, Officer. Treat him like any other common criminal."

The sheriff smiled thinly. "We know how to deal with these bad apples." He nudged him toward the squad car. "Move along, shorty."

"Don't call me shorty, fat-ass. And what about Curt? Why isn't he coming?"

The sheriff opened the rear door to the squad car and pushed him inside. "Don't worry about him. You got enough to worry about." The door slammed shut.

Frank glared at Curt through the rear window as the squad car pulled away. Sirens blared and the blue lights swirled in the darkness. They drove fast, like a real emergency. They ran every stop sign all the way to the station. Frank felt important. He imagined he was president—or better yet, someone who'd killed the president and his entire family.

The stockade was in a part of town that Frank had never seen. No trees, no grass. Just boarded-up buildings and garbage in the gutters, and lots of mean-looking dudes on every street corner standing in circles and sharing short little cigarettes. They were frightening to Frank in the shadowy streetlights, but he refused to let it show. The squad car stopped at the busted-up curb. The sheriff got out and led Frank upstairs into the station.

Inside, people were moving in all directions, mostly men. Some wore uniforms and some street clothes. One guy with no clothes was chained to a bench and puking on his feet. Every desk was cluttered with files and newspapers. Three guys in the back were shooting hoops into the wastebasket. The others were jabbering back and forth, making enough noise for a thousand conversations. It reminded Frank of homeroom and driving the teacher crazy.

"Whatta we got here?" asked the intake officer behind the counter.

"Kiss my ass," Frank said defiantly.

The cops exchanged smiles. "Tough guy, huh," said Nettle, as he removed the electrical tape binding Frank's wrists. "Hands on the palm prints."

Frank leaned against the wall, but he had to raise

his arms way up over his head to reach the black out-lines that marked the spot for prisoners to place their hands, like a vertical game of Twister. As the sheriff patted him down and searched his pockets, Frank noticed how much bigger the outlines were than his own hands.

"Solitary confinement for this one," Nettle told the intake officer. "Real dangerous character."

"My own cell? Cool. I can jerk off then."

The officer did a double take, then checked the register behind the desk. "We can put him in tank eleven. Hornsby ate one of the lightbulbs again, sent him to the hospital this morning." He glanced at Frank. "Some guys'll do anything to get outta here for a few days."

Frank made a face and narrowed his eyes. "Aren't you jokers gonna fingerprint me first?"

Nettle just shook his head. "What for? You ain't never gettin' outta here. Alive."

The intake officer punched the button behind the counter, and the heavy metal door slowly clanked open. Nettle retaped the prisoner's wrists behind his back even tighter than before and led him down the chute, past a row of holding cells for the night's arrests.

It was noisy and crowded inside the cells, worse than Frank had ever seen on television or in maga-zines. The iron bars seemed thicker, the cement walls felt colder. It smelled bad, like the time he plugged up the toilets in the locker room at school. Looking straight down the corridor to the end of the cellblock, he could see hands and arms sticking out between bars. It was as if the walls had limbs. He tried not to look at any of the prisoners, but one caught his eye. He was crouched on the floor with his shirt off and his hands in his underwear. Frank looked away, but his eyes met the woman in the opposite cell. She was ugly with stringy blond hair, more makeup on her face than the Catwoman, and tight stretch pants that looked two sizes too small. He winced as she blew him a kiss.

His heart raced faster, but he bit his lip to control it. "Bunch of losers," he said with bravado. "I *deserve* my own cell."

They stopped at the end of the hall in front of one of the internal cells with no window to the outside world. The sheriff unlocked the door with a key from his belt, then flipped the switch outside the cell. The light by the door went on, but the bulb over the sink was missing. Just like the other cop had said. Hornsby ate it.

"Get in," said Nettle.

Frank stumbled inside. There was a rust-stained sink standing in the corner and a hole in the floor that smelled like a sewer. A cot stretched the cell's entire length. The sheriff sat beside him on the edge of the bed and removed the tape from his wrists that had cuffed his hands. They could hear two men arguing about something at the end of the hall. Then, suddenly, a third voice started up—a man, obviously deranged, making what sounded like animal sounds. Frank's hands started shaking as the tape came off. The sheriff contained his smile, then spoke in a low, somber tone. "Know what they do in here to nine-year-old tough guys?"

"What?"

"They turn them into girls."

He rubbed his wrists, helping the blood flow. "They can't turn *me* into a girl."

The sheriff wadded up the tape into a ball and shoved it in his pocket. "That's what the last boy we had in here said. But he wasn't talking at all when he left. We put him next to one of those greasy, smelly people you see wandering around the streets downtown. Kind of like those characters right across the hall. And as soon as we turned out the lights, the big guy snuck in the kid's cell. Know what he did then?" He paused for effect, making sure Frank was listening. He leaned a little closer and spoke in a hoarse whisper. "Sonofabitch opened his zipper and did it right in the kid's mouth. Poor bastard couldn't talk anymore after that."

Frank swallowed hard, trying to stay tough. "Why couldn't he talk?"

The sheriff's expression turned deadly serious. "Because it tasted so bad, the kid cut his own tongue out."

Frank instinctively touched his tongue, believing every word.

The sheriff smirked with satisfaction, then stepped toward the door. "Sleep tight, Frank." He closed the cell door and switched off the light.

The cell turned black. Suddenly, Frank didn't feel so invincible. He rushed to the bars to be closer to the light, but the dim bulbs in the corridor left the rear cells in darkness. It was so dark he couldn't even see to the other end of the cell. His heart raced, but he fought to control it. No one was going to scare *him* into being a Goody Two-shoes. No way. In fact, he'd made up his mind. He was going to do anything he wanted, when he wanted. And one thing was damn sure, he'd never again get caught. Because he'd make sure there were no witnesses. If someone did see him and tried to snitch, he'd hurt them bad.

He froze, thinking he heard something. He gasped, thinking he'd heard it again. Maybe it was coming from the cell next to him. His short, panicky breaths were so loud it was hard to hear, so he held his breath and listened harder. There it was again—footsteps drawing closer . . .

The bathroom light switched on over the shower stall, giving Hannon a start. His head was pounding from the twenty-year-old memory. He turned off the shower and listened.

"Charlie?" a woman called out. "Is that you, babe?"

He was so wrapped up in his thoughts that, for a split second, he nearly forgot that "Charlie" was the alias by which she knew him. He wrapped himself in a bath towel and stepped from the steamy shower. "Hi, Valerie."

She was a plain but attractive brunette in her late forties, with the figure of a woman who was constantly on a diet. Her winter suntan was phony but perfectly even, and her legs looked great in her short white tennis dress. Indoor doubles, Hannon figured, since it was forty degrees outside.

"I wasn't expecting you back so soon," she said with a smile. "How'd the project go?"

"Uh—okay, I think. I got their system up and

running. Those people don't need an independent computer consultant, though. They need to get over to the library and check out *Computers for Dummies*."

She moved closer and glided her hand lightly over his well-defined chest. "Well, not everyone appreciates how brilliant you are. But as long as you've got your Valerie, it doesn't matter that they don't pay you what you're worth."

"Did you miss me?"

She smiled seductively with her eyes and planted a light kiss on the corner of his mouth. "Let me show you how much." She tugged at the towel around his waist and led him to the bedroom, stopping at the foot of the four-poster bed. His leather travel bag was spilled out on the fluffy down comforter. She noticed the book in middle of the pile. *How to Put Power and Passion into Your Relationships*.

"Are you *still* reading this?" she asked incredulously.

He wrapped his arms around her and playfully bit her earlobe. "I told you. I don't really read it. I just hold it up and stare at it in public places until a good-looking woman comes along and talks to me."

"You tramp," she said as she fell back on the bed and pulled him on top of her. Her breath quickened as her thighs opened. Her hands brought him toward her pelvis. She desperately wanted just to yank away the towel and feel his naked body, but she knew the *only* way he'd please her.

"Why don't you put on some underwear," she whispered in his ear. "And make me scream for my Charlie."

She gently caressed his face, trying to relax him. He suddenly tickled her, making her jump. She screamed playfully, then inadvertently nicked him on the chin with her diamond. It bled like a razor cut.

"I'm so sorry, honey," she said, rubbing the little wound.

He shrugged, as if it didn't matter. He brought her hand to his lips and gently kissed away the little red drops from the ring he'd given her on his return from Atlanta—a heart-shaped diamond in a platinum setting with two emerald baguettes on either side.

He smiled at a thought, but he kept it to himself: It wasn't the first time there'd been blood on these stones.

Chapter 29

from the penthouse balcony overlooking Biscayne Bay, Mike could see it was a cool and crisp morning, the February-in-Florida version of a strong Arctic cold front. Inspired by the chill, he threw on his jogging shorts, T-shirt, and Nikes and went out for a run.

He headed up the asphalt path north along Bayshore Drive, a busy tree-lined street through Coconut Grove that wasn't exactly on the water, but more or less followed the irregular coastline. He passed the marina and waterfront shops to the east, with several blocks of towering condominiums across the street to his left. Oaks and long-limbed royal poinciana trees offered plenty of shade. Morning traffic was heavy, but a light breeze from the bay made the exhaust fumes unnoticeable.

A hundred yards ahead, near the entrance to the waterfront park, a midnight blue Mercedes turned off Bayshore Drive and skidded to halt in the gravel parking lot. The windows were tinted dark, so he couldn't see the driver inside. The motor was still running. Mike slowed nearly to a walk. The Mercedes didn't move. Black diesel exhaust was still pouring out of the tailpipe. It seemed to be waiting.

Mike stopped, straining to recall whether he'd written any particularly biting articles about drug dealers lately. Curious, he propped his leg up on the fence post and did a few stretches, keeping one eye on the car. It wasn't going anywhere, and the motor was *still* running.

He jogged off the path and crossed the street. The car, he noticed, pulled out of the parking lot and back onto Bayshore Drive. Mike turned down a side street into an upscale residential area. It was like heading into a tunnel. The expensive homes had no front yards. Crime what it was, each one had a seven-foot stone wall built up along the street and an iron gate barricading the driveway. Halfway down the street he glanced back over his shoulder. The midnight blue Mercedes was turning off Bayshore, following right behind him. His heart raced. The stone walls on either side left no place to turn. A sudden burst of adrenaline propelled him forward at full speed, like a sprinter out of the blocks. The car came faster. Mike was huffing and puffing at a dead run, and his legs felt like lead.

The engine roared behind him as the Mercedes barreled down. He whizzed past gate after iron gate, all of them locked. The car was just twenty feet away when Mike reached the street corner. He faked left then cut right, but the driver didn't go for it. The car screeched to a halt in the middle of the intersection and Mike nearly ran right into it. The passenger door flew open.

"Get in," Aaron Fields said sharply.

Mike was sweating and panting, barely able to speak. "Why the hell are you chasing me?"

"Why the hell are you running away from me?" he snapped. "Now get in the car."

Mike took a deep breath, then slid into the passenger seat and closed the door. Aaron pulled away slowly, heading back toward Bayshore Drive. Mike directed all the dashboard vents right at his sweaty face and cranked up the air-conditioning full blast. "You know," he said, sucking in the cool air, "I'd much rather you fire me than stalk me."

"I'm not stalking you. I called from my car phone on my way downtown, and your roommate said you were out jogging down Bayshore. When I saw you I pulled off and waited—and then you headed off in another direction, like you didn't want to talk to me. Which only makes me think there might be some truth to the rumors."

"What rumors?"

He stopped the car at the corner and shot Mike a look. "That you're holding out on me. I got a call this morning from Charlie Gelber. Tenth body turned up this morning in Virginia. And you didn't print the story."

"This is the first I've heard about it," he said with surprise.

"I'd like to believe that. But the word down at the newsroom is that you're pissed because I put you on probation."

The Mercedes pulled back onto Bayshore Drive, merging into the morning traffic. "Wait a minute," said Mike. "You think I got a call from my informant, like usual, and that I blew the exclusive just to get back at you."

He grimaced, as if he hated to levy the accusation. "Do you expect me to believe it's coincidence that your informant stopped calling on the same day I put you on probation? Put yourself in my shoes."

"No. Put yourself in *my* shoes. I came to you and Charlie with this proposal because I thought you'd care as much about stopping a serial killer as I did. The minute something went wrong you put *me* on probation."

"You're still covering the story."

"Oh, thank you very much for letting me continue to write and pump up sales."

The car rocked as Aaron steered off to the shoulder of the road and slammed on the breaks, bringing them to a screeching halt. Two purple veins stood out on his temples. "Is that what you think, after thirteen years we've known each other? That I'm *using* you?"

"No," Mike said with a sigh. "It's just that . . . this whole experience has me feeling like you've changed, or I've changed, or maybe it's the whole damn profession. Back when you were editor in chief, we took risks, sure—but not the kind that made me question our own motives. There's just a lot more emphasis on selling papers these days."

Aaron shook his head. "And what the hell is so wrong with a publisher who wants to sell newspapers?"

"Nothing, so long as that's not the only thing you care about."

"What do *you* care about, Mike?"

"I care about the people I write about."

"Really? You *care* about them?"

"Sure. My wife even commented the other night, how she's heard me talking on the phone to them for hours. Victims. Their families. Witnesses to crimes. I've spent hours talking with them, consoling them. Karen sounded almost jealous about it."

"Okay. And out of all these thousands of people you've consoled over the years, how many have you called back after the story ran in the newspaper? You know, just to see how they're doing. How they're making out."

Mike looked down.

Aaron smirked. "That's what I thought." He sighed heavily, then laid a paternalistic hand on Mike's shoulder. "I'm not trying to make you feel like a shithead, Mike. All I'm saying is that you don't care as much as you think you do; and by the same token, I'm not as interested in money as people think I am. We're journalists. We care about the story. And if we're good journalists, we care about the truth. If, along the way, we make a little money and make a few friends, that's a bonus. But those incidentals aren't what drive us. They can't be, or they get in the way of telling it the way it is. You and me, Mike, we're driven by the same thing. That's why I'm on my third marriage," he said with a half-joking smile. "That's why you've never worked for another publisher."

Mike ran a sweaty hand through his hair, and

goose bumps covered his arms. He'd always liked Aaron, but the thought of being *like him* was suddenly disquieting. He reached for the handle and popped open the door. "I promise you, Aaron: I'm not holding out on you. If I hear from this guy, the *Tribune* gets the story."

He smiled as Mike stepped down from the car onto the gravel shoulder. "That's my boy," he said with a wink.

Mike forced a return smile, then quickly closed the door. He was suddenly thinking about the secrets Karen had never told him, and the way he was always rushing off at the beck and call of people like Aaron whenever she tried to talk.

Still damp with sweat, he stood alone in the cloud of dust, feeling that he'd just gotten more than a workout.

Chapter 30

frank Hannon woke at ten minutes till two that afternoon. He found a note on the lacy white pillow beside him on the bed. Valerie had a luncheon at the country club, then shopping at the Chevy Chase Mall. She probably wouldn't be back until dinnertime. Perfect.

He stepped naked across the polished oak floors to a walk-in closet that was bigger than most bedrooms. Her slacks hung neatly from a rod that ran from one end to the other, with another for party dresses and two more for casual wear. A wall of shelves displayed shoes and purses. Along the far wall was a set of built-in drawers with Plexiglas facades, making hose, belts and underwear impossible to lose. A tiny quadrant in the back was the precious space Valerie had given him, but it was all he needed.

He put on a pair of khaki chinos and a blue oxford-cloth shirt with button-down collar—the preppy look that had melted Valerie's heart. Yesterday's high temperature had been in the fifties, so he took the Ralph Lauren jacket with the plaid lining that she'd bought for him, then grabbed the car keys from the nightstand and headed for the garage.

He stopped at the kitchen table, where Valerie had left her copy of the *Washington Post* beside an empty cup of coffee with red lipstick on the rim. He flipped through it with interest, noticing immediately that he'd made the front page. *Tongue-Murderer Strikes Capitol Area*, read the headline. *Tenth Victim Found in McLean, Va.*

He skimmed the story, smiling. Nowhere was Mike Posten or the *Miami Tribune* mentioned. That confirmed it: Rollins was definitely the source.

He grabbed a V-8 from the refrigerator and walked with purpose from the kitchen. He'd left the space heater on inside the garage all night, so it was nice and warm. Valerie's Jaguar was still there, which meant one of her snooty friends had picked her up. He took the Volvo and drove to the strip mall just a few blocks away.

A light rain started to fall as he pulled into the parking lot. The hypnotic sound of the wipers streaking across the windshield had him thinking back again, to that night he'd spent in jail. It brought back all the old feelings, his hatred for cops, his old man— and Curt. . . .

Twenty-some years ago, the very morning he'd gotten out of jail, he went right to Curt—the rat. The night in jail was supposed to teach him a lesson, his father said. It had. And he went right to Curt's house to teach *him* what he'd learned.

Curt had spotted his friend coming up the drive-way and tried to run, but his crutches didn't take him far. Frank tackled him behind the house. The crutches flew as they tumbled to the ground. He ripped Curt's pant leg and tore off the bandage. Curt screamed, but it only excited him. With his bare hands he gouged the stitches from his leg. Curt cried out for his mother, as if to invite more. Frank punched him wildly in the face, beating him to near unconsciousness, stopping only when the blood from his nose and mouth completely covered his face. He was panting with exhaustion, but his rage still hadn't subsided. Curt was on his back, moaning. Frank was on top, pinning him to the ground. The sheriff's story about that other boy cutting out his own tongue was still fresh in his mind, feeding his anger and giving him strength. He grabbed Curt by the hair and spoke right into his face.

"You're a girl!" he shouted. "A little girly tattle-tale."

"They made me tell," Curt grunted, barely able to speak. "They *made* me—"

Frank spit in his eye. "They made you into a *girl*! They thought they could do the same to me, but they couldn't, and they never will." He grabbed Curt by the throat, and his voice seethed with new menace. " 'Cuz if anyone *ever* rats on me again, I swear I'll rip the tongue right out of their mouth."

Frank jumped up and kicked Curt in the leg, leaving him on the ground writhing in pain. . . .

The rubber wipers screeched across the wind-shield, rousing Hannon from his thoughts. The rain had stopped, so he killed the wipers. He parked the

Volvo in a secluded no-parking zone by the Dumpsters, off to the side of the strip mall. Plastic bread crates and a stack of compressed cardboard boxes from the supermarket towered over the car like a big castle wall. He walked around the side of the building, past the automatic doors at the supermarket entrance. In the busy pet shop next to the liquor store, a pack of two-week-old Collies tumbled in the display window. A little girl watched with glee, but Hannon didn't seem to notice as he stepped inside. It took him only ninety seconds to get what he needed. He carried the cardboard box out by the handle and headed back to the car.

He checked over his shoulder as he dug the keys from his pocket. Seeing no one, he popped the trunk open. His cargo stirred in the sudden burst of light. He was hog-tied, hands and feet bound behind his back. Silver duct tape covered his mouth. The syringe and bottle of ketamine, an animal tranquilizer that Hannon had used to render him unconscious, were lying at his feet. Rollins was staring right up at him, still groggy, still wearing his black rubber wet suit. His eyes squinted painfully in the daylight. The smell of urine filled the air.

"You stink like hell," he said with a snarl. "Keep it up, and you'll have the hounds after us." He opened the cardboard box, smiling deviously with his eyes. "This should throw them off the trail."

He pitched the box like a bucket, and something furry flew out. Rollins squirmed and let out a muffled cry as one landed on his chest and the other scampered down his leg.

Hannon laughed to himself, looking down with

disdain. "They're just rodents. Harmless, little white lab rats." His black eyes narrowed, showing utter contempt. "Think of them as family, Curt."

He slammed the trunk closed, then got behind the wheel and quickly drove away.

Chapter 31

the winding mountain road reached a dead end at a thick stand of birch and bare elm trees. In summer the foliage blocked the view of the lake in the valley below, but in February the leaves were a soggy, decaying carpet on the forest floor. Sunset was less than an hour away, and the overcast sky was as dreary and gray as the rounded granite peaks of the Shenandoah Mountains bulging above the evergreens.

Frank Hannon steered left into the muddy entrance drive, following the signs to the Merry Moose Inn and Cottages. The Volvo rocked like a dune buggy as it splashed from puddle to pothole. The access road was nothing more than an extrawide footpath twisting through the forest. He chuckled to himself, imagining Rollins and his furry companions bouncing around in the trunk. At the clearing in front of the inn he killed the engine and stepped out of the car.

The inn was an old mountain home with a stone facade, high-pitched roof and screened-in porch. The rushing sound of a nearby brook filled the chilly air. There wasn't a car in sight, just a fishing boat on a trailer beneath a canvas tarp.

The screen door squeaked as Hannon stepped through onto the porch. He peered through the diamond-shaped window on the door, seeing nothing. He knocked once, then again, giving it a good pounding. Just as he'd hoped: closed for the winter.

He got back in the car and drove farther down the road, past the main inn toward one of the more secluded cottages closer to the stream. The road twisted and grew more bumpy. He stopped at the fourth cottage, which was surrounded by evergreens. Even his car would be hidden from the inn and other cottages.

It was a small, wood-frame cottage with shutters on the windows. The door was padlocked, but it had plenty of play. Hannon put his shoulder into it, and with two powerful shoves the lock ripped from the doorframe. He brushed the cobwebs aside and stepped inside. There was one main room with a rustic wood floor and an old wood-burning potbelly stove. In back was a separate kitchen area and bathroom. The bed frame on the other side of the room had no box spring or mattress. A wood table and chairs were stacked neatly in the corner for storage. He flipped the switch, but the electricity was off.

He went back to the car and took a duffel bag from the floor in the backseat. From under the front seat he pulled a revolver. He checked the chamber, making sure he had six bullets. Then he went around the back and opened the trunk.

A foul odor escaped, forcing him to step back. One of the rats squeaked as it scurried beneath the spare tire. Rollins lay still, bound and gagged. He looked up pathetically, squinting at the sudden burst of daylight. He whimpered through the tape over his mouth as Hannon pressed the barrel of the gun against his temple.

"Shut up," said Hannon. He reached down with his free hand and untied the rope around his ankles. "Get out."

Timidly, Rollins threw one leg over the back of the car, then the other, sliding out of the trunk. His legs wobbled, and he couldn't seem to stand up straight. Hannon put the gun to the back of his head and gave a quick shove from behind, toward the cottage.

"Inside," he ordered.

Rollins stumbled forward. Hannon followed right behind with the gun in one hand and the duffel bag over his shoulder. He shoved Rollins to the floor as they crossed the threshold. He fell against a vertical support beam in the middle of the room. He sat on the floor with his back against the post. Hannon tied him tightly to the post with a rope from the duffel bag. Then he pulled a kitchen chair from the stack of furniture in the corner and sat facing Rollins with his back to the wall. He leaned forward and in one quick motion ripped the duct tape from Rollins's mouth.

Rollins grunted at the sound of whiskers ripping from his face, then stretched his mouth open like a man trying to yawn.

"Hungry?" asked Hannon. He took a pack of Fig

Newtons from his bag and shoved one in Rollins's mouth. The prisoner gobbled it up, so he fed him a few more. They went through half the pack before Rollins finally spoke.

"What are you gonna do with me?" he said as he chewed his last mouthful.

He stuffed the rest of the Fig Newtons back in his bag and opened a bottle of Pepsi. "Thirsty?" he said.

Rollins tilted his head back as Hannon poured. Some of it spilled down his chin, but he chugged down most of it. He looked up warily at Hannon and swallowed hard.

"Can I use the bathroom?"

"No."

"Why not?"

"Because I'd rather have you pissing in your pants than walking around the room. Think of it as a control thing."

Their eyes locked, then Rollins looked away. "I want to know. What are you gonna do with me?"

He leaned back in the chair and folded his arms smugly, saying nothing.

Rollins licked a drop of Pepsi from his lip. "Don't kill me, okay. Please don't kill me."

"Funny," he said with a confident smirk. "In thirty seconds I could have you begging me to kill you."

Rollins's eye twitched, and he answered in a nervous, shaky voice. "You don't want to do that, man. I've been thinking while I was in the trunk, you know. You and me. We could be partners in this thing. Split the money, you know, fifty-fifty."

"Partners?" he said with amusement.

"Yeah. I got a quarter million out of those suckers at the *Miami Tribune* already. We can keep this up forever. You're smart. You'll never get caught."

"That's real interesting. The problem, though, is that two people have to trust each other to be partners. There has to be honesty, openness."

"I could have turned you in a long time ago. I didn't. Why would I turn you in now? You can trust me, man."

Hannon sighed and shook his head. "I can't really trust you or anything you say. Only one thing can change that."

"What's that?"

He reached inside his bag, past the Fig Newtons and empty Pepsi bottle. Slowly, he pulled out a long shiny diving knife with a serrated edge.

"Pain," he said, brandishing the knife before Rollins's eyes. The steel blade flickered in the last remaining daylight. "Pain is an *amazing* truth serum."

Rollins squirmed. "Come on, man. What you want to do this for? Really, you can trust me. I've always been your friend, always respected you. Even when we were in school I never even teased you, not like the other kids did."

Hannon shot a quick, piercing glance. "Remember what they used to call me?"

"Sure. Kids can be cruel, man."

"All because I grew thirteen inches in eleven months. Fucking old man made me wear that back brace. Made me walk like a monster. Frank-Hannon-stein," he said bitterly. "That was me."

"Look at you now. You look like a stud."

"That's not what you told Mike Posten," he said sharply. "Your profile said I was impotent."

He smiled awkwardly. "Okay, I said that. But that's the beauty of this scheme. I keep feeding them enough correct details about the murders so they keep on paying me, but I give them totally wrong information about *the murderer*, so you'll never get caught. I been throwin' 'em off the trail from the very beginning, when I called that yokel in Georgia and pretended like *I* was the killer. It's like I said, man: We can keep this up forever."

"Or until you rat on me."

"I won't."

"You ratted on me before."

"We were just kids. Nine years old. I learned my lesson after you . . . well, you know."

Hannon's eyes suddenly lit up. "That's how you knew it was me, isn't it. The threat. I told you I'd cut out your tongue."

Rollins's mouth curled into a clever smile. "I heard about the murders on TV—and, yeah, it rang a bell. So I checked up on you, found out you'd just gotten out of prison, right about the time these tongue murders started. Tracked you down and started following you. That's when I got the brainstorm. I figured I'd scope out your next, uh, target in advance—and sell the story to some news creep."

"Posten certainly fills the bill," Hannon said dryly.

Rollins recognized dangerous territory. He decided to steer past the remark. "I figured you'd kind of be tickled by what I was doing, actually. You know, seeing as how the whole thing added to the publicity the killings were getting."

"Looking after my best interests, were you?" Hannon said. His eyes narrowed. "You don't fool me. Once that well ran dry, you'd turn me in—for the big reward."

"No. I was never going to rat on you."

"Why should I believe you?"

"Because . . ." He swallowed hard, racking his brain for an answer. "Because there were lots of other times I didn't rat on you, when I had the chance."

"When?"

"Back in school. I was onto you, Frank. You may have got good grades, and maybe you even had your old lady fooled into thinking you wanted to grow up to be a vet, like her. But I knew it wasn't a future career in medicine that made you wanna—you know, do those things. Like, remember in eighth grade, when somebody broke into the biology lab and cut off all those snakes' tongues? Principal never found out who did it. I knew it was you. But I didn't tell."

Hannon ran his finger lightly along the sharp blade. "Snakes," he said with a bemused smile. "Did you know that if you cut out a snake's tongue, it can't smell a thing? Even the most dangerous snakes get completely disoriented, can't find their prey. A snake couldn't hurt a flea without its tongue." His eyes turned cold as he looked right at him. "Kind of like a snitch."

"Listen to me, man,"—Rollins's voice shook—"I'm not a snitch. I hate snitches. I went to fucking jail as a cop for selling the names of government informants to the cocaine cowboys. I was never gonna turn you in. This is about money, pure and simple. It's business, that's all."

Hannon scooted to the edge of the chair and leaned forward, bringing the tip of the knife to Rollins's chin. He turned the blade slowly, drawing tiny drops of blood as it nicked a quivering lower lip.

"Please," Rollins whimpered.

"Business, huh," he said in a low, steady voice. "If that's all it is, I'd say you're about outta business— permanently. Unless you tell me exactly where that money is."

Chapter 32

i t took several hours for the Fairfax County Sheriff to request assistance from the FBI, but by midafternoon Victoria finally got her orders. She drove right from her office in Quantico to the busy crime scene in McLean. Overcast skies darkened the brown winter landscape in the day's waning moments. Two county sheriff cars were parked across the street from the redbrick house with the brown shingle roof. A deputy with a flashlight was directing traffic, both cars and pedestrians, keeping the rubberneckers moving along. A van marked FAIRFAX COUNTY CORONER'S OFFICE was blocking the driveway. Victoria parked her Oldsmobile at the curb, just on the other side of the bright fluorescent police tape that marked off the front lawn. She flashed her credentials to the deputy on the street. He directed her to the sheriff, who was standing by the coroner's van. Victoria buttoned her coat and approached him directly, but cordially.

"Victoria Santos," she said, extending her hand. "FBI."

"Sheriff Woodson," he said brusquely, "busy as hell." The baritone voice matched his heavyset frame. He had a clean-shaven, clean-cut look, right down to his polished shoes, pressed pants. Victoria guessed he was ex-military, probably a Vietnam vet. He turned away, returning his focus to the crime scene diagram on his clipboard.

She moved closer, glancing over his shoulder. "You've marked off a fairly large crime scene for a homicide that took place inside the house. Was the victim abducted outside and brought inside?"

His nose stayed in his clipboard. "Maybe."

She smiled to herself. *Another local sheriff who isn't about to be overrun by the FBI.* "I hear there may be a witness," she said.

He flipped the page and scribbled in the margin. "Maybe. The victim was Pamela Barnes, a thirty-three-year-old divorced mother who lived with her eleven-year-old-son, Alex. The boy wasn't hurt. The killer locked him in the closet, drugged him."

"What kind of drug?"

"Blood test showed ketamine. Special K is what they call it on the street."

"I know. It's an animal tranquilizer. I'm beginning to think our killer may have some veterinary training, or at least some connection with animals. That's the second time we've seen that same drug."

The sheriff looked up from his clipboard, showing his first sign of interest. "Where'd you see it before?"

"We had a similar situation out in San Francisco—

the Timothy Copeland murder. The killer drugged the victim's roommate and put him in the closet. Unfortunately, Copeland's roommate didn't remember a thing."

The sheriff tucked the clipboard under his arm. "Well, this may be a little different situation."

"How's that?"

"The boy seems to remember something."

Her heart thumped. "What does he say?"

"At this point he's basically incoherent. Which is understandable—he's pretty traumatized. But I think he knows a lot more than he's able to tell. A lot more than he probably wants to remember. The question is how to draw him out of his shell."

She thought for a moment, then her eyes lit with an idea. "I know just the right person to help you with that. One of the polygraph agents in Washington is a friend of mine. We went through the Academy together. She's trained in hypnosis, and she's excellent with children. We've used her in some of our abduction cases."

"Hypnosis? I don't want no hocus-pocus. I'd rather just wait and see if the kid remembers something."

"This isn't the kind of case where you can wait around for anything. We have a killer who we *know* is going to kill again."

"Maybe," he grumbled. "But that doesn't mean we should hold a séance."

"It's not a séance. We don't conjure up spirits or pump him full of drugs or anything like that. It's just a psychological tool to help the boy relax, remove his anxieties. If nothing else, do it for the boy. Let's find out what he knows right now, before the nightmares, so the counselors can help him deal with it."

He sighed, but her last point had seemed to make an impression. "I'm still not too keen on this."

"Let's leave it up to his father," said Victoria. "The boy's a minor. We'll need parental consent. If the father will go along—will you?"

He paused, mulling it over. "I suppose. But we've been working with this boy all day. Let's at least give him and his dad a night to grieve. We can meet in the station tomorrow morning."

"What time?" said Victoria.

"Say ten o'clock?"

"I'll call my friend. We'll be there."

The sheriff nodded. Victoria was gone in an instant, headed for her car phone before the sheriff could change his mind.

At dusk the mountain air had dropped below forty degrees. The cabin was cold enough to steam Rollins's breath, yet little beads of sweat had gathered on his upper lip. A trace of blood trickled from the corner of his mouth. He was still seated on the floor, braced against the post, hands tied behind his back. Hannon sat in the chair facing him, tapping the flat side of the blade into his gloved hand as he spoke.

"This is your last chance, Curt. How'd you hide the money?"

Rollins licked his dry lips, then swallowed hard. "It's like I said. I've seen lots of money laundering as a cop, so I knew how to do it."

Hannon dragged the blade like a razor over the whiskers on Curt's chin. "I want details."

Rollins's lips quivered. "I didn't think Posten would call in the cops, but just in case he did, I couldn't take cash from him in a suitcase. They might mark it. So I had him deposit it in Citibank. The first fifty thousand was cash, but the bigger deposits I had wire-transferred, so Posten wouldn't look like a drug smurf toting all that money. I withdrew some of it with my ATM card, just to get my hands on some cash. But for the bulk of it I wanted to do it right."

"What does that mean—doing it right?"

"Doing as many wire transfers as I could without eating up my funds, to throw any tracers off the trail. Three thousand to a bank in Wyoming, seven thousand to a bank in New York, and so on, every day. When I got to a quarter million, I wired it all offshore to Antigua. If anyone *was* tracing it, they sure couldn't get through Antigua's bank secrecy."

"How do you get it back?"

Rollins swallowed, felt his terror rise. He knew that if he gave Hannon the means to secure the money, he'd be issuing his own death sentence.

"I asked you a question, Curt," Hannon repeated, bearing down on each word. The tip of his knife pricked Rollins's skin.

"Antigua," Rollins said desperately, "I go to Antigua, withdraw the cash, buy a two-hundred-and-fifty-thousand-dollar boat for cash money, and sail it back to Miami." He was hyperventilating now. "The IRS doesn't track big cash purchases outside the United States. If the bank secrecy laws don't throw the stiffs off my trail, turning the cash into a yacht sure will. Then I either keep the boat, sell it, use it as collateral for another loan. Whatever I want."

"Where are all the account records?"

Rollins's eyes lit with faint hope. "My apartment in Brooklyn. Hey," he said, trying to smile, "I'll take you there, man. Come on, you and me. Like old times. Buddies. Partners."

Hannon looked at him coldly, then rose from the chair. His six-and-a-half-foot frame towered over the prisoner. He bent down and slowly lowered the knife. With a quick flick of the wrist he cut the ropes from Rollins's hands.

Rollins was shaking with fear and giddy relief. He rubbed his raw wrists and looked up gratefully.

"Let's go," said Hannon. "I want the records."

"I know you do," said Rollins as he wobbled to his feet. The apparent reprieve was allowing him to think more clearly, and he found himself improvising. "Of course, you know that without me the records won't do you any good. This isn't a normal bank with a checking account and ATM card. I went there personally to open up the account, and I set it up with special restrictions so that *I* have to go there *personally* to close it out. You can't wire it out or ask for a check in the mail. You *need* me. I'm the only guy who can walk into the bank and withdraw the funds."

Hannon's eyes narrowed. "You're a pretty good bluffer, considering the circumstances."

"It's no bluff. There are too many feds who want that money back. I couldn't take the risk that one of them would just walk in and withdraw it." He looked for signs that Hannon was buying his explanation, then continued. "Come on, old buddy. This will be a beautiful partnership. Let me show you the records, and then we'll talk about how to keep the gravy train running."

Hannon stared coldly, then his mouth curled with a semblance of a smile. "All right. You've bought yourself some time."

"Good. *Now* can I use the bathroom?"

"'Fraid not," he said, shaking his head. "Back in the trunk."

Rollins grimaced. "All the way to Brooklyn? Come on, man. It smells like those rats you threw in there."

Hannon was deadpan. "Like you, Curt. You smell exactly like a rat."

Chapter 33

hannon reached Brooklyn before 10:00 P.M. and parked the Volvo on the street outside the old brownstone flat. It was a mild night for February, much warmer than the Virginia mountains. The streets were wet, but the scattering of white that at first looked like snow was actually trash that had collected in the gutters. Several streetlamps were burned out, and the row of parallel-parked cars across the street looked as if they hadn't moved since Reagan was president. Fifty years ago it had probably been a quaint neighborhood, but times had changed.

Hannon saw no one walking the sidewalks, but he didn't want to risk opening the trunk. The Swedish car had a small hatch that opened in the middle of the backseat so that snow skis could lay flat, partly in the trunk and partly in the backseat. He popped the latch, then winced immediately at the pungent odor.

"Where's the key, Curt?" he said as he waved off the stench.

"Untie me, okay? I can't stand it in here."

"Shut up or I'll gag you again. Where's the key?" Seconds passed as Rollins shifted around in the darkness. The odor was getting worse. "Curt!"

"There's no key. Combination padlock. Twenty-eleven-seventeen."

Hannon closed the latch, crawled out of the car and headed up the cracked sidewalk. Rollins had the basement apartment, down the cement steps behind the black iron gate. It reminded Hannon of those stairs in Atlanta where he'd cut off that woman's finger for her diamond ring. The front door was padlocked, like Rollins had said. There was a hole where the old key lock had been. It looked like somebody had taken a crowbar to it.

He popped the lock and the door opened to an efficiency apartment that smelled nearly as bad as the trunk of his Volvo. It was garbage. Strange, he thought, the way everyone's garbage seemed to smell the same. He switched on the light and went straight to the kitchen, the source of the odor. He picked up the trash basket and dumped the mess in the middle of the floor. Old coffee grounds, milk cartons, tin cans and a big glob of something that looked like a year's supply of creamed corn spilled onto the linoleum. He shook everything out, then looked inside the can. As Rollins had promised, fastened securely to the bottom of the garbage can was a watertight pouch with something inside.

Hannon took the pouch to the counter and opened it carefully. Inside were three big manila envelopes. The first contained bank records. A detailed log showed a series of wire transfers through FedWire, CHIPS, and SWIFT, all funneled to a secret numbered account at Charter Bank in Antigua. Two hundred and fifty thousand dollars. It wasn't exactly like winning the lotto, but it gave him the option to ditch Valerie if she got too nosy. In truth, the amount wasn't the issue. It was simply *his* money; he'd earned it by giving old Curt something to snitch about.

The second envelope contained a birth certificate, Florida driver's license and Social Security card for a man named Ernest Gill. The picture, however, was Rollins with big eyeglasses, a heavy mustache, and added gray to his hair that made him look older. *The Citibank account.*

The third contained similar ID for "Eric Venters," including a U.S. passport, voter's registration and New York driver's license. Again, the picture was Rollins wearing a convincing disguise. *The Antigua account.*

Hannon smiled as he stuffed the envelopes back in the pouch. Decision time. He could let Rollins be Venters and withdraw the funds, or *he* could become Venters and do it himself. The birth certificate and Social Security card were reusable—no photo, and they looked legitimate. All he needed was a passport, which in New York was as easy as finding pastrami on rye. He could become Venters before the sun came up.

The open issue, of course, was the height. Rollins was five feet ten inches tall, and as he was being put back into the trunk back at the lodge he'd mentioned that the bank had some record on file with the customer's—Rollins's—height on it. That could be true. But from what Hannon knew about offshore banks, they'd be unlikely to focus on height—and even if they checked, what were the chances they'd challenge him?

That left just one question: What to *do* with Curt.

Hannon sealed up the pouch and started toward the door, smirking at the possibilities.

Just after 11:00 P.M. Valerie St. Pierre returned home. An afternoon of shopping at the mall had turned into dinner and a movie with her girlfriends. Her face was flushed red from a little too much wine, and she was humming a tune from *Phantom* when she dropped the bags from Lord & Taylor on the kitchen table.

"Charlie?" she called out.

The house was quiet. She checked the den, then flipped on the hall light and started upstairs to the bedroom.

"Honey, come look what I bought you."

The bedroom was dark, and so was the bathroom. A puzzled look came over her face, then she noticed the message light blinking on the answering machine. She sat on the edge of the bed and hit the play button.

"Hi, babe, it's Charlie." She perked up immediately at the sound of Hannon's voice. "I'm really sorry, but I got an emergency call from that accounting firm I did the network for. Some weird computer virus has the whole system running slower than shit. Anyway, I had to drive to Pittsburgh this afternoon. Not sure when I'll be back. But I'll make it up to you. Promise."

She switched off the machine and fell back against the pillows, sighing with disappointment. She reached across the comforter for the television remote on the nightstand, then stopped as she noticed his leather flight bag resting in the corner. It was still lying where he'd tossed it this morning, beside the skimpy white tennis dress he'd ripped right off her. He'd always taken the bag with him on his other trips. She wondered why he hadn't this time.

She slid across the bed, then knelt on the floor beside the bag. She felt a little like a snoop and hesitated, but her excitement grew as she ran her finger lightly over the leather straps. Slowly, she unzipped it and peeked inside.

There was a razor and toothbrush and other uninteresting stuff. She smiled to herself as she sniffed his cologne. The extra pair of baggy boxer shorts triggered a smirk. He was too embarrassed to wear the bikini briefs she'd given him. Not much of a bulge for such a big man. That didn't bother her, however. He knew what she really liked, and whenever he buried his face between her thighs he was her golden boy with the magic tongue.

Magic, and tireless. Lustful thoughts of him putting her flat on her back brought tingles inside. His muscular body would glide over her breasts and stomach and slowly disappear below the vaginal mound. She imagined him sliding the pillow gently beneath her ass, then grabbing both cheeks with his huge hands and pulling her toward him as her body arched to receive his kiss. On impulse, she touched herself through tight designer jeans. Lightly at first, then gradually harder, rubbing back and forth in the way he liked to tease her. Her heart pounded at the first sign of wetness, but her hand quickly pulled away. The drapes were still open, she suddenly realized, and with the bedroom lamp shining brightly someone outside could easily see her.

For a split second that possibility seemed strangely exciting. Still on her knees, she was frozen between this titillating new freedom and her old feelings of embarrassment that had always cramped her fantasies. She took a deep breath, afraid of her own feelings. No man had ever driven her so far. She'd wait, she decided. Maybe he'd come home early.

She rose to one knee to close the drapes, then stopped. In the bag's side pocket she noticed that self-help book again—the one he'd joked about never having read. Her eyes brightened with renewed curiosity as she slid the book from the pocket and cracked it open. Strangely, the pages felt stiff, like maybe he really hadn't ever read it. She flipped to the page marked by the cocktail napkin. It looked used, like he'd had a drink. A message was scrawled on the back in ballpoint pen. She lifted it carefully from between the pages and read it to herself. *Don't be a stranger. Victoria . . . 555-9511.*

Her eyes flared, and the napkin shook in her hand as she read it one more time. Tears welled in her eyes, but she looked like she wanted to scream, not cry. She threw down the book and fell back on her butt.

"You slut," she said in a voice filled with anger. "Keep your hands off *him.*"

On Thursday morning Hannon headed through Long Island City in western Queens on his way to La

Guardia Airport. Outside it was clear and comfortably cool, but with the Volvo's heater cranked up to eighty-five degrees, he was sweating through his shirt and sticking to the leather seat. He would have liked to crack a window, but he didn't want to chance it. His precious cargo had to stay warm.

He stopped at the light at the busy intersection of Jackson Avenue and Vernon Boulevard, the commercial center of the neighborhood. Huge four-barreled stacks of the old Pennsylvania Railroad generating plant towered above butcher shops, diners and modest shingle homes. A steady stream of commuters rushed along the sidewalks, disappearing into the subway like rats into their holes. *Rats, all of them*, he thought. Like Curt.

He turned down a side street by a deserted warehouse, scoping for a secluded place. A stretch of boarded-up buildings ahead looked promising. He slowed as he rounded the corner, then turned quickly down a narrow alley. The car came to a stop behind an oversized Dumpster filled with planks, charred roofing shingles and twisted pipes that had been yanked from the buildings.

Hannon left the motor running and the heat blasting as he stepped from the car and closed the door. He raised his arms up over his head. The cool air felt good on his sweaty pits. He walked around back and popped the trunk.

Rollins grimaced at the sudden burst of light; Hannon winced at the overwhelming stench. A white rat scurried beneath the blanket.

"Where are we?" asked Rollins weakly. All that time in the trunk had taken its toll.

"Antigua."

Rollins blinked hard as his eyes struggled to adjust to the morning sunlight. He didn't even have the strength to parry Hannon's sarcasm with a reply.

"Sorry about the accommodations, *partner*," Hannon said.

Rollins lay on his side, hands behind his back. He looked up anxiously, then managed a semblance of a smile. "Does that mean you'll untie me?"

He placed his foot on the bumper, raised his pant leg and unsheathed the knife. "What do you think?" he said flatly.

Rollins swallowed hard, his eyes nervously darting back and forth from the diving knife to Hannon's stoic expression. With lightning speed Hannon lunged forward. Rollins squealed, then gasped at the sight of the little white rat impaled on the knife. Hannon flung the bloody rodent aside, then wiped the blade clean in the blanket.

"Like I said, we're partners now," he said with a flat smile. "You and I are going to Antigua."

Rollins sighed so heavily he trembled with relief. "You mean it?"

"You bet I do . . . Mr. Venters."

Rollins smiled smugly. "Pretty clever, huh? All that stuff's first quality. I went to the Social Security office myself to get the card issued. Come on," he said as he pointed with a nod. "Cut me loose."

Hannon cut the ropes from around his ankles, then from the wrists.

Rollins extended a hand. "Help me outta here."

"No way," said Hannon. "We may be partners, but

I refuse to ride in the front seat with you smelling like a rat."

"Shit, man. I can't stand it in here no more."

"Just a few more minutes. I promise. This is the last time you'll ever have to ride in the trunk."

Rollins grumbled, then sighed with resignation. "All right. But if I'm in here more than five minutes, our fifty-fifty split becomes sixty-forty."

"Whatever you say, partner." They exchanged smiles as he closed the trunk.

Cautiously, he opened the rear door on the driver's side. The wave of heat hit him in the face like a blast from the tropics. A large canvas bag stretched across the entire seat, draping partially onto the floor. The cold air from outside set it in motion—a slow, rolling motion, like lovers in a sleeping bag.

EXOTIC PETS OF QUEENS, the bag read.

Hannon snugged up his leather gloves, then took the knife and cut the drawstring at the near end. The motion increased, and part of the bag slid up from the floor and onto the seat. He made an opening the size of his fist, being careful to point it away from him. Out popped the head of a Burmese python.

He grabbed it from behind. It flicked its tongue.

"That's it, boy. Get that tongue going. Smell the rat." He opened the latch in the backseat that led to the trunk. This time, the strong odor pleased him. He could feel the snake pulling toward the trunk. Its tongue flicked again and again, picking up the scent. He'd handled plenty of snakes as a teenager while helping his mom at the veterinary clinic, and he could always tell the aggressive ones. It was clear now that the pet shop owner hadn't lied: This one had been raised on *live* prey.

"Dinner time, Monty. Go get the rat."

He released the head, and the snake speared through the opening. He watched with fascination as all thirteen feet slithered through the hole. Its skin was smooth and beautifully patterned. The body was skinny, then fat—as big around the middle as a good-sized watermelon—then skinny again.

A bloodcurdling scream emerged from the trunk. "Frank, *no!*"

Hannon slapped the latch closed. He laughed to himself as the screams grew louder and more horrific. Lots of kicking and thrashing about, like Tarzan wrestling the giant anaconda in some jungle stream. It lasted nearly a minute.

Then all was quiet. Eerily quiet.

Hannon imagined the snake coiling around Curt's body several times, pinning his arms at his sides, squeezing tighter and tighter each time its prey gasped for air. A death grip. Right about now, the distensible jaws were unlocking. Snakes, he knew, always swallowed their prey headfirst. Curt might even be alive as its gaping mouth covered his hair, slithered over his face and wrapped around his throat. It would hold him that way for hours, trying to work its mouth around his shoulders and swallow him whole. It would probably never get past his head, but it would die trying. Dinner for this carnivore was the biggest piece of meat it could fit in its mouth. To it, Curt was nothing but a big fat rat. Snakes could be so stupid.

Almost as stupid as Curt.

Chapter 34

V ictoria and her friend Freeda Schnabel arrived at the Fairfax County sheriff's office promptly at 10:00 A.M. They'd met ten years ago during their initial sixteen-week training session at Quantico, where they shared a dorm room. After graduation they'd gone to different field offices—Victoria to New Orleans and Freeda to Sacramento—but they'd kept in touch over the years, keeping tabs on each other's career paths. They'd ultimately landed a relatively few miles apart, but the gap between the Training Division in Quantico and Headquarters in Washington wasn't necessarily measured in miles.

As Victoria had expected, Freeda did a first-rate job of convincing the boy's father that hypnosis was the way to go. Freeda was five years older than Victoria, a mother of three who had worked as a family counselor in Los Angeles before joining the FBI. She hadn't lost her touch.

At 10:40 A.M., a red light blinked on over the door to the police interrogation room. It was a signal from

Freeda. She'd wanted no one but herself and the father in the room with the boy while he was going under. Victoria and Sheriff Woodson quietly shuffled into a cubicle adjacent to the interrogation room. Hidden behind a one-way mirror, they could see inside the room, but they couldn't be seen. That way, if the boy suddenly woke up, he would see only Freeda and his father—not a roomful of strangers.

Eleven-year-old Alex Barnes was slouching in his chair, eyes shut, as if he were fighting sleep. He was a thin boy with freckles on his cheeks and a little turned-up nose. He wore blue jeans and an oversized shirt. His high-top, Velcro-strap sneakers were the expensive and cool kind that kids could pump with air for a better fit. Victoria wondered how happy it had made his mother to be able to buy them for him.

Freeda sat directly across from Alex, with the boy's father right at her side. He was a plain fellow, somewhat on the chubby side and lacking a chin. Alex took after his mother, thought Victoria.

The sheriff glanced at Victoria and said quietly, "You think we'll get anything?"

"I don't know. My guess is that the killer wasn't quite sure how much ketamine to give to a child. He apparently didn't give him enough. The boy could have heard something he wasn't supposed to hear."

The sheriff reached across the table and switched on the speaker. Victoria could suddenly hear everything that was said on the other side of the one-way mirror.

"Alex," Freeda said in a soothing voice. "What do you see?"

The boy just shook his head.

"Can you see anything?"

"It's dark," his voice quivered.

"Where are you?"

His shoulders shrugged. "I dunno."

"How do you feel?"

"Sleepy."

Behind the mirror, the sheriff glanced at Victoria and rolled his eyes. "Of course he feels sleepy. He's hypnotized."

"No," said Victoria. "It's the tranquilizer the killer gave him. She's taking him back to the closet."

Freeda moved closer to her subject. "I want you to think hard, Alex. Think about what you can hear."

He shrugged again, this time in a very exaggerated motion—like a child who is hiding something.

Freeda paused, then asked, "Can you hear anything?"

The boy said nothing, didn't move.

"Tell me what you can hear, Alex."

His body went rigid. "Time," he said in a very faint voice.

Freeda moved closer, modulating her tone. "Time for what, dear?"

His little face shriveled into a pained expression. "Need to know . . . time. Tell him! Just tell him, Mom!"

His sudden shrillness chilled everyone in the room. He took several short, panicky breaths, and then there was silence. Cautiously, Freeda pressed forward. "What else, Alex?"

His lips quivered, seemingly with fear. "Color."

"You're seeing colors?"

"What color! *What color was it!*" He was shouting at the top of his lungs, squirming in his chair. In a split second he cowered and covered his ears—shaking but saying nothing.

Freeda backed away, allowing him to recover. Victoria watched with trepidation from behind the glass.

"What the hell kind of gibberish is this?" the sheriff muttered into Victoria's ear.

"It's not gibberish," she said quietly. "It sounds like he overheard some kind of interrogation—the killer talking to his victim."

"You've got a serial killer who wants to know what time it is?"

"Just listen," said Victoria.

As the boy sobbed and sunk lower in his chair, the room filled with an uneasy silence. His face grimaced, as if he were shutting out sounds, trying *not* to listen. Suddenly, in spastic motion, he screamed and fell to the floor.

"Mom!"

His father sprang from his seat and rushed forward. "That's enough!"

The boy came to, roused by the sound of his father's voice. Victoria closed her eyes as the man hugged his trembling son.

"Well," said the sheriff, "that was good for nothing. Unless you call a traumatized child 'progress.'"

Victoria didn't feel like arguing with the sheriff about whether it was better for the boy to open up than to keep it inside. For the moment, she just wanted to be *away* from it. She headed out to the lobby and disappeared into the ladies' room.

Two minutes later, Freeda caught up with her. "You okay, Victoria?"

She was leaning over the sink, staring at her tired face in the mirror. She glanced at Freeda in the mirror. "Yeah, I'm fine."

"You don't look fine."

She straightened up, still looking in the mirror. "You know me. I'm usually pretty stoic. But every now and then, it gets to me. Seeing an innocent child like that, emotionally scarred for life." She paused, then turned and looked her friend in the eye. "It reminds me of a niece I used to have."

Freeda's eyes clouded with sympathy. "I'm sorry. I didn't know about that." She moved closer. "Was it recent? Your losing her, I mean."

"Seems like it. It's actually been quite a while. She was eight. She'd be twenty now. Twenty and beautiful and with her whole life ahead of her." She blinked hard, suddenly full of memories. "Everyone used to say she looked a lot like me."

Freeda laid her hand on her shoulder. "You want to tell me what happened?"

Victoria took a deep breath to regain her composure, then shook her head. "Let's just say it wasn't the serial killers that made me want to work for the Child Abduction and Serial Killer Unit."

She flashed a sad smile of gratitude, then headed for the door.

*   *   *

Hannon left New York at noon, one o'clock Antigua time. In Puerto Rico he changed planes to the Antigua-based LIAT, short for Leeward Islands Air Transport, locally known as "Luggage in Another Town."

Luggage, however, wasn't a concern. He traveled lightly with just an overnight bag. He'd burned all his clothes back in New York, along with the big rat, the little rat and a thirteen-foot snake. By now the Volvo was in a thousand pieces, having gone to a chop shop in Queens for a quick two grand. It was his cardinal rule: Destroy all evidence. Once the deed was done, never drive the same car, wear the same shoes, or even use the same toothpaste—*ever*, again. True to form, his khaki slacks, cordovan shoes and navy blue blazer over a pink oxford-cloth shirt were all brand-new, purchased just that morning with cash from Rollins's apartment. It was typical West Indies business attire.

The plane landed in Antigua at 5:22 P.M., about an hour before sunset. Bird International Airport was a busy hub for air traffic between islands, the O'Hare of the Caribbean, but that was like calling Little Rock the New York of Arkansas. A steady stream of small one- and two-engine propeller planes took off and landed as he walked across the runway and into the terminal. Inside, the customs officer didn't even stamp his passport. Turned out, United States citizens didn't need one. A driver's license and birth certificate were good enough.

"Purpose of your visit?" asked the customs officer inside the glass booth. He had a hint of an English accent. The tone, however, was decidedly mechanical, as might be expected on a tiny island of ninety thousand people that was besieged by half a million tourists each year.

"Business," said Hannon. Then he smirked with an afterthought. "*And* pleasure."

He rented a Jeep at the airport and drove south across the island. The British leeward islands had a much flatter terrain than the volcano-scarred windwards, so the roads had fewer treacherous curves. Potholes, however, were a nuisance, and as he swerved from side to side to avoid the craters he had to keep reminding himself to drive on the left, like in England. Through the island's dry interior he passed rolling scrub and the hollow cones of decaying old windmills. They were among the few remaining structures from the dark days of slavery and sugarcane plantations. Even then, as now, the spectacular coastline was the main attraction. Antigua boasted 366 beaches in all.

Hannon took a room at the Admiral's Inn, a restored eighteenth-century Georgian inn that was the centerpiece of touristy Nelson's Dockyard. The dockyard was a historic compound of restored shops, hotels and restaurants on famous English Harbour, like a small-scale Williamsburg, Virginia, with a nautical flare. Rooms at the Ad were away from the best beaches, so they were relatively cheap by Antiguan standards. More important, he was just a short drive away from the Charter Bank, where at nine o'clock Monday morning there would be a quarter million dollars for Eric Venters.

Hannon left his garment bag and jacket in the room and headed to the outdoor bar on the elevated terrace. The sunset crowd was enjoying tropical drinks and dancing to melodious steel drum music beneath shady Australian pines. The bartender was a lively woman who moved behind the bar with rhythm in her step. She was in her mid-twenties, Hannon guessed, with long brown hair and a pink hibiscus blossom tucked behind her ear. Her dark, mysterious look exuded a kind of exotic beauty found in island women of mixed ancestry. She had every man's attention in her tight white shorts and flower-print shirt knotted beneath her rounded breasts. Hannon liked what he saw, and he started a casual round of across-the-room eye contact. She broke away from a regular customer at the other end of the bar and came his way.

"How about a fig daiquiri, mate?" she said.

He made a face, like it sounded gross.

She laughed. "It's okay. In Antigua a fig's a banana."

"All right. You talked me into it: I'll buy one for you."

She smiled. "Sorry. Can't drink while I work."

"How about after work?"

"Maybe." Her tone was encouraging. She put a napkin on the bar and casually brushed his hand, as if by accident. "So what do you usually drink?"

"A belt-and-suspenders martini."

"What's that?"

"Shaken *and* stirred."

She cracked a smile and reached for the blender. "Tell you what, if you don't like the fig daiquiri, the martini's on me."

"Can I trust you?" Hannon asked.

"Of course," she said. "The question is, can I trust you?"

"Only one way to find out," he said, grinning.

She burrowed her tongue into her cheek and gave him a sly look. Her smirk turned seductive as she leaned into the bar and gave him an eyeful of cleavage. "You're pretty bold," she said coyly.

He chuckled lightly and looked her right in the eye. "You'd be surprised. I guarantee it." The smile slowly faded from his face, and he turned serious.

She smiled awkwardly, blinking at his stare. She poured his daiquiri, then glanced toward the far end of the bar. "Be back in a sec," she said.

"Hey, what's your name?" he said as she started away.

"Dominique," she replied, glancing back over her shoulder.

He nodded, as if he liked it. He watched as she walked toward the other customers, then turned his attention to the long strand of black hair in his hand. She hadn't even noticed his plucking it from her head. Their eyes connected again from a distance, and she blushed with a smile. He smiled back suavely as he rolled the strand of hair between his thumb and finger. Then, discreetly, he turned his head and tucked it beneath his tongue.

Chapter 35

On Saturday afternoon Victoria dropped her muddy baseball cleats at the kitchen door, then shuffled across the linoleum floor in stocking feet to the refrigerator. Softball season was still eight weeks away, but a sudden burst of springlike weather had given her coach a brainstorm for a Saturday scrimmage. Her hair was twisted in a ponytail, flowing out the hole in the back of her cap. Across the front of her jersey in bold red script was the team logo, *Long Balls*, a name that could conjure up some rather obscene images until you finally visualized a long *fly* ball sailing out of the ballpark.

Considering she hadn't played since Labor Day, she'd made a decent showing in a losing effort. Two for four, three RBIs, and a big red strawberry on her left buttock from sliding into third base like an idiot on semifrozen ground. Starting at the waist, she carefully peeled down the tight pants for a peek, wincing with pain at the bruised and bloody proof that buns of steel weren't always an advantage.

Now that she'd seen the damage, it hurt like hell.

She hobbled to the freezer and grabbed a bag of frozen peas. She'd had the same bag for months; frozen veggies made great ice packs. She leaned over the kitchen table, cringing and cooing as she held her home remedy in place. Her left cheek was sending mixed messages, as if it couldn't decide whether the cold was worse or made it feel better. It would definitely keep down the swelling, however. By Tuesday, she might even be sitting again.

The phone rang. It was hanging on the wall, completely across the room. She laughed out loud, suddenly imagining herself in one of those happy-smiley telephone commercials, unable to get to the phone because she was slumped over the kitchen table with a bag of frozen peas slapped on her ass. Don't *you* wish you had call return?

She heard her machine answer, but the caller hung up. A minute later, the phone rang again. Someone obviously didn't want to talk to her machine. She tossed the peas aside and darted for the phone.

"Hello," she said through clenched teeth. She was in that "only-hurts-for-a-little-while" phase, like when the Band-Aid takes your hair with it.

"Is Charlie there?" It was a woman's voice, one Victoria didn't recognize.

"I'm sorry, there's no Charlie at this number." She grimaced and was about to hang up.

"I know he doesn't *live* there. I just want to know if he's there."

Victoria hesitated. The tone sounded accusatory, agitated. "Who is this?"

"A friend of Charlie's. Are you a friend of his too, Victoria?"

"How'd you know my name?"

"Because you gave Charlie your phone number."

Her skin was tingling, her mind racing. "I told you: I don't know a Charlie."

"That's a lie. I saw your little message on the cocktail napkin. 'Don't be a stranger.' And you wrote your name and number."

Victoria blinked hard, confused. She remembered *that,* of course. But he'd said his name was Mike, not Charlie. "I have no idea what you're talking about. But if you ever call here again, I'm calling the police." She slammed down the phone and took a deep breath.

You idiot, she thought. She'd taught self-defense classes to women, warning them never to give their phone number to strangers. Three vodka tonics had apparently turned her into Agent "Do as I say, not as I do." He'd seemed charming and was very good-looking, but that was no excuse. She felt like that skydiving instructor she'd heard about on the news who'd jumped out of an airplane without his parachute. Worrying about the safety of others is a good way to forget about your own.

Part of her said just to ignore it, but if she'd run into an insanely jealous spouse or girlfriend, it might make sense to take precautions and do a little damage control. She hobbled across the kitchen floor and into the master bedroom, where the caller ID box rested on the nightstand between the telephone and a framed snapshot of her mother. She hit the retrieve button. Names and corresponding phone numbers instantly appeared on the digital display terminal, identifying her last three callers. The last two, counting the hang-up, were from the same woman. The name, however, meant nothing to her.

She picked up the phone and dialed a friend who was an investigative analyst with the Bureau.

"Hi, Sam, it's Victoria Santos."

"Hey, how's it going? Long time."

"I know it probably seems like I only call when I need a favor, but I need another one."

"Okay," he chuckled. "I'll put it on your tab."

"I just got this strange call at home," she said pensively. "Don't know who it was. I was hoping maybe you could do a background check. Valerie St. Pierre is the name."

"Sure. When do you need it?"

She thought for a moment, and the more she thought about it, the more it tickled her instincts. There was something *really* weird about that call.

"As soon as you can get it."

Hannon slept alone in his room until one o'clock that Saturday afternoon. The driving, flying and searching for Burmese pythons over the past few days had finally caught up with him. He purchased a pair of cotton chino shorts, sandals and a plaid madras shirt from the men's shop in the hotel, then showered, dressed, and ate a late lunch in his room while looking over the documents for the account at the Charter Bank.

At four-fifteen he reached over to the nightstand and picked up the cocktail napkin on which Dominique had written her phone number. Her shift last night had run past midnight, but they'd talked for an hour or so, until he was able to coax her number out of her. She was off tonight, so he called to see if she'd show him around the island.

"It's a date," she said, and Hannon chuckled at the way she'd put it.

He picked her up in his Jeep from her St. Johns apartment around five. She was wearing cutoff jean shorts, with a white fishnet shirt that covered a yellow bathing-suit top. Her breasts seemed fuller and rounder than he'd remembered, and she seemed to like the fact that it was so obvious he'd noticed. The pink hibiscus flower was gone from her hair, but the long brown locks draped over her shoulders, caressing her skin with her every move.

Hannon helped her with the blanket and cooler she'd packed. "To the beach?" he asked.

"No. Boggy Peak. There isn't time to tour the whole island, but you can see lots from up there. I thought we'd drink a few beers and watch the sunset."

He smiled with approval, then steered into traffic, shooting her a glance every now and then to admire the way the wind blew her hair in the open Jeep.

The road from St. Johns skirted the coastline, past some of the island's finest west coast beaches, in the lee of the Shekerley Mountains, Antigua's biggest hills. Dominique took them up the southern entrance, a steep road inland from Cade's Bay. Fields of black pineapple stretched on either side of the road, while baked mud roads twisted inland through the island's lushest and most attractive area. The southwest hills were the closest thing Antigua had to a rain forest. As they climbed Boggy Peak to thirteen hundred feet they were soon surrounded by elephant ear and colorful tropical flora.

They parked at the end of the road, then walked the rest of the way through a stand of tall trees and thick bushy undergrowth. The path, if one existed, was indiscernible. She led the way through the overgrowth, but with his height Hannon was banging his forehead on low-hanging branches. Finally, they reached a small clearing on the side of the hill, with a view of the Caribbean that stretched south to Guadaloupe and north to St. Kitts. To the west, straight out, the sun was an orange ball hovering over the sea.

Dominique spread the blanket out and tossed him a cold beer. "Greatest show on earth," she said. "Come sit."

Hannon sat beside her on the blanket. She was leaning back on her elbows, her long legs stretched out in front of her. The hike had them both perspiring a little, and he could see her brown nipples faintly through her top. They sipped cold beer as she pointed out the sights. Frye's Point, Darkwood Beach, and Johnson's Point were the nearest beaches, mile-long strips of sand that had yet to be developed.

"When I was a little girl, there were lots of beaches like those right down there. If your family drove up for a Sunday picnic and somebody was already there, you just left them alone and drove on to the next one. These days, you're lucky to find only one *hotel* per beach." Her eyes drifted slowly toward the horizon, where the sun was beginning to dip into the glistening Caribbean. "This is truly my favorite place in the whole world," she said with a nostalgic grin. "Sometimes I wish I could just stay here forever."

Hannon smirked, then finished his beer and opened another, staring down at the sailboats below. From this height, they cut across the blue-green waters like graceful white swans.

"Hey," she said, her eyes brightening. "Maybe we'll see the green flash."

"What's that? Some Antiguan comic-book hero?"

"No," she laughed. Then she sat up quickly, excited he'd never heard of it. "It's an island tradition. A little ribbon of green color stretches across the horizon just as the last bit of sun slips away for the night. You can only see it in places like the Caribbean, where there's no dust or pollution. Even then, it's hard to see it. But if you do, they say it brings you luck."

He shot her a glance, thinking her enthusiasm peculiar. "I don't really believe in luck."

"You should," she said as she scooted closer to him on the blanket. Her eyes were playing games with him. "I bet you have all kinds of luck and don't even know it. Has anyone ever read your palm?"

He shook his head.

"Mind if I do?" she said with a sly smile.

He hesitated, then relaxed his hand as she took it gently in hers and uncurled his fingers. She was sitting cross-legged, staring down into his palm.

"Wow," she said as she dragged her nail along one of the creases. "I can see you're going to be a rich man. Or maybe you are already."

"Soon," he quipped, thinking of the Charter Bank.

She sipped her beer, then found another crease. "Here's your lifeline, right here."

"Long?"

"Looks to me like you should've keeled over yesterday. Kidding," she said, giving him a friendly elbow. "Yes, it's long. And I'd venture to say it's a happy one, too."

"What makes you say that?"

She flattened her hand against his, comparing size. "Because you've got the biggest hands I've ever seen," she said, eyebrows dancing. "A girl doesn't have to be a palm reader to know what *that* means."

He quickly withdrew his hand. His expression turned cold as he stood up, towering over her.

"What's wrong?" she said, looking up nervously.

He was sneering, all traces of warmth having vanished from his face. "That's what you think, isn't it? Big tall guy. Must be hung like a mule."

"I was just teasing."

"I don't like to be teased."

"Sorry, mate. Let's just drop it, okay?"

He drew a deep breath, but his face flushed red. "That's what you came out here for, isn't it?"

"What?"

"To see the biggest cock you've ever seen."

"No," she winced. Her lip started to quiver, a combination of fear and anger. "I don't care about that."

His eyes narrowed and filled with contempt. "You *liar*."

She swallowed hard, suddenly afraid to speak. "I—

I think I want to go home now." She pushed herself up, but he knocked her right back down.

"*Siddown!*" She started to squirm away, but he stepped hard on her ankle, pinning her on the spot, as if he had a rat by the tail.

"You're hurting me." She reached for her ankle, but his look made her back off.

"What did you think, this would be some kind of X-rated freak show? Something you could go back and tell your girlfriends about?"

She cowered against the blanket. Her voice trembled. "Take it easy, all right? I won't tell anyone anything. Just let me go."

"Don't *lie* to me! You talked. I know *you talked*!"

A tear ran down her cheek. "I don't even know you! What are you talking about?"

"I'm talking about me! You fucking talked about *me*."

Her fear became panic as she watched his expression turn steadily colder, to something beyond reason. It was as if he were speaking to someone else.

She brushed a mosquito from her hair, then finally forced herself to look him in the eye.

"Look," she said in a desperate tone, "I'm sorry if I said something wrong. Please. I'll walk myself back. I know the way. Just let me go."

"Go?" he said with a sadistic scowl. "I thought you said you wanted to stay here forever."

Her mouth opened, but the words didn't come. It was getting darker, harder to see, but she watched closely as he reached into his pocket.

"Forever's a long time, Dominique."

Her eyes were locked on the hand slipping from

his pocket. He had something wadded in a white cloth napkin.

His voice became lower, more threatening. "Forever," he said. "Hasn't anyone ever warned you to be careful what you ask for?"

He dropped the napkin, revealing the knife.

She was about to scream, but he was right on top of her, pinning her to the ground. She couldn't shout, couldn't bite, couldn't even breathe. Her skull seemed to flatten beneath the pressure, against the ground. It covered her entire face, half her head, from chin to crown.

It was the biggest hand she'd ever seen.

Chapter 36

the Charter Bank of Antigua opened for business at nine o'clock Monday morning, but Hannon didn't want to draw too much attention to himself by being the first customer of the day. He ate a leisurely English breakfast of poached eggs and tomatoes alone in his room while reviewing the bank records he'd taken from Rollins.

At five minutes till ten, he started to apply the disguise.

His Aryan complexion was already darker from the Clinique self-tanner he'd applied before going to bed. Brown contact lenses covered his icy blue eyes. A latex cap and brown wig went over the sandy blond hair. The epoxy irritated his nostrils, but he shook it off, knowing that the rubberized nose would make his chiseled profile unrecognizable. The padding strapped around his waist gave him a middle-aged paunch. Finally, a thick brown mustache and tortoiseshell eyeglasses made him look almost Middle Eastern.

He fumbled in his briefcase for the right passport. The disguise was hot for the tropics, not something he'd want to wear all day. Accordingly, he had two sets of identification. He'd entered the country as Charles Ackroyd, "Charlie," the Nordic god who had won over Valerie's heart and wallet back in Maryland. He would enter the bank, however, as Eric Venters—the tall, dark, and not so handsome creation staring back at him in the mirror. *Perfect.*

Around 11:00 A.M. he arrived by Jeep in St. Johns, the island's capital and only real city. Nearly a third of the island's population resided in the old city that had stood for centuries on gentle slopes above the large bay. Near the boatyard, fishermen made lobster pots and mended their nets. Many older streets were still lined with traditional two-story buildings of wood and stone with balconies that hung over the narrow, cracked sidewalks. The Charter Bank was in a modern strip mall near a cluster of clothing shops and computer stores.

Hannon parked his Jeep in a space directly in front of the bank. He was dressed in the same khaki slacks and blue blazer he'd worn on the plane from New York, but he had a fresh white shirt and conservative striped necktie for added credibility. The drive along All Saints Road had been comfortably cool in the open-air Jeep, but now that he'd stopped he was feeling the heat. He dabbed the sweat from his brow and started toward the mall.

Hannon stopped at the curb, somewhat surprised by what he saw. The Charter Bank didn't appear to be much of a bank at all. It shared a main entrance with a dozen other banks, all with their small signs posted outside the door—everything from "Charter Bank of Antigua" to something as silly as "Joe's Bank of the Caribbean." He'd heard of offshore havens, but somehow this was on a much smaller scale than even he had anticipated.

He opened the glass door and stepped inside. It had no leather couches, expensive artwork or rich wood paneling. The walls were bare beige and the furnishings simple. Two women were busy at computer terminals on metal desks. A man dressed in casual slacks and a short-sleeve shirt was talking on the telephone near the fax machines. Hannon noticed no tellers, guards or security cameras. He felt as if he'd entered a travel agency rather than a bank.

One of the women rose from her desk. "Can I help you, sir?"

"Yes," he said with assurance. "My name's Eric Venters. I'm here to close my account. But first I'd like to enter my safe-deposit box."

"I can handle the box for you," she said. "You'll have to see Mr. Jeffries about closing the account. Come with me, please."

Hannon followed her to a cubicle in the corner. It was a small area of privacy where one customer at a time could enter his safe-deposit box. Hannon bristled as she checked his identification—passport and driver's license—against the records on file, fearing she might focus on the height discrepancy that Rollins had warned him about. It went smoothly, however. As he'd expected, the bank had a written application, but no picture ID on file with which to compare his passport.

That kind of formality would definitely have scared away the drug-smuggling, money-laundering clientele that kept this particular offshore haven in business. In two minutes she returned with a rectangular metal box. She placed it on the table in front of him.

"Just signal me when you're through," she said.

"Thank you." Hannon looked around discreetly before entering the box, to make sure he had total privacy. He slid open the metal top and smiled as he peered inside. It was completely empty, save for a 9mm pistol and three ammunition clips.

Without question, the most dangerous part of Rollins's plan was the physical retrieval of the money. As yet, there was no reason to believe that the *Tribune* had called in the FBI. Even if it had, Antigua's bank secrecy laws probably would keep them off the trail. It was no secret, however, that bank secrecy could conceivably be broken by well-paid informants. Even Rollins had been savvy enough to make sure he was armed in case something went wrong.

Hannon removed his jacket and wrapped it around the gun and ammunition clip. It muffled the distinctive sound of a gun being loaded. He put the jacket back on and tucked the loaded gun in his breast pocket. The two other clips went in his pants pocket. He closed the box, then stood up to signal that he was finished. It took a moment to get the woman's attention, since the bank was very sensitive to its customers' privacy. Finally, she came.

"Mr. Jeffries will see you about closing your account now," she said.

Hannon nodded with appreciation and headed

across the room. Jeffries was a portly man, roughly twenty years older and a foot shorter than Hannon. He had thin, jet black hair but a salt-and-pepper mustache that obviously didn't get the same dye he used on his head. He greeted Hannon with a firm handshake and polite smile, then offered the chair facing his desk.

"Mrs. Flannery told me you wish to close your account with us," he said in a distinctly West Indian accent.

"Yes. I'd like the balance in cash, please. American dollars."

"Cash," he said with a slightly troubled look. "I see. Well, that shouldn't present too much of a problem, I hope. At all events, I've taken the liberty of pulling up your account information. We show a balance of two hundred thirty-eight thousand dollars. Pity how those wire transfer fees add up, isn't it?" he said with a banker's smile. Drawing no response from Hannon, he slid three standard forms across the desk. "If you'll just sign here, here, and here, please."

Hannon looked it over, then signed carefully. He'd practiced for more than an hour that morning, trying to get it perfect.

The banker smiled. "All right. If you'll excuse me for a moment." He rose and headed across the room, then disappeared through a locked door to the back. Hannon sat quietly, but he remained alert. He presumed the bank was checking the signature on file. After a minute the door opened, and Jeffries was still smiling. A good sign.

He laid a friendly hand on Hannon's shoulder. "I

need just another moment," he said. Then he headed for the computer terminals across the room.

Hannon watched out of the corner of his eye. He couldn't see the terminal screen, and he wasn't sure what he was doing. Jeffries had said he'd already taken the liberty of pulling up his account information. He glanced across the desk to see what was there. The account application, a record of account activity—and a photocopy of the signature card. He felt a tug of suspicion. If the signature card was here, what had Jeffries been doing back *there*?

He glanced again across the room. Jeffries was on the telephone. He was too far away, however, to overhear the conversation. Hannon tried to read his lips or even the expression on his face, but the banker turned his back. Finally, he hung up. He was dialing again— yet another phone call. Hannon glanced at the two women at their terminals. Neither made eye contact with him. Jeffries was now off the phone and walking toward him. He was still smiling, but it seemed more plastic than ever.

"Everything is all set, Mr. Venters. I pulled a few strings. It should only take about forty-five minutes."

Hannon grimaced. "Forty-five minutes for *what?*"

"Your cash, of course. As an IBC, we don't keep any cash on the premises. It has to be delivered from the Eastern Caribbean Central Bank. I'm sure we explained that to you when you opened your account."

Hannon smiled uneasily. "Oh, of course. It must have slipped my mind."

"Can I get you some coffee or something while you're waiting?"

"No, thank you." Hannon sighed and leaned back in his chair, thinking.

Jeffries reached for his phone, then stopped and smiled. "I don't mean to be rude, Mr. Venters. But I have some business to conduct on behalf of other customers. Private matters of course. Would you mind waiting over there?" With a nod he pointed to the chair by the door.

"Not at all," said Hannon as he rose from the chair. He had an uneasy feeling as he slowly crossed the room. Rollins hadn't said anything about there being no cash on the premises. Then again, it would have been just like that idiot to leave out the most important detail. Hannon lowered himself into the armchair and exchanged glances with Jeffries from across the room. The banker was still wearing his plastic smile. *It's so fucking annoying, that plastic smile.*

Hannon picked a magazine from the coffee table. He pretended to read, but his eyes roamed above the pages as he carefully cased the exits. The front door appeared to be the only way out. The door to the back was locked—Jeffries had used a key. There was no telling where it might lead, or even if there was an exit out the back. Hannon glanced back at Jeffries, then at the women at their terminals. They all seemed to be doing exactly what they'd been doing all along. Nothing unusual. Then again, if Jeffries had called the cops, that's exactly what they would have told him to do until they got there.

Hannon checked his watch. Ten minutes had passed. It was ghastly hot beneath the wig. He was sweating. His gut wrenched at the sudden thought of his rubber nose and mustache coming unglued. *Paranoia?* he asked himself.

He glanced across the room, trying to remain calm. One of the women got up from her desk and went to the back room. It was the woman who'd checked his identification against the records on file. Maybe she *had* noticed the height discrepancy. Or maybe she remembered Rollins from when he'd opened the account. *Maybe I should have kept that ass-hole alive.*

Twenty minutes passed, and the woman still hadn't returned. The other one got up and disappeared through the same door. They both were gone. It was just him and Jeffries, all by themselves. Hannon scooted to the edge of the seat. His antennae were up for the smallest aberration. Suddenly, he heard the rumbling noise of a big truck pulling up right outside the door.

Jeffries looked up from his desk. "That must be them," he said. "How about that? Nearly twenty minutes early."

Hannon felt a rush of adrenaline. Nothing *ever* happened *early* in the islands. The door swung open. Two men in uniform led the way, both with sidearms in their holsters. Hannon didn't like the looks on their faces. They had to be cops. On impulse, he reached for his weapon.

"Gun!" shouted Jeffries as he ducked behind his desk.

The lead guard drew his gun from his holster, but Hannon was quicker. The room exploded in gunfire. He hit the guard with two shots in the chest before he could fire. His white shirt erupted with a bright crimson stain.

The second guard dove for cover behind the potted plant. Hannon fired repeatedly while running for the door. The guard crashed into the computers and landed in a heap beside the plant. The women in the back screamed at the gunshots, but Hannon never stopped. He burst through the door and ran through the parking lot, digging for his keys. The Jeep started right up and squealed away. He was standing on the accelerator all the way down the road, pushing the needle past 150 kph, flying past cars, pedestrians, and a herd of stunned goats.

PART
THREE

Chapter 37

ike was critiquing the eleven o'clock news from the couch, channel surfing among three different networks that all claimed to have the same "exclusive" lead story, when the phone rang. He hit the mute button just as the wide-eyed anchor launched a "shocking live report" of a neighborhood disturbance involving "scores of angry residents," most of whom could be seen in the background laughing and slapping high fives after managing to get their faces on television. The oblivious reporter kept right on sensationalizing. It suddenly hit Mike that if anyone was wondering what "cacophony" *looked* like, they should just watch the evening news with the sound turned off.

He reached across the coffee table and grabbed the portable on the half-ring. It was Zack from Key West, calling to say he wouldn't be back for a few days. Mike could hear a live band and laughter in the background. Zack sounded a little drunk and breathless, like he'd been dancing.

"One other thing," said Zack. "Very important. The maid comes tomorrow, and I think I left my BFR out on the dresser. Can you stash it away for me?"

Mike smirked. The BFR was Zack's "big fucking ring." He was forever paranoid that the maid would find it, hock it, and use the proceeds to buy her own third-world country. "I'll check just as soon as I hang up," he lied. "Have fun."

He switched off the phone and hit the television remote, bringing the audio back to the news. He was just about to cut away from a story on Princess Di—the sum and substance of what most American newscasts pawned off as "international news"—when a blurb on Antigua caught his attention.

"In a bizarre but tragic story," said the anchor, "two security guards were gunned down by an American man who was withdrawing his own money from a bank in Antigua."

Mike quickly remembered what Victoria had said about the money having disappeared in Antigua. He leaned forward with interest and increased the volume.

"The gunman, who police describe as a white male in his thirties, approximately six foot six inches tall, arrived at the Charter Bank of Antigua this morning to close an account of nearly a quarter million U.S. dollars. When security guards arrived with his money, the man inexplicably pulled out a pistol and opened fire, killing both guards. He then fled without the money. Crazy world out there, isn't it? The suspect remains at large.

"Finally in international news, Kitty Van Dorn, our world news correspondent from Milan, has this exclusive Channel 8 interview with Italian supermodel—"

Mike switched off the set, but he kept staring straight ahead at the blank screen, his mind awhirl. The man was American. He was withdrawing a quarter million dollars, the same amount of money he'd paid to his informant. The bank was in Antigua, exactly where Victoria had said the money had landed. It couldn't be coincidence. It had to be their man.

Mike quickly organized his thoughts. He'd want to see the police file, possibly a sketch of the suspect. He'd want to interview the bank employees, any witnesses to the shooting.

He picked up the phone and started to call Victoria, then stopped. If the story had already reached the nightly news in Miami, the FBI must have known about it by now. Victoria must have made the same connection he had. Yet she hadn't called him.

Fine, he thought. If that's the way she wants to play it. Every man for himself. He canceled her number and dialed another.

"Yes," he said, "I'd like information on flights from Miami to Antigua. Tonight, please. One passenger."

Karen was getting ready for bed when Mike stopped by on his way to the airport. She still hadn't completely forgiven him for the way he'd rushed off to see Aaron Fields the last time he'd come by, but the worried look in his eyes made her put that aside. She sensed he simply wanted to hear from someone he trusted that he was doing the right thing, for he stayed just long enough to explain why he was going. It wasn't just a matter of finding the money. The money was the only connection to his informant, and the informant was the only connection to the killer. *This* was the only lead he had.

He made it sound so logical, the same dispassionate way some of her partners at the law firm might have approached it. She wondered for a moment if that weren't the inherent flaw in their marriage, this peculiar shared ability of lawyers and journalists to put their emotions aside and be so damned objective. Marriage didn't amount to much with emotion on the side.

She was still wide awake by 2:00 A.M., lying in the dark and listening to a stiff wind beat against the house. Shadows moved across the bedroom as bending tree limbs played tricks with the streetlamp outside her window. She thought some old reruns on Lifetime might help her sleep, but it only depressed her to think that everyone on *thirtysomething* was now forty-something pushing fifty. She switched off the set and sank into the pillows, well on her way to a night of staring at the ceiling.

The wind blew harder, rattling the French doors that led to the pool. The shadows grew longer and shook more violently. Even though she and Mike had been living separately, knowing that he was leaving the country made her feel more alone, more vulnerable. As a little girl, she used to pull the covers over her head to hide from the monsters lurking in the closet. Now, however, the demons were in her head. They'd been there since college, when that man had crawled in her window and forced her into bed. . . .

He was finally pulling away. Not fast enough for her, but she didn't dare push him off and set him off again.

The cold barrel of the revolver pressing up beneath her chin and pointing at her brain kept her perfectly still, lying on her back. She'd willed herself numb during the act, but she was starting to feel ripped from a lack of lubrication. Rug burns covered her elbows and knees from the attack in the hallway, and her head was still throbbing from the way he'd slammed it against the wall when entering from the rear. Her right eye was completely swollen shut, and the salty taste of blood trickled down the back of her throat from a gash on her lip. She'd put up a fight and paid the price.

Her eyes fluttered open as she finally felt the weight of his body lift from on top of her. His wide face was a blur, sweaty and distorted beneath a dark nylon stocking. His breath still wreaked of stale bourbon. Even in the darkness, she could see the stains of her own blood on his Bon Jovi T-shirt. Her own nightshirt lay in a shredded heap at the foot of the bed. She prayed it was over as the room slowly came back into focus.

He was upright on the bed, kneeling between her legs and towering over her as the gun finally pulled away from the base of her chin.

"Move and you die," he said.

She stared up at the ceiling, hoping for the sound of him buckling his pants and zipping his fly—some signal that it was over. But she didn't hear it. She lowered her eyes, and her line of sight cut slowly across the ceiling, over to the fan, down to the top his head, to his shoulders and below. Her eyes locked on his groin. He was spitting on himself to make up for her dryness. *He's coming back again!*

Her throat went dry and her whole body shook, but she clenched her fist to regain control. She grimaced without making a sound as he probed between her legs, inserting his saliva. Out of the corner of her eye she glanced at the nightstand. Instinctively, her hand began to slide beneath the pillow at her side. It moved at a patient, imperceptible pace, until she'd stretched her entire arm as far as she could. She gripped the edge of the mattress and took a deep breath, coiling up her strength.

"You be rubbin' me raw, bitch," he said as he used his wet hand to bring back his erection.

In his moment of distraction she shot up like a flash and in one quick motion grabbed the telephone and slammed it hard against his head. Her knee went up and crushed his groin. Before he could react she swung the phone again, knocking the revolver from his hand. It flew across the room and landed on the floor in front of the closet.

He cried out in pain and tumbled off the bed with his pants around his knees. Karen was naked, kicking and screaming as she scrambled for the gun. They were swinging and grabbing at each other as they tumbled across the floor. She clawed his face with her nails, feeling his blood on her hands as she gouged at his eyes. She dove for the gun and grasped it in her hand, but in the tangled brawl he had one hand on her throat and the other on her wrist. The gun waved in every direction as she struggled to break free.

"Drop it!" he shouted, but she bit him fiercely on the arm.

A shot rang out in a deafening explosion. A hot

burst of blood drenched her face. His limp body came crushing down on top of her with a weighty thud.

She tried to scream, but nothing came out. With all her strength she pushed up, launching him off of her. The body landed in a contorted heap on the rug beside her. She scampered away on hands and knees to the farthest corner, as far away as possible. Her body heaved in hysterical sobs as she curled up and sat on the floor with her knees up, covering her nakedness. The gun seemed terribly heavy in her hands, but she wouldn't let go. She watched from ten feet away in the darkness. He lay absolutely motionless. Finally, she looked away, unable to look back. Tears flowed, and she didn't even try to stop them as she buried her face in her hands.

Then, a strange sound cut through the silence, sending icicles down her spine. She raised her head and listened. It was a faint, fading voice.

"Help me."

Her heart was quickly in her throat. With an unsteady hand she pushed a bloody strand of hair out of her eyes and peered through the darkness. Puzzled and frightened, she listened intently, until it came again—this time a little stronger.

"Please. Help me."

Squinting through tears, she could see bubbles of red saliva percolating from his mouth. "Oh, my God," she muttered. "You're still *alive*. . . ."

A shrill noise suddenly filled the bedroom, and her heart stopped as she shot up in her bed. It was just the alarm clock. She let out a heavy sigh of relief, but she was trembling as she wiped her sweaty palms in the sheets. Exhausted, she reached across the bed and swatted the noisy alarm. Six-thirty. Time to get up. Time to go to work.

Time to keep pretending that none of this had ever happened.

Chapter 38

Clouds rolled in a few hours before dawn, blocking out the stars and half-moon over southeast Antigua. A warm, steady breeze kicked up a few whitecaps in the inky black waters near English Harbour. The scarred Atlantic coast, beaten by waves over the millennia, was very unlike the scalloped white sandy beaches that laced the island's gentle Caribbean side. Jutting headlands of jagged limestone enclosed countless bays and secluded coves that smugglers had exploited for centuries.

An armada of recreational sailboats was anchored offshore, some for the night, others for the season. Each had a rubber dinghy floating alongside or mounted up on deck to shuttle sailors to and from shore. Every kind of craft—from little one-designs to hundred-foot cruisers—rocked sleepily in the waves, flying under the flags of the United States, Great Britain, and every sailing nation in between. Windmills for electric generators on some of the decrepit old houseboats spun silently in the breeze, but all else was still. At this small hour not a sailor was in sight, so that the deserted decks and towering bare masts seemed part of a floating ghost town.

A hundred yards offshore, Frank Hannon swam quietly toward a thirty-foot sloop, cutting through the water like a crocodile stalking its prey.

He was nearly sixteen hours into a contingency plan that his pretty friend from the bar at the Admiral's Inn had unwittingly helped form. Dominique had shared all kinds of details about the island—hiking, exploring, her favorite secluded spots—before he left her forever at her very favorite spot, a place so secluded that no one would ever find her.

Minutes after having fled from the bank, he'd hopped on the back of a vegetable truck and headed out of the city back to Boggy Peak, which Dominique had told him was Antigua's version of a tropical rain forest. He'd spent the daylight hours in the highlands, hiding on lush slopes covered in elephant ears and course fig trees, well away from the airport and harbors that would be crawling with police. At dusk he'd continued on foot toward the nautical centers in the southeast, trudging along the coast beneath the tangled limbs and thick, leafy canopy of the mangrove clusters. As a natural defense to erosion and hurricanes, the mangroves weaved land and sea together into what often seemed an impenetrable thicket. They grew right along the marshy shoreline in a foot or so of water—which meant the dogs couldn't pick up his scent. There was no escape, however, from the swarms of mosquitoes and annoying little sand flies called "no-see-ums," which had been bearable only because of his long pants and his long-sleeved shirt. Hunger, by comparison, had been a minor problem. Dominique had warned him about the little applelike fruit of the manchineel tree, which was deadly poisonous. The green bananas on Fig Tree Hill had proved tasty enough, far better than the tree oysters and shell-less snails clinging to the submerged roots of the mangrove trees.

By nightfall he'd picked his spot on a hill overlooking a secluded bay, his point of departure. It was too risky to approach the ocean freighters in the commercial harbor, or the yacht clubs and deep-sea fishing charters, where the police had undoubtedly warned everyone to be on the lookout. Although he'd worn a disguise to the bank, his height and build were still distinctive. Any six foot five American trying to leave the country was bound to be a suspect. His only way off the island, he figured, was one of the hundreds of boats that had dropped anchor off the coast, away from the marinas, beyond police protection.

Hannon swam a very controlled and quiet breaststroke as he neared the stern, making not a sound. A rear approach was best, where a ladder led to the dinghy. He grabbed the bottom rung to begin his ascent.

The boat rocked gently in rolling waters made black by the overcast night. Halyards tapped against the mast in the light breeze, emitting an incessant hollow ping, like a squeaky box spring. Hannon climbed slowly and steadily, hand over hand, inch by inch, with the strength of a gymnast on the rings spreading into an iron cross. He kept silent as fog, realizing that one kick to the hull or bang of the ladder would thump like a drum inside the cabin. It would surely wake the owner—who probably owned a gun.

One leg went over the polished teak rail, then the other. In complete silence he was a mere shadow on board. He crouched into a ball toward the aft of the cockpit. Looking straight ahead, he could see down into the main cabin. The companionway door had been left wide open for ventilation. It was dark below, but he could make out the stove in the galley and an empty starboard berth. The portside berth looked lumpy, occupied. When he closed his ears to the surf he could even hear breathing. Snoring. The lonely captain was asleep.

Hannon clutched the long fish filet knife he'd stolen from behind the back of the fisherman at the pier and moved quietly toward the open cabin door.

The adrenaline flowed faster with each step forward. He knew exactly what was going to happen, just as he had with all the others. He never attacked without mapping it out first, seeing it through to the bloody end in his world of fantasy, pursuing his dream of the perfect crime. For the first time ever, this was nearly as titillating as the fantasy. *I am perfection.*

Hannon leaned over him as he slept, waiting for him to sense the intrusion. With a wrinkled sheet pulled up around his neck, the man had the weathered look of a salty old sailor. A scraggly two-day growth of whiskers covered his pudgy face. Hannon brought the knife to his fleshy nose and tickled the little hairs in his nostrils, smirking with sadistic amusement as the man shooed away imaginary gnats in his sleep. He dragged the blade lightly across his lips and paused, as if considering his next move. With a quick jab he poked him in the cheek.

"Oww! What the hell!"

Hannon grabbed him by the throat and shoved the knife before his eyes. "Flinch and you die."

He blinked hard, not fully comprehending. His whole body shook as it became frightfully clear that this was real, not a nightmare. The eyes bulged with each desperate gasp for air.

"Whatever you want," his voice trembled. "Take it."

Hannon pressed the blade against his cheek, then spoke in a low, threatening whisper. "I want to see Puerto Rico. And I want *you* to take me."

The layover in San Juan had been longer than expected, making Mike's flight from Miami a tiring nine hours. The plane touched down at Bird International Airport just a few minutes before 10:00 A.M. Mike had only an overnight carry-on bag with him, so he went straight to customs and immigration. He queued up in the longer line, since the guy at the end of the short one looked like he might be carrying a bazooka in his bag and would probably hold things up.

The customs and immigration officers wore dark blue uniforms with military-style caps. One sat behind a counter, checking documentation. Another stood at the end of the conveyor, visually inspecting baggage, but he'd yet to open a single suitcase. Given the lax security, the line seemed to be moving very slowly. When Mike's turn finally came, he slipped his passport across the countertop.

The young black woman in uniform checked the photograph, then looked up at Mike. He smiled awkwardly, then glanced casually at the other officer at the end of the conveyor. He showed no expression. Mike glanced back at the woman behind the counter, who was now reviewing a computer printout. Undoubtedly that was the reason things were moving so slowly. Some kind of fugitive list, he presumed. With the murder at the Antigua bank just twenty-four hours old, border control couldn't be too careful.

Finally, she looked up. Mike smiled, expecting his passport back. She didn't return the smile or the passport. "Can you come with me, please?" she said matter-of-factly.

He was momentarily stunned. "I'm sorry. What's the problem?"

Her eyes narrowed. "Come with me, please," she said more sternly.

Suspicious glares came from the others in line. The old woman right behind took a gigantic step back, making it clear they weren't together. He didn't want a scene. "All right," he said with a shrug. "Let's go clear this up."

She called over two other officers—two big guys with barrel chests, thick necks, and impressive sidearms in their holsters. The three of them—one behind him and one at each side—escorted him down a sterile hallway with a polished cement floor, bright fluorescent lights, and no doors or windows. Their footsteps echoed against the bare walls.

"Do you mind telling me what this is all about?" asked Mike.

No one replied. They turned the corner, then stopped at a door at the end of the hall. The woman took a key from her belt and unlocked the door. She pushed it open, then pointed inside with a jerk of her head. "This way, please."

He chuckled nervously. "What's this, the interrogation room?"

"Yes," she said flatly.

His forced smile faded. "Look, Officer. I don't want to make trouble, but I really don't see what right you have to detain me. Am I being arrested?"

"That's up to the police. They'll be here any minute. In the meantime, I suggest you sit down and cooperate."

He glanced at all three of the stone-faced guards. "Can I make a phone call first?"

"Later," she said.

The biggest guard took a half-step forward, as if telling him that it was time either to walk into the room or be thrown into it. He sighed with resignation as he passed through the doorway. The door closed behind him, and the keys tinkled on the outside, locking him inside.

"Welcome to Antigua," he said to himself, alone in the room.

Chapter 39

two hours passed before the door finally opened. In the open doorway stood a well-groomed man wearing a navy blue blazer, gray slacks, and a Scotch-plaid tie that seemed to draw out the red freckles on his black skin. Like many Antiguans, his family tree had both African and Anglo-Saxon limbs. He was much shorter than Mike and probably twenty years older, pushing sixty. He reached inside his breast pocket and flashed his badge. "Detective James Dewberry," he said in an English colonial island accent. "Antigua Police—Homicide."

Mike's heart raced, but he said nothing. Dewberry took the metal folding chair on the other side of the rectangular table, facing him. He pulled a small spiral pad from his breast pocket and clicked his pen.

"Tell me, Mr. Posten, what brings you all the way to Antigua?"

"I hear the diving's terrific."

He nodded slowly. "It is. We take it very seriously

down here. Almost as seriously as homicide." His expression soured. "Two security guards were murdered yesterday morning in the Charter Bank of Antigua. We have reason to believe you have information that may lead us to the killer."

Mike suddenly found himself wondering about their tongues, but he didn't want to ask the kind of question that would reveal how much he knew. "Me? Why me?"

"Have you ever heard the name Eric Venters?"

"Never."

"Surely you've heard the name Ernest Gill."

Mike fell silent.

Dewberry scooted forward to the edge of the couch. "Allow me to explain something before we get tangled up in the usual dance. We know that someone using the name Eric Venters—we're certain it's an alias—opened an account at the Charter Bank in St. Johns. He arrived yesterday morning to close the account and withdraw the funds. Nearly a quarter million U.S. dollars. Of course, a bank like the Charter Bank doesn't keep that kind of money on the premises. Normally, customers call in advance to make an appointment, so that the money is waiting for them when they arrive. Either Mr. Venters didn't know that or, more likely, he simply didn't want to give anyone advance notice of his arrival. The bank officer did his level best to get the money to him as quickly as possible from the central bank. As best we can gather from our witnesses, the phone calls and apparent delay made him very suspicious. When the security guards finally arrived with the funds, he evidently mistook them for police officers, smelled an ambush and opened fire. Two of them ended up dead."

Mike sighed and shook his head. "I'm very sorry to hear that."

"I suspect you'll be even be sorrier to hear that by murdering the guards, Mr. Venters created a legal basis for the police to pierce bank secrecy."

"I'm not sure I follow you."

"In Antigua, bank secrecy is absolutely inviolable except when the authorities are investigating conduct that constitutes a crime under Antiguan law. Tax evasion, money laundering—those aren't crimes in Antigua. Homicide, of course, is."

"So, because of the murders, you've been able to trace the funds."

"All the way back to a gent named Ernest Gill. And ultimately to you. That's how the immigration officials had your name on their list, right along with Ernest Gill and Eric Venters."

Mike nodded, understanding. "What do you intend to do with me?"

He leaned back in his chair. "I'm not going to put bamboo shoots under your fingernails, if that's what you're wondering. Antigua, after all, is a very civilized country. You seem very civil for an American. I'm hoping you'll come back to the station with me on a voluntary basis to talk to our lieutenant. We'd also like you to look at the composite sketch of the killer we've created from the witnesses at the bank. And," he said firmly, "we'd very much like you to submit to a polygraph examination."

"And what if I don't feel like cooperating?"

"That would be a bloody shame. I feel as though I've been very forthcoming, and I was hoping we could conduct ourselves like gentlemen. Like I said: I can't force you to talk to us. But by the same token, you can't force us to keep word of your involvement to ourselves, either."

"What are you implying?"

His voice grew lower, more serious. "Let there be no doubt that you *will* have to explain why the man who murdered two security guards in an Antiguan bank was in the process of withdrawing two hundred and fifty thousand American dollars that can be traced directly back to you. You can come with me to the station and explain it quite privately to our investigators on the case. Or you can get on an airplane and explain it to your colleagues in the American press—who, I'm sure, would be most interested to know that I have a quite remarkable follow-up to your latest professional embarrassment concerning payments to informants."

Mike felt a dryness in his throat, remembering how Aaron Fields had bailed out before at the first sign of bad publicity. He stared back at the smug detective, waiting for him to blink, to show some sign of bluffing. It didn't come.

"All right," he said without heart. "I'll go with you."

Dewberry smiled for the first time, albeit faintly. "I knew you'd make the right choice."

"I didn't know I had one," Mike said as he started for the door.

* * *

A squad car was waiting at the curb outside the airport with a stiff, uniformed cop behind the wheel on the English side. Mike and the detective piled into the backseat. The tiny blue-and-white sedan merged quickly into traffic, and Mike was struggling for legroom when he caught a glimpse of his own reflection in the driver's-side mirror. His hair was flat, and he needed a shave. He looked tired, like a man who hadn't slept in forty-one hours. Or was it forty-two? He set his watch ahead one hour to 1:00 P.M., local time, as they dodged the potholes on the road from the airport.

He noticed no road signs or distinguishing landmarks along the way, just flocks of white egrets dotting the flat, scrubby landscape and a few tin-roofed shacks with twisted TV antennae. Feeling lost was undoubtedly part of the island charm for tourists on scooters with no particular destination, but for a man peering out the window from the back of a police car it was just added anxiety.

At the fork in the road was a wood arrow-shaped sign nailed to a telephone pole that read, ST. JOHNS 3 KM.

"St. Johns," said Mike. "Funny, I just came from San Juan."

Dewberry glanced at the sign, then said dryly, "He got around." They rode the rest of the way in silence.

The police headquarters was downtown, up the hill and away from the more touristy shopping sections along the waterfront. Dewberry escorted him directly to the interrogation room, an interior beige office with a small Formica table and four metal chairs. The walls were bare—no pictures, no clock.

With the door closed and blinds pulled shut, it was the kind of room where, after a few hours, discerning the time of day was purely a matter of taking the interrogator's word for it.

Mike sat on one side of the rectangular table. Dewberry sat across from him, sipping hot tea from a Styrofoam cup. For more than an hour he peppered him with questions that could easily have been asked at the airport or in the car coming over, which left Mike with the impression that he was merely softening him up for the real interrogator. Just before five o'clock entered a lanky man in his early forties who, for a cop, spoke with a very proper English accent.

"Lieutenant Brenford A. V. Scot," he said stiffly, offering his hand.

Mike shook his hand, thinking he *looked* very much like a Brenford A. V. Scot, or at least the West Indian version thereof. He was formal and polite, with a distinct air of conceit. His thick black hair was parted on the side, and he had an affected way of brushing the long curls from his eyes every minute or so. The hairstyle seemed a bit young for a man his age, though his dark, handsome face was on the boyish side. He sat beside Dewberry, directly across the table from Mike.

"This can be a very short meeting," said Scot. "Or it can be a very long meeting. It's up to you, Mr. Posten."

Mike sighed. Scot seemed to be expecting some kind of witty rejoinder, but the energy wasn't there.

"With the aid of Interpol," the young lieutenant continued, "it has come to our attention that you've written a rather smashing collection of articles about a certain serial killer. As well, we understand that some unsavory accusations have been levied against you publicly, to the effect that you've paid goodly sums of money to a confidential informant. True or not, we know for a fact that you did indeed deposit two hundred and fifty thousand dollars into a Citibank account for a gentleman named Ernest Gill. And of course we now know that a gentleman using the name Eric Venters killed two security guards while trying to withdraw those very same funds from the Charter Bank here in Antigua."

Mike was stone-faced, confirming nothing.

"Now," Scot continued, "let me tell you what we *believe*. We believe Eric Venters is Ernest Gill. We believe Ernest Gill is your informant." He leaned forward on the table, his expression very serious. "And we believe you will tell us how to find him."

Mike rubbed his tired face, fighting off a yawn. "Believe whatever you like. But I can't tell you who my informant is, and I can't tell you how to find him."

Scot smiled politely, but without a trace of sincerity. "Please, don't misunderstand us, old boy. We're not asking you to confess to having paid a confidential source. We simply wish to know his identity."

"I'm not refusing to tell you. I just don't know who or where he is."

Scot raised an eyebrow, emphasizing his skepticism. "That's terribly convenient, isn't it, Mr. Posten."

"I'm not playing games."

"Neither are we," said Scot.

Dewberry rose slowly and leaned across the table,

glaring at Mike. "I know your type," he said in a low, angry tone. "One of those cocky, self-righteous American journalists who like to get their face on the evening news by going to jail to protect the identity of their sources. Well, you'd bloody well not pull those stunts with us."

Mike returned the glare, sizing up his opponent. Dewberry seemed to be waiting for him to make a false move, just looking for an excuse to blow a gasket. Mike sensed that this was one cop who'd been skewered by a reporter or two.

Scot leaned forward, as if to separate the two of them, reeling his partner back into his chair. "What Detective Dewberry is trying to say, Mr. Posten, is that in Antigua it isn't unheard of for journalists to land in jail. In point of fact, it was Detective Dewberry who personally arrested the editor and proprietor of a newspaper called the *Outlet* back in 1985 for a positively libelous article that accused our own government of kidnapping a child and whatnot. The arrest caused quite the international stir—perhaps you even heard of it. Eventually, the British House of Lords overturned the jail term. However, I don't suppose you'd care to lodge here in one of our cells until your barrister can press your appeal all the way to England. Would you, Mr. Posten."

Mike rolled in his seat, taking on a more aggressive posture. "Like I said, Lieutenant. I can't reveal my source, because I don't know who he is. But I will say this. Your very eloquent speech, complete with legal precedent, has convinced me of one thing."

Scot smiled with his eyes, as if expecting a sporting

concession of defeat from a worthy opponent. "What's that, old boy?"

Mike looked him straight in the eye. "Even if his name were tattooed on my forehead, you'd be the last to find it."

The conciliatory smirk ran from his face, and his face flushed red with indignation. "We'll see about that." He glared at Mike, then glanced at Dewberry. "Looks like we have ourselves a guest. Lock him up."

The detective was quickly at Mike's side, pulling him up from his chair and using more force than necessary to cuff his hands behind his back. Mike started to resist, then stopped himself and just took the pain.

"Where do you want him?" he asked the lieutenant.

Scot was still seated at the table. He looked up, paused for a moment, then narrowed his eyes. "You know where to put him."

Mike bristled at the way they exchanged glances, like two clever insiders savoring the same thought. He didn't give them the satisfaction, however, of asking the obvious question.

"I'd like to call my wife," said Mike.

Dewberry ignored the request, then shoved him out the door. "Straight ahead," he barked. He trailed right behind Mike down the hall, pushing him repeatedly on the back and shoulders, until they reached an old elevator with a metal, accordion-style gate.

"Into the lift."

The two men entered and stood shoulder to shoulder as Dewberry yanked the gate shut and hit the button. There was a loud hum but little sense of movement. Mike was beginning to wonder whether they'd actually left the ground when they finally jerked to a halt on the second floor. The detective pulled back the gate and pushed him out.

With his back to the lift, Mike was surrounded by thick black bars. Dewberry prodded him forward, and their footsteps echoed off the smooth cement floor. It reminded him of a tour he'd taken of Alcatraz, except the tropical air was stale and hot. A cockroach scampered through bars, into the darkness. They stopped at the metal gate that led to the cellblock, and Dewberry removed the handcuffs.

An armed guard sat on the other side of the bars, enclosed in his own protective cage behind a panel of levers and controls. He greeted the detective with a familiar smile, then pulled a black lever. A metal tray appeared through the bars, containing a dark blue prison uniform and beach thongs.

"Put those on," said Dewberry. "Your things go in the tray."

Mike emptied his pockets and stripped down to his underwear, putting everything in the tray. The uniform was a little small, and it smelled like someone had been sick in it. Dewberry slapped the metal cuffs back on his wrists. The guard retrieved his belongings, then pulled another lever. The main iron gate slid open, clanking like a rickety old roller coaster.

Mike was staring straight down a dimly lit corridor. He counted twenty cells, ten on each side. Each was about the size of a typical walk-in closet. It was too dark to see inside all of them, but the nearest one seemed to be housing at least four prisoners.

"We're putting him with Watts," said the detective to the guard.

The two men exchanged that same curious look he'd seen Scot give Dewberry a few minutes ago.

"Away from the bars!" the guard shouted down the hall. He pushed a button on his panel, and a bell rang out.

A low rumble filled the cellblock. In the dim lighting, Mike could see only shadows as the prisoners shuffled toward the rear of their cells. When the rumbling stopped, Dewberry nudged him from behind. Together, they started down the hall.

"Eyes straight ahead," said Dewberry.

Mike caught a glimpse of a few prisoners as they passed each cell. One with long dreadlocks. Another naked from the waist up, covered with tattoos, another with arms like tree stumps. He felt like jail was their fraternity and they couldn't wait to initiate him. A dryness filled his throat as he reached the end of the hall. They'd passed all twenty cells, but he had yet to meet his cellmate.

"So, which one is Watts?" he asked finally.

Dewberry nodded toward the dark gray wall—but it wasn't the wall, Mike suddenly realized. It was a solid metal door fitted right into the wall. There was an open slot in the middle just big enough for a dinner tray. Through it, Mike could see only darkness.

Dewberry gave the door a swift kick. A chilling shriek came from within, something primal, beginning with a piercing scream and ending with a howl.

"That's Watts," he said with a smirk.

Another scream, and Mike cringed. It didn't

sound human. "This is pointless, you know. You could put me in there with Charles Manson and I still wouldn't be able to come up with the name of my informant. I really *don't* know."

"Sure you don't," he said as he pushed him toward the door. "And if you're still saying that in the morning, we might even believe you."

Chapter 40

Lieutenant Scot was in his office early that morning, sitting at his desk, reviewing a signed statement taken from one of the employees of the Charter Bank. A crumbled blueberry muffin lay on a napkin to his right, beside an empty teacup and a mountain of paperwork spilling out of his in box. Lines of fatigue rimmed his eyes, but his crisp white shirt was buttoned to the wrists, and his tie was straight and knotted snugly, fit for Sunday services.

His assistant poked her head through the open doorway. "An American woman is here for Michael Posten," she said in a soft, unintrusive voice.

Scot looked up curiously from his desk. "His wife?"

"No. She says she's with the FBI."

"The FBI? *Here?*" He froze for a moment, then jumped forward in his chair, tossing the muffin wrapper in the trash, stuffing the dirty teacup in a drawer, straightening the papers atop his desk.

His assistant rolled her eyes, as if she'd seen her

image-conscious boss in his neatnik mode before. "I'll send her in."

"Yes, do," he said, frantically running a hand through his hair. "And bring Dewberry round as well."

Detective Dewberry arrived first, and the two men greeted Victoria with gracious smiles. She was wearing a gray business suit that looked a little warm for the islands, but it seemed befitting of the FBI. Eduardo Ortega, a handsome young Latin agent from the Miami Field Office, was standing at her side. After quick introductions she declined the tea and sat on the sofa beneath the window, with Ortega still at her side. Dewberry took the Old English oak chair facing the desk.

"I must say," said Scot from behind his desk. "I'm a bit surprised to see someone from the FBI."

"Well, you *did* request our assistance."

"We did?" he said, glancing at his partner.

"Uh, yes," said Dewberry. "In a manner of speaking. You can imagine our excitement, miss, upon discovering two distinct sets of fingerprints for Mr. Venters at the bank. Unfortunately, the data bank at Interpol turned up nothing a-tall. Since he was a Yank, we were hoping the FBI data bank might provide a match." He glanced at Scot, as if he were speaking more for his benefit than Victoria's.

She smiled thinly, instantly aware of who was *really* in charge here. "Well," she said, "you gentlemen have yourselves a match."

"Splendid!" Scot was smiling widely, but the grin soon faded. "But . . . why did you and Mr. Ortega have to come all the way to Antigua to tell us?"

"Because there's a rub," she said. "I'm authorized to deliver the results to you on one condition only."

"Which is . . . ?" he said cautiously.

"You give us custody of Michael Posten."

Scot shifted uneasily. "How did you even know we had him?"

"That's really none of your concern, is it?"

"Why do you want him?" Dewberry interjected.

"We believe he may have assisted in structuring wire transfers to offshore banks in violation of U.S. currency laws."

Scot leaned back in his chair, thinking. "Truth be told, the only reason we were holding Mr. Posten was in the hope that he'd tell us who Mr. Venters is. If the FBI will tell us whose fingerprints we have, I suppose we no longer need him."

Dewberry gave him a subtle nod, as if approving his analysis.

"Then I can have him?" said Victoria.

"Certainly," the lieutenant said with a shrug. "Just show us your bounty."

Victoria shot him a curious look.

"The fingerprints," he explained, nervous with embarrassment.

Victoria confirmed their agreement with a firm nod, then opened her briefcase and removed a file. "As you say, the fingerprints do belong to an American citizen. A convicted felon, in fact." She rose from her seat and laid the open file on the detective's desk.

The Antiguans eagerly leaned forward, inspecting it with interest.

"His name is Curt Rollins."

*   *   *

The door to isolation cell number two opened with a clank and a thud. At the first crack of light, Mike jumped up in the darkness from his place in the corner.

The howling resumed.

Watts was shirtless and barefooted, wearing only dark prison pants that fit loosely like pajamas. His ragged beard and a matted coat of thick body hair made it impossible to guess his age, somewhere between twenty-five and forty-five. He had a habit of using feces like a styling gel, rubbing it through his long hair, making it stand on end—straight up, like a man who'd stuck his finger in a light socket. Mike figured that was the reason they called him "Watts." His arms and shoulders were broad and muscular, but his belly protruded grossly over his belt line. A thick pink scar ran nearly the entire length of his right arm, presumably from a knife fight. Mike noticed two tattoos. The one on his arm read, NO LIFE LIKE LOW LIFE. The other was centered on his forehead—a third eye.

As the door opened, Watts jumped forward, then snapped back like a dog at the end of its leash. His waist and ankles were chained to the wall, allowing him only a few feet of movement.

Mike squinted as his pupils adjusted to the light. His clothes were splattered with wet brown stains. Wads of wet toilet paper dotted the walls around him. The cell reeked of strong disinfectant and human waste.

Dewberry stood in the doorway, covering his

mouth to contain his laughter. "I see Mr. Watts has emptied the latrine for us again, one handful at a time. His aim's improving a mite, as well."

Mike glared at him, completely nonplussed. "Get me out of here. *Now.*"

Watts growled and swung his arms like a bear, but the chains kept him safely on the other side of the cell.

"You're a lucky chap, Posten. Tonight we were going to unchain your cellmate."

"What made you change your mind? Amnesty International?"

"The FBI. They've come to arrest you."

His mind raced. It had to be Victoria—but *arrested?*

The detective grabbed his arm and led him from the cell down the hall to the showers. He waited as Mike quickly showered and put his street clothes back on. Dewberry then led him through the gate, past the guard and down the prehistoric elevator. The door opened on the first floor, where Victoria was waiting beside a tall Latin gentleman who Mike guessed was also an FBI agent. Mike was about to say something, but she quickly cut him off.

"Is this Posten?" she said to Dewberry.

Mike looked confused at first, but in half a second he realized she was signaling to him. The supposed arrest still had him leery, but whatever her plan was, it had to be better than another night with Watts.

"He's all yours," said Dewberry.

Victoria watched as the detective removed the old metal handcuffs. Once they were off, she made a big show of grabbing his arm and securing both hands behind his back with her plastic flex-cuffs. She cinched them up extra tightly, pinching his wrists.

"Oww!" He glanced at her sharply, as if to say, "You did that on purpose."

She smiled with her eyes, then said sternly, "Don't try anything funny, Posten."

She thanked Dewberry profusely, then quickly pushed her prisoner through the lobby and out the front door before anyone had the chance to change their mind. She had Mike's right arm, Agent Ortega had the left. They were still pushing their prisoner when they hit the cracked and busy sidewalks of downtown St. Johns. Victoria steered the threesome in and out of pedestrians and around the ornate wrought-iron posts that supported the old Georgian-style balconies hanging overhead. A block away from the station, she yanked him to an abrupt halt at the BMW parked at the curb.

With a quick yank she removed the plastic handcuffs.

"Oww, dammit! Will you cut that out?"

"Just get in," she said as she flung open the car door. Mike ducked into the passenger seat, rubbing his wrists. Ortega jumped in the backseat. Victoria ran around to the driver's side, then pulled away quickly from the curb. She was pounding the clutch like a test driver, racing in what Mike seemed to remember was the general direction of the airport.

"I want to know what's going on."

She darted into the passing lane, flying by a rusted old flatbed Ford. "You already know most of it. Like us, you figured out these murders at the Charter Bank were no coincidence. Since I told you we'd lost track of the money in Antigua, I had a feeling you might get curious enough to come here and see what you could find out. So we put a tail on you," she said, glancing toward her colleague in the backseat. "Ortega's been shadowing you. Good thing, too."

"What's this business about an arrest?"

She checked traffic, then rolled through a stop sign. "We haven't told the Antiguan authorities anything about your cooperation with the FBI. The last thing I wanted was yet another jurisdiction brought into the loop on this serial killer. I'm having trouble enough coordinating the domestic authorities. But I had to tell them something to get them to turn you over to me. So I made them think we were after you for currency violations."

"That would be a fitting end," said Mike. "The checkbook journalist who's so stupid he even figures out a way to blow the benefits of Antiguan bank secrecy." He shook his head, then sighed. "They locked me up, you know. They wanted me to tell them who some guy named Eric Venters really is."

"I told them. That's why they let you go."

"How do you know who he is?"

"The Antiguan police asked for the FBI's assistance in analyzing two sets of fingerprints they lifted from the Charter Bank. One was from the safe-deposit box, left behind on the day of the murders. The other was from the application forms filled out several months ago by whoever opened the account. Our database came up with a match on both."

Mike caught his breath. "Is it one guy, or two?"

"Two."

He sighed, not sure whether that was a good or bad thing. "Who are they?"

Victoria glanced over, then turned her eyes back to the road. "The only way I can tell you is if this is a two-way dialogue. I don't want to hear any excuses about how you can't tell me anything about them because they were one of your old sources, or some other confidential baloney."

Mike blinked hard. He'd hardly slept in the last forty-eight hours, and he wasn't sure if he was clear-headed enough to make that kind of ethical judgment. Curiosity, however, put his mouth in gear. "Just give me the names."

"The prints on the bank application forms probably belonged to your informant, since he's the one who opened the account. His name is Curt Rollins."

Mike paused, searching his memory. "Sorry. Never heard of him. Maybe if you told me something about him, it would come to me."

She glanced over, as if to make sure he wasn't holding out. "He's thirty-two years old, former cop. After three years on the Chicago police force, he was convicted of selling the names of the government's confidential informants to drug dealers. Served five years of a seven-year sentence in Joliet maximum security prison—which, for a cop, is eternal damnation. Basically he was an unemployed lowlife living in a basement apartment in Brooklyn since his release."

"Kind of strange, isn't it? A guy who was actually *convicted* for selling out informants becomes my confidential source?"

"From what we've been able to gather from his parole officer and prison psychologist, Rollins is basically a big-time loser who's been at psychological war with himself over this whole idea of being an informant. On one level, he's always hated snitches. He was in a gang as a teenager, with a string of juvenile arrests—burglary, arson, car theft. He was always getting caught, basically because he wasn't very smart. Lucky for him he was never convicted as an adult, or he never would have been able to become a cop. Still, according to his parole officer, Rollins believes he is a victim of snitches. Even when he went before the parole board, he still showed a lot of anger over the way he seemed to get caught every time he broke the rules, while all the other crooks seemed to get away with murder. It seems that fear of getting caught is the only thing that kept him from growing up to be a criminal in the first place. Jealousy of more successful criminals, so to speak, is what made him become a cop."

"So, he wanted to bust people not because they were breaking the law, but because it killed him to see other guys break the law *and get away with it.*"

"Exactly. In my opinion, it was that same jealousy that made him want to inform on others, despite his hatred of the people who snitched on him."

Mike shook his head, drawing a blank. "It all makes sense, I guess. But none of it sounds at all familiar."

"I'm not surprised. If you two had crossed paths before, I have to believe it would have come out somehow in all those phone conversations you had with him. Incidentally, you're not likely to hear from him again, either. We searched his apartment in Brooklyn.

Looked a little ransacked. Garbage strewn all over the kitchen floor. No sign of him. Neighbors haven't seen him, and he missed his appointment with his parole officer. Apparently he was quite the mama's boy, too. Her birthday was last week—no card, no call."

"You think he's in hiding?"

"My opinion? He's dead. If he were alive he would have gone to Antigua and gotten the money himself, especially after all the trouble he went to to get it out of you. We probably won't know for sure, though, until we catch up with the guy who left his fingerprints on the safe-deposit box."

"Who's that?"

She paused. "Again, Mike. I haven't even given the Antigua authorities his name yet. I want to make sure this is handled exactly right—as a search for an intelligent serial killer, not just some loony who had a gunfight with two security guards in an Antiguan bank. If I tell you his name, you can't repeat it. And you have to tell me everything you know about him. No journalistic privileges."

"I already gave you my word, dammit. Tell me his name."

She glanced his way, as if expecting a reaction. "Frank Hannon."

His expression went cold. He sat in silence for a moment, then simply said, "Hannon." There was no real emotion in his voice, just a hint of recognition.

"You know him?"

He looked away, feeling a pain in his gut as he looked out the window. "I don't think anybody really knows Hannon."

Chapter 41

their plane landed at Miami International Airport that afternoon on BWIA, direct from St. Johns. Victoria stayed over in Miami just long enough to interview a couple of people on her Miami list who might know something about Hannon. She left on a late-afternoon flight for Washington National, arriving in the early evening, then drove straight to the FBI Academy in Quantico.

At 8:00 P.M. the full team of agents assigned to the case met in the north conference room on the second floor. Victoria sat at the head of the table beside the large empty chair for David Shapiro, her unit chief. Steve Caldwell and Arnold Freeland, the CASK Unit profilers, sat on one side of the table. On the other side sat two field agents working on the case, both men. Victoria had thought they'd be bursting with questions, but the group sat in silence, waiting for Shapiro. A sense of importance lingered in the air, despite the austere government furnishings filling the room. Cloth office chairs rimmed a simulated walnut table with chipped corners of exposed particle board. Glossy white walls and fluorescent lighting made the room far too bright. The American flag draped limply from a pole in the corner.

The major intrusion in the room was a three-by-five-foot white display board resting on an easel near the head of the table, closest to Shapiro. On it was a diagram for an ocean line cruise ship, the *Peninsular II.* There were seven different ovals on the board, each a different size, each displaying the floor plan and cabin configuration for one of the ship's seven different decks.

Shapiro rushed in at two minutes after eight and took the seat beside Victoria. "Let's hear it," he said.

Victoria bristled at his brusque tone. It seemed to punctuate the silent treatment from the rest of the group. Apparently there were a few men in the room having a tough time handling the fact that Victoria's infamous memorandum to Assistant Director Dougherty had been exactly right: The informant was *not* the killer. For now, though, she'd leave that out of things.

She took the long rubber-tipped pointer from the chalk rail behind her and moved toward the board.

"Twelve years ago," she began, "Frank Hannon raped a twenty-two-year-old woman in cabin 503 of the *Peninsular II.* It's located here," she pointed, "on the Lower Deck. He was arrested, convicted, and served twelve years of a twenty-year sentence before being paroled eight months ago. The first in the series of so-called tongue murders happened just one month after his release."

Freeland rolled his eyes. "This is beginning to sound like that old Willie Horton commercial," he muttered, just loud enough for everyone to hear.

Victoria ignored it. "Now that we know Frank Hannon's involved, the common thread connecting the victims has become obvious: They were all passengers on the *Peninsular II* on the night he committed the rape."

She laid the pointer on the table and picked up a red-tipped marker. "Not only were they on the same ship, but they were staying on the same deck, in the adjacent cabins. These were basically inexpensive single-passenger accommodations on the lowest deck, below the waterline, so the cabins didn't even have portholes. They appealed to vacation bargain hunters, people on a budget—like the young woman who was raped. She was in cabin 503," she said, circling it in red.

"Hannon's first homicide victim was in cabin 501." She marked it in red, this time with an X. "Next was 502. He skipped 503, his rape victim, then went to 504, 505, and on down the line, right in sequential order."

"Question," said Caldwell, raising a professorial finger. He spoke in trademark fashion, with his unlit pipe clenched between his teeth. "How did Hannon secure the passengers' names?"

"When we checked the court files from Hannon's rape trial, we found that his lawyer had subpoenaed the passenger manifest in pretrial discovery. We presume he was simply fishing for a list of potential witnesses, or other potential suspects."

He raised an eyebrow like a learned old judge, then leaned forward as he removed his pipe. "If a document existed that actually listed the names of the victims, why didn't *somebody* make a connection somewhere along the line?"

Victoria glared. He was clearly implying she'd overlooked something. "The only person who might have been able to link this list to the victims is Hannon's defense lawyer, and he's dead. Cancer, eight years ago. Even if he were alive, I doubt even *he* would have made the connection. These passengers weren't really a part of the trial. They were just names on a defense lawyer's very long list—three thousand names, if you include staff and crew members. None of them ever testified at trial, because the few passengers who *were* interviewed all said they saw nothing. You have to remember, too, that these passengers never knew each other before the cruise, and they all went their separate ways afterward. Think about it: Do you remember the names of the people who were in the hotel room next to you on your vacation twelve years ago?"

"I suppose not," Caldwell grumbled. "Anyway, now that we've identified his potential targets, what's being done to notify and protect these people?"

Shapiro spoke up. "I made that call. We're not going with a media blitz, if that's what you're wondering. That would just send him into hiding—or worse, send him on a killing spree. I don't want to do anything to tip our hand to Hannon that we know he's the killer. We're working discreetly through our field offices to contact everyone on the Hot List first—

which is everyone on the same deck where the rape occurred—and ultimately everyone who was on the ship, both passengers and crew. We're keeping the media out of it."

Caldwell made a face. "I'd be a lot more comfortable with the clandestine approach if we knew *why* he was targeting these people."

"We do know why," said Victoria, casting a long look across the table. "That's where Michael Posten fits in."

The garage light was burned out, but the old Coleman lantern gave Mike all the reading light he needed. Although he'd moved out after the separation, his files had stayed behind in their place of honor—the garage. The entire east wall, from the garden tools in the corner to the washer-dryer at the opposite end, was a floor-to-rafters collection of stacked banker's boxes, containing every file on every story he'd written in thirteen years as a *Tribune* reporter. There were marked-up drafts, handwritten interview notes, some old phone messages. Somewhere in there was even his first issue as editor in chief of his college paper, the *Independent Florida Alligator*.

Mike was sitting cross-legged on the cement floor, surrounded by a semicircle of old boxes he'd pulled down from the wall. A stack of yellowed papers lay scattered before him. The lantern rested on the floor at his side, lighting a small area like a campfire, so that he and his selected boxes seemed shrouded in a ball of light in the dark garage. The lantern's gas-fired mantles gave off a faint but steady hiss, the only break in the heavy silence. A hungry mosquito buzzed in Mike's ear, then lighted on his cheek. He swatted it, splattering the blood on his chin without ever looking up from the yellowed clippings at his feet. He simply turned the page.

He was reading one of his stories on Frank Hannon, written for the *Tribune* twelve years ago.

A passing shadow suddenly broke his concentration. He caught his breath as he quickly checked over his shoulder.

"Karen," he said with a sigh of relief. "What are you doing up?"

She was wearing a white silk robe, cinched at the waist. With the backlight from the lantern, Mike noticed the curve of her breasts underneath. Her hair was mussed, as if she'd been at war with the pillow. She sat on top of a stack of boxes near the lantern.

"I couldn't sleep. Not after what you told me about Hannon."

"Sorry. I wasn't trying to spook you. I just thought you should know."

"Don't be sorry. Not knowing is worse." She smiled thinly, appreciatively, then glanced at the clippings spread out across the floor. "So, what are you looking for?"

"This is so frustrating," he said with a sigh. "I feel like I should have known it was Hannon. Hell, I'm the guy who passed the tip along to the police that got him convicted."

"Don't blame yourself. With all the stories you've written, twelve years ago is like ancient history. You didn't know any of the victims, so there was nothing to trigger any memories of him. As far as you knew, Hannon wasn't even supposed to be out of prison for another eight years."

Mike grimaced cynically, shaking his head. "The parole board called him a model prisoner. Can you imagine such a thing?"

"If he was such a good prisoner, they should have left him in prison." She caught his eye, then tried to smile. "I'm worried about you. Why don't you try to get some sleep?"

"I can't. Hannon's on a revenge rampage. It's clear to me he's determined to find the source of my information. It may be futile, but I have to go over this stuff, just to see if there's anything I've overlooked. I *have* to figure out who my source was before Hannon does."

"You really have no idea who she was?"

"No. It was a totally anonymous call. She was scared to death to get involved. That's why I never wrote a story based on the tip—just follow-up pieces. I couldn't verify who she was, so I just passed her information along to the police, for whatever they thought it was worth." He looked away, then glanced back curiously. "How'd you know it was a woman?"

She shrugged. "I guess I just assumed a woman would be more fearful of retaliation from a rapist, that's all. She might think it's safer to make an anonymous call to a reporter. The guy might come after *her* if she went to the police."

Mike nodded. "The one good thing is that Hannon knows less about my informant than I do.

Based on the way he's selected his victims, he's apparently assuming that whoever saw him coming out of the victim's cabin was staying on the same deck, probably in one of the cabins nearby. That's probably a reasonable assumption, given the way it happened in an isolated cluster of cabins at the end of a dead-end hall, where the only people who had any business being there at three o'clock in the morning were the passengers in the area. But he obviously doesn't know whether it was a man or a woman, black or white, old or young. His victims have been just about every combination of race, sex and age. Basically everyone who was staying in that little area."

Karen moved to another box, closer to Mike and more at eye level with him. "There's something I don't understand about all this. Why is Hannon focusing on the anonymous source? You'd think he'd be more angry at the judge or the jury or the witnesses who actually showed up at trial."

"That's the whole point. Without the informant there never would have been a trial. The police didn't even have a suspect when the investigation started. They collected a small amount of semen from the victim's vagina, but they couldn't very well run blood and DNA tests on all two thousand male passengers and crew members, looking for a match. The big break came when the informant called me with the physical description of the man she saw leaving the victim's cabin. She focused the entire investigation on Hannon. Once the police knew he was their man, it was just a matter of collecting circumstantial evidence that linked him to the crime. Blood test matched.

Fibers matched. A pubic hair matched. And when the DNA matched, they didn't need the informant's testimony."

Karen turned pensive, staring off to the darkness. "Are you afraid?"

"I've dealt with some pretty scary people. Hannon is definitely the scariest."

"I meant, are you afraid he might come after you? Maybe he'll try to get you to tell him who your informant was."

Mike shook his head. "He *knows* I don't know who my informant was."

"How?"

"Eventually it became public knowledge that I didn't know. The police issued a statement after Hannon's arrest, praising me for passing on the tip. It was explained that I didn't run with the story because I couldn't verify the source."

"I hope he bought that explanation," she said in a hollow voice. She was silent for a moment, then glanced up from the articles at his feet. "So, what do you think he'll do now?"

"It depends on what the FBI does. I think he may lay low for a while, maybe change his identity, wait for the manhunt to scale back a bit. He knows that not even the FBI can keep the intensity up forever."

Her voice softened. "You think he'll keep on killing?"

Mike blinked, then looked her in the eye. "Truthfully? I don't think he'll ever stop. Not even after he finds the informant. Not until somebody stops him."

Chapter 42

The night sky was a cloudless blanket of stars from every galaxy, the sea a gentle scape of blackness with white foamy waves. A steady east wind filled the mainsail and jib on a broad reach toward Puerto Rico. Hannon was shirtless, wearing only a pair of Bermuda shorts he'd taken from the captain. He was at the helm, manning the tiller. He closed his eyes, then opened them, enjoying the cool sea air on his face.

The captain sat at the other end of the cockpit, facing Hannon. His hands were tied behind his back. A rope around his waist kept him secured in place. Navigational charts lay on the seat beside him, showing the way from Antigua to Puerto Rico. He was still in the same nightshirt he'd been wearing when Hannon had come aboard twenty-six hours earlier. He hadn't slept since then, though he'd watched Hannon get his fair share. All he could do was watch, since Hannon had tied him so securely. The man looked much older than his sixty-one years. Part of it was a life at sea, part of it was the present circumstances. His eyes were growing heavy now, and he was fighting sleep.

"You ever heard of Ted Bundy, Captain?"

He stirred from his state of semi-sleep. His lips smacked, but he said nothing. The waves gently splashed against the starboard side.

"Hey," Hannon snapped. "I'm talking to you. I said: Ever heard of Ted Bundy?"

The captain licked the sea salt from his shriveled old lips. "Yeah. I heard of him. The killer."

Hannon smiled to himself, more like a condescending smirk. "That's a real test of fame, isn't it? Some ignorant old fart floating around the world in a sailboat knows who you are." He shook his head in amazement, then glanced back. "How many people you suppose a guy has to kill to get that famous?"

The captain shrugged without interest. "I wouldn't know."

"Come on. Ten? Twenty?"

"I said I didn't know."

Hannon ignored his surly tone. "I see it this way. Bundy was like the first guy to break the four-minute mile. The world was in awe. Everybody knew his name—until faster runners came along, and people expected more. You remember the name of the first guy to run a four-minute mile?"

The captain shook his head.

"Of course you don't. Nowadays, he's no more famous than the *last* guy to run a four-minute mile. So tell me, Captain. What does a guy have to do *these days* to be as famous as Ted Bundy? Is it a numbers game, or do you get points for originality?"

The old man narrowed his eyes, seemingly building up courage. "A murderer gets famous the same way as always, I suppose."

"How's that?"

"By getting caught."

Hannon shot him a glance, then looked off in the distance. The lights of a cruise ship shined on the horizon. Several minutes passed, then he pointed with a nod. "That's a pretty sight, isn't it. A cruise ship at night."

The captain turned his head to look. His eyes brightened, like the Bird Man of Alcatraz peering out at freedom.

"Makes you wish you were on it, doesn't it?" Hannon taunted.

The captain looked away.

Hannon let the silence linger. "I was on one once. A cruise ship, I mean. Raped a girl, right in her cabin."

The captain bristled, then scowled. "I wish they'd caught you."

"They did. Thanks to some snitch who talked to a reporter. Didn't even have the guts to give him a name." His expression turned serious as he gave the captain a steely glare. "Someday I'll find out who it was."

"Hey, don't take it out on me. I ain't never even been on a cruise ship."

"Don't shit your pants, okay?" Hannon said. He forced himself to calm down. "I know it wasn't you. You're not on the list."

The wind kicked up, then died. The sails luffed in the shifting breeze. Hannon pushed the tiller toward port, until the sails filled again.

"What do you mean, a list?" asked the captain.

"A list of passengers who might have been the snitch. I narrowed it down to thirty-seven people. John Wayne Gacy killed thirty-three. Puts me ahead of him."

"You're just gonna kill thirty-seven people?"

Hannon's face was deadpan. "I don't just kill them. I rip their tongues out."

The captain cringed, withdrawing as far into the corner as the ropes would let him go.

"Don't be so squeamish. It's not like it's gratuitous violence. It's just the most fitting way I know of to get a rat to admit he—or *she*—is a rat."

"Seems more like a way to get people to confess whatever you want them to confess."

"No, it wasn't like that. I didn't just say, 'Were you the person who ratted on me?' I asked specifics. Like, what time was it? What color shirt was I wearing? Which way did I turn? Only the real McCoy would know the answer to those questions."

The sails luffed in the shifting breeze. The captain looked at him curiously, as if he weren't quite sure Hannon was for real. The mainsail was beginning to flap like a bedsheet in the breeze. "You need to tack," he said finally.

Hannon used his foot to steer, taking the jib sheet in one hand and the main sheet in the other. "Helm's away," he said, pushing it away with his foot. The captain ducked as the boom swung overhead. The boat rocked from starboard to port as it came about. Hannon found the wind, then tightened the sheets. He smiled with satisfaction as the boat settled into its new tack.

The troubled look returned to the captain's face. "You ain't really killed all those people, have you? You just yankin' my chain with all that tongue stuff, right?"

Hannon stared without expression, then smiled like a drinking buddy. "You're too smart for me, Captain."

The old man sighed with relief.

"But I did rape that girl."

Their eyes locked, as if the captain were trying to discern whether it was true. "What you do that for?"

"Why'd I rape her? Complicated question. You ever heard of Marfan's syndrome?"

His brow furrowed. "No."

"You're looking at it."

He swallowed hard.

"Would you like a closer look?"

"No," his voice shook.

"Liar. You'd *love* a closer look. You're just afraid. That's the way people are. The happiest people in the world aren't looking at life through rose-colored glasses. They're peering into their neighbor's bedroom with telescopes and binoculars."

"Not me. That's why I'm on the ocean. I couldn't give a shit about other people."

Hannon nodded. "You're all right, Captain. There's hope for you yet."

His eyes flickered. "Does that mean you'll let me go?"

"Of course I'm gonna let you go."

The captain smiled awkwardly. "Really?"

"Really. In fact, I'll let you off right here." In two quick steps he was across the cockpit. He took the fish filet knife from his pocket and cut the rope around the captain's waist. He grabbed the captain by the shirt collar, then yanked him to his feet. "Come on, old man. It's time to go."

His hands were still tied behind his back. His nervous smile faded. His lips quivered with fear. "Why you want to hurt an old man in the middle of the ocean? I'm no snitch. I just mind my own business. I won't tell anyone I even met you."

"There's really only one way to make sure of that, isn't there."

"Please. We're still twenty miles from shore. I'll drown."

Hannon grabbed the man's shoulder, turned him around, and quickly cut his hands free. The captain rubbed his wrists. He was almost giddy at the thought of going free, but gasping with fear. "We're still too far out. I can't swim this. I'll drown, I tell you."

Hannon clutched the knife. With a quick slash he opened a deep, long flesh wound down the length of each of the captain's arms. Blood immediately ran from the old man's shoulders to his wrists.

The captain cried out, though the blade was so sharp it was more shocking than painful. "What— what'd you do *that* for!"

Hannon was deadpan. "Now you won't drown. The sharks will eat you."

With a quick shove the man tumbled backward into the ocean, head over heels. He went under with a splash but came up quickly, bobbing with bloody arms flailing, coughing up salt water. The white sails caught the wind, sending the boat knifing through the waves.

The captain's desperate cries for mercy grew more faint and distant as the boat forged ahead.

Hannon glanced up at the stars, then out across the waves. The black ocean was deceptive, seemingly peaceful, but with so much activity hidden beneath the waves. With his foot on the tiller Hannon looked back in amusement, knowing that the crimson trail was as long and wide as the sailboat's wake—and that nighttime was feeding time.

Chapter 43

the stale smells of burned coffee and pipe tobacco lingered in the conference room as six tired agents pushed on through dawn. The buildings in Quantico were all no smoking, but Steve Caldwell seemed to bring the scent of Royal Copenhagen wherever he went. Mini-blinds on the east window slashed the early-morning sun into horizontal stripes. Files and transcripts covered every inch of Formica on the table, with empty Styrofoam cups scattered about. A pile of crumpled candy wrappers gathered at David Shapiro's elbow. The diagram of the *Peninsular II* had a few more circles and arrows, reflecting the collective wisdom regarding which cabin might be Hannon's next target. Jackets and ties lay draped over the backs of chairs. Caldwell was resting on the couch, still awake, sucking on his unlit pipe. The others were resting on their elbows, still hashing things out at the table.

Arnold Freeland ran a hand through his hair, perplexed. "One question still tugs at me. If Hannon wanted to know who the source was, why didn't he just go to Posten the day he got out of jail, put a gun to his head and force it out of him?"

Caldwell, as usual, was the first to offer an answer. He rose from the couch, packing his pipe and pacing peripatetically. "Too risky, Arnold. Picture it. He goes to Posten and demands the name of his source. Posten tells him, or doesn't tell him—either way, Hannon has to kill him. The murder comes right on the heels of Hannon's release from prison. Hannon is the prime suspect, since Posten supplied the information that landed him in prison. His scheme never gets off the ground."

Shapiro grimaced. His shirtsleeves were rolled up to the elbows, and flecks of a powdered-sugar doughnut dotted the tie hanging loosely around his neck. "That may be part of it, Steve. But I think the real reason Hannon hasn't gone after Posten is that he accepts that Posten doesn't know who his informant was." He fumbled for a manila file in the mound of material on the table. "Wasn't it reported in the press that Posten couldn't verify his source?"

Freeland nodded. "Even if Posten did know the source, Hannon had to realize that no reporter would serve up his source on a platter to be slaughtered by a psychopath bent on revenge."

"Those are all very logical explanations," said Victoria. "Which is why I think they're all wrong."

"What a surprise," said Caldwell, his voice filled with sarcasm. "Why don't you just write another memo to Assistant Director Dougherty?"

Her eyes were like lasers. "Much in the same way

you enjoy insulting me, Steve, I think Hannon simply *enjoys* the killing. Every time he rips out somebody's tongue, he's experiencing the fantasy of finding his informant. That's what drives psychopaths—the fantasy. Truth is, seldom does a serial killer direct his anger at the person he really resents."

Shapiro sipped his cold coffee. "He was in prison for twelve years. That's a long time for somebody to harbor resentment about an informant."

"You have to consider the circumstances."

"Oh, no," Caldwell groaned. "I hear another lesson in pop psychology coming on."

This time, Shapiro shot him a look. "Let me remind you, Steve: It was the pop psychologist who was right the last time."

His teeth clenched his pipe, but he said nothing.

"Okay, Victoria," said Shapiro. "What's your fix on Hannon?"

She nodded at her boss with appreciation. "Let me just say straightaway that this isn't just off the top of my head. Yesterday in Miami I had a pretty in-depth conversation with the prosecutor who handled Hannon's rape case, and he had some keen insights of his own.

"Anyway, I see Hannon as a handsome, personable man who women find attractive. He probably dated in college, but I doubt it ever led to sex. He had a physical deformity that made him the subject of teasing as a schoolboy. The same deformity made him paranoid about taking his clothes off with a woman he'd have to see again. He was convinced she'd make fun, tell everyone, embarrassing him. He tried intercourse only with women he would never see again. He may have turned first to prostitutes. Then to rape—which gave him the power to have any woman he wanted, totally anonymously.

"His rape trial, though, stripped him of his anonymity in the worst way imaginable. The victim never got a look at his face. Basically, all she could say about her attacker was that he was a large white man with a remarkably small penis.

"The prosecutor couldn't force Hannon to show his penis to the jury; it would be self-incrimination. But he did introduce into evidence Hannon's medical records showing that he had Marfan's syndrome as an adolescent. It's a disease that makes the bones grow fast, but it stunts the growth of the genitals. The end result is a tall man with a very small penis. For Hannon, it was bad enough being convicted. Even worse, however, the world suddenly knew his most humiliating secret.

"He spent twelve years in jail, searching his mind for someone to blame. He didn't blame the victim; he's the one who got *her* involved. The police were just doing their job, as were the judge, jury and prosecutor. Even the media was just doing what the media does. His anger focused on the one person who went out of her way to hurt him. She didn't have to get involved. And if she hadn't gotten involved, he never even would have been arrested in the first place. He blames the informant."

Silence filled the room. Victoria scanned all eyes around the table, waiting for someone to poke holes. No one said a word.

Finally, Caldwell sprung from the couch. "I *knew* I was right! There *is* an underlying sexual motivation for these murders." He was pacing again, waving his pipe. "This is what I've been saying all along: Serial killers are psychopathic sexual sadists. Haven't you heard me say this before, David?"

Shapiro glanced at Victoria and rolled his eyes, then looked back at Caldwell. "Siddown, Steven."

Caldwell stopped in his tracks. Silence again lingered in the room, but it was more tense than expectant.

Shapiro rubbed his face, then sighed heavily. "We all need to get some rest," he said. "But before anybody moves, let me tell you where *I* think we are. Victoria, we need you to get Posten to give us the name of his source, assuming he knows. It's obvious that Hannon is after the informant he used on that story."

"David, I don't think Posten is being cute with us. He told me he doesn't know, and I believe him."

"Why?"

"Because of the relationship we've developed, for one thing. But the main thing is that he didn't just shut me out and say, sorry, I can't tell you anything. He seemed to tell me everything he knew about this informant."

"What did he tell you?"

"Enough for me to reach the same conclusion he did: Whoever she is, she's not likely to reveal herself to anyone, ever—not under any circumstances."

"Why is that?"

She grimaced, struggling for the right way to say it. "Sometimes when you deal with a confidential source, a perfect stranger, they become very forthcoming, very trusting. I've seen that with some of my own informants. Anyway, Mike and his informant had a very brief phone conversation, just long enough for her to give him Hannon's description. She had a sock or something over the receiver, disguising her voice. He tried to get her to tell him who she was, but she wouldn't. He passed her information on to the police and figured that was the end of it. But a few months later, he heard from her again. They developed some kind of dialogue—still anonymous. I don't know the details, but it got to the point where she was totally open. Too open for her own good."

Shapiro arched an eyebrow. "What do you mean she was totally open?"

"She confessed something very private about herself. The kind of thing that, in my opinion, would make it impossible for a woman to ever admit she was his informant."

"What did she say?"

Victoria hesitated, then looked Shapiro in the eye. "She told him she'd killed a man."

Chapter 44

a t ten after eight Karen put on her robe and
walked into the living room. The reading light
was still on, just a glowing globe in a room
already bright with streams of morning sunlight. Mike
was asleep on the couch, with his head on one armrest
and his feet hanging over the other. His shoes were off,
but he was still wearing his shirt and blue jeans.
Obviously, sleep had crept up on him.

Karen hadn't slept much last night. She'd lain
awake, wondering about a lot of things. She'd wondered, in particular, whether to invite him to bed. She
missed the time they used to spend holding each other,
talking in the dark. They might not have made the
whole world right, but for a brief, safe moment, it
would at least be irrelevant.

She stood over him and watched him sleep. She'd
seen him like this before, more in a state of exhaustion
than rest. He'd always been the type to put work ahead
of sleep. He'd run for days on pure adrenaline, chasing

down some story. Eventually, his body would shut down and scream "Enough!" When that happened, he could sleep through Mardi Gras.

She sat on the edge of the coffee table, then leaned over and stroked his head. She smiled as he stirred. Then she stopped suddenly. A weathered page of handwritten notes at the top of the stack of papers on the floor caught her eye. She recognized Mike's handwriting marking it CONFIDENTIAL.

The date in the margin said it was twelve years old.

She looked at Mike. Still asleep. Discreetly, she picked it up.

His eyes blinked open just as she started reading. She quickly hid the notes behind her back, as if she'd been caught snooping.

"Morning," he said with a disoriented smile. He propped himself up on one elbow.

She smiled and tossed her hair nervously. One hand was still behind her back. "Morning. I was just, uh . . ."

"Watching me sleep?"

She smiled sweetly, but her anxiety showed. "Yeah. That's all."

He smirked. He could read her face. "What's behind your back?"

She sighed and rolled her eyes, slowly producing the letter. "I *really* was just watching you sleep. It just caught my eye, okay?"

He stretched and sat up on the couch. He smiled at first, then turned serious. "It's okay. Those are just some notes I jotted down after my last conversation with—you know, the informant from back then."

Karen looked away for a moment, then glanced back. "You kept the notes all these years?"

"Yeah," he said, shrugging. "I guess when somebody really opens to you . . . Well, it didn't seem right to throw them away."

She nodded, seeming to understand.

He sat up and faced her. "I only talked to her twice. The first time she told me about Hannon. Very brief. I didn't hear from her for another eight months, the day they picked the jury in Hannon's trial. She was an absolute wreck."

"What do you mean?"

"She was still trying to disguise her voice, and on top of that she was sobbing and breaking into tears. At times I could hardly understand what she was saying. But I understood what she was going through."

"You did?"

"Yeah. She was terrified Hannon would go free because she wasn't testifying at trial. She felt like she was turning her back on the woman he'd raped by not having the courage to do everything she possibly could to help convict him. I think she just wanted me or *someone* to understand why she was afraid to go to the police, why she couldn't come forward and testify at trial. Why she had to be anonymous."

"Is that something you could understand?"

"Sure. I told her that on the phone. We talked for a while, I really don't remember how long. Naturally, I was pretty surprised by what she said. But I think it was cathartic for her to tell me, get it off her chest. Then that was the end of it. I never heard from her again."

"Did you ever try to find her?"

"I was confused about that. I wasn't sure it was ethical for a reporter to search out someone who wanted to be anonymous. I spoke to Aaron Fields. He wanted me to pursue it. He thought maybe there'd be a story there."

Her eyes clouded. "So this woman poured her heart out, and the only thing that crossed your mind was maybe there'd be another story?"

He looked her straight in the eye. For a split second he thought of that recent morning in his publisher's dark blue Mercedes, with Aaron telling him they were exactly alike. "No," he said in all sincerity. "That was Aaron. I'm not like that."

He scooted to the edge of the couch, leaned forward and took her hand. "Remember when we were in Maine, and you told me, 'The only people who can be truly open with each other are lovers and strangers'? That's so true. This woman was a total stranger, but she told me secrets she'd never told anyone before. She was in a lot of pain, and she had to tell *someone* what was inside her. And you know what? It felt . . . right. It seemed completely natural that *I* was the one she told. Who else could she turn to? I was the only one who knew her dilemma."

Karen grimaced, then lowered her eyes. "So this woman told you everything. But your wife keeps secrets."

He tried to smile, but it was a painful one. "I don't fault you for that. For all I know, this women was married. I may know things about her that even her husband doesn't know."

"Maybe," she said as she squeezed his hand. "But maybe it's time my husband knew mine."

He didn't move. Their eyes locked for what seemed a very long time, and then she began. For ten astonishing minutes, he just listened. Her body shook as she told him, but she told him everything. The curtains blowing in the open window. The brutal beating in the hallway. The unspeakable acts in the bedroom. And finally, the struggle for the gun and the shot that rang out.

Saying it aloud made the final moments more vivid. She could see herself crawling on hands and knees across the floor, drawing closer to her rapist. His splattered blood covered her naked body. A gaping wound glistened like a crimson rose through his T-shirt. She touched his arm, and he groaned, causing her to start. She squeezed the gun in her hand. It felt so *big*. A sucking, gurgling sound came from his mouth. Still on her knees, she slid closer to him, then raised the gun with shaking hands, pointing it at his head. Then, once again, he spoke.

"Help me," he said.

Her arms shook, her whole body trembled.

Mike watched in rapt silence as she told her story. She seemed almost in a trance.

"Help me," she said, repeating the man's words.

There was a long pause. Mike sighed, not sure whether she wanted to continue—whether she *should* continue. "What did you do?" he asked.

She bit her lip, and her face swelled, as if something inside were about to burst. "It wasn't self-defense," she said flatly. "It was revenge."

He blinked hard, trying not to judge. "Anyone would understand what you did."

Her voice was shaking. "No. Anybody would have understood if I'd just fired a second shot in the heat of the moment, out of fear or confusion or even anger."

"That's not what you did?"

"No. *No!* I listened to him plead. He begged me to call an ambulance. He begged me to give him the phone, to let him call. But I wouldn't let him. Something inside me wouldn't let him. Don't you understand? All I could think about was what he'd done to me. I wanted him to suffer. I told him I'd shoot him if he so much as twitched a finger. I just sat there and watched him die."

"Lots of women would have done exactly what you did. He raped you, beat you bloody. Who's to say he wouldn't have killed you?"

"He did kill me," she said in a hollow voice. "Right before he died."

He paused, then asked, "What did he do?"

She swallowed hard and hugged him as tears filled her eyes. Her chin rested on his shoulder as she spoke, as if she could only look past him, not at him. Her shaky voice cracked with emotion. "He looked at me and said, 'Please, lady. Don't let me die. I'm only fifteen years old.'"

Mike didn't move, couldn't move. Her whole body shook violently in his arms. He fought back his own tears, feeling her pain. He held her close, with all his strength, then brushed her wet cheek. "It's okay. Everything will be all right." He spoke softly, shutting his eyes tightly.

Then his eyes blinked open, as the full weight of her words sunk in. He remembered that painful telephone conversation twelve years ago. The woman with the disguised voice who'd seen Frank Hannon. The woman who'd called to explain through tears why she couldn't come forward to testify against him. The woman who'd confessed to having killed her own rapist.

The informant.

"It's okay," he said with a lump in his throat. "I'm very protective of my sources."

Chapter 45

the luxury cruise ship MS *Fantasy* sailed from the Port of San Juan at 10:00 A.M., bound for Miami. Gray-white smoke curled from the stacks into a cloudless blue sky. Foghorns bellowed as legions of smiling tourists clad in straw hats and sunglasses waved from crowded decks on five different levels. In the harbor below, brown-skinned men treading crystal-clear waters waved back eagerly, diving for the pocket change the passengers deigned to throw. In thirty minutes, the big white ship was gliding out to sea.

The *Fantasy* boasted eleven different onboard bars and lounges. The Tiki Bar was a shaded outdoor bar on the Pool Deck, done in a Tahitian bamboo and palm tree decor. Seated on a stool at the end of the bar was a calm and collected Frank Hannon, comfortably disguised in full tourist regalia.

Hannon knew Antigua was a member of Interpol. He wasn't sure what kind of international manhunt they'd mounted, but he was taking the necessary precautions. His alias was now Keith Ellers, taken from the sailor he'd fed to the sharks. Big mirrored sunglasses and a broad straw hat covered most of his face. Purple zinc oxide distorted his nose. Rubber sandals, Bermuda shorts and a loud Hawaiian print shirt completed the ensemble, with a frothy piña colada in a hollowed-out coconut shell for good measure. Even with his height, people would mistake him for Norton on *The Honeymooners* before they'd spot Frank Hannon the serial killer or Eric Venters the bank robber.

Hannon had debated whether to fly or sail back to the United States. With the captain's credit card, he could have afforded either. Flying was faster, but he knew immigration was tighter at the airports. Seaports were notoriously lax border-control points.

Hannon glanced toward the women sunbathing at the pool. A shapely young brunette smearing lotion on her thighs caught his attention. The television was playing behind the bar, and he whirled around quickly at the sound of his name.

Flashing on the screen was a grainy color photograph of a blond-haired man with blue eyes and a well-groomed beard that hid most of his face. Hannon recognized it as his old mug shot.

"According to exclusive CNN sources," said the anchorwoman, "all of Hannon's alleged victims were passengers on the cruise ship *Peninsular II*, which sailed twelve years ago on a three-day cruise from Miami to Nassau on April sixteenth, seventeenth, and eighteenth. Reportedly, the FBI is now secretly making contact with all passengers and crew from that specific three-day cruise, for their own safety.

"In addition to the ten so-called tongue murders, CNN sources reveal that police are also investigating Hannon's possible connection to the robbery of an Atlanta woman in which the perpetrator mutilated the victim's hand.

"You're watching *Headline News* on CNN. More news in a minute."

Hannon stared blankly at the screen as the news broke for a commercial. He sipped his piña colada, deep in thought.

It was no time to panic. The good news was that he was in no immediate danger of being recognized. In the old mug shot, he was fifty pounds heavier. The extra weight, together with the full beard and mustache, hid most of his facial features. He'd grown facial hair after the rape precisely for that reason, just in case the victim had gotten a look at him. He wasn't sure whether they'd connected him to the Antigua murders, since he'd missed the first part of the broadcast—but even if they had, the disguise he'd worn would have had them looking for a Middle Eastern–looking man named Eric Venters.

Too, he reminded himself he was *just* a suspect. Somehow, somebody had figured out that all of the victims were passengers on the cruise ship where he'd committed a rape. But it took more than motive to prove a man a killer. One thing was certain: The police would never find any physical evidence linking him to the murders. His were the *perfect* crimes.

He was smiling, about to order another drink, when his expression went cold. He suddenly realized that he'd overlooked the fact that, as CNN had just reported, the police had somehow linked the serial killings to the woman in Atlanta from whom he'd taken the diamond ring.

Valerie had the ring.

He closed his eyes, regretting the day he'd given it to her. It had seemed like a harmless, titillating little ploy at the time—mutilating one woman to win the heart of another. He'd resisted those fetish urges with each of his tongue murders. He'd forced himself never to take anything from the crime scenes, having heard of too many serial killers who'd been caught with their "trophies"—jewelry, photographs, body parts. He'd never dreamed, however, that they'd connect an isolated robbery in Atlanta to the killings.

He sighed, considering his options. He could do nothing and hope that Valerie would never realize the "Charlie Ackroyd" she fell in love with was actually Frank Hannon. She wasn't *that* stupid, though. The average person might never recognize Hannon from the photographs on CNN, but Valerie *knew* him—up close and very personal. What would she do, he wondered, if she saw a resemblance? Having heard nothing from him in more than a week, she'd probably get suspicious. She'd start to wonder about all of his out-of-town trips on supposed interviews. She might even hire a private investigator to check out "Charlie Ackroyd"—to find out who he was, and where he'd gone. The investigator would tell her that Ackroyd never existed. Then she'd go to the police.

But if she heard his voice—Charlie's voice—she'd be reassured. She wouldn't get suspicious, and she'd never call the police.

Hannon slid off the barstool and headed inside, convinced there was only one thing to do. He composed himself as he headed toward the bank of telephones on the main deck, considering what he'd say. Then he closed the door to the phone booth, paid for the ship-to-shore call with Captain Ellers's credit card, and dialed the number.

"Valerie, it's me."

"Charlie! Where've you been? I was so worried."

Hannon felt a rush of relief. She obviously hadn't been watching the news, or at least she hadn't made any sort of connection. "Sorry I haven't called. Something terrible has happened."

"What!"

He sighed audibly, as if it were difficult to tell her. "It's your Volvo."

"Did you have an accident? Are you okay!"

"I'm fine. But the car was stolen. I'm really sorry. I've been working with the police, trying to track it down. I know I should have called, but I just—I was just putting off calling you, hoping they'd find it. But it's gone. I'm sorry, Val. Will you forgive me?"

"Oh, Charlie," she gushed. "I don't care about a stupid car. I was so scared. I thought you were dead or in a hospital, or . . ." Her voice cracked, then trailed off.

Hannon sensed her anxiety. "Or what?"

"That you'd left me. I thought you were with another woman. I found a napkin in your book, where she'd written her phone number. Someone named Victoria."

Hannon blinked hard, hiding his anger. "Victoria?"

he said, pretending not to know it. "I did meet a Victoria at an airport a few weeks ago. We just talked. I never asked for her phone number. She must have just stuck it in there when I wasn't looking. You know how pushy some women can be."

"I really want to believe that."

"I would never lie to you."

There was still only silence. Hannon took a deep breath. He could sense she was on the fence. The wheels turned quickly in his head, searching for the right words. *The ring—of course!* He softened his voice, the way he did on the night he'd come back from Atlanta and given it to her. "Valerie, I gave you my own mother's engagement ring. The only thing of value I own in the whole world. Doesn't that mean anything?"

She was sniffling. "Of course it does, darling."

"So," he said coyly, "you won't change the locks on me?"

She sniffled again, laughing with affection. "No. Come home, darling."

"Two more days."

"Why so late? Come now."

"I've been running around so much trying to find the Volvo, I've hardly scratched the surface on that computer virus."

"Well, then . . . why don't I come up and stay with you?"

"No," he said firmly. "You know how I get when I'm working."

"It'll be good for you. Come on, Charlie, don't you want to see—"

"I said *no*, damn you."

The tone was extremely harsh, like something from his other side. He drew a deep breath, calming himself. "Sorry, Val. I'm just under a lot of pressure right now. All these accountants screaming at me. I'm doing everything I can to get their computers back up to speed. It just wouldn't be good for you to come. But I'll work fast. I've got four days of work left; I'll cram it into two, three at most. Then we can be together. Okay?"

"Okay," she peeped.

"Just try not to touch yourself between now and then. I want you to really want me."

"Charlie!" she said with mock astonishment.

"Love ya, babe."

"I love you, too."

"Gotta go," he said, then hung up the phone. He sighed, then rolled his head, loosening the muscles in his neck.

His hand was still gripping the phone as he sat in the booth, thinking. A part of him—a very small part—wished there were some other way to handle the only woman who'd never embarrassed him, who'd never pressured him for something he simply couldn't deliver. She'd been perfectly content with his tongue and the vibrator, never even trying to coax him out of his underwear. She'd just always known when to dim the lights, close her eyes, and turn her backside submissively, where he could have his way with no one watching, where the fit was tight no matter the size.

There was no erasing from her mind, however, the little things that could convict him. Cybil Holland's ring. His supposed business trips out of town that, if anyone were to check, would turn out bogus and would coincide with the murders. And now the FBI agent's phone number.

The only question left was *how* he would kill her.

His eyes brightened as he walked away from the telephone, and his mouth curled into a smile of anticipation. *Might as well enjoy it*, he thought.

Chapter 46

One floor directly below the Academy's gun vault, Victoria was at her cluttered desk eating an early lunch or, quite possibly, a late breakfast. For all she knew it was dinner. Her watch said eleven-fifteen, but her internal clock still thought she was in Antigua sparring with the local police. This morning's shower had been at the locker room at the Academy, and she was wearing the spare suit she kept in her office closet. She wasn't sure when she'd be home again. This was why she had no pets. Hell, this was why she had no life.

While sipping a Diet Coke she scanned complete background checks on the passengers on the Lower Deck of SS *Peninsular II*. Ten had already been killed at the hand of Frank Hannon. Another six had died of natural causes. Her eyes popped when she saw the report on cabin 515.

She immediately dialed Mike's pager. He called back in thirty seconds.

"Nice exclusive you guys gave to CNN," he said. "I would have thought I at least rated a courtesy call."

"I'm in no mood for shit from anyone, okay? I would have called you if it had been our plan to take this story to the media, but it was a damn leak from one of our field offices that put it on CNN. Believe me, that was the last thing we wanted. We've lost the element of surprise. It'll be ten times harder to catch him now. Anyway, don't be giving me hell about not calling *you*. Why didn't you call *me* about passenger Karen Malone—your wife's maiden name?"

Mike sighed, chagrined. "I was about to call you."

"She's on our 'Hot List'—people within Hannon's targeted area. Her cabin was across the hall from the rape, down just a few doors. She's in potential danger, Mike."

"More than you think. She was my informant."

Her jaw dropped, but she said nothing.

Mike spoke first, heading off her anger. "I haven't been playing games with you. I just found out this morning it was her. That's between me and Karen, and I don't want to get into all that. The only thing you need to know is that she's the one who saw him. It was three o'clock in the morning. She was a little seasick and couldn't sleep. She thought she heard a scream and looked out the peephole. That's when she saw Hannon coming out of 503."

Victoria's brow scrunched in thought. "Could Rollins have known your wife was the source? Is that why you were the reporter he chose to feed his information to?"

"I considered the possibility, but it's too much of a

stretch. Rollins probably did make the connection between the choice of victims and Hannon's rape conviction—it would have been easy enough to get hold of Hannon's police record. But prior to the pay-offs, his financial situation wasn't healthy enough to permit background checks on all the likely passengers. Remember, just following Hannon from place to place was expensive. My guess is, Rollins came across my name in the coverage of Hannon's trial, and picked me as a kind of dig. It has the smell of one-upmanship. It's possible the two knew each other and there was no love lost."

"It makes sense," said Victoria. She glanced up at the ship diagram with the cabin configurations. "Better that Rollins never knew, I'd guess, because Hannon might have wormed it out of him. If I had to guess, the only reason Karen's still alive is because Hannon hasn't figured out yet that Karen Malone is Karen Posten."

"I know. That's why I've been brainstorming for a way to throw him off the trail. Maybe I could write an article saying my informant is deceased. I don't know. There's ethical issues there, too. I'd be writing a lie."

"Just don't do anything, okay? I think he's in a down cycle right now, after the Antigua murders and the CNN coverage. If he reads that the informant is dead, you could set him off into a rage that's worse than anything we've seen."

"Yeah," he said pointedly. "That's a possibility. The other possibility is that Karen Malone is the next name on his list. Do you really expect me to sit around and do *nothing*?"

Victoria sighed. "Just talk to me before you do anything. Please."

"Deal. So long as *you* talk to *me* before the FBI does anything."

"You know I can't do that."

"And you know I can't give you a veto over what I print and don't print."

"All right," she said with a reluctant sigh, "I'll give you this much: You won't know everything, but from here on out, you won't hear a thing on CNN that you don't already know."

"Sure," he said. "You know how to reach me."

They said good-bye, but as Mike hung up the phone he had no illusions. He knew what she was really saying.

From here on out, she wasn't telling *anyone* squat.

The phone conversation with Mike left Victoria with an uneasy feeling. She wondered whether, with his wife a potential target, he could simply report events and not try to influence them.

She managed just two bites of her pita-pocket sandwich when a young agent with his ID clipped to his white shirt appeared in the doorway.

"I have the Hannon photos you asked for," he said proudly.

She smiled politely and waved him in. He couldn't have been more than six months out of the Academy, and he looked about six months out of high school—something that Victoria took as a sure sign of her aging.

"Thanks, Marc," she said as she took the manila envelope. "Shapiro went ballistic when he saw that CNN broadcast this morning. I think the only thing that pissed him off more than the leak was the lousy old photograph CNN dug up. They might as well have run that old sketch of the Unabomber. Probably about as good a likeness."

He watched eagerly as Victoria opened the photo envelope and removed the glossies. "The top one's from his high school yearbook, which is pretty old," Marc volunteered. "But at least he doesn't have a beard and mustache, like he does in his mug shot and prison photo."

"He also looks thinner," said Victoria.

"Yeah. The lab guessed he put on about fifty pounds after high school. That's why the real gems are on the bottom, the face-aged computer likeness created by headquarters. They based it mostly on the old high school yearbook photo, since he's covered with facial hair in every picture we have that's more recent. The computer enhanced the lines in his face, made the skin a little less pink, gave him a more contemporary haircut."

Her expression froze as she stared at the image. The hair was blond, the eyes were blue. But she could see past the things that hair dye and colored lenses could easily change. "It's him," she said quietly, almost to herself.

The young agent looked at her curiously. "Of course it's him."

She stared at the computer image, not really listening. Her mind was racing, and the pieces were finally fitting together. "Now I'm certain of it," she said, still staring at his image. "I've seen him before."

She looked up. Marc was about to speak when she sprang out of the chair and bolted out the door, face-aged photograph in hand.

"Where you going!" he shouted, chasing after her.

She was streaming down the hall at full speed, her two-inch heels clicking on the hard tile floor. She hit the stairwell without slowing down, never responding, never once looking back.

It was just one flight up to the auxiliary surveillance center. She slid her access card through the electronic security checkpoint and rushed through the doorway. The technician behind the counter knew her by sight. He was a skinny old black man wearing a short-sleeve dress shirt and incredibly wide tie. His warm smiled faded as she rushed toward him. She slid to a halt and leaned across the counter, speaking right into his face.

"I want the transcripts," she said, still trying to catch her breath, "from the phone tap I put on Valerie St. Pierre."

Chapter 47

a three-foot tail of perforated computer paper flapped behind her as Victoria ran back downstairs and down the long corridor. It had only taken a few minutes for the surveillance department to print out a verbatim transcript of Valerie's telephone conversations, and in just a few seconds Victoria realized she had exactly what she needed. Her hair was falling and her face flushed with excitement as she landed at the door to David Shapiro's office on a dead run. She gave one quick knock, then rushed inside.

"I've got him!" she blurted.

Shapiro flashed a startled look from behind his desk. Steve Caldwell was seated on the couch beside his boss's potted prickly cactus plant. His mouth was hanging open as if Victoria had caught him in midsentence.

"He's on the MS *Fantasy*—a cruise ship out of San Juan."

The two men exchanged glances. "How do you know?" asked Shapiro.

"Long story."

"Make it short," he said with urgency.

She stepped farther inside and closed the door, then spoke quickly. "Last month, I met a guy in the airport bar in San Francisco. We got to talking, and I gave him my phone number, thinking he was a nice guy. I never heard from him, but a week ago I got an angry call from some woman claiming to be his girlfriend—very jealous type. She scared me a little, so I retrieved her name and phone number from my caller ID service and wrote it down, just in case she kept harassing me."

"What does this have to do with Hannon?"

"At the time, I didn't think it had anything to do with him. But then, fast-forward: Two days ago, I saw Hannon's mug shot and prison photo. It didn't hit me at first, because the beard and mustache made it hard to make a comparison, but the longer I stared at the photographs, the more I saw a resemblance between Hannon and the guy at the airport. That's when I really started to think about it. He was the right height, the right age. We were both flying out of San Francisco, right after the Copeland murder. And what really got me thinking was . . ." She stopped for a moment, measuring her words. "Well, we talked about his penis."

Shapiro looked at her strangely.

"In an innocent way," she said defensively. "He was just saying things like how his ex-wife didn't seem to notice he had one. It's not like he came out and said he had Marfan's syndrome, for crying out loud."

Caldwell smirked. "Gee, Victoria. You never asked *me* about my penis."

"You see, dammit?" she said angrily, shaking her head. "That's *precisely* the reason I didn't want to say anything about this. I didn't want it to turn into the next big Victoria joke, and then for the next ten years have to put up with the bullshit from every penis in the Bureau. So I pursued it on my own. Once we focused on Hannon, I had a reasonable suspicion that he was the guy I'd met at the airport, but I wasn't sure. So I just had surveillance tap the girlfriend's phone in Maryland, figuring that if something panned out, then I'd bring it to your attention. Well, it *did* pan out. Frank Hannon is on the cruise ship. And here's the transcripts that prove it."

"Transcripts of what?"

"Just this morning, a guy using the name 'Charlie' called his girlfriend from the cruise ship. Charlie is the guy who I met at the airport."

"I still don't see how you make the leap to Hannon."

"It's his old high school yearbook photo and the face-aged computer image," she said, spilling them onto his desk. "I just saw them this morning. Now that I've seen Hannon with no beard and mustache, I'm convinced that he was the guy I talked to at the San Francisco airport. That means 'Charlie' is Hannon. And Charlie's on the ship."

Shapiro gave her an assessing look. "Are you a hundred percent on this?"

"I don't know. The high school shot is almost sixteen years old. The computer image has Hannon blond and blue-eyed, and the guy in the airport had brown hair, brown eyes. But that's an easy disguise. I'm ninety-five percent sure, I'd say."

He nodded pensively, seeming to mull it over. It took just a few seconds until he looked her in the eye. "Get your sunscreen, Victoria. We're going on a little Caribbean cruise."

At Karen's invitation, Mike spent the rest of the morning at the house. He borrowed one of her disposable razors and showered in the guest bathroom. The *guest* bathroom—a tantalizing reminder that he wasn't quite home yet.

He still had some clothes buried deep in the walk-in closet, just things he'd left behind to make their separation seem temporary. Most of them had been mothballed for years, like the pastel linen jackets with colored T-shirts and rolled-up sleeves from the heyday of *Miami Vice*. He wasn't sure which was harder to believe, the fact that he'd once worn them or that Karen had actually allowed them into her closet. Fortunately, he found some khakis that still fit and a timeless old tennis shirt.

Since Victoria's phone call this morning, Mike had been bursting inside. He sensed something was afoot, and it wasn't his style to sit around waiting for the telephone to ring. But he could see in Karen's eyes that she didn't want to be left alone. For once, he was determined to put her first without telling her he was doing it.

They made a team effort at lunch. Karen cooked the fusilli pasta and created the dressing while Mike chopped up the tomatoes, carrots and broccoli. He pretended she was out of cauliflower; the broccoli was compromise enough. They ate at the blond knotty-pine table in the breakfast nook. Karen kept the room like a miniature greenhouse, with plants draping down from the skylight like ever-growing tentacles.

"I was thinking about my grandfather last night," said Mike, going heavy on the grated Parmesan.

Karen sipped her iced tea. "What about?"

"Remember toward the end there, the way his mind was kind of slipping?"

She raised an eyebrow. "You mean before or after he asked me to marry him?"

Mike smiled. "He was like a schoolboy, with those crushes he developed. I was thinking about how nuts he was for Diane Sawyer. He thought she was the total woman. A beautiful, smart journalist. Personable. And to top it all off, an incredible cook."

"Diane Sawyer can cook?"

"I doubt it," he said with a shrug. "But who had the heart to tell poor old Grandpa that the woman on television with all those great recipes was actually Martha Stewart?"

She laughed to herself. "A perfectly honest mistake for a ninety-seven-year-old man."

"Hey—he was in love, he was happy. I could have set him straight, if I'd wanted to. But you have to make a judgment call on these things." He paused to catch her eye. "Telling the truth isn't always better. The important thing is that your intentions are good."

Her smile faded. She lowered her eyes toward her pasta salad. "Nice try, Mike. But what I did to you isn't even in the same cookbook."

He looked at her with concern, until finally she looked up. A soulful expression filled her eyes.

"I was twenty years old," she said, "a punky little sophomore on spring break from Cornell. When I got off the ship I saw your article in the *Tribune* about the rape, saying the police had no suspects. That's when I decided to call you. How could I know that five years later I'd actually lay eyes on you, when I almost literally ran into you at that fund-raiser for the Miami Ballet? My first reaction was to get the hell out of there."

"But you didn't."

"No. It was a strange feeling. Your being a stranger, really, and yet knowing my deepest secret. I guess I felt like I had the right to know something about you. At least talk to you a little, find out what kind of person you were."

"It must have been a shock when I asked you out."

Her eyes widened. "Boy, was it."

"Well, at least now I know why you turned me down."

"But then when I ran into you at happy hour the next week, I started to think it was fate or something. It wasn't until after I finally said I'd go out with you that my friend Terri told me you'd called her to find out where I went after work on Fridays."

"Reporters," he said. "Can't trust 'em."

"That was sweet, really. And for the first few dates I was able to put the history aside, even though in my heart I really wanted to tell you the truth."

"Why didn't you?"

"I was afraid. I was never publicly connected to the rape or the shooting. The newspaper in New York had a policy against printing the names of rape victims, and . . . well, he was technically a juvenile, so his name wasn't printed either. I left Cornell and moved closer to home. The only people who really knew anything were my parents, and even they didn't know that what I had done was as much revenge as it was self-defense."

"Call it whatever you want. It doesn't change the way I feel about you."

"Back then it might have. What if we'd broken up? I didn't want you—a *reporter*—knowing who I was and what I'd done. So I kept putting off telling you the truth about how we met. I said to myself, I'll tell him if we date six months, if we date nine months, if we get engaged. By the time we got married, I'd kept it secret for so long that I *couldn't* tell you—not after having concealed it for so long. Keeping the secret became as bad as the secret itself."

"You're too hard on yourself."

"Really? The truth is, if Frank Hannon hadn't gotten out of prison and murdered ten people, I don't know if I ever would have told you."

He paused for a moment, then reached across the table and touched her hand. "If you had believed our marriage was strong enough to survive it, you would have told me. Keeping the secret isn't what made our marriage weak. I had a little something to do with that."

They exchanged a long, warm look. "Thank you," she said.

He nodded, then smiled wryly. "That's quite a

trick—when a guy can get a 'thank-you' for screwing up his marriage. I also do lifelong friendships and extended families, if there are any of those you'd like busted up."

She threw her wadded napkin at him, smiling as she shook her head. "That's the problem with you, Posten. You take life too seriously."

They talked well past the lunch hour. The phone rang at two-forty-five, just as Mike was loading the dishwasher. He answered in the kitchen.

"Victoria," he said, loud enough to let Karen know who it was. She was sponging off the table and stopped in midswipe. "Are you actually making good on your promise to call *me* before CNN?"

Her tone was strictly business. "I just wanted to reiterate what I said this morning. Please don't print anything about Hannon, the serial killings or your informant. It's extremely important."

"You already told me that."

"But now it's more important than ever. We're in an extremely delicate situation. Anything you write could set Hannon off, jeopardizing the lives of agents and civilians."

"If you're asking me to put public safety over the public right to know, I think I have a right to know what I'm balancing."

She sighed, struggling. "I'm sorry, I can't give specifics. All I can tell you is that Hannon doesn't know it yet, but we've got him cornered. Anything you put in print could tip him off or provoke him."

Just then, Mike heard a long, low-pitched background noise over the line, like a bassoon in the distance. He winced with confusion. *Where the heck is she calling from?*

Her voice was suddenly nervous. "I have to go. I hope I can count on you."

His mind raced as he hung up the phone. Karen stepped quietly into the kitchen. From the look on her face, he could tell she'd overheard the conversation.

"Something big is going down, isn't it," she said.

He nodded. "They've got Hannon cornered."

"Where?"

"She wouldn't say. But—" He stopped himself in mid-sentence. His expression changed, as if something had just hit him. "It was a ship's whistle."

Her faced scrunched with confusion. "What?"

"I heard a noise in the background while we were talking. It was faint, in the distance, but it was definitely one of those obnoxious horns from a ship. I think she was calling from a seaport."

"So?"

"So, where do you think they have Mr. Hannon cornered? We know he was in Antigua, because that's where he killed the guards. He's eager to get back to the United States, so he can continue his search for the informant. Victoria says they have him cornered, and I just heard a ship's whistle in the background. Right now, I'll bet he's on a ship heading for the States."

She shook her head, confused. "Why would he come by ship?"

"Antigua's over twelve hundred miles from the

United States. It could take a month in a little sail-boat, and flying would mean having to deal with air-port security."

"What kind of ship, though? Freighter? Cruise ship?"

He stopped to think. "Freighters are slow, and it's not exactly easy to know where they're headed. A cruise ship, as we know, is more his style. Some of them hold over two thousand passengers, so it's easy to get lost in the crowd. And security is nowhere near as tight as it is at the airport. The *Tribune* did a feature story a couple years ago, on how illegal immigrants come into the United States on cruise ships. One retired customs inspector estimated there were hundreds, every week. And it's no small wonder. When the ships stop in their ports of call, you don't even need a ticket to get back on. All it takes is a pass and a hand stamp, which you can get on the black market pretty easily. On some ships, the only passengers who ever got their passports checked were the ones who voluntarily presented themselves at the immigration desk onboard. The INS flat out admitted to us that it didn't have the resources for full dockside inspections."

"You think he jumped a cruise ship in Antigua?"

"Possibly." A sly smile came to his face. "If we jump on the Internet, I bet we could even figure out which one."

"You nerd. I swear I'm gonna get you a pocket pro-tector." She smiled, then led the way to her office and switched on the computer. They watched as the color-ful logo for America Online filled the screen. Karen typed in the keyword CRUISE, which prompted a big color photo of a cruise ship and a menu with several choices. She clicked on CARIBBEAN ITINERARIES.

"Yikes," she said. "Look at 'em all."

"There can't be that many departing from Antigua."

Karen scrolled down the list. "You're right. There aren't *any*. The only port of origin not on the U.S. mainland is San Juan, Puerto Rico. I see some with Antigua as a port of call, though."

"He wouldn't take any of those. Think about it. Two bank guards are murdered in Saint Johns. Some guy hops ship in the middle of a cruise, going one way, back to the United States. He might as well strap on a lightning rod. If I'm Hannon, I'm looking for a cruise that *originates* in the Caribbean. That way I can just board right along with two thousand other passengers."

"Let's see, if we eliminate everything out of Miami . . . Fort Lauderdale . . . New York." The list shortened with each click of the mouse. "Still, fourteen ships originate out of San Juan."

"I'll bet most of those just circle the Caribbean. Hannon needs one with at least one port of call on the U.S. mainland."

"There can't be very many of those," she said, scanning the screen. "Here's one: *Pacific Princess*. Originates in San Juan, goes through the Panama Canal to Los Angeles. Thirteen days."

"Too long," said Mike. "Besides, look at the sailing dates. Right now it's on its way *from* LA to San Juan. It doesn't sail back to California for another eleven days. What else is there?"

She scrolled down further. "Just this one. Round-trip from San Juan. Sails northwest to the Bahamas, then to Key West, around Cuba to Grand Cayman and Jamaica, then back to San Juan."

They looked away from the screen and locked eyes, sharing the same thought. "So Hannon boards a round-trip cruise from San Juan," he said pensively, "then gets off in Key West and never comes back to the ship."

"From there, it's straight up U.S. 1 to wherever he wants to go."

"What's the name of the ship?"

With a click of the mouse, Karen brought a close-up image of the ship on the screen. Its name stretched across the stern in bold red letters: MS *Fantasy*.

Mike stared at the screen, seeming to imagine the killer somewhere deep inside. "Print it."

She pushed a button, and the itinerary printed out, along with the ship's tonnage, capacity and vital information. Mike read as the paper curled from the printer.

"Well," said Karen, "what are you waiting for?"

He looked up from the printout. "What do you mean?"

"It's your story, isn't it? Don't you want to be there when they arrest Hannon?"

His mouth fell open, unsure what to say. Regrets came to mind over the way he'd rushed off to Aaron Field's house to argue over his probation, the last time he and Karen had seemed to be getting back on track. "I think it's more important that I stay here."

"*Please*," she said with a roll of her eyes. "You've

been a wonderful husband the last couple of days. Don't spoil it by shooting for sainthood."

He smiled. "Okay, if that's the way you feel about it. But the ship's in the middle of the Caribbean. How would I even get there?"

She switched off the computer. "If we're right, Hannon won't try to make a run for it until he hits Key West. You could fly to Nassau tonight, maybe try to board when the ship stops there tomorrow morning."

"It's a total long shot. I could get all the way on the ship and be wrong."

"Do you think you're wrong?"

He thought for a moment. "No. I think he's on that ship."

"Then go."

"You really want me to?"

She nodded. "You earned this exclusive. And there's not a person on earth who can call it checkbook journalism."

His heart swelled, as if he suddenly had something to prove. He did a half-turn, then stopped short and looked back at her. His expression was warm, but serious.

"I love you."

She blinked, a little surprised. "I can't remember the last time you said that in three words, instead of four."

"What do you mean?"

"I'm not usually the one who gets to say, 'I love you, *too*.'"

They exchanged smiles, then he "knocked wood" on his forehead as he headed for the door.

Chapter 48

a t 3:30 that afternoon the sun was shining down
brightly on the Miami seaport. From the Pool
Deck of the cruise ship MS *Rhapsody*, the sister
ship of the MS *Fantasy*, Victoria took in the view of
the Miami skyline across the bay. Downtown Miami
had essentially erupted in new construction since her
early childhood memories of "Freedom Tower," the
classic old skyscraper due west of the port that had
served as a processing center for Cuban refugees back
in the sixties. The tallest buildings were now to the
south, at the mouth of the Miami River. From a fifty-
five-story glass-and-granite peak, the cityscape sloped
steadily downward like a mountainside, as if its most
undesirable elements couldn't help but slide to the
crime-ridden areas on the north side of town. From the
deck of a cruise ship, however, even the north side
looked beautiful, as Victoria's eyes settled on the
imposing waterfront headquarters of the *Miami
Tribune*. The irony of the moment intrigued her. She

could practically wave to the reporters rushing around the fifth-floor newsroom, yet none of them had a clue that the biggest story of the year was happening right under their nose. *Unless, of course, Mike had figured it out.*

The ship was moored in its usual slot, facing east, toward the Atlantic, directly behind one of Carnival Cruise Line's floating hotels. The MS *Rhapsody* had just returned from a nine-day cruise to the Virgin Islands, and up until an hour ago the crew had been preparing for the next voyage. It was deserted now, save for a team of ten FBI agents and forty-eight-year-old Bill Odoms, the cruise line's director of security.

Odoms had the look of a tough ex-cop, someone whose first job in "security" had been as a bouncer at a bar in college. He wore a police academy ring on his right hand and a Rotary Club pin on the lapel of his navy blue sport coat. His hair was thin and combed straight back, but when the breeze blew it revealed a sunburned scalp. The tinted lenses in his gold-framed glasses had darkened in the sunlight, obscuring his eyes and a good part of his face. Still, Victoria could sense the intensity of his stare as he spoke to the group of agents.

"The *Rhapsody* is virtually a carbon copy of the *Fantasy*," he explained. "It's just two years older, and its home base is Miami, rather than San Juan. At ninety thousand gross registered tons apiece, these two beauties are our megaships. To give you a point of reference, the original *Queen Elizabeth* went into service in 1940 at eighty-three thousand gross registered tons. Our ships, however, have things you didn't even see in hotels back in 1940. There's a seven-story atrium lobby, fourteen passenger elevators, a fiber-optic lighting system and a twelve-thousand-square-foot health club. It has eleven hundred cabins, two double-deck dining rooms with full ocean views, a double-width promenade that completely circles the ship. Almost fifty percent of the seven hundred ocean-view cabins have private verandas with glass balustrades for unobstructed ocean views."

"What are the basic dimensions?" asked Shapiro.

"Nine hundred feet in length, a hundred twenty feet in width. There are twelve teak-planked passenger decks, with the highest at a hundred and forty-five feet above the waterline. The very top of the funnel is two hundred ten feet above the waterline."

"What's the cruising speed?"

"Twenty-one knots."

"Is there any difference in floor plan between the two ships?"

Odoms shook his head. "Everything you see here this afternoon is exactly the way you'll see it on the *Fantasy*. The only difference, of course, is that you'll have close to two thousand passengers and nine hundred crew aboard. And I want to reemphasize: Their safety is my primary concern—even if it means that your serial killer escapes."

Shapiro nodded, as if to reassure. "This is not designed as a Rambo operation. Our goal is simple: identify the suspect, watch him, and then arrest him only when we can get him in an isolated situation. If all goes well, he won't know what hit him until the cuffs are on his wrists. We've kept the team relatively small so as not to tip him off. The last thing we want to do is force him to take a hostage. If something does go wrong, however, we have all the talent and firepower we need. Victoria spent five years in hostage negotiation before joining our serial killer unit. If it becomes a life-threatening situation, we have some of the finest men from the Hostage Rescue Team—kind of the ultimate SWAT team within the FBI's Critical Incident Response Group."

Odoms was deadpan. "I still don't see why anyone needs to board before it's in port. The ship arrives in Nassau in twelve hours. Seems to me you could all just board then."

"In twelve hours Hannon could spook and get off for good in the Bahamas. With seven hundred islands in an area roughly the size of Connecticut, he could disappear forever. We can't take that chance. Only five of us are boarding at sea; the rest will board in port. Believe me, we'll do it in a way that won't raise an ounce of suspicion."

"Just bear in mind that gunfire isn't good for business."

"Ninety-nine percent of what we do, let alone *talk* *about*, is purely precautionary. But if we do reach a worst-case scenario, I need to know the best place on the ship to place my sharpshooters. If he's running down the hall from point A to point B, my team needs to know how to get there before he does. So—if you will, please: Let the tour begin."

Odoms sighed, seemingly uncomfortable. "Follow me."

He led them past the pool, speaking to Shapiro. The rest followed behind in groups of two and three.

Kevin McCabe, a sharpshooter and HRT squad leader, ambled up alongside Victoria. She vaguely remembered him from years ago, at the Miami office. He'd distinguished himself in the drug enforcement squad, with a bumper sticker on his desk that read SO MANY COLOMBIANS, SO LITTLE TIME. He was about her age, the thick-necked and square-jawed type that didn't appeal to her. He was smiling and chewing gum with his mouth open.

"So," he said with a cocky toss of the head, "I hear you and Mr. Hannon had an interesting little anatomy lesson at the airport."

A look of concern crossed her face. It hadn't taken long for the "penis" talk to circulate. "What about it?" she said flatly.

"Nothing," he said, still smirking. "I just thought that, under the circumstances, I should get your permission before going for a head shot."

"No problem. If you want to shoot yourself in the head, women everywhere will be rejoicing."

Two men behind them chuckled at the rejoinder. McCabe's face reddened with anger.

"Very funny," he snapped. "But when this creep puts a steak knife to some babe in a bathing suit, you're gonna beg me to lead the charge."

"Easy, McCabe. You're just backup. No one takes out Hannon unless we have to."

His stare tightened with intensity, and his tone was deadly serious. "Got news for you, sister, this animal isn't about to walk peacefully off the Love Boat. He's smart and, remember, he's got nothing to lose."

She blinked hard as he walked ahead, but her gut

wrenched with a sinking realization that McCabe was absolutely right. A hostage negotiator's book of "favorite phrases" wasn't going to bring in Hannon. Only force was likely to do that.

Chapter 49

from an altitude of eleven hundred feet, the MS *Fantasy* looked like a toy boat cutting across a beautiful blue carpet. Peering down from the Coast Guard HH-60J Jayhawk helicopter, Victoria could see why its sister ship was nicknamed "Rhapsody *on* Blue."

Victoria was strapped in the rescue swimmer EMT's jump seat in the rear compartment with McCabe, who was posing as flight mechanic, and two other members of the Hostage Rescue Team. David Shapiro was in the cockpit beside the Coast Guard pilot. The five agents were dressed exactly alike in dark blue jumpsuits, flight boots and metallic blue helmets. An embroidered patch stitched on their right arm identified them as members of EMERGENCY MEDICAL SERVICES—AIR LIFT. On the floor behind Victoria lay a gurney cart covered with white sheets and blankets. Beside it was a red-and-white cooler marked HUMAN BLOOD, a silver tank marked OXYGEN, and a small red "crash cart" for cardiopulmonary resuscitation, which looked like a tool chest rigged with an IV pole and a Hewlett-Packard cardiac defibrillator.

Shapiro glanced back over his shoulder to catch her eye. He gave her a "thumbs-up" as the helicopter eased back on its cruising speed of 160 knots and began its descent.

The pilot's monotone suddenly crackled over the radio implanted in her flight helmet. "Coast Guard HH-60 Rescue 37 with five crew from OPBAT ready to rendezvous with MS *Fantasy* for medevac."

As the ship grew larger, Victoria noticed scores of passengers on the decks looking up and pointing at them. She checked her watch. Right about now, she figured, a message was being broadcast throughout the ship, assuring passengers not to be alarmed about the "medical emergency."

Victoria glanced around the six-foot-wide cabin, but each of the other agents sat with his head down, deep in thought, as if running through the plan in their head. They'd been that way since takeoff from the Coast Guard's OPBAT Unit in the Bahamas. She peered out the window. They were flying just a hundred feet above sea level, parallel to the ship, even with the Main Deck. The seas were calm, so that the ship's rocking motion was barely perceptible. The helicopter raced ahead of the ship, then slowed to a dead-even pace as the pilot struggled to synchronize the speed. Once he had it exactly right, the chopper moved laterally toward the helipad on the bow. It hovered for a moment, then touched down perfectly on the big black "H."

The door slid open and the team sprang into action.

The chopper filled immediately with warm, salty sea air, and four whirling rotor blades made it impossible to hear anything. Two men jumped out and lifted the gurney onto the deck. Victoria handed down the blood cooler and the oxygen tank, which they placed on the gurney. She and McCabe unloaded the red crash cart, then jumped down to the deck. She grabbed the handle on one side and McCabe grabbed the other, and they sprinted for the entrance. Shapiro and the men with the gurney were right behind.

The ship's physician met them at the door. He was wearing a white lab coat with a stethoscope draped around his neck, to make sure that anyone watching would recognize him as an MD.

"This way!" he shouted. He sprinted down the hall, leading the pack of paramedics.

The team rushed down the long, narrow hallway, then up an impressive wide staircase that seemed more befitting a hotel than a ship. Curious onlookers peered out of their doorways as the paramedics raced up two flights to the Aloha Deck, where the largest and most expensive suites were located. The doctor opened the door to a cabin suite, waving his arm as he directed them inside. Shapiro was the last to enter, and the door slammed behind him.

Waiting inside were six cruise line employees: a tall woman, three white men and a black man—the same makeup as the team of FBI agents—plus an old man whose face had been powdered a chalky white for a sickly pallor. Victoria and her team quickly stripped out of their Coast Guard jumpsuits and handed them over to their respective "doubles." McCabe pulled the

blanket back on the gurney, then tossed a fully auto-
mated M16 rifle to each of his hostage rescue team-
mates, keeping the 308 sniper rifle for himself. Victoria
pilfered the drawers on the crash cart for the handguns—customized .45-caliber pistols for each of the
men and a 9mm SIG-Sauer P-228 for herself. She
dumped the cooler on the bed, spilling out five hundred rounds of hollow-point, hydroshock service
ammunition.

"Let's move it!" barked Shapiro.

The agents quickly helped their doubles on with
the dark blue jumpsuits and orange crash helmets. The
old man lay on the gurney with a phony oxygen hose
clipped to his nose. In thirty seconds the new team was
ready. The agents moved to the far side of the room,
away from the door.

"Go!" said Shapiro.

The physician flung open the door, and the new
team rushed out with their patient strapped in the gurney, retracing the path back to the helicopter. The
hallways were filled with more onlookers now, and the
physician shouted to clear the way. They were down
the two flights of stairs and out the door in ninety seconds.

A crowd had gathered on the Pool Deck, looking
down on the helicopter. Most were wearing bathing
suits and sipping tropical drinks, smiling and chatting,
as if the chopper were a welcome source of excitement.

From above, Frank Hannon leaned against the
rail, watching, completely unamused. He was still
wearing his touristy straw hat and sunglasses.

"What's going on?" he heard someone ask from behind.

It was a fat man in an electric blue bikini, sucking down a week's worth of calories from a hollowed-out pineapple. He was talking to an old woman with orange hair and a floppy hat who had been watching the whole thing through a pair of opera glasses.

"Oh, we see this at the condo all the time," she said in a nasal New Yawk accent. "Heart attack, faw shaw. They gotta ahrlift him outta here."

"Did they get here in time?"

She smacked and waved her hand. "He looked fine, thank the Lawd. It was the same bartenduh who was just yestuhday laughin' and servin' drinks to me and my guhlfriends. Such a nice man."

Hannon watched carefully as the helicopter lifted away from the bow, his eyes narrowing with suspicion.

Chapter 50

a t 5:00 P.M. Victoria and David Shapiro met with the ship's chief of security and twelve carefully selected crew members in the linen storage room. It was a secluded area of the ship below the waterline, off-limits to passengers. Sheets, towels and pillowcases filled rows of floor-to-ceiling shelves, surrounding them in white. Victoria could feel the steel floor vibrating beneath her feet as the ship's huge engines churned in the hull below.

The crew stood in a semicircle, facing Victoria. They were dressed in the traditional black pants and white jacket of the old cruiser cabin boys, though five of them were women. All were young, in their twenties. Eight were Indonesian, and four were Jamaican. Each had in hand a glossy photograph of the old and new Frank Hannon.

"You've been handpicked by your director of security," Victoria told the group. "One lead cabin steward from each of the twelve passenger decks. You were

383

selected primarily because your employer believes you can be trusted to keep this operation completely confidential. Do I have your agreement on that?"

They glanced at one another, then nodded slowly in unison.

"Each of you will be responsible for inspecting the cabins on your deck. We're looking for a white American male who is six feet five inches tall. Apart from his height, however, he could look like anyone. He could have shaved his head or dyed his hair. Contact lenses might change the color of his eyes. He could make himself look fat or old, or he could even be traveling as a woman."

"Question," said one of the young Jamaican men. He was noticeably skinny, even in the face, but his rather aggressive stance conveyed more confidence than the others.

"Yes," said Victoria. "What's your name?"

"Leddy Coolidge. Most people just call me 'Cool'."

"You wish," cracked one of the women.

"What's your question?" said Victoria.

He spoke with a laid-back island accent, but his tone was slightly sarcastic. "If this mon can be dressed up lookin' like anybody, then what in the world we sposed to be lookin' for?"

"The one thing he can't disguise is his height. So the first thing you need to do is make a note of anyone who appears to be over six feet tall—man or woman."

"Dat could be five hundred people, mon," he scoffed.

"Which means we've eliminated over a thousand people with just the first cut. Next, you need to be alert for any suspicious circumstances. A wig or hair dye in the bathroom would be an obvious clue, but look for more subtle things. For example, someone who eats dinner in the cabin instead of the dining room. Someone who doesn't interact much with other passengers, never says 'hello' in the hallway."

The Jamaican raised his hand, making a face like he was sucking lemons. "Shouldn't we be focused on the single cabins?"

"You can't limit yourself to that. We do believe he's traveling alone, but the ship's reservation system matches up single passengers with other same-sex singles in double cabins, so he could have a male roommate. It's conceivable he hired himself a prostitute in San Juan as a cover, so he could be with a woman. Or maybe he bought a double cabin for himself and a companion who doesn't exist. Every time you enter a double cabin, therefore, you should look for signs that there really are two people staying there. Don't be obvious about it, but—"

"Excuse me." It was him again. This time his peers glared, as if they all thought he was asking too many questions.

"Yes?" Victoria said patiently.

"What should we be doin' if we think we spotted him?"

Shapiro interjected. "Above all, you must keep your routine as normal as possible. If you notice anything suspicious, let us know. We'll take it from there. We're not looking for any of you to become heroes."

One of the Indonesian women shifted uncomfortably.

"Just how dangerous is he?" she asked, her voice cracking with concern.

Victoria glanced at Shapiro, then looked back at the group. "Extremely," she said in a serious tone. "We'd prefer to use FBI agents, but frankly we don't have enough aboard yet. Even if we did, I would expect Hannon to have already made note of his cabin stewards and everyone else who works on his deck or who has access to his cabin. We wouldn't want to make any personnel changes that might alert him."

"What if he attacks one of us?" the woman followed up.

"This ship is an escape route for Hannon," said Victoria. "We don't believe he'll attack anyone—unless he's provoked. In case of emergency, however, each of you will have an electronic beeper. Carry it with you at all times. If you get into trouble, hit the button, and we'll immediately know exactly where you are." She paused to scan their faces, sensing the tension. "Does anyone feel like they're not up to the task?"

The group was silent.

"Good," said Victoria. She finished the discussion with a final reminder on confidentiality, then collected the photographs before everyone left. They didn't want any of their materials circulating around the ship.

"Thank you, all," she said, dismissing the group.

The stewards filed out in silence. The ship's chief of security stood at the door, personally thanking each of them as they left. Victoria and David Shapiro stood alone, behind a stack of towels and away from the others.

"You worried about any of them?" Shapiro asked quietly.

"Only Mr. Twenty Questions. I have this nagging sense he's a James Bond wanna-be."

"We have to trust the cruise line's judgment on these things. They know their employees. He'll be all right."

"I hope so," she said with a sigh. "For his sake. And ours."

Mike had a travel-weary look on his face as he retired to his hotel room in Nassau. He hadn't been to the Bahamas in nearly a decade, and he'd spent most of that last trip lying on Paradise Beach or cruising on mopeds, dressed in a bathing suit and purple tank top that said, HEY MON. Tonight, though, he felt like anything but a tourist.

He pitched his travel bag on a chair by the tiny closet, then kicked off his shoes and flopped on the bed. It squeaked with his every movement—including, it seemed, when he merely blinked his eyes. Finding a decent room in high season with no reservation was no easy task, and this ground-floor special with the peeling cabbage-rose wallpaper was far less than decent.

He rolled onto his elbow—squeaks galore—and picked up the phone on the nightstand. He'd told Karen to leave her portable on, just in case the FBI was still listening to their home telephone. He dialed her number, and she answered on the third ring.

"Well, I got here okay," he said.

"That's good," she said, but her voice had a nervous edge to it. "Are you going to be able to get on the ship?"

"It's completely booked, so I couldn't get a ticket. I had to buy a pass on the black market."

"What does that mean?"

"The ship gives out passes to its passengers when they're in port so they can get back on the ship. It's like I was telling you earlier. There's a black market in these passes, mostly for illegal aliens who want to get into the United States. The only problem is I don't have a cabin."

"What?" She winced.

"It's only one night until we reach Key West. I can hang out in the casino, sleep in a deck chair if I have to."

"Isn't that dangerous?"

"Nah. If I get caught, Captain Stubing'll just throw me overboard."

She chuckled nervously. "No. I mean sleeping in a lounge chair. Seems kind of risky, with Hannon on board."

"You have to put it in perspective, I guess. Think of the war correspondents who crashed the beach on D day or waded through rice paddies in Vietnam."

"I don't want you wading through rice paddies any more than I want you sleeping in a deck chair. Why don't you just go aboard for the day, while the ship's in port?"

"You sound a little spooked."

"No, I'm fine." She sighed heavily. "Okay, I'm a little creeped out. After you left, I started thinking about all those innocent people Hannon killed. The horrible way they died. One of them was staying in the cabin right next to me. It could have been me, so easily. Hell, if I'd kept my maiden name I'd probably be dead now."

"Maybe I should just come home."

"No. You went all the way down there to get the story. So stay there and get it. I want you to."

"What are you going to do tonight?"

"Lock all the doors," she said, "and leave the lights on. Those guys who were protecting me said it's safe, not to worry, but—"

It suddenly occurred to him that Hannon might not be on the ship—or that somehow he might get off. "Why don't you go over to Zack's penthouse and stay in my room? The condo has a security guard. You'll feel a lot safer."

Her phone chirped, signaling a low battery. "I'm about to lose you," she said.

They both paused. It was clear she was talking about the dying battery, but the way she'd put it made them both uneasy.

"I meant the battery," she said.

"I know. I'll be careful, okay?"

"Love you," she said as the line disconnected.

He was about to reply, but the signal was dead. His heart sank with an empty feeling as he reached across the bed and hung up the phone. He lay back against the headboard, thinking that Karen had been no more fooled by their words than he. They both knew he hadn't hopped a plane and finagled his way onto a cruise ship just to get a story. It wasn't that he didn't trust the FBI to do its job, and he wasn't even sure he could be of any help. But with Karen so high on a serial killer's hit list, he was sure of one thing.

He had to make sure they got Frank Hannon— whatever it took.

Chapter 51

a t sunrise, the MS *Fantasy* docked at pier number 3 on Prince George's Wharf, beside two empty berths. Heavy ropes as thick as an elephant's thigh moored the towering vessel to oversized cleats on the old wood pier. Gentle waves from Nassau Harbor lapped at the barnacles clinging to the hull.

The cruise from San Juan had been fairly smooth, but Hannon didn't even have to get out of bed to tell they were in port. The cabin had lost all sense of motion, as if the ship had run aground.

There was a light knock on his cabin door. "Room service," came a muffled announcement from out in the hall.

Hannon sat up in bed and checked his watch. Seven-thirty. Exactly on time. He rolled out of the double bed and slipped into a terry-cloth robe. He started for the door, then stopped and looked around the room. He still had a tinge of concern over the medical emergency yesterday, and he felt the need to be extra careful.

"Just a minute," he shouted.

He checked his face in the mirror. No one onboard had seen him without a hat and sunglasses, but he couldn't very well be seen walking around the room that way first thing in the morning. He thought fast, then rushed to the bathroom. He dug out his shaving kit and ran some hot water, then lathered his face with thick white shaving foam. He picked up the razor and took a couple swipes, to make it look like he was in the middle of it.

Perfect, he thought. He went to the door and opened it.

"Good mornin'," said Leddy Coolidge in a friendly Jamaican accent. "I'm sorry, sir. Did I catch you shavin'?"

"No problem." The sweet smell of French toast and hot syrup filled the air. Hannon stepped aside, allowing the steward to pass.

He rolled the cart inside and positioned it in front of the television set. It was a warming cart with cabinets underneath to keep the food hot in transit from the kitchen, and it also had moveable leaves that folded up on top so that it could be converted into a dining table. The steward opened the lower cabinets and removed one tray, but paused as he reached for the second tray, seeming to do a double take.

"Should I keep the second meal in the warmer until Mrs. Ellers returns?"

"Huh?" said Hannon. "Oh, yeah. She's in the bathroom. No problem."

The steward hesitated again, remembering what the FBI agent had said about a tall, single male in a cabin for two. He glanced at Hannon, then looked away quickly. "I'll just leave it right here for her," he said, then started for the door.

"Don't I need to sign anything?" asked Hannon.

The steward stopped. His smile was nervous as he took a leather-bound pad from his pocket and presented it to Hannon. "Just sign anywhere."

Hannon signed the name "Keith Ellers." He noticed the steward's hand was shaking as he retrieved the pen.

"Thank you, sir," said the Jamaican.

Hannon nodded, then watched carefully as the steward left the room. He was trying not to be paranoid, but the steward had seemed exceedingly nervous. He took the cloth napkin from the table and wiped the shaving foam from his face, thinking. The CNN report yesterday. The airlift to the ship. A nervous cabin boy this morning. His instincts were telling him to get the hell out.

On impulse, he grabbed the suitcase from the closet and threw it on the bed. He checked the zipper pouch along the side flap. Inside a lead-lined Kodak photography film-protector bag, impervious to X ray, was the stainless-steel Smith & Wesson .45 ACP caliber pistol he'd purchased from a gun shop in San Juan. He cracked open a box of hollow-point ammunition and removed twelve rounds. His eyes brightened at the sound of the double-stack magazine clicking into place.

He wheeled quickly and pointed the pistol at the

full-length mirror, like a gunslinger on the draw, as if taking aim at his enemy. Slowly, his aim drifted down toward the color brochure on the dresser, which featured a bronzed young couple in skimpy bathing suits, hugging and smiling as they stupidly proclaimed the islands' official tourist slogan: *It's better in the Bahamas*.

"We'll see about that," Hannon said with a smirk.

Mike couldn't bring himself to eat in his fleabag surroundings, so he headed for Bay Street, Nassau's busy main avenue on the waterfront. He had a light breakfast at the old British Colonial Beach Resort, an imposing pink edifice on the beach with a view of the cruise ships at Prince George's Wharf. At 8:00 A.M. he took the ten-minute walk along the Western Esplanade, passing restaurants and shops on one side of the street and pink sand and palm trees on the other. A warm, salty breeze greeted him at the end of pier number 3.

Even from a distance, the *Fantasy* looked about as big as the hotel he'd just left. A gangplank with an arching blue canvas canopy joined it to the pier. The tentlike booth at the end of the gangplank was where the attendant would check the passes, Mike presumed. A steady stream of passengers was already filing off the ship, besieged by the tourist industry from the moment their feet hit the ground. A friendly man in dreadlocks and a New York Yankees jersey greeted them with shouts of "Taxi, taxi!" Women in loud print dresses hustled straw hats and junk jewelry. T-shirts were available at every turn. The passing tourists just smiled at the commotion, flashing their teeth and American dollars.

Mike was dressed in shorts and polo shirt, with a tourist bag slung over his shoulder. A baseball cap and dark sunglasses were enough, he felt, to keep from being recognized. He stopped near an old man selling hand-carved statues that were made in Taiwan. He wanted to board the ship, but he realized now wasn't the time to try his bogus shore pass. Passengers were only coming *off*. He would have to wait a few hours, closer to lunch, when the traffic would flow in both directions. In the meantime, it wouldn't hurt to watch for a while, maybe catch a glimpse of something to confirm his guess that the *Fantasy* was the right ship.

As the parade of passengers continued down the gangplank, he wondered whether Hannon himself might come out with the morning rush. Out of curiosity, he started singling out every tall man who came down the plank. He was surprised to find how few he could say were definitely *not* Hannon. It chilled him to think he could be looking right at Hannon and not even know it. The corollary, however, turned the chill to a shiver.

Hannon could be looking right at *him*.

Frank Hannon wore a broad-brimmed hat and mirrored sunglasses as he headed down the hall toward the atrium lobby. His suitcase had a shoulder strap, and with his height it looked no bigger than the camera bags most of the other tourists had slung over their shoulders.

From the housekeeper's closet at the other end of the hall, the cabin steward watched as Hannon headed toward the stairs. He'd been ashamed of the way he'd lost his nerve at breakfast—the way he'd gotten so scared he didn't even look around the room. He could have counted the number of suitcases or looked for women's clothing, or even just glanced at the bed to see if it looked like two people had slept in it. He did none of that. He knew the FBI had told him to report anything suspicious, but the *only* thing he knew was that a tall guy had ordered room service. He couldn't really say there'd been no Mrs. Ellers sitting in the bathroom.

Nobody was going to call Leddy Coolidge a fool. Back in Jamaica, they just called him "Cool"—or at least that's what he told everyone. He wasn't about to blow his image by going back to the FBI with absolutely nothing to tell them. It was easy enough to go back for a minute and check out the cabin, the way he should have in the first place.

He watched as Hannon disappeared down the staircase, then waited a few minutes, just to make sure he was really gone. When the hallway was clear, he started toward the cabin. He stopped outside the door to check left, then right.

He drew a deep breath, then took out his key and opened the door.

The early shift for breakfast was just about over, and a flood of land-hungry tourists was flowing from the dining room. Hannon planted himself in the middle of the crowd and shuffled toward the exit. He could see blue sky through the opening in the side of the ship. The crowd, however, soon reached a bottleneck. He was inching forward, pressed between some starry-eyed honeymooners and a pack of gray-haired fossils who belonged on a tour bus outside the Vatican. He bent slightly at the knees as he waited his turn, so that he wasn't the tallest in the crowd.

It took several minutes, but they finally turned the corner. The gaping exit was in plain view, straight ahead. People were marching off in pairs down the narrow gangplank. Hannon stopped just twenty feet from the exit.

"Come on, buddy," someone groused from behind.

Hannon stepped aside, allowing them to pass. His face showed concern. There was a security camera.

Was that thing there when we boarded in San Juan?

He couldn't remember, but he had a sneaking suspicion that it had been mounted just for him. He moved farther to the side, letting still others go around him. The glare from outside made it tough to see, but he could swear that on the doorframe opposite the camera there were little red markings every inch or so—like those height scales in the doorways at convenience stores that measured the height of robbers on their way out.

Hannon felt that twinge in his gut again—that instinct that had never failed him. He needed to think through his options. Coolly, he broke from the crowd and started back toward his cabin.

Leddy Coolidge had stood in the open doorway for nearly a minute, searching for the nerve to step inside.

It suddenly occurred to him that there might really be a Mrs. Ellers, and that she might be inside or out on the private veranda. The last thing he needed was to be accused of breaking and entering. He rapped lightly on the door and called inside.

"Cabin steward," he announced, then waited. The cabin was perfectly still.

"Anyone here?" he asked politely. He waited a few moments, but no one replied. Finally, he closed the door behind him and switched on the light.

He stepped carefully, as if he were afraid that with one false move he might knock something over. He checked the bathroom first—where Mr. Ellers had said his wife was. There was no makeup or hair spray on the counter. He checked the tub. No little containers of women's shampoo or conditioner.

Carefully but with a little more speed, he moved toward the main part of the cabin. The curtains were drawn shut—unusual for someone who'd paid extra for an ocean view cabin with private veranda. The bed was a mess, making it impossible to tell how many people had slept there. He checked the closet. No women's clothes.

His brow furrowed with concern. He'd almost seen enough, but the room service cart caught his attention. Only one tray was on the tabletop, but they might possibly have put the other one back. Curious, he knelt down beside the cart and opened the cabinet. Sitting in the warmer was the second breakfast, completely untouched.

His heart raced as he rose from his knee. He started toward the door, then froze in his tracks. He could hear the key in the lock, and the door swung open.

He retreated quickly, even considered jumping off the balcony to the Lido Deck below. Just as he reached for the door to the veranda, Hannon had him in his sight.

"What are you doing here?" Hannon said sharply.

Coolidge stood frozen behind the cart. His throat went dry, and his voice cracked as he answered. "I, uh—I wanted to see if I could bring anything more to Mrs. Ellers."

Hannon shot a steely glare across the room, then closed the door and locked it. He took just three steps forward—large steps, the kind that nearly gobbled up the room. He stopped just a half-step away, towering above him, close enough to enjoy the fear in the young Jamaican's eyes.

"You and I both know my name's not Ellers," he said as he reached for the silverware resting on the tray.

Chapter 52

the double bed was stripped, and what was left of the sheets lay in a shredded heap on the floor. Heavy blackout drapes were drawn across the glass door to the veranda, and a bath towel stretched across the threshold to block out light and sound. The FBI's emergency beeper lay atop the room service cart, beside Hannon's half-eaten plate of French toast. The coffee cup was empty, the fork and spoon lay crisscrossed on the tablecloth.

Hannon clutched the serrated butter knife in his right hand.

Leddy Coolidge sat erect in the guest chair, gagged and bound at the hands and feet with narrow strips of cloth cut from the bedsheets. His right eye was swollen shut. A trickle of blood ran from the corner of his mouth to the base of his chin.

Hannon dragged the knife across the steward's lower lip, scraping away dried blood. "I can think of nothing worse than being dissected with a dull knife."

Leddy's eyes widened, and his teeth clenched nervously around the red-soaked gag.

Hannon's voice was calm but threatening. "I'm going to remove the gag now. You're going to tell me who put you up to this, where they are, and what they know. If you shout for help, or even talk a little too loud, you're going to be *begging* for a bullet. Understood?"

Leddy nodded nervously. Hannon reached behind his head, unknotted the gag, and pulled it from his mouth.

"It's the FBI," he blurted, before Hannon even asked the question. "Please, just let me go."

"How many?"

"I dunno. A woman named Victoria Santos, lotsa others."

Hannon's face flushed with anger. He rose and started pacing, thinking fast. The ship was probably crawling with FBI. No way were they going to let a man his size just walk right off. He was going to have to negotiate—and one hostage was not enough. He pulled his gun, then rushed to the door and peered out the peephole. He saw no one. He reached for the knob, then stopped. For all he knew there were FBI agents sitting at each end of the hall. He couldn't risk another venture outside the cabin. He put the chain on the door, came back to the telephone, and dialed 7.

"Housekeeping," a young woman answered.

Hannon put on his most charming voice. "Hello, this is Mr. Ellers in cabin nine-twenty-one. This is somewhat embarrassing, but my wife and I were having a nice romantic breakfast in bed and—well, the breakfast is now spilled all over the sheets. Could you please bring us a fresh set of linens?"

"Of course."

"Oh, and it *is* rather urgent. Today's our anniversary."

"Right away, sir," she said, giggling at the lovebirds.

"Thank you. You're very kind." *And very stupid*, he thought as he hung up the phone.

At nine-forty Victoria and David Shapiro were on the Main Deck, standing side by side in the windowless communications center of the MS *Fantasy*. Both were disguised as tourists, so they could walk freely around the ship. Victoria wore a tropical wrap-skirt and matching blouse, and she'd dyed her hair blond for a whole new look rather than wear a wig in the tropics. Shapiro looked ready for shuffleboard in sneakers and plaid shorts.

Bill Odoms, the director of security who had given the FBI a tour of the *Rhapsody* in Miami, was facing the control panel. He had boarded ship that morning with two of the FBI's technical agents, both of whom were also in the room, both from "El-Sur," short for Electronic Surveillance. They were part of the Engineering Division's busy "TS Squad," a dual-purpose acronym that meant "Technical Support" for the requests they met, and "Tough Shit" for the ones they didn't.

One entire wall was covered with seventeen-inch television screens, each with a different view of the ship sent back by security cameras. All eyes, however, were focused on the electronic equipment stacked on the table in the center of the room. For nearly half an hour, the two tech agents had been splicing wires and talking in some technical lingo that only they understood.

"That should do it," said one of the techies. He stepped back from the mound of wires and equipment and flashed a look of admiration, like Michelangelo and his *Pietà*.

"Let's see," said Victoria.

With a flip of the switch on the circuit board, the security screens on the control panel suddenly went black, then brightened. The pictures, however, had changed.

"Allrrrright," he said with a smile.

"What are we looking at?" asked Shapiro.

"We left the ship's existing security cameras in place," he explained. "Your dining rooms, purser's office, and main entrance to the ship are all on screens one, two and three, just like before. The six screens on the bottom are taking the signal back from twenty-four new cameras we added this morning, two for each deck. Now you have a complete view of each hallway. You can leave the system on roam, so that the image on the screen changes every eight seconds. Or you can zero in on one specific deck. Of course, the new cameras are completely hidden in the air-conditioning ducts. No one will know we've added a thing."

"How soon can we be sending pictures back to the mainland Operations Center?" asked Victoria.

"Should be up and running now," he said. "They'll get the same signal we're getting. Hell, we've got enough equipment onboard to set up our *own* Op

Center. The agents who came on the ship today have brought everything we need. When you're simply augmenting an existing security system that's as good as the one already on this ship, it's really not that big a job."

Shapiro glanced up at the changing images flashing on the screens. "With these cameras roaming like this, how do we know what we're looking at? The hallways tend to all look alike."

The techie shrugged. "You'll just have to get used to the sequence. It's on the Atlantic Deck now. In a few seconds—there it goes—it switches to the Dolphin Deck, then Caribbean and so on, bottom to top."

They watched for a moment as the cameras worked through the sequence. The team's interest had already waned, however, by the time the cameras flashed to the Tropical Deck. Not that it was anything out of the ordinary, but no one really seemed to notice the attractive young woman in the housekeeper's outfit rushing down the hall with a set of fresh linens tucked under her arm.

Hannon stirred at the gentle knock on his cabin door.

"Housekeeping," came the voice from the hallway.

He gave Leddy a threatening gaze. The hostage was still tied to the chair, but Hannon had moved him to the other side of the room, closer to the bathroom, so that he couldn't be seen when the door opened. The gag was tight, but he wore no blindfold. Hannon could see the fear in his eyes, see what he was thinking.

"Not one peep," he muttered to his prisoner. With the pistol cocked he headed for the door.

"Just one second," he said as he peered through the peephole. She was a petite brunette, maybe twenty years old. She looked cute in her white blouse and blue jumper, thought Hannon, and he liked the way the darts at the waist showed the curve of her figure. She reminded him a little of Dominique in Antigua, but with lighter skin.

He picked up the towel he'd laid at the threshold to help soundproof the cabin, then removed the chain. He opened the door and stepped behind it, with his back against the wall.

"Sorry," he said with an impish smile, exposing only the top half of his face from behind the door. "You caught me and my wife in the shower, and I'm afraid I'm not really decent. Could you just lay the linens on the bed there, please?"

She smiled again, thinking of the romantic anniversary couple. "Sure."

She took three steps into the short entrance hallway, but the curtains were drawn and the lights were off, making it uncomfortably dark and difficult to see. The door slammed behind her. She stopped out of instinct, suddenly afraid. Instantly, a hand covered her mouth and she was knocked to the floor, facedown, as the sheets flew out of her arms and across the cabin.

"Scream and you die," he said, pressing the barrel of the gun against the back of her head. He was sitting on her kidneys. She was completely pinned, yet her body trembled beneath his weight. He quickly gagged her and tied her hands behind her back with strips from the bedsheet.

She was shaking, starting to sob. He noticed tears as he covered her eyes with a folded hand towel.

"Don't be afraid," he said in a calm, even tone. "This blindfold is going to save your life. It's absolutely essential that you never see how many people are in the cabin, where we sit, where you sit, how the furniture is rearranged—nothing. You're my bargaining chip. Behave yourself, and you'll get out alive. But if you see anything, then the FBI will make you draw a blueprint once I let you go. I can't let you be a snitch. Do you understand?"

Her lips quivered around the gag in her mouth, but she slowly nodded her head.

"Good." He lifted her to her feet, checked the blindfold once more, and switched on the light. As he tied her to the desk chair with the strips of bedsheet, he noticed that Leddy was trying not to watch. Still, the fright was evident in his uncovered eyes, as if the hostage already knew that he'd seen too much.

He stepped slowly toward Leddy, then leaned forward and whispered, "Sorry, Jamaica man. You and I are gonna be a long way from this cabin before I can let *you* go."

Victoria and David Shapiro headed up to the stateroom to check on Kevin McCabe, who was taking inventory. In addition to the materials they'd snuck aboard in the mock medevac operation, FBI agents in plainclothes had been coming and going all morning, smuggling additional supplies—radios, tear gas, body armor, Kevlar riot shields, weapons and ammunition.

There was a knock on the door. Shapiro unlocked it, and Bill Odoms, the cruise line's director of security, rushed inside. His face flushed with excitement as he spoke. "I got him on the phone!"

"Who?" said Victoria.

"Hannon."

"My God," said Victoria. "You didn't tell him we're here, I hope."

"He's *knows* you're here. He asked for you by name. And he wants to speak to you. *Immediately*."

"Do you know where he is?"

"Yeah. All calls to security display the cabin number automatically. He's in nine-twenty-one, Tropical Deck. Says he has a hostage."

"Dammit!" said Shapiro.

Victoria stayed focused. "Tell me exactly what he said."

"Basically, 'This is Frank Hannon, I got a hostage. Put on Victoria Santos, or the hostage is gonna scream.'"

She and Shapiro exchanged glances, as if they knew Hannon was a man of his word. "Let's go," she said.

The tiny, windowless office for the chief of security was down just one flight, next to the purser's office. Odoms led the way with Victoria and Shapiro on his heels. The three of them gathered around the phone on the desk. The orange HOLD button was blinking like a warning light.

Victoria took a deep breath as she reached for the phone, then stopped. "We need this on tape."

The men looked at each other and shrugged. Odoms rifled through the desk drawer and came up with a pocket Dictaphone. He laid it on the table beside the telephone.

"I don't want to talk on speaker," she said. "It might inhibit him."

"Just hit the SPEAKER button and then the star sign," said Odoms. "That'll put him on speaker, but you can talk normal into the receiver, so he won't know it."

Odoms laid the Dictaphone on the desk beside the phone, then clicked the RECORD button. Victoria picked up the receiver and hit the right buttons to activate the special speaker.

She took a deep breath, then answered in a cordial tone. "Hello, Frank."

There was a brief pause. "I told you I'd call. You really shouldn't give your phone number to strangers at airports."

"I guess you're just irresistible, Frank. I wish you'd called sooner."

"Well, I've been kinda busy."

"Really? Why don't you tell me about it, Frank?"

He chuckled to himself, but his tone suddenly sharpened. "Why don't you go fuck yourself?"

"There's no need to get nasty, Frank. We got on pretty well last time, I thought."

"Cut the small talk, and stop using my first name in every sentence, like you're some kind of FBI hostage negotiating genius. Here's what I want. One: Pull the ship away from the dock and out to sea. Nobody boards, nobody leaves. I'm sure you've got enough law enforcement onboard already. Two: Stay by the phone, and stay away from my cabin. I'll be in touch. You got ten minutes."

"Wait," she said. "I can't just agree to anything like that. These things take time. I have to check, get clearance."

"Clearance, my ass. I know how the FBI works. It's better to ask for forgiveness than for permission. Just do it, Santos. I want this ship *moving*."

"Who's your hostage, Frank?"

"Who said I only have one?"

"How many *do* you have?"

"More than enough."

"I need names."

Hannon grunted. "For now, just *one* name—Mr. Coolidge."

"Can I talk to him?"

"He ain't talking."

"I need to know he's alive."

"I said he ain't talking. None of my guests are talking till I say so. Now quit stalling!"

She glanced at Shapiro, as if wondering how far to push it. She suddenly remembered the meeting in the linen room. "Ask Leddy what everybody calls him," she said. "His nickname."

There was a muffled sound, as if Hannon were covering the receiver. He was quickly back on the line. "They call him 'Cool,'" he said.

Victoria sighed—Hannon had himself a hostage all right. She wondered how many others might be involved. "I want to talk to Cool."

"Keep it up, and you're gonna turn Cool into one cold corpse. Now float the boat. You're down to nine minutes."

"Wait—" she said, but the line clicked. The room

went silent. She laid the phone in the cradle and clicked off the recorder. She glanced at Shapiro. His face was ashen.

"Put the snipers on notice," she said.

"Snipers?" balked Odoms. "Not yet. I told you the cruise line wouldn't authorize a gunfight."

"That's not what we're doing," said Victoria. "We just need them on notice. Not a shot will be fired until we've exhausted all efforts at negotiation."

"Wrong," snapped Odoms. "Not a shot will be fired until we get every last passenger off this boat. Most have already gone ashore for the day, but my company is legally if not morally responsible for the lives of nine hundred passengers and crew who are still onboard."

Victoria shook her head. "Hannon gave us nine minutes to be at sea. We don't have time for everyone to disembark."

"Stall him."

She looked at Shapiro, as if appealing. "We can't stall. It's not like he asked for a million dollars in diamonds or political asylum in some third-world nation. He made a very simple demand, but that demand is so important to him that he called us on the phone, *knowing* it would reveal his position. He would never have done that if he weren't convinced that more and more law enforcement is flooding onto the ship with every passing minute, and that he has to put a stop to it. If we try to stall, he'll *know* we're stalling. That's where hostage negotiations turn fatal—especially when dealing with a man who's already butchered ten people. It won't take much to provoke number eleven."

Shapiro rubbed his fingers through his hair, sighing heavily. "What do you propose, Victoria?"

"He's in cabin nine-twenty-one, Tropical Deck. That's in the bow. This ship has two double-deck dining rooms and six lounges in the stern. Let's get the ship sailing, and move everyone aft."

Odoms shook his head. "It'll be pandemonium. You'll have nine hundred people trying to dive overboard."

"If we need to unload them, we can board them in the starboard lifeboats. Hannon's cabin is portside. He won't even know it's happening, so long as we keep the ship moving."

"I don't like it," said Odoms. "I don't mean to be mercenary, but Coolidge is a crew member. No one wants to see him killed, of course. But frankly it's a bigger disaster for this cruise line if one of our passengers turns an ankle stepping into the lifeboat."

Victoria just glared. "That's not the way the FBI operates, sir. Plus, you're assuming Hannon's lying about having other hostages."

Odoms's face showed irritation. He seemed about to say something, then reconsidered it.

"How about it, Odoms?" Shapiro interjected. "Are you willing to risk the possibility that our serial killer actually has a passenger locked in that cabin?"

Victoria and Odoms locked eyes in a tense, silent pause. Seconds passed slowly, but neither said a word. Finally, Shapiro spoke up again.

"Move the ship, Mr. Odoms. *Now*."

Chapter 53

he sea was up as the MS *Fantasy* sailed out of Nassau Harbor, with nine-foot swells that tested even the most seasoned of sea legs. A strong northwest wind blowing across the Gulf Stream off the Florida coast was kicking up a blustery tropical disturbance. At ten knots the megaship was cruising at less than half its normal cruising speed, but the gusts on the Pool Deck were nearly twice that strong. The ship's course, however, remained steady: south-by-southwest, toward the Florida Keys.

Fifteen additional members of the FBI's Hostage Rescue Team had managed to board at Prince George's Wharf, all in plainclothes, each with his gear and weapons concealed in his luggage. Posing as ship employees, they immediately went door to door, rousing passengers from their cabins and directing them toward the aft dining room and lounges. On eleven of twelve passenger decks, the halls echoed with cries of protest from angry and confused passengers. Some had left friends behind in the Bahamas. Most just wanted to know what was going on.

An old couple from Iowa wondered about afternoon bingo. The team worked quickly, allowing passengers no time to gather up their belongings.

The mood was entirely different on the forward half of the Tropical Deck. Cabin 921 was nine doors from the forward end of a straight and narrow hall that stretched half the length of a football field. At one end of the hall was the auxiliary stairwell; at the other, the main stairwell leading to the seven-story atrium lobby at midship. Nautical art was fastened to the walls, above a polished teak handrail that stretched the entire length of the hall. Cabin doors were evenly spaced at fifteen feet apart.

Special Agent McCabe and two other members of the Hostage Rescue Team lay crouched in the main stairwell at midship, like soldiers in a foxhole. Another team of three lay in the auxiliary stairwell at the bow. They wore full SWAT regalia, including helmets and flak jackets. Their eyes were at floor level as they peered down the empty hallway. Their M16 rifles seemed trained on each other, as the enemy hid between them.

McCabe kept an eye fixed on the door to cabin 921 as he switched on the headset inside his Kevlar helmet and spoke into the microphone.

"Team one in position," he said.

"Copy," said Victoria. She was back in the ship's communications center with Shapiro and Odoms. The three of them were watching live shots of both teams on the black-and-white security monitors positioned on the control panel.

"What's the head count so far?" said McCabe.

"We believe he has at least two hostages," said

Victoria. "Both crew. In addition to Coolidge, there's one housekeeper we can't account for. Shelly Greene, nineteen years old. We still don't know if he has any passengers."

"What's the passenger status on the Tropical Deck?

"We've made contact by telephone with every passenger between you and team two. All those on the starboard side are being evacuated off their private verandas, down to the Lido Deck directly below them. Portside passengers have been instructed to lock themselves in the bathroom and not to venture out of their cabin under any circumstances."

"We need everyone out," said McCabe.

"It's too risky to have passengers climbing off balconies on the same side of the ship as Hannon. We have team three watching his veranda from inside a lifeboat on the Lido Deck, but they can't guarantee he won't get a shot off from behind the curtain. The safest thing is for portside passengers to stay put. I'm sending down a list of which cabins are occupied."

"I can get them out."

"You could get them killed."

"Or worse," he scoffed, "I could get *Hannon* killed. Then you and your brain trust up in Quantico wouldn't have any sickos to interview. What a pity that would be."

"Kiss off, McCabe. We're doing this my way. Understand?"

"Sure," he said as he trained his sights on the cabin door. "Just let me know when you want it done the *right* way."

*   *   *

The double-deck dining room was already filled to capacity as still more passengers were streaming in. Tables that were designed for parties of eight, four and two were filled with ten, six and four, respectively. People were carrying in deck chairs just to have someplace to sit. FBI agents disguised as crew directed traffic at both the port and starboard side entrances. Most of the waiters and busboys had gone ashore in Nassau, but a skeletal crew was hustling back and forth from the kitchen with platters of cold cuts and appetizers to appease a contentious crowd.

A few lucky passengers had spilled over to the Luna Lounge, just down the hall from the dining room. It was one of the ship's "after-hours" hot spots, complete with a disco ball suspended above the dance floor. The ceiling was painted like the Milky Way, and the wallpaper displayed a bad astrological motif, as if the entire lounge were built around the worst pickup line ever, *What's your sign?*

Mike Posten was sitting on a barstool munching peanuts. CNN was on the television behind the bar, but he had his nose in his notepad, frantically scribbling down details of what he'd been observing. At the moment, he was trying to figure out which members of the so-called crew were FBI agents, and who would be the most likely to talk to him.

Drinks were on the house, as a matter of public relations, and the crowd was getting louder. Mike was half listening to the television and half listening to little clusters of conversations at the tables around him as people speculated about what was going on. Suddenly, videotape of the MS *Fantasy* appeared on the television screen.

"Quiet!" the bartender shouted.

Mike and everyone else in the room turned quickly toward the television.

"This just in," said the anchor. "Foul play is suspected as hundreds of passengers on the cruise ship *Fantasy* were left stranded in the Bahamas. With absolutely no explanation from the cruise line, the megaship left port more than eight hours before its scheduled departure with most of its crew and nearly eleven hundred of its two thousand passengers still ashore. In this video footage obtained exclusively by CNN from a fishing charter boat, the outer decks of the ship appear completely empty, and a handful of men can be seen preparing lifeboats. So far, the cruise line has refused comment. Stay tuned for further details."

The room fell completely silent. Mike swiveled on his barstool and looked into scores of stunned faces. Finally, a man with a Budweiser broke the spell. "They know more *off* the damn boat than we do on it!"

"That's right!" said another, belting back his drink. Others joined with similar complaints, each a little louder than the last. In fifteen seconds the raucous din had returned to its previous level.

Mike turned away and looked back at the television. It angered him that the hecklers were right. People off the ship did seem to know more than those who were on it. Except that he was convinced he knew who was behind it.

The CNN anchor was back on the screen, closing down *Headline News* for the half hour. "More on that cruise ship in the Bahamas just as soon as we receive it," he said.

Mike just shook his head and muttered sarcastically into his Coke: "Nice going, CNN. I'm sure you've got Hannon glued to his TV set."

Suddenly, his whole expression changed as a thought occurred to him. He grabbed his travel bag from the bar, spilling a bowl of peanuts as he jumped off the stool and rushed from the lounge.

In cabin 921 Hannon sat on the edge of the bed, staring angrily at the television. He hit the MUTE button on the remote control, got up and turned toward Coolidge, who was still gagged and bound to the chair.

Leddy cowered, as if fearing that Hannon would take it out on him.

"It's your job to watch the screen," he said. "The second anything comes on about us, grunt. Otherwise, I don't want to hear a peep out of you. Got it?"

Leddy nodded.

Hannon pulled the pistol from his belt and stepped toward the glass door to the veranda. The mattresses and box springs from both beds were standing on end, braced up against the door by the couch. Hannon pulled back the couch and slid the mattresses a few inches to one side. With his back to the wall, he peered outside, through the half-inch crack of daylight between the doorframe and the hem of the blackout drapes. Straight out was the blue but choppy Atlantic. He pressed his face flat against the wall for a side view of the ship. Because his cabin was in the bow, the curve of the ship allowed him to see all the way back to midship. Directly above were the bottoms of verandas from the state-suite cabins. On his own deck, he could see into the verandas for every cabin between him and midship. When he closed one eye and flat tened his cheek against the wall, he could see down to the Lido Deck directly below. It was a little wider than the Tropical Deck, so as to accommodate the storage of the ship's lifeboats. Looking back toward midship, Hannon counted nine lifeboats, but he saw none of the preparations going on that CNN had just reported.

Must be on the starboard, he thought.

Just then, the lights and television blinked off, and the mini-bar hummed to a halt. Hannon froze and listened in the darkness. A shaft of sunlight streamed in behind the curtain's edge. He jumped up on a chair and stuck his hand in front of the air-conditioning vent. Nothing.

He rushed to the bathroom and swung open the door. Shelly Greene flinched at the sudden noise. She was lying in the tub, blindfolded and tied to the shower safety rail.

"Don't make a sound!" he shouted. In the darkness he fumbled for the faucet and turned it. It made a gurgling sound, spit out a few drops, then went dry. "Those bastards!"

He untied her and pulled her from the tub, leaving her blindfolded with hands tied behind her back. He pushed her on the bed and snatched up the phone. There was still a dial tone. He angrily dialed security.

The phone rang once in the main security office, then transferred automatically to the communications center. Victoria, Shapiro and Odoms jumped at the ring. The display on the telephone showed it was from cabin 921. She hit the speaker and star button so the men could overhear, then picked up.

"Hello," she said.

"Get away from the lifeboats," he said in a gravelly voice.

Victoria paused. The CNN report had prompted them to cut off the power, but she'd hoped Hannon had missed the broadcast. "I'm not sure I know what you're talking about. But if anyone's out there, I'll take care of it."

"Someone *is* out there. Starboard side. I just saw it on CNN."

She glanced at Shapiro, as if to curse the media.

"And put the power back on—*including* the television. Or Coolidge dies. I've got another hostage. I don't *need* his ass."

He yanked the gag from Shelly's mouth and stuck the phone in front of her. "Say something!"

"Please," she whimpered, "don't hurt me."

He cinched up the gag and took back the phone. "You hear that, Santos? Don't hurt her."

"I'm listening, Frank. But you're not telling us something we don't already know. Her name's Shelly Greene. She's a housekeeper. We know everything. You can't make a move, Frank. The ship's loaded with FBI agents. Come on now, you're a smart guy. Let's talk about this."

"Enough talking. Get away from the lifeboats and get the power back on."

"You're asking an awful lot for a guy who gives nothing in return."

"Nothing! You say I give *nothing!* Let me ask Mr. Cool about that. Hey, Mr. Cool, you want the power back on!"

Victoria cringed as she heard a light thud, then silence, as if Hannon were laying down the receiver. Suddenly, a shrill, tortuous scream rattled her speakerphone. She closed her eyes in anguish. It sounded too real to be staged.

"Just as I thought," said Hannon, back on the line. "Mr. Cool *really* wants the power back on. And let me assure you: That's his final word on the matter."

"I'm warning you, Hannon. Do *not* harm those hostages."

"He's fine, bitch. It was just a fingernail. But the rest is totally up to you. Now here's the deal. First, I want two extralarge wet suits, some black greasepaint and two full sets of scuba gear. Tanks, fins, mask, regulator, weight belt—the whole ensemble. I know they rent diving equipment from the ship's sports center, so don't give me the runaround. Second, I want the ship to change course. Steer for Mexico, the Yucatán Peninsula. When you're a half mile offshore, steer north and follow the coastline."

"We can't just sail into Mexican waters. We'll need time to clear it."

"I don't care what you have to do. Just get it done. Call me when you've got my equipment."

"Wait. You don't need two hostages, Frank. Let the girl go, and then we'll talk about the equipment."

He scoffed loudly. "What do you mean, let her go? Go *where*? There's no safe place on this ship. You're *all* hostages. So don't tell me what you need, don't jerk me around and above all, don't walk through the wrong door—or this entire tub blows, along with everyone on it."

The phone slammed in her ear. Victoria looked at the others, but no one spoke for a second, as if they weren't quite sure whether to believe their ears.

"Call Quantico," said Shapiro. "It's a whole new ball game."

Chapter 54

Victoria dialed David Shapiro's direct supervisor in Quantico, the Assistant Special Agent in Charge of the Critical Incident Response Group. In twenty seconds she explained the latest demand. As she'd predicted, the assistant didn't want a decision this big on his head. Victoria waited on hold while he tried to conference in Adam Levanthal, the Special Agent in Charge, himself. She wasn't holding her breath.

The house phone rang as she waited. Victoria picked up, with one ear still trained for Levanthal's voice over the speakerphone. "Communications center," she said.

"This is Agent Kozelka, down in the kitchen."

Victoria could barely hear. The rumble of the unruly crowd in the ship's main dining room was more than just background.

He spoke loudly over the noise. "Your reporter friend from Miami is here."

Her mouth fell open. "*Posten?*"

"Yeah. He wants to speak to you."

She stammered, unsure what to say. "Yes. Put him on."

The agent lowered the receiver and waved Mike forward. He took the phone.

"Hey," said Mike. "Bet you're surprised to hear from me."

"What the hell are you doing?"

"I'm here to talk Hannon into surrendering."

"Since when did you become a hostage negotiator?"

"I'm not. But with a little imagination I could become an informant—*Hannon's* informant. Or should I say *mis*informant. Interested?"

She hesitated, but she was thinking hard. "Put the agent back on," she said finally. "I'll have him bring you up."

In thirty seconds Adam Levanthal, the Special Agent in Charge of the Critical Incident Response Group, was on the speakerphone. Odoms was excused from the room as Victoria and David Shapiro gave a full briefing. Kevin McCabe, the Hostage Rescue Team leader, stood by and listened.

"Does Hannon seem to have a coherent plan?" asked Levanthal.

Victoria grimaced. "I think he's making it up as we go along, but he's come up with a fairly decent one. The Yucatán coastline is pretty rugged and desolate for long stretches on both the Gulf and Caribbean sides. I went to Cancún a few years ago on vacation, and from what I remember most of the peninsula is just a thick mat of jungle. I presume he intends to jump from the ship in full scuba gear and swim underwater to shore. He's probably correct in assuming we'll have some difficulty coordinating with Mexican authorities and getting American law enforcement into position. If he slips into the jungle we may never find him. He could head for Central or South America, or come north to the States."

"Have the snipers take him out when he jumps," said Levanthal.

McCabe chimed in. "Not to underestimate my own men, sir, but I don't think that's possible. That's why Hannon asked for *two* sets of scuba equipment. My guess is that in the middle of the night, we're going to see two people flying off that balcony simultaneously, clinging to each other like Romeo and Juliet. We won't know which is the hostage and which is Hannon. I assume that's why he asked for black greasepaint, so we can't single out the white guy. Even if we could tell one from the other, we couldn't risk a shot. If the bullet were to rupture his scuba tank, the compressed air would cause a huge explosion, like the exploding shark at the end of that first *Jaws* movie. With a full tank, you're talking three thousand pounds of pressure per square inch. Our hostage would be killed right along with him."

"What about the bomb threat? Is he bluffing?"

Victoria grimaced. "Possibly. I think he boarded this ship purely as a means of escape, with no intention of blowing it up. I doubt he came aboard packing explosives. One thing, however, does give us concern.

When our agents were preparing the lifeboats, we noticed that one was missing a flare gun and the spare tank of gasoline. A five-gallon container."

"Five gallons," Levanthal said with concern. "That's like five sticks of dynamite. Does his background show any familiarity with explosives?"

"Possibly," said Victoria. "He did have some arson activity as a juvenile."

Shapiro leaned toward the speaker. "It wouldn't take an expert to blow this ship up. She's probably carrying a hundred thousand gallons of fuel in her tanks. Blow that up and you might take the whole Bermuda Triangle right along with you."

"But how would he detonate it?" asked Levanthal.

"The flare gun?" she speculated.

Shapiro shook his head. "He's not suicidal."

"I think he's got something rigged up so he doesn't have to pull the trigger," she said. "He told me, 'Above all, don't walk through the wrong door.' The only reason he would say that is because he wants us to be too scared to make a move. That makes me think he set up some kind of makeshift spring gun, like store owners use to protect their property from burglars after hours. He could have soaked a closet or storage room with gasoline, then rigged up the flare gun to the door handle. If somebody opens the wrong door, it fires the flare gun. Five gallons of gasoline in one of these tiny cabins would be a major explosion. If it's below the waterline, it could rupture the hull and sink the ship. If it's anywhere near the main fuel tanks, it could blow us all to kingdom come."

Levanthal's sigh crackled over the line. "Put the

agents on notice to sniff for gasoline before they open any doors. But let's not paralyze ourselves. The gasoline and flare gun could have been missing from that lifeboat for six months. At this point, all we have from Hannon is a vague threat."

"That's true," said Victoria, "but he's got enough victims to prove at least one thing: He's never threatened anything he couldn't deliver."

McCabe grimaced and moved closer to the phone. "Sir, Agent Santos just made my point. We have a hostage taker who is a known killer, not a negotiator. It's time to be more proactive. He's already tortured one of the crew, ripped off a fingernail. His tongue might be next. My men are ready to go in."

There was silence on the line as Levanthal mulled it over.

Victoria was suddenly getting bad vibes. She could sense his decision going the other way, and flaming images of the Davidian disaster in Waco were filling her head. "Sir, before we pull the plug on negotiation, let me try one more strategy. I just found out Mike Posten's on the ship."

"The reporter?" he said.

"Yes. Maybe we can do something with him as a third-party intermediary. It's worth a try."

There was silence again. Finally, Levanthal spoke. "All right. Use him. But whatever you do," he said in a serious tone, "don't you dare *lose* him."

Chapter 55

Just after 4:00 P.M., Hannon was kneeling in front of the mini-bar, trying to decide between peanut M&M's and the last package of shortbread cookies. The second breakfast on the room service cart had gotten him through lunch, but dinner pickings were looking slim. Suddenly, the mini-bar kicked back on, and the cabin lights were back. Hannon wiped the sweat from his brow and reached up to the air-conditioning duct. They had power.

Leddy Coolidge grunted loudly through the gag in his mouth. Hannon shot him a look, then glanced at the television. An aerial photograph of the MS *Fantasy* was filling the screen.

"Good job, Mr. Cool," he said as he grabbed the remote and switched on the volume.

It was a different CNN anchor this time, an attractive woman with a serious expression. She was in midsentence when the volume switched on.

". . . late-breaking developments on the cruise

ship MS *Fantasy*, which unexpectedly left Nassau a few hours ago with only half its passengers and crew aboard. We now have word that the ship has veered from its normal course and is headed in the direction of Mexico. Michael Posten, a reporter for the *Miami Tribune*, is aboard the ship and has made contact with us by portable telephone."

Hannon's eyes lit with anger as a photograph of Mike suddenly flashed on the screen.

"Michael," she said, "can you tell us what is going on down there?"

The words LIVE, BY TELEPHONE, flashed beneath Mike's photograph. The line crackled as he spoke, like a bad connection.

"Right now, rumors are flying, but it appears as though the ship has indeed been hijacked by an American named Frank Hannon. We're told that Hannon has taken at least two hostages, which is a matter of grave concern. As I'm sure you're aware, the FBI just yesterday identified Hannon as the prime suspect in ten serial murders committed over the past few months across the country—the so-called tongue murders."

"What does Hannon want?" she asked.

"That's not entirely clear," said Mike. "What is clear, though, is that capture is inevitable. The ship is loaded with FBI agents who boarded in Nassau wearing civilian clothing. All of them are well armed and well trained in hostage rescue. They're doing an excellent job of keeping the passengers calm and protected. The only question is whether Hannon will surrender peacefully without senseless bloodshed, or whether he'll make a suicidal attempt at escape."

"But if he's wanted for murder, what would Hannon have to lose by making a desperation move?"

"Much more than he thinks," said Mike. "Ironically, should he kill one of his hostages, it would be the *only* murder authorities can actually link to him. While the FBI at first believed that Hannon was the serial killer, they're now focusing on another man named Curt Rollins. As you may know, I wrote a number of exclusive stories on these serial killings for the *Miami Tribune*. All of the stories were based on information I obtained from a source who professed to be very knowledgeable about the crimes. Curt Rollins was that source. An abundance of physical evidence connecting Rollins to the murders has been found at each of the crime scenes. I'm told there's little, if any, physical evidence connecting Hannon."

"Are you saying that Hannon has been framed by Rollins?"

"According to my sources, that's what the FBI is thinking at this point. The only item linking Hannon to the crime is apparent motive. All of the victims were potential sources for the prosecution at a rape trial Hannon was involved in twelve years ago. I might add that Hannon was convicted—though he always maintained his innocence. The list from which the victims was selected was easily obtainable, and may have been used by Rollins to act out some sort of grudge against Hannon, to set him up. At this point, it's difficult to imagine the authorities making a murder charge against Hannon stick."

"Granting that Hannon is blameless, why would he take hostages?" the reporter asked, puzzled.

"One theory is that he believes he won't get a fair shake because of his past criminal record, that he's convinced he's being railroaded."

"Michael, can you—"

The line crackled. "I have to leave you," said Mike. "The FBI has prohibited any phone calls, and I believe I've been spotted."

"One more thing," the reporter tried, but the line went dead. "Well, I believe we've lost contact," she said to her television audience. "Once again, that was Michael Posten aboard the MS *Fantasy*."

Hannon sat on the edge of the bed, listening for any further coverage. When a colorful weather map appeared on the screen, he hit the MUTE button. He sighed and smiled thinly.

"Welcome aboard, Posten."

Victoria walked into the ship's communications center with Mike at her side. They'd made the call from an outside deck for better reception on Mike's portable telephone. Inside, Shapiro was standing near the control panel beside the same FBI technical agents who'd installed the additional security cameras in Nassau.

"How did it come out?" asked Victoria.

"Perfect," said the techie. "We relayed CNN's closed-circuit signal from Atlanta through the Operations Center in Miami. It was a scrambled FBI frequency on both ends of the transmission, so I'm sure no one but this ship picked it up. I temporarily blacked out the televisions in the bar and dining room, so our passengers wouldn't see it. I can virtually guarantee you that the only person on the planet who saw the broadcast was Hannon. The way we coordinated it with the restoration of power, he'll never know there was a break in the regular CNN signal."

"Good," said Victoria. "Remind me to write a little thank-you note to CNN."

Mike cleared his throat pointedly.

She smiled. "And to the *Miami Tribune*."

He smiled back, then turned serious. "Do you think Hannon will bite?"

"I don't expect him to come walking out with his hands up, but it might make him think twice before killing his hostages. Your pitch played right to his psychological profile. Hannon believes he's capable of committing the perfect crime. When he heard you say there was no physical evidence linking him to the crimes, I'm sure he believed that. I'm also sure he'd enjoy the notoriety of going to trial and being found innocent. The problem with the frame-up theory, though, is that it would force him to give someone else credit for his own work. I'm not sure he's willing to do *that*, even if it means saving his own life. Either way, you deserve an Academy Award."

"Thanks."

The phone rang. The display panel flashed cabin 921.

"Should I leave?" Mike asked.

Victoria shook her head. She hit the buttons that allowed the others to overhear on the speaker, then picked up the phone.

"Hello."

Hannon had a lilt to his voice, as if he were

amused. "For a print journalist, Mr. Posten delivered a very compelling report, don't you think?"

"We just realized Mr. Posten is here, and he's in a lot of trouble," Victoria said, keeping up the charade. "That report was completely unauthorized."

"Unauthorized?" Hannon snickered. "I doubt it. It wasn't even thought provoking, actually. I've known all along you can't prove anything."

"Then why don't you let the hostages go? Why risk a murder charge that can stick?"

"With my record, a conviction for kidnapping alone would mean life in prison. There's nothing to gain by turning myself in now. And there's nothing to lose by killing Mr. Cool and the girl."

"There's a big difference between life imprisonment and the electric chair."

"Not in my book. My only option is getting off this ship. And our star reporter's going to help me."

"How's that?"

"He's the only person on this ship who I can say for certain is *not* an FBI agent. That's why I want *him* to bring me my scuba gear."

She glanced at Mike, then shook her head. "We can't involve a civilian—"

"He's *already* involved!" Hannon shouted. "Now"—his voice returned to normal—"do you want to see the hostages alive, or don't you? Oh, and let's not forget: There is the little matter of that bomb you haven't found yet."

"I don't believe there *is* a bomb, Frank."

"I don't believe you can take that risk. Nor can Posten."

"No one in his right mind is going to set foot inside your cabin."

"There's the rub. I would have to be out of *my* mind to step into the hall and pick up my gear. If the FBI is doing its job, I'm sure you've got snipers lined up at both ends."

"What are you proposing?"

"Send Posten—alone. He'll probably need a cart to carry all the equipment. When the cabin door opens, he simply wheels the cart across the threshold. I never go outside. He never comes inside. There will be a cart and a hostage between the two of us at all times. When the door closes, Posten leaves. No one gets hurt. I'll be expecting him at six o'clock."

"I can't promise he'll come."

"He'll come. Hold on just a second, okay?"

Victoria bristled at the sudden pause. "Don't you dare hurt the hostages."

Hannon said nothing. He kept the phone at his chin, so Victoria could hear him, but he spoke to the housekeeper. "Get up, Shelly."

She rose slowly from her chair. Her hands were tied behind her back. The blindfold was still in place. With a nudge, he turned and faced her toward the door. Then he reached for the knife on the room service cart. "Do exactly as I say, Shelly."

Victoria's heart raced at the other end of the line. "What are you doing to her, Frank?"

Again, he ignored her. With a quick flick of the knife, he cut her hands free. She gasped at the sound of the tearing knife.

"Now walk, Shelly. And keep walking until I tell you to stop."

She took a small step, then another. She was tentative, still wearing the blindfold.

"That's good," said Hannon. "Nice and slow. Straight ahead. Stop!"

Shelly froze right in front of the door. Hannon was standing twenty feet behind her, deep inside the room. He crouched behind the dresser, tucked the telephone under his chin and aimed his pistol at the back of her head. "With your right hand, Shelly, take the chain off the door."

Her hand shook as she reached out for the chain like a blind woman. She found it, then removed it.

Hannon's eyes narrowed as he focused his aim. "Now open the door."

Back in the communications center, Victoria grabbed the radio that linked her to the Hostage Rescue Team, adjusting the receiver in her ear.

"Cabin door's opening," came the message from the HRT agent parked at the end of the corridor on the Tropical Deck.

Victoria looked at Shapiro, confused. One of the technical agents adjusted the security monitors on the wall, training all six cameras on the long corridor that led to cabin 921, Tropical Deck.

Victoria leaned over the table and spoke into the speakerphone. "Frank, what are you doing?"

"Just watch," said Hannon, speaking into the phone tucked under his chin. He peered out over the top of the dresser. Shelly was standing in the open doorway, framed in the rectangle of light that led to the hallway. "Shelly," he said loudly, "take one step forward, then get on your knees."

Her chest heaved with an anxious sigh. The first step took her to the threshold. Kneeling put her body just outside the cabin, but her feet were still inside. She was shaking in her blue-and-white uniform. The hand towel covered her eyes and the top half of her face.

Victoria suddenly got another message in her earpiece from the Hostage Rescue Team. "Hostage in the hall. Alone." Victoria glanced at the monitor. The picture confirmed the report.

Hannon's voice was back on the speakerphone, filling the communications center. "Decision time," he said in a bemused tone. "I can show good faith and free a hostage. Or I can show you I mean business and blow her brains out. Ask Posten what he wants me to do."

Victoria's gut wrenched. "Just let her go, Frank."

"Is he coming?" he said, cocking his pistol. "Or isn't he?"

Mike checked the television monitors on the wall, focusing on the black-and-white image of the long corridor leading to Hannon's cabin. He and Victoria exchanged glances.

"It doesn't feel right," Victoria whispered to Mike. "There's a chance he found out about Karen before it all went downhill for him. If so, you're his payback."

"What's it gonna be!" said Hannon.

In the communications center, all eyes were on Mike. Calmly, he reached over and snatched the receiver from Victoria. "Hannon, this is Posten. You've got yourself a delivery boy."

Back in cabin 921, Hannon smiled. "How nice," he said. He focused again on the doorway. "Shelly," his voice boomed. "Back inside! On your knees!"

Victoria took back the phone. "You said you'd let her go, Frank."

"I will. Just as soon as Posten keeps his word. If he comes, Shelly leaves with him. If he doesn't . . . well, let's just say she would have been *much* better off had he just said 'no' and let me put a bullet in her head."

The telephone line clicked. All eyes in the communications center turned to the monitors, watching helplessly as Shelly walked backward on her knees, retreating into the cabin. The door swung shut.

Victoria looked away from the monitor. "That *bastard*."

Mike swallowed the lump in his throat.

Shapiro looked him in the eye. "You sure you want to go through with this, Mike?"

He glanced at Victoria, then back at Shapiro. "I don't see that there's much choice. I'd hate to think what he'd do to that girl if I backed out now."

Victoria sighed, knowing he was right. "Let me check with our sharpshooters. Maybe they can give you a fighting chance."

Chapter 56

kevin McCabe was nearly running as he reached the communications center. Mike was standing outside the door, so that the FBI agents could confer among themselves. McCabe gave him a wink as he opened the door and stepped inside. David Shapiro was pacing in front of the wall of television screens. Victoria was sitting at the table. In five minutes Victoria explained everything. McCabe had a gleam in his eye as he spoke.

"We can view this two ways," he said. "We can be on the defensive and simply protect Posten. Or we can use this as our entrée for a quick offensive."

Shapiro made a face. "I won't have a civilian leading the charge into the den of a psychopath."

"Of course not," said McCabe. "Let's leave Posten out of it. *I'll* wheel the cart down the hall. We'll put another agent inside the cart, like a Trojan horse."

"We can't make substitutions. Hannon knows what Posten looks like. That's why he chose him. He can take one look at Posten and know he's not dealing with an FBI agent."

"All right," said McCabe. "We're stuck with Posten. He can still be of help to us. For example, when he delivers the equipment, he could discreetly take a look inside the cabin. I'd like to know where the hostage is positioned, whether any furniture has been moved around. That would be of value to us if we do decide to go inside at some point."

"Mike can't be looking around," said Victoria. "He needs to be focused on Hannon, period."

"Okay," said McCabe, "here's another possibility. While he's focused on Hannon, he could talk to him, try to lure him out of the cabin so that the snipers could get a shot."

"It's too dangerous for Mike to strike up a conversation, and Hannon is too smart to be lured out of his cabin anyway."

"You're right," he said. "That leaves us with no choice but my favorite option. In any hostage situation, the moment of the exchange is a moment of distraction. We should take advantage of that. The instant Posten shoves the cart inside, we should send a rescue team in the back door, through the veranda."

"That's *extremely* high risk," said Victoria. "Posten could end up shot by one of our own HRT agents."

McCabe bristled, obviously annoyed. "Look, I'm trying to be constructive here, and all you're doing is shooting me down like a protective mother hen. Now, either you got a thing for this guy, or that blond dye job has made you really stupid."

"Get a grip, will you?"

"No, you get a grip. If we don't go in, our hostages are dead. Hannon said it himself: He has nothing to lose by killing them. He wouldn't even let you talk to Coolidge on the phone. I'd be surprised if the poor kid still has a tongue."

Shapiro stopped pacing and faced them both. "You're right, McCabe. It looks like we *will* have to go in. But Victoria's right, too. We can't do it with Posten standing in the doorway."

McCabe grimaced. "If we don't go when there's some kind of distraction, you're making it ten times more risky for our rescue team."

"The best way to reduce everyone's risk," said Shapiro, "is for Posten to give us an advance look inside the cabin. I agree with Victoria that Posten can't be looking around. But let's see if our technical support can hook up a camera on him. Even though he's not going inside, these cabins aren't that big. We may get a great picture from the hallway."

Victoria nodded. "I'm okay with that."

"Fine," said McCabe. "We'll stay on the defensive. But if Posten gets into trouble, any realistic rescue has to come in through the veranda. I'm the best man for the job. I want to lead it."

Shapiro gave him an assessing look. "All right. But no one goes in without a direct order from me or Victoria. I won't have Posten used as a decoy."

"Fair enough," he said with a confident smirk. "Call in your paperboy, Victoria."

Chapter 57

annon's cabin was closer to the bow than midship, so Victoria used the deserted casino in the bow as their staging area. Along the far wall, a row of one-armed slot machines stood in silent salute. Two crap tables stretched in isolation beneath a picture window that framed an ocean view. Blackjack and roulette stations were scattered about the interior on a royal blue carpet. The overhead lights were up to full intensity, giving the place a level of scrutiny that most of its night-owl patrons could never have endured.

"How do you feel, Mike?" she asked.

"Like a guy with a five-dollar limit playing at the fifty-dollar table."

She smiled only slightly, sensing he was half-serious. Two other agents were nearby, retrofitting a room service cart, loading on the scuba gear. She helped Mike with the body armor.

"This is the most inconspicuous full-coverage

armor we have. It's made of Kevlar 129. Front, back, side, groin, shoulder and upper-arm protection, with an extra steel trauma plate covering the sternum. This getup would get you through a prison riot. It bulks you up a little, but with a baggy shirt no one can tell." She pulled the Velcro strap snugly around his waist, below the belt line. "Too tight?"

"Only if I want children."

She gave him a half-inch of slack, then pulled an extra large Hawaiian print shirt from the box beside her. It was a ghastly mixture of red, green, yellow and orange tropical flowers.

He made a face. "Dear God, please don't let me die in that."

"Don't even joke about it," she said, her voice shaking slightly.

"You getting soft on me or something?" he jested.

She bit down on her upper lip. "I just want you to be *careful*," she said. She looked down self-consciously as he worked his arms into the shirt.

"It must be hard," he said, slowly doing the buttons.

"What are you talking about?"

"Always keeping up that tough-as-nails exterior."

Her eyes met his. The moment hung there. "Sometimes," she said. "Sometimes it is."

Then the connection was gone and she was all business. "Our technical agents wanted a loud color print shirt to hide the video camera," she said. "The lens is sticking through this patch of begonias here on the breast pocket. It's such a busy pattern, there's no way Hannon will notice any of the electronics. All you have to do is face the open doorway, and we should get a nice wide-angle view of the cabin."

"Is it bulletproof?"

"No. But in addition to your vest, we're mounting a Kevlar shield on the room service cart. If bullets start to fly, just duck behind it. Don't try to run unless I tell you to."

"How will I hear you?"

"With this," she said as she tucked a LASH unit into the utility pouch beneath his shirt. A clear wire channeled through the vest to an electronic collar around his neck that looked like a thick, gold chain. She plugged the tiny receiver into his ear. "Just talk in a normal voice and I'll hear you fine. I'll be giving you instructions all the way through, from the moment you start down the hall until you get back safely. There's a microphone around your neck, so I'll be able to hear everything you or Hannon say."

"What about a gun?"

"Sorry. We can't risk letting another weapon fall into his hands."

His eyebrows arched. "You want me to go up against Hannon completely unarmed?"

"Not at all. You've got two Hostage Rescue Teams on either end of the hall. My guess is that if you actually see Hannon, he'll be holding the hostage at gunpoint. If you notice the barrel turning toward you, even in the slightest, just hit the deck. We'll shoot the door right off the frame. We won't have the angle to hit Hannon, but he sure as hell won't come running out of the cabin after you."

"Then what do I do?"

"Just lay on the floor and pin yourself against the wall. The rescue team will come flying through the back door, off the veranda."

"They know I'm one of the good guys, right?"

"Of course. They can be pretty bad guys themselves sometimes, but at times like these, I'm glad they're on my side. If you just listen to my commands, however, it won't come to that."

"What are you going to do, call a time-out?"

"I'm serious, Mike. If we get any inkling that he chose you for any reason other than to deliver the gear, I'm pulling you out. We're letting you do this only because we *think* he has no idea of the role Karen played in his rape conviction. If he does *anything* to suggest he does know—or even suspects—you're pulling back immediately."

One of the agents from the Technical Support Squad came up and said, "Cart's all set."

Victoria looked at Mike. "Ready?"

He took a deep breath. "I guess so. But if this turns out badly, can you do me a favor?"

She looked at him reprovingly. Her eyes were getting glassy again. "Name it."

"Tell CNN to find a better picture of me."

The last swirl of color from a glowing sunset had just faded into the dark ocean as the Hostage Rescue Team silently moved into their outdoor positions. Outfitted in SWAT tactical armor, they were three black silhouettes in the night. Their ballistic military vests came with inflatable flotation devices, in case they were swept overboard, and radio channelization for two-way communication with Victoria. Black Nomex body-suits, gloves and tactical hoods made them virtually invisible in the darkness. Each was armed with a Heckler & Koch MP5 submachine gun, and an FBI .45 HRT pistol holding thirteen rounds of .45 ACP ammunition for ample backup.

McCabe was the first to step out onto the veranda to state-suite 1021, one deck above Hannon's cabin. Twenty feet below was the narrow teak-planked Lido Deck and lifeboats. Beyond that single tier was a sheer hundred-foot drop to the black ocean below. The brisk wind beat against their faces, filling the air with salt spray. The ship rocked gently with the rolling swells. The noise from wind and waves would have made conversation difficult.

McCabe waved the other two men forward to the glass balustrades, where they huddled in a crouched position. He checked his watch, then raised three fingers and jerked his arm forward three times. Without a word, the others nodded in silent confirmation.

In three minutes, the team was going in.

Chapter 58

Mike took a deep breath and started walking from the bow stairwell. The cart rolled smoothly across the carpet. Two sets of scuba tanks lay on top. Wet suits, masks and fins were tucked in the shelves below.

The narrow corridor stretched more than a hundred feet to midship, like a long, straight tunnel. The walls were covered with nautical art, with teak and brass accents. Were it not for the slight sense of motion from the sea, Mike would have thought he was in a luxury hotel. Straight ahead, he could see a team of snipers crouched in the main stairwell. They seemed closer with each step, which was a momentary comfort, until he realized that the closer he got to them, the farther he was from the home base behind him.

The cabin doors were evenly spaced, each one exactly like the other. Odd numbers were on portside; even, on starboard. Mike counted them off, knowing he'd pass five of them before reaching cabin 921.

Victoria's voice was suddenly in his earpiece. "Slow down a little, Mike."

He drew a deep breath, calming himself. With the adrenaline pumping, he hadn't noticed how fast he was going. He was beginning to sweat beneath his Kevlar vest.

"Slower still," said Victoria as he reached cabin 925.

Two more doors. Thirty feet to go.

His throat went dry as he passed 923, the last door between him and Hannon's cabin. He felt a sudden urge to turn back and forget it. But then he thought of the stories he'd written about Hannon and his victims—Gerty Kincaid in Georgia, Timothy Copeland in San Francisco, and all the others. He thought how close Karen had come to being on that list. He imagined Shelly Greene and Leddy Coolidge on their knees in the cabin, begging for mercy, praying for a miracle. Most of all, though, he remembered telling Aaron Fields how much he really cared about the victims he wrote about each day—and how he hadn't stayed in touch with a single one of them *after* the *Tribune* had run their story.

The cart stopped directly outside cabin 921. His earpiece buzzed again.

"Don't stand in the line of fire when the door opens," said Victoria. "Stand to the right side, so that if you have to run, you can run back to me without passing in front of the door."

Mike positioned the cart facing the door, then stepped to the right. He checked his watch. Six o'clock exactly—Hannon's designated time.

"Are you out there, Posten?" came the voice from behind the door.

His heart leapt to his throat. Hannon even *sounded* large. "It's me. I'm alone."

"Come out where I can see you through the peephole. And don't even think about shooting at the door. You've got a fifty-fifty chance of hitting my hostage."

Victoria jumped in. "Take the Kevlar shield from the cart, Mike. Stand behind it, so he doesn't shoot *you* through the door."

Mike detached the shield from the front of the cart. It was solid black, except for a clear window that revealed his face. He held it like a cop marching on a riot as he stepped in front of the door, directly behind the cart. He stared at the peephole, wondering if Hannon was staring back.

"No need to be a hero," said Hannon from behind the closed door. "I know this is personal, but keep your head."

Mike winced at the "personal" remark. Victoria's voice was suddenly in his ear. "Don't get sucked into a dialogue, Mike. Just deliver the goods, get the hostage and get the hell out."

He licked his dry lips. He'd heard her plainly, but he couldn't resist letting Hannon talk. "What do you mean, it's 'personal'?"

There was a long pause, then Hannon replied: "I know it was your wife who got me convicted."

Mike bristled, but said nothing.

"When I dropped that sailboat in Puerto Rico and started hunting for a cruise ship, I knew I'd be making my way back home through Florida. There was just one Floridian left on my list, so I figured I might as well take advantage of being there. Imagine my surprise when I dialed Mrs. Malone of Clearwater to check on her daughter's whereabouts for the alumni association and learned she'd gotten hitched—to a Mike Posten, no less. Now don't even try to tell me it's a coincidence that my old shipmate and my favorite reporter ended up tying the knot. You wouldn't be here, Posten, if it was a coincidence."

Mike's heart raced, but he stood his ground, staring at the door. Victoria's voice blared through the earpiece.

"Step *back*, Mike. Abort. I repeat: Abort!"

Slowly, Mike's right foot slid back an inch—then stopped. Her command made sense; Hannon was obviously out for blood. But something told him he had to play this out. Take his chances. Even before he'd walked down the hall, he knew there'd be no turning back.

He waited for Hannon to make his move.

A hundred feet away, Victoria cursed and stared helplessly at the scene that was unfolding.

Suddenly, Mike heard the chain lock coming off the door inside. But it didn't open.

"We're moving away from the door," said Hannon from inside the closed cabin. "Count to five, slowly. Then open the door and push the cart inside."

Mike drew a deep breath. "One."

Victoria was on one knee, watching intensely. "McCabe, stand by. He's entering in five seconds."

"Two."

"McCabe, do you copy?"

"Three."

Her voice shook with urgency. "I need confirmation *now*. Digital if not verbal."

"Four."

"*Dammit, McCabe!*"

"Five," Mike said as he swallowed hard and opened the door.

At that same instant, McCabe yanked open the door to enter from the veranda, and a drapery cord that was tied to the handle snagged the trigger on the missing flare gun, which was aimed at the fuel tank stuffed behind the mattresses.

The spring gun triggered a fiery explosion that obliterated the veranda. The major force was directed outward, away from the mattresses and through the open doorway. A tube of flame shot out the side of the ship like water from a hydrant. A shock wave shattered windows and glass balustrades on neighboring cabins. Little pieces of the veranda splashed into the ocean. McCabe landed with a thud on the Lido Deck below.

Inside the cabin, the blast sent everything flying toward starboard. Mike slammed against the door across the hall, then tumbled to the ground. He cried out in pain as the cart landed on his leg. His clothes were shredded down to his Kevlar vest, and his body was blackened with ash and debris. Thick black smoke filled the cabin and the hallway. He sat up and choked on the heavy smoke, so he laid flat on his back for the fresh air down low. The sprinklers came on throughout the corridor, soaking him with cold water.

Victoria stood at the end of the hall, drenched from the sprinklers, yelling into her receiver. No answer from McCabe. Nothing from Mike. The smoke and spray had filled the hallway like a foggy thunderstorm, reducing visibility practically to zero.

"Snipers, hold your fire!" shouted Victoria. From their positions at the end of the hall, it was impossible to tell Hannon from Mike, from Coolidge or even from Shelly.

Victoria grabbed a flashlight and goggles from the equipment box, then drew her gun and headed up the hall. An HRT agent in SWAT regalia was flanking her. Two people suddenly burst through a cabin door into the smoky hallway.

"Freeze!" she shouted—but it was an elderly couple, two of the portside passengers they'd been unable to evacuate earlier. Two other doors flew open with still more passengers who were coughing from the smoke that had seeped into their cabins. Victoria looked at her HRT escort. "Get the passengers out of here!"

He broke away quickly to tend to the passengers. Victoria was suddenly on her own.

The smoke began to clear as she forged ahead, and the sprinklers were producing more of a mist than a shower. The hallway lights, however, were completely blown out within fifty feet of the cabin. Victoria ran to the edge of darkness, then halted. She waited a moment for her pupils to dilate. With her back to the wall, she quickly scanned the debris. She could see the cart and scuba equipment. Thankfully, the tanks hadn't ruptured and compounded the explosion. The

Kevlar shield lay scorched on the floor—hopefully, it had saved Mike's life. But there was no sign of him.

Victoria inched closer to the gaping hole that was once the doorway to cabin 921. She stopped just at the edge of the hole. She noticed a charred smell, which didn't bode well. She could hear a crackling sound every three or four seconds, like a leaky pipe dripping onto hot coals. She crouched, then wheeled on one foot and peered inside.

It was worse than she'd expected.

The back wall and veranda were completely gone, making the cabin look like the back of a dollhouse. Through the gaping hole, she was listening to the ocean and looking at the night sky and stars on the horizon. The moon lent the cabin an eerie light. The interior looked as if someone had taken a flamethrower to it. Scorched wallpaper was peeling off the walls. Half the ceiling had been blown away, exposing a portion of the cabin above. The shell of a television and mini-bar lay amid the blackened remains of a bed and dresser.

Cautiously, she stepped inside. She pointed her gun toward the bathroom, then switched on the flashlight. Damage was minimal, but there was still no sign of Mike, Hannon or his hostages. She turned away from the bathroom and stepped toward the closet. Again, she pointed her gun and switched on the flashlight. Nothing. It was just as scorched as the rest of the cabin. She left her flashlight burning and scanned the rest of the cabin. She could quickly discern that the main blast had gone out the door that led to the veranda. Inside, however, she saw no trace of human life or remains.

It was then that she noticed the side door that presumably led to an adjoining cabin.

She switched off the flashlight and reached for the brass handle. It felt warm through her gloves, but it didn't burn. With her gun drawn she turned the handle.

A burst of gunfire splintered the door. Two shots missed, but one hit her in her Kevlar vest, knocking her backward. She was stunned for a second, then got up quickly. She was about to make a run for it when the side door flew open with the force of a hurricane, nearly swinging off its hinges. Hannon stood in the doorway right behind Mike, holding a gun to Mike's head.

Victoria froze.

"Drop the gun!" said Hannon.

Her mind raced with a flood of bad news. Her back was to the gaping hole in the ship and ocean beyond. The only way out was on the other side of Hannon. Mike was between her and Hannon. And he was naked from the waist up—Hannon was wearing his vest.

"I said, drop the gun!"

Victoria was in the classic stance: her arms extended out in front of her, both hands on the gun to steady her aim. For a split second, she saw herself in Mike's shoes, back at Quantico, staring down the barrel of a gun as some nervous cop in training decided what to do.

"Where are the hostages!" she shouted.

"In the next cabin. Some people have enough sense to leave before a cabin explodes."

"You son of a bitch. You left while Mike was counting down. You set us up."

"You set yourself up. Now drop the gun."

She aimed at his forehead. He was only slightly taller than Mike, giving her an opening of just a few inches. She wanted to wait for backup or a better shot, but she could see the gun slowly sliding forward on Mike's head, angling toward her. Hannon had no intention of letting either one of them out alive.

"Drop it!" he shouted again.

"Drop dead," she whispered.

On instinct, she fired off a shot that sounded like thunder. In an explosion of red both Mike and Hannon tumbled backward. They landed side by side on the charred remains of the cabin floor.

Neither one moved.

Victoria rushed toward them. "Mike, are you okay!"

Mike sat up in a daze. He brought his hand to his head, as if checking for a bullet hole. Then he glanced back at Hannon. He was motionless, eyes open. The top of his head was gone. Not a pretty sight—then again, it *was*.

"You could have blown my head off," he said in disbelief.

"Or I could have stood by and watched Hannon do it."

He sighed, then smiled thinly. "You're right. Thanks. I owe you."

"For saving your life, or for killing Hannon?"

His mouth curled into a wry smile. "For getting me the exclusive on that bastard's obituary."

Epilogue

mike filed his firsthand account of Hannon's demise by modem from the ship, in time for the early edition of the *Miami Tribune*. The reaction in the newsroom was fairly predictable, with overly eager editors who didn't know the facts trying to rewrite his story. He had a brief ship-to-shore argument with one editor who wanted to harp on Agent McCabe's death as evidence of yet another botched FBI operation, followed by a few words with Aaron Fields, who urged him to take more personal credit than Mike thought was due. Ultimately, he wrote a piece that, in a perfect world, might well have put Victoria Santos on the short list of candidates for the next FBI Director.

The news, of course, wasn't all good. The stolen credit card Hannon had used to purchase his cruise and the alias he'd used aboard ship had police searching for the real Keith Ellers, the old sailor who was last seen in Antigua and whose boat was found in Puerto

Rico. Likewise, customers at the Admiral's Inn in Antigua recalled having seen the young bartender, Dominique, talking with a man who looked like Hannon, and she hadn't returned to work since. Both were presumed dead, bringing Hannon's death toll to seventeen, counting Agent McCabe and the two security guards at the Charter Bank—eighteen, if you wanted to count Curt Rollins. The only consolation, Mike wrote, was that there would never be another.

What he didn't write, however, was his biggest consolation: Karen was forever off Hannon's hit list.

The MS *Fantasy* docked at the Port of Miami the following morning, distinguished from all the other white and shiny cruise ships by the charred black hole in its side that marked the explosion. Mike walked off the ship beside Victoria and David Shapiro, followed by the rest of the FBI team. They all looked battle weary, but their eyes glowed with the smile of victors. Victoria looked up and waved as eleven hundred grateful passengers and crew cheered from the decks above, sending them down the gangway to the pier. It was like a parade, she thought, without the ticker tape.

Legions of reporters were waiting on the pier, peppering them with questions as they headed for the terminal. Victoria chuckled to herself as she overheard a beaming Leddy Coolidge talking to a television reporter from one of the national networks.

"The name's Coolidge," he said proudly. "Most folks just call me 'Cool'."

David Shapiro stopped in the main lobby for a makeshift press conference. A huge media circle formed around him and Victoria, and the two of them took questions from every direction. From a distance, she and Mike exchanged thin smiles of good-bye. He started away, then forced his way through the wall of flesh. Victoria discreetly edged her way over as Shapiro was speaking to the crowd.

Mike spoke softly, so only she could hear. "I just wanted to say, you make one hell of an FBI agent."

She smiled with her eyes. "You make a lousy one. Stick to reporting."

He smiled back, then turned and slipped away. A few reporters tailed after him as he headed quickly up the inclined corridor, back toward the main security checkpoint inside the terminal. He was only half listening to their incessant stream of questions. His mind had one focus—finding Karen.

At the end of the hall he finally saw her.

She was just fifty feet away, standing on the other side of the gate, where the guards had stopped everyone but members of the press. She was squeezed between dozens of anxious friends and relatives of the remaining passengers. Their eyes met immediately. She tried to burst through the gate, but the security guard restrained her. Mike sprinted the last bit of distance between them. The pushing and shoving from the crowd nearly turned their embrace into a head-on collision, but neither of them seemed to mind. They just threw their arms around each other and squeezed with all their strength.

A microphone suddenly came between them. "Mr. Posten, how do you feel?"

He glanced at the reporter, then looked into Karen's eyes. "Let's get outta here."

Hand in hand they weaved a path through the crowd, toward the exit. As the crowd thinned they picked up speed. Their fast walk became a jog, and they were running and grinning like fugitives as they broke through the doors and cut across the parking lot. Karen pitched him the car keys. The doors flew open and they jumped inside. In thirty seconds they were at the stoplight, looking across eight lanes of traffic on busy Biscayne Boulevard. He was about to turn south toward downtown, but Karen pointed north.

"Get on the interstate."

He looked at her quizzically. "How come?"

"I packed a bag for you. We're going to the airport."

He smiled as he steered onto the entrance ramp, picking up speed as they merged into traffic. "What's this all about?"

"There's a lead we need to track down."

"What kind of lead?"

"You know that woman you married eight years ago?" she said coyly.

He glanced up from the road. "Yeah. I kind of miss her."

"Well . . . she wants to talk to you."

"Really? Where is she?"

"Paris. At the Plaza-Athénée."

Mike nodded slowly, then stepped harder on the accelerator.

"That's a relief," he said as he reached across the console and took her hand. "For a second there I thought you were going to say Antigua."

Enjoy an excerpt from
BEYOND SUSPICION
by James Grippando,
the stunning sequel to THE PARDON,
available now
from HarperCollins Publishers

Outside her bedroom window, the blanket of fallen leaves moved—one footstep at a time.

Cindy Swyteck lay quietly in her bed, her sleeping husband at her side. It was a dark winter night, cold by Miami standards. In a city where forty degrees was considered frigid, no more than once or twice a year could she light the fireplace and snuggle up to Jack beneath a fluffy down comforter. She slid closer to his body, drawn by his warmth. A gusty north wind rattled the window, the shrill sound alone conveying a chill. The whistle became a howl, but the steady crunching of leaves was still discernible, the unmistakable sound of an approaching stranger.

Flashing images in her head offered a clear view of the lawn, the patio, and the huge almond leaves scattered all about. She could see the path he'd cut through the leaves. It led straight to her window.

Five years had passed since she'd last laid eyes on her attacker. Everyone from her husband to the police had assured her he was dead, though she knew he'd never really be gone. On nights like these, she would have sworn he was back, in the flesh. His name was Esteban.

Five years, and the horrifying details were still burned into her memory. His calloused hands and jagged nails so rough against her skin. The stale puffs of rum that came with each nauseating breath in her face. The cold, steel blade pressing at her jugular. Even then, she'd refused to kiss him back. Most unforgettable of all were those empty, sharklike eyes—eyes so cold and angry that when he'd opened his disgusting mouth and bit her on the lips she'd seen her own reflection, witnessed her own terror, in the shiny black irises.

Five years, and those haunting eyes still followed her everywhere, watching her every move. Not even her counselors seemed to understand what she was going through. It was as if the eyes of Esteban had become her second line of sight. When night fell and the wind howled, she could easily slip into the mind of her attacker and see things he'd seen before his own violent death. Stranger still, she seemed to have a window to the things he might be seeing now. Through his eyes, she could even watch herself. Night after night, she had the perfect view of Cindy Swyteck lying in bed, struggling in vain with her incurable fear of the dark.

Outside, the scuffling noise stopped. The wind and leaves were momentarily silent. The digital alarm clock on the nightstand blinked on and off, the way it always did when storms interrupted power. It was stuck on midnight, bathing her pillow with faint pulses of green light.

She heard a knock at the back door. On impulse, she rose and sat at the edge of the bed.

Don't go, she told herself, but it was as if she were being summoned.

Another knock followed, exactly like the first one. On the other side of the king-sized bed, Jack was sleeping soundly. She didn't even consider waking him.

I'll get it.

Cindy saw herself rise from the mattress and plant her bare feet on the tile floor. Each step felt colder as she continued down the hall and through the kitchen. The house was completely dark, and she relied more on instinct than sight to maneuver her way to the back door. She was sure she'd turned off the outside lights at bedtime, but the yellow porch light was burning. Something had obviously triggered the electronic eye of the motion detector. She inched closer to the door, peered out the little diamond-shaped window, and let her eyes roam from one edge of the backyard to the other. A gust of wind ripped through the big almond tree, tearing the brownest leaves from the branches. They fell to the ground like giant snowflakes, but a few were caught in an upward draft and rose into the night, just beyond the faint glow of the porch light. Cindy lost sight of them, except for one that seemed to hover above the patio. Another blast of wind sent it soaring upward. Then it suddenly changed direction, came straight toward her, and slammed against the door.

The noise startled her, but she didn't back away. She kept looking out the window, as if searching for whatever it was that had sent that lone leaf streaking toward her with so much force. She saw nothing, but in her heart she knew that she was mistaken. Something was definitely out there. She just couldn't see it. Or maybe it was Esteban who couldn't see it.

Stop using his eyes!

The door swung open. A burst of cold air hit her like an Arctic front. Goose bumps covered her arms and legs. Her silk nightgown shifted in the breeze, rising to mid thigh. She somehow knew that she was

461

colder than ever before in her life, though she didn't really feel it. She didn't feel anything. A numbness had washed over her, and though her mind told her to run, her feet wouldn't move. It was suddenly impossible to gauge the passage of time, but in no more than a few moments was she strangely at ease with the silhouette in the doorway.

"Daddy?"

"Hi, sweetheart."

"What are you doing here?"

"It's Tuesday."

"So?"

"Is Jack here?"

"He's sleeping"

"Wake him."

"For what?"

"It's our night to play poker."

"Jack can't play cards with you tonight."

"We play every Tuesday."

"I'm sorry, Daddy. Jack can't play with you anymore."

"Why not?"

"Because you're dead."

With a shrill scream she sat bolt upright in bed. Confused and frightened, she was shivering uncontrollably. A hand caressed her cheek, and she screamed again.

"It's okay," said Jack. He moved closer and tried putting his arms around her.

She pushed him away. "No!"

"It's okay, it's me."

Her heart was pounding, and she was barely able to catch her breath. A lone tear ran down her face. She wiped it away with the back of her hand. It felt cold as ice water.

"Take a deep breath," said Jack. "Slowly, in and out."

She inhaled, then exhaled, repeating the exercise several times. In a minute or so, the panic subsided and her breathing became less erratic. Jack's touch felt soothing now, and she nestled into his embrace.

He sat up beside her and wrapped his arms around her. "Was it that dream again?"

She nodded.

"The one about your father?"

"Yes."

She was staring into the darkness, not even aware that Jack was gently brushing her hair out of her face. "He's been gone so long. Why am I having these dreams now?"

"Don't let it scare you. There's nothing to be afraid of."

"I know."

She laid her head against his shoulder. Jack surely meant well, but he couldn't possibly understand what truly frightened her. She'd never told him the most disturbing part. What good was there in knowing that her father was coming back—*for him?*

"It's okay," said Jack. "Try to get some sleep."

She met his kiss and then let him go, stroking his forehead as he drifted off to sleep. He was breathing audibly in the darkness, but she still felt utterly alone. She lay with eyes wide open, listening.

She heard that sound again outside her bedroom window, the familiar scuffle of boots cutting through a carpet of dead leaves. Cindy didn't dare close her eyes, didn't even flirt with the idea of sliding back to that place where she'd found the cursed gift of sight. She brought the blanket all the way up to her chin and clutched it for warmth, praying that this time there'd be no knocking at the back door.

In time the noise faded, as if someone were drifting away.

Jack Swyteck was in courtroom nine of the Miami-Dade courthouse, having a ball. With a decade of experience in criminal courts, both as a prosecutor and a criminal defense lawyer, he didn't take many civil cases. But this one was different. It was a slam-bang winner, the judge had been spitting venom at opposing counsel the entire trial, and Jack's client was an old flame who'd once ripped his heart right out of his chest and stomped that sucker flat.

Well, two out of three's not bad.

"All rise!"

The lunch break was over, and the lawyers and litigants rose as Judge Antonio Garcia approached the bench. The judge glanced their way, as if he couldn't help gathering an eyeful of Jack's client. No surprise there. Jessie Merrill wasn't stunningly beautiful, but she was damn close. She carried herself with a confidence that bespoke intelligence, tempered by intermittent moments of apparent vulnerability that made her simply irresistible to the knuckle-dragging, testosterone-toting half of the population. Judge Garcia was as susceptible as the next guy. Beneath that flowing black robe was, after all, a mere mortal—a man. That aside, Jessie truly was a victim in this case, and it was impossible not to feel sorry for her.

"Good afternoon," said the judge.

"Good afternoon," the lawyers replied, though the judge's nose was buried in paperwork. Rather than immediately call in the jury, it was Judge Garcia's custom to mount the bench and then take a few minutes to read his mail or finish the crossword puzzle—his way of announcing to all who entered his courtroom that he alone had that rare and special power to silence attorneys and make them sit and wait. Judicial power plays of all sorts seemed to be on the rise in Miami courtrooms, ever since hometown hero Marilyn Melian gave up her day job to star on *The People's Court*. Not every south Florida judge wanted to trace her steps to television stardom, but at least one wannabe in criminal court could no longer mete out sentences to convicted murderers without adding, "You *are* the weakest link, goodbye."

Jack glanced to his left and noticed his client's hand shaking. It stopped the moment she'd caught him looking. Typical Jessie, never wanting anyone to know she was nervous.

"We're almost home," Jack whispered.

She gave him a tight smile.

Before this case, it had been a good six years since Jack had seen her. Five months after dumping him,

Jessie had called for lunch with the hope of giving it another try. By then Jack was well on his way toward falling hopelessly in love with Cindy Paige, now Mrs. Jack Swyteck, something he never called her unless he wanted to be introduced at their next cocktail party as Mr. Cindy Paige. Cindy was more beautiful today than she was then, and Jack had to admit the same was true of Jessie. That, of course, was no reason to take her case. But he decided it wasn't a reason to turn it down, either. This had nothing to do with the fact that her long, auburn hair had once splayed across both their pillows. She'd come to him as an old friend in a genuine crisis. Even six months later, her words still echoed in the back of his mind.

"The doctor told me I have two years to live. Three, tops."

Jack's mouth fell open, but words came slowly. "Damn, Jessie. I'm so sorry."

She seemed on the verge of tears. He scrambled to find her a tissue. She dug one of her own from her purse. "It's so hard for me to talk about this."

"I understand."

"I was so damn unprepared for that kind of news."

"Who wouldn't be?"

"I take care of myself. I always have."

"It shows." It wasn't intended as a come-on, just a statement of fact that underscored what a waste this was.

"My first thought was *You're crazy, doc. This can't be*."

"Of course."

"I mean, I've never faced anything that I couldn't beat. Then suddenly I'm in the office of some doctor who's basically telling me, *That's it, game over.* No one bothered to tell me the game had even started."

He could hear the anger in her voice. "I'd be mad, too."

"I was furious. And scared. Especially when he told me what I had."

Jack didn't ask. He figured she'd tell him, if she wanted him to know.

"He said I had ALS—Amyotrophic Lateral Sclerosis."

"I'm not familiar with that one."

"You probably know it as Lou Gehrig's disease."

"Oh." It was a more ominous sounding "oh" than intended. She immediately picked up on it.

"So, you know what a horrible illness it is."

"Just from what I heard happened to Lou Gehrig."

"Imagine how it feels to hear that it's going to happen to you. Your mind stays healthy, but your nervous system slowly dies, causing you to lose control of your own body. Eventually you can't swallow anymore, your throat muscles fail, and you either suffocate or choke to death on your own tongue."

She was looking straight at him, but he was the one to blink.

"It's always fatal," she added. "Usually in two to five years."

He wasn't sure what to say. The silence was getting uncomfortable. "I don't know how I can help, but if there's anything I can do, just name it."

"There is."

"Please, don't be afraid to ask."

"I'm being sued."

"For what?"

"A million and a half dollars."

He did a double take. "That's a lot of money."

"It's all the money I have in the world."

"Funny. There was a time when you and I would have thought that *was* all the money in the world."

Her smile was more sad than wistful. "Things change."

"They sure do."

A silence fell between them, a moment to reminisce.

"Anyway, here's my problem. My *legal* problem. I tried to be responsible about my illness. The first thing I did was get my finances in order. Treatment's expensive, and I wanted to do something extravagant for myself in the time I had left. Maybe a trip to Europe, whatever. I didn't have a lot of money, but I did have a three-million-dollar life insurance policy."

"Why so much?"

"When the stock market tanked a couple years ago, a financial planner talked me into believing that whole-life insurance was a good retirement vehicle. Maybe it would have been worth something by the time I reached sixty-five. But at my age, the cash surrender value is practically zilch. Obviously the death benefit wouldn't kick in until I was dead, which didn't do *me* any good. I wanted a pot of money while I was alive and well enough to enjoy myself."

Jack nodded, seeing where this was headed. "You did a viatical settlement?"

"You've heard of them?"

"I had a friend with AIDS who did one before he died."

"That's how they got popular, back in the eighties. But the concept works with any terminal disease."

"Is it a done deal?"

"Yes. It sounded like a win-win situation. I sell my three-million-dollar policy to a group of investors for a million and a half dollars. I get a big check right now, when I can use it. They get the three-million-dollar death benefit when I die. They'd basically double their money in two or three years."

"It's a little ghoulish, but I can see the good in it."

"Absolutely. Everybody was satisfied." The sorrow seemed to drain from her expression as she looked at him and said, "Until my symptoms started to disappear."

"Disappear?"

"Yeah. I started getting better."

"But, there's no cure for ALS."

"The doctor ran more tests."

Jack saw a glimmer in her eye. His heart beat faster. "And?"

"They finally figured out I had lead poisoning. It can mimic the symptoms of ALS, but it wasn't nearly enough to kill me."

"You don't have Lou Gehrig's disease?"

"No."

"You're not going to die?"

"I'm completely recovered."

A sense of joy washed over him, though he did feel a little manipulated. "Thank God. But why didn't you tell me from the get-go?"

She smiled wryly, then turned serious. "I thought you should know how I felt, even if it was just for a few minutes. This sense of being on the fast track to such an awful death."

"It worked."

"Good. Because I have quite a battle on my hands, legally speaking."

"You want to sue the quack who got the diagnosis wrong?"

"Like I said, at the moment, I'm the one being sued over this."

"The viatical investors?"

"You got it. They thought they were coming into three million in at most three years. Turns out they may have to wait another forty or fifty years for their investment to 'mature,' so to speak. They want their million and a half bucks back."

"Them's the breaks."

She smiled. "So you'll take the case?"

"You bet I will."

The crack of the gavel stirred Jack from his thoughts. The jury had returned. Judge Garcia had finished perusing his mail, the sports section, or whatever else had caught his attention. Court was back in session.

"Mr. Swyteck, any questions for Dr. Herna?"

Jack glanced toward the witness stand. Dr. Herna was the physician who'd reviewed Jessie's medical history on behalf of the viatical investors and essentially confirmed the misdiagnosis, giving them the green light to invest. He and the investors' lawyer had spent the entire morning trying to convince the jury that, because Jessie didn't actually have ALS, the viatical settlement should be invalidated on the basis of a "mutual mistake." It was Jack's job to prove it was *their* mistake, nothing mutual about it, too bad, so sad.

Jack could hardly wait.

"Yes, your honor," he said as he approached the witness with a thin, confident smile. "I promise, this won't take long."